The WITCHES OF Bramberry FOREST

VESSELS OF THE GODS
III

KATERINA STEVENS

First Paperback Edition October 2025

Cover art by Tina @tcdesigns271 [Instagram]

Interior art by Katerina Stevens

[Canva Pro & Inkarnate Commercial License]

Editing by Rattle the Stars PR

ISBN Paperback: 979-8-9985657-5-5

ISBN E-book: 979-8-9985657-4-8

To the millennials who dreaded turning thirty...
And then realized being in your thirties is actually freakin' awesome.

The Witches of Bramberry Forest is a thrilling dark fantasy with morally grey characters, friendly-*ish* beasties, magic, and kingdoms in peril. As such, this story includes elements that might not be suitable for all readers. Violence, gore, bodily injury, blood, murder, ritualistic sacrifice, death (including the death of a parent and siblings), imprisonment, dealing with loss & grief, perilous situations, sexual activities, alcohol, graphic language, manipulation, witchcraft, torture, drowning, religious trauma, and mentions of war are depicted. Readers who may be sensitive to these elements, please take note, and prepare to enter the hauntingly enticing depths of Bramberry Forest...

OBSIDIAN KINGDOM

OPAL KINGDOM

IRRIDESSEN

LARIMAR ISLANDS

THE SEVEN KINGDOMS OF

SLATE KINGDOM

TERRAMERE

VESSELS OF THE GLOSSARY

Mini Recap of Gods, Places, & Characters

Gods and Goddesses:

Aella (ay-luh) – Goddess of Destruction

Akash (uh-cash) – God of Air

Alke (al-key) – God of Strength

Balint (bay-lint) – God of Healing

Beyos (bay-yos) – God of Water

Carra (car-ruh) – Goddess of Salvation

Eek (eek) – God of Riddles

Faune (fawn) – Goddess of Life

Massis (mas-sis) – God of Chaos

Moirai (moi-rye) – God of Sight

Phades (fay-dees) – Goddess of Death

Realms:

Aurramere – The god realm. Currently sealed so no god can leave. All of the gods are trapped here except for Phades and Massis.

Avamere – Ruled by Massis. Filled with his demon horde. Currently sealed.

Minmere – Ruled by Phades. The afterlife for all souls regardless of species. Currently sealed.

Terramere – The realm of the living. Home to fae, gargoyles, humans, witches, and beasties!

Kingdoms of Terramere & current rulers: (mentioned so far)

Jade – ?

Larimar (Islands) – ?

Obsidian – Queen Esmeray & King Keerian

Opal – Queen Sparrow & King Laurent

Ruby – King Eamon & Prince Cillian

Slate – King Dalen & Prince Feydor

Topaz – King Wei-Li, Queen Yan, & Princess Yin

Major Players in QOSAS & QOWF:

Adara (adah-ruh) – Half-fae, half-gargoyle. Esmeray's fraternal twin. Lineage gift water wielding. Heritage gift siphoning. Murdered her parents, the King and Queen Absolute, and took over Irridessen until Esmeray stopped her. Now on the run after escaping the Soul Keeper's Cell. Current whereabouts unknown.

Briar (brye-ur) – Sparrow's identical twin. Was destined to be Merrick's soul tied mate but died from a Martyrshade thorn as a faeling.

Cillian (ki-leeuhn) – Fae. Lineage gift protection magic. Planning a coup against his father that isn't going well at the moment. Has major heart eyes for Orla. Not a poet.

Eamon (ee-muhn) – Fae. Lineage gift air manipulation. Has the Book of Aella and wants the Book of Carra. Blame him for that stellar cliffhanger in Queens of Woven Fates.

Esmeray (es-mur-ray) – Half-fae, half-gargoyle. Lineage gift of illusions. Vessel of Death. Soul tied to Keerian. Enjoys having powerful enemies.

Hale Moyo (hay-l moi-yo) – Half-fae baker with an affinity for translating dead languages. In love with Lenna. Currently held prisoner in the Ruby Kingdom.

Keerian (ki-ree-uhn) – The Golden Gargoyle. Soul tied to Esmeray. Best friends with Merrick and Laurent. Fearlessly, wickedly, and completely supports Esmeray and her wild schemes.

Laurent (lor-ruhnt) – Fae. Lineage gift fire. Heritage gift portal creation. Soul tied to Sparrow. Ex-Spymaster of Irridessen.

Lenna Poryadok (le-nuh por-rih-ah-dok) – Human. The Oracle of Terramere and a seer. Thankfully ditched her ex-husband Leon. (Leon sucks.) In love with Hale. Currently held prisoner in the Ruby Kingdom.

Leon (lee-on) – Lord of Doortan. He suuuuucks. Currently in the Slate Kingdom and probably up to something sinister.

Merrick (mair-rik) – Traumatized gargoyle. Is straight up not having a good time after King Eamon tortured him.

Neci (nes-sea) – Witch. Broke Adara out of the Soul Keeper's Cell. Double crossed King Eamon. Current whereabouts (and loyalties) unknown.

Orla Grey (or-luh gray) – Fae. Lineage gift fire. Bonded a two-headed (courtesy of King Eamon) hydra named Seysei. Fled the Ruby Palace during the Autumnal Equinox/Culling with Dimas and Soren. Very glad Cillian is not a poet.

Sparrow (spair-roe) – Fae. Resurrected Merrick after he died. Vessel of Life. The extent of her gifts is a secret she hasn't revealed. Soul tied to Laurent. Best friend to Esmeray.

We'll catch up with most of these characters in Book 4. Now, prepare to meet *The Witches of Bramberry Forest*!

Part One

FORGOTTEN

Chapter One

DOVE

HAVING BLIND FAITH IN an omnipotent power could be interpreted as either pure devotion or sheer stupidity. And as I tipped my head back, feeling the ice-cold pinpricks from the drizzle of rain above, I wondered if the gods would ever forgive us, or if we were thoroughly damned in their eyes with no chance at redemption for the actions of our long-dead ancestors.

As if the gods decided at that exact moment to turn their eyes to me and punish my disbelief in their ways, the torrent of rain strengthened with a roar, driving me from the meadow and back towards the cover of the Bramberry Forest behind me.

Darting into the tree line cut off the barrage of rain from drenching me further. The sky had been clear this morning, but the billowing green clouds told me the rest of the day would be wet and gloomy. I removed my headscarf, twisting the water from it, before tucking it into my soaked skirt. One look at my boots told me my dash to cover included stepping directly into a mud pit.

The gods above must be laughing their divine asses off on my account.

With practiced movements, I unwove my hair from its loose knot. The sudden downpour turned my dark brown hair nearly black, and as I fought to tie it into a thick braid, the slick-straight and water-logged tresses annoyingly stuck to my arms.

Though the Autumnal Equinox only passed a fortnight prior, winter wanted to arrive early. The storms were simply the beginning. If they kept up this intensity, the rain would turn to sleet within weeks. Leaning against one of the thick oaks, I rummaged in my pocket, confirming my flee from the meadow hadn't allowed any of my collected stones to escape.

I ran my finger over each smooth rock, the cool, grainy texture soothing. Finding the smallest, I wrapped it in my fist, a little jolt of energy passing from myself to the pebble. The slightly dizzying sensation of my meager heritage magic settling into the hard surface of the stone was another reminder that the gods truly didn't give a fuck about witches.

Over the *drip, drip, drip* of rain drenched leaves, the rustling sound of shoes against damp pine needles told me I wasn't alone. My muscles tensed.

I was a ten-minute walk from the outskirts of town, so when my magic felt a presence at the edge of my consciousness, I knew I had mere seconds to prepare before I was ambushed.

Prowling behind the trunk, I held my breath, waiting until the patter of feet moved closer. An unnatural tendril of shadow wove past me, and I crouched low, bunching the wet fabric of my skirt in one hand so it wouldn't hinder my movement. Slowly, I peered around the trunk of the tree, and let out a soft breath, allowing my hunter to hear me.

A flash of light brown hair told me my trap worked, and I launched from my hiding place, using my free hand to snatch up the witchling shrieking in surprise, the wisps of shadows hovering around him dissipating with a *poof*.

"*Dove!*" While he erupted into hysterical giggles, his bright green eyes filled with mischief, I squeezed him in a tight hug. At eight years old, Elijah manifested his heritage gift and feared nothing - to the sheer frustration of his mother.

Loosening my hold on him, I combed my fingers through his damp hair, affectionately smoothing the ruffled pieces back into place. He was dressed in a matching deep blue shirt and pants, the hems sodden from the puddles covering the ground.

"Where's your mother?" I admonished lightly, flicking the tip of his nose with my finger as I stooped down, releasing him from my arms. He jumped around me, completely ignoring my question in favor of a fat caterpillar inching along a low branch. "You're not old enough to be wandering around during a thunderstorm."

"I'm here." An amused voice slipped through the trees ahead of me, and I exchanged wicked grins with Elijah as we moved out from the dense forest. Polina appeared, her youngest son, Henir, balanced on her side. Her honey-blonde hair was swept up in an intricate bun, and her smile widened as she beheld Elijah and I. My sister was my best friend. Polina and I were both adopted by our Coven Mother as babies, and though we weren't blood-related, family was what you made it, and I loved my family fiercely.

Elijah bolted away with a giggle, shadows swirling around his heels. Polina and I watched as he ran down the path towards the village. "Go *home,* Elijah, or you won't get to play outside after dinner," Polina called sternly, sighing in defeat as her oldest howled excitedly in the distance. "I don't know what I'm going to do with him, Dove. The last thing I anticipated was him manifesting *shadow* magic. And he's still *so young*."

I chuckled, "You manifested at nine. It's not a huge difference."

Polina let out a soft laugh, but I could tell she wasn't really listening.

"We'll find him a teacher," I reassured her, knowing exactly why Polina was so worried about her oldest son.

Unlike the magic the haughty and brutal fae inhabiting the majority of Irridessen and Ingotheria flaunted, witch magic was no longer a lineage gift given by the gods. We had no *acat* inked on our skin, no individualized, divine blessings that filled our souls with magic. Witches scraped and fought for every piece of power needed with our ability to siphon that came from our ancestral heritage – passed down from lineage gifts bestowed by Massis, the God of Witches.

Before the Witch War, Massis bestowed *acatis* and his siphoning gifts onto fae and humans. Bestowing gifts to humans created witchkind, though the intricate, silver-hued tattoos of his first gift were now reduced to hand-drawn depictions in old tomes and heritage magic that weakened and faded with every new generation.

After the fae turned their backs on him, Massis began experimenting, finally creating two new lineage gifts. Half of his witches received light magic that worked similar to a fae's battle magic, and the other half was given shadow magic.

Shadow magic gave witches the ability to siphon energy from darkness and wield the darkness into physical form. Their only weakness was that they couldn't power most runes, though the disadvantage rarely hindered them throughout history.

Polina and I were light witches, though either her or her husband carried both gifts in their bloodline since Elijah manifested shadow magic a week ago, becoming the youngest, and only, shadow witch in Bramberry Coven.

"Maude was asking for you," she said quietly. I pursed my lips, my plans to curl up on my couch with a new book were now moot. When the Coven Mother of the Bramberry Forest called, we answered.

Maude's word was law, and as the strongest witch in the Coven, her laws were *not* up for debate.

Maude Koroleva raised me after my own mother abandoned me in the half-destroyed temple near the edge of Bramberry Forest. I was incredibly fortunate to have Maude, and there wasn't much I wouldn't do for the woman.

"Did she say why? I was going to visit her tomorrow."

Polina shook her head. "She didn't say, but I knew if I didn't come for you, she'd send Juliette."

I reached into the pocket of my skirt, fishing out the largest of the four rocks I found, handing it to Henir. He was almost three, and as I handed it over, his chunky fingers snatched it from my hand. He cooed, shaking the stone wildly, almost smacking Polina in the face. I stifled a laugh at Polina's flat look that said, *Thank you for giving my child a weapon.*

The storm had let up to a light drizzle, and the canopy of thick, sprawling branches snatched the last bit of rain from the sky greedily to feed their ancient roots.

Fine by me – since every stitch of clothing I wore was now freezing and damp.

Turning the bend that led to town, Polina's cottage came into view. A cobblestone half wall separated her well-maintained garden from the fiercely untamed brush of the Bramberry Forest, and wide river rocks lay embedded in the soft soil, creating a walkway up to her door. Through the sheen of mist, I glimpsed Elijah inspecting bugs in the garden.

"Here, this seems like a good runestone." Polina held out her hand, offering me the rock back from Henir.

I waved her off. "Keep it, I found three more."

"Fine, I'm not going to argue that." Polina shrugged lightly, passing the stone back to Henir who shrieked with glee. "Gods above and below know I don't have time with these two heathens running around."

The river rock was smooth with no chips or cracks – an ideal stone for rune work. It took a few hours to find four with good symmetry and no fissures. Additionally, imbued sigils increased the weight of the object it was placed on, so hunting rocks that wouldn't be annoyingly heavy once filled with power added another layer of complexity to my search.

Sigils could be etched or painted onto the surface and light witches could store the raw power they siphoned into the stone – which turned it into a runestone. Light witches used runestones to carry more power with them than what their soul could hold.

When they could siphon no more, or if their well of magic was low, a light witch could use an imbued runestone and fill their soul with power once more.

High-tier light witches could use runestones to perform much more advanced magic. Though I'd spent years studying a multitude of different sigils, I was painfully limited by my meager heritage gift as to which ones I could successfully power.

There were runes to find lost objects, runes for tracking, runes to contain beings or items into a certain spot, runes to learn hidden truths – even death runes. Sigils could be painted or etched on surfaces other than rocks and gems, though those needed more power to imbue and were leagues above what I was capable of.

Most witches could only power basic runes, though the majority of sigils were *far* out of my magical range. I was still begrudgingly coming to terms with that twenty years after my heritage gift manifested.

"Children seem...fun," I replied sarcastically as Henir twisted and wailed in Polina's arms until she relented and put him down. The moment his toes touched the moss-covered ground, he tore after Elijah, his springy golden curls flying about. With a wild growl that was just too adorable coming from his mouth, he charged after Elijah on stocky legs, the stone clutched tightly in his fist.

We shared a chuckle as the brothers tussled in the grass, their clothes quickly becoming dirt flecked and wrinkled. Promising to come for supper tomorrow, I embraced Polina and headed towards town, Elijah and Henir's delighted screams following me down the path, sounding as if they found a particularly disgusting insect to admire.

With a soft laugh, I upped my speed. I needed to change and make myself presentable to visit Maude. Showing up on her doorstep damp and ragged was a surefire way to piss her off.

The winding path took me further into the village, where the dense forest thinned enough for our Coven to build homes between the ancient trunks. The rain had fully dissipated as I hustled to my own doorway, the shadowy exterior reminding me that I left the porch lamp unlit.

With the heavy tree canopy above, and grey, rolling clouds blotting out the setting sun, the temperature continued dropping, causing my neighbors to scurry into their homes and leave the cobblestone street deserted.

Grumbling a curse, I reached into my pocket for the runestone I'd pushed some magic into, reluctantly pulling the little morsel of power back out. The soft light hovered in my palm for a moment before I flicked my finger to the glass bulb cradled in a thick iron casing. The pale blue orb darted from my hand, settling into the bulb and lighting the threshold just enough for me to find the keyhole and unlock my front door.

Without a cache sigil etched onto the rock to hold the raw power, the bit of magic had already dwindled significantly. Frustration mounted in my chest.

I wasn't strong enough to siphon much from the meadow on the outskirts of Bramberry Forest, yet the field of wildflowers was my favorite place to be – even though it was grown for the purpose of harvesting power.

Our Coven Laws dictated where light witches could siphon. The sacred Bramberry Forest trees were extremely off-limits, but the meadow and any rapidly replenishing plant-life was fair use.

Light witches *could* siphon energy from any species with magic – such as gargoyles, fae, or other witches, though it portrayed witches as parasites. Treaties were drawn up a thousand years ago by the other six Kingdoms after our exile, calling for live siphoning to be punishable by death. But we were self-governing and cut off from the rest of Terramere, so it became more of a *'don't fight dirty...unless they do first,'* moral guideline.

Witches were peaceful beings. Unless that peace was threatened.

Shaking my head, I stripped off my soggy clothing, throwing them into a heap by the bathroom door. I purchased this tiny, one-bedroom townhouse with the money I made helping around the Manor. Though it was old and rickety and the roof leaked constantly, it was mine. Pivoting, I smiled warmly, reminding myself of all the good I had in life.

The deep, earthy green hue I painted on the walls the first week I moved in.

My little collection of teacups that hung proudly in my kitchen.

The full bookshelf next to the stone hearth.

Leaving my muddy boots by the front door, I hopped over the raised floorboard that swelled during rain and rarely failed to trip me. Padding barefoot to my wardrobe, I chose a ruby skirt that swayed against my ankles and a loose, cream-hued sweater.

I untangled my three favorite necklaces, the river rock pendants bumping against my sternum. Wearing runestones that held stored magic was common among light witches, though the wealthy preferred to etch cache runes into jewels and gemstones – a practice I loved, and would never be able to afford.

Dressing quickly, I restrained my hair with a leather ribbon before adding a linen scarf, tying it behind the nape of my neck to keep my damp roots hidden from my mother. I side-eyed the wet bundle of clothing on the floor before begrudgingly sacrificing the hem of my discarded skirt in an effort to wipe the majority of mud from my sole pair of boots.

I knew Polina would let me wash clothes at her house, but I hated feeling like I was a burden to her and her family. Though we lived together for almost twenty years under Maude's roof, Polina always knew exactly what she wanted from life, and nothing ever stood in the way of her determination.

On the eve of her twenty-fifth birthday, she'd swung down from the top of the bunk bed we shared and proudly announced that she'd be married and have a baby by this time next year.

And she had.

Polina set her sights on the kind – and very rich – cobbler who'd silently yearned over her for years, and to no one's surprise, Elijah appeared earthside eleven months later. The wedding took place the evening before she turned twenty-six, and though I knew the tears in her eyes as she stood on the marriage altar were from pure happiness, there was a sort of smugness to her too that made me laugh.

Her self-confidence sometimes terrified me, and while she was one of the most powerful witches in our village, Maude always said Polina was too headstrong to be a Coven Mother – too brash and audacious to ever take a vow to selflessly lead our people.

Hurrying down the dirt path to Maude's, the night had truly fallen, and the thick shadows on the ground hid the residual puddles the earth hadn't yet swallowed. The storm left a cool breeze behind, but I barely noticed the brisk temperature as I rounded the last corner and spied the large Manor nestled into the thickest grove of the Bramberry Forest.

A sense of ease skittered through my bones as I climbed the stairs to the wide porch. Bramberry Manor had been my home for twenty-eight years, and though I moved out three years ago to begin treading my own path in life, I would always hold love in my heart for this place...and for the Coven Mother who was currently standing at the threshold with a scowl on her face.

Fuck.

CHAPTER TWO

DOVE

"You took your time getting here, my Dove," Maude sniped.

"I needed to change. The rain caught me by surprise in the meadow."

Maude huffed, striding into the Manor and silently requested I follow. As always, she appeared perfectly polished and formal in a pale blue pantsuit, her tight bun of grey hair glinting silver under the lamplight illuminating the wood-paneled hallway.

Our Coven Mother was at least four hundred years old – if not older – though whenever she overheard witchlings whispering about her age, she'd snap at them for being *impolite*. Any spare breath in our lungs should be used begging the gods to shine blessings upon witchkind once more, *not* wasted pondering ridiculous questions.

She was family. I loved her *and* her no-nonsense act that rarely faltered since she found me among the ruins of Carra's temple and adopted me. I was raised as Maude's daughter – as was Polina. We'd been given her surname, though Polina's changed with her marriage to Arthur Sova. After I took my Coven Vows, Maude offered me a job with the academy based out of the Manor. By no means was I a teacher or a scholar – but while creating lesson plans, cleaning classrooms, and building course schedules for the witchlings to follow, I quietly dreamed of becoming an expert in a field of study to teach my own class one day.

Every witch in our Coven completed schooling and trained their heritage gifts in these hallowed halls. Some witchlings stayed in the Manor dorms while finishing their studies, like Polina and I had. Others simply came to the Manor for lessons and lived in town with their families.

"These witchlings make my bones ache," Maude grumbled as she strode towards her private study. "Twice today I've had to redirect their focus from idle gossip to chores. Half the kitchen was late serving breakfast."

I chuckled, reminiscing on fond memories of being sixteen with Polina. We'd stay up late, talking about everything and nothing, until Maude rapped on our bedroom door and berated us for wasting magic keeping the lights on too long.

"Young witches must broaden their minds with stories if they're ever going to contribute well in society," I chastised, rewarded with a small flick at the corner of her pursed lips – the closest to a smile Maude revealed.

"That explains why Polina and yourself stuck your noses into everyone's business, always up to mischief. I knew you'd blossom into a wonderful, polite witch that stayed away from trouble. But my Polina...she's too crafty for her own good."

I rolled my eyes instead of commenting. If Maude declared the grass was green, Polina would siphon every speck of power from the brush until it withered just to tell our mother *that* grass was brown.

Thankfully, their relationship improved once Polina finished her studies and moved out of Bramberry Manor. Elijah and Henir's births also helped tremendously. Maude was instantly smitten with the boys, spoiling them incessantly as any grandmother would. Polina and I were the only two orphans Maude ever adopted, though the Manor housed any child in need – human *or* witch.

Maude delicately cleared her throat as she entered the large kitchen where two teenaged witchlings hovered over a romance novel propped open on the counter. In sync, their heads snapped up, the book vanished, and the witchlings hurriedly began chopping vegetables, identical blushes flaming their cheeks. I tried smiling at them as we passed, but with every step closer to Maude's study, uneasiness over *why* I was abruptly called to the Manor grew, making it difficult to do anything other than grimace.

Throwing a pointed glower over her shoulder to the witchlings, Maude escorted me through another long hallway, towards the lone door at the end of the corridor. With a flick of her finger, the brass knob turned, and I was quickly ushered into her private study.

Candles scattered along the bookshelves flared to life with magic as Maude stalked across the room, rounding her giant desk, and gestured me to the leather seats positioned in front of it. "I asked you here to talk about the day I found you in Carra's temple."

I sat up straighter, interest piqued. "There's more to my story?"

That flicker of bright curiosity dimmed as Maude assessed me, her face falling into a somber expression. "This is not a happy tale, my Dove."

Biting back the frustrated demand for clarity that begged to spill from my lips, I kept silent, but godsdamned – I was not a child. At thirty-one years old, I was a full-fledged witch, vowed to my Coven, and though my magic wasn't *incredible*, I was proud it was mine.

I tucked my skirt around my thighs as I sat, wiping clammy palms against the fabric. In Cravic, our ancestral language that only a handful of witches still spoke, Maude started, "The day I found you, I was called to Carra's temple by Hanna, the Mother of Rummerock Coven. When we approached the ruins, I heard the mewling of a babe and rushed to investigate."

The ruins of Carra's temple were poised on the rim of Bramberry Forest, though the witches of Rummerock Valley visited often since our Coven land bordered theirs.

"When I entered the chamber...there was so much blood." The wobble in her voice made my breath hitch. I rarely saw my mother lose composure, so that tiny tremble spoke volumes. "Yet there you were – bundled in a white cloth and hidden behind a wall, not a speck of blood on you."

"I didn't see the young woman atop the altar at first." Maude flinched. "There was nothing we could do; she was already in Minmere. But the lacerations carved into her flesh haunt me to this day."

Tears slipped down my cheeks. Over the years, I'd casually wondered who my birth mother was, though growing up alongside other orphans in the Manor, I never expected to learn anything about her. In stunned grief, blood-stained answers processed agonizingly slow.

Maude made the sign of respect for the dead. "The moment I held you, you stopped crying and peered up at me with your beautifully unique eyes. From that moment, you were mine, my Dove. My peace. I felt it in my soul. And when we lit the memorial pyre for your mother, I vowed that I'd always keep you safe."

I blinked back a wave of tears to focus on the black-bladed spinel sword displayed on the wall behind Maude's massive desk. My eyes were definitely unique. One iris was a light, coppery brown, the other, a dark, steely blue – like a churning sea after a storm. Numbly, I wondered what color my birth mother had.

As if she read my haunted thoughts, Maude sighed, "Her eyes were the same hue as your right iris, my Dove."

Copper brown, then. The conclusion didn't bring peace.

"Who was she?" I asked bleakly as Maude leaned across the desktop to offer me a handkerchief. Accepting it gave my shaky hands something to do.

"We aren't sure," Maude broke gently. "The woman recently arrived in Rummerock – though no one knew where she'd come from, only that she appeared to be running from something."

Blotting tears away, I inhaled slowly through my teeth, recentering myself. Maude dutifully skimmed over part of the story. The body on the altar. Blood. Lacerations on the flesh...

"Dove, you –"

"Were there runes carved into her body?" I interrupted. Normally, I'd never speak so brazenly, but I mourned a woman I'd never had the chance to know. "Were they true blood runes?"

"Dove," Maude scolded, though the reprimand held none of her usual sharpness, "Speaking of blood runes is...improper."

"But there *were* blood runes?" I hedged. Maude frowned.

Witch blood was extremely potent. It boosted the efficiency of any rune, though true blood runes could *only* be cast in witch blood, and typically held sinister purposes – hence the reason true blood runes were highly illegal. In times of peace, witches steered clear of blood casting, and the practice fell out of favor swiftly after the Witch War a thousand years ago.

"Maude," I pleaded, unable to elaborate how desperately I needed to know more.

In that moment, I loathed the way Maude paused. She was searching for the right words to appease me while holding back information she deemed too horrid.

Irritation prickled down my spine. Growing up, Maude supported my thirst for knowledge, encouraged my desire to study advanced topics.

However, getting a straightforward answer from her was frustratingly difficult.

Maude pinned me with a stern look that made me scream internally. I squeezed my fists in my lap until my palms ached from nail pricks. Sure, my heritage gift was weak. That didn't mean *I* was, too.

"The witches used *her* blood to cast runes."

My mother's silence said enough.

"What did they cast?"

"Runes for a ritual that demanded witch blood to complete –"

Obviously. I bit back my retort.

"– surrounded by black ash and carved near major arteries. No burns, just ash."

I smothered my surprise over Maude's detailed answer. It was much more than I expected her to reveal. *Yet, it still pointed towards one specific sect of witches.* The ones I already suspected.

"It was...heretics?"

Heretic witches were zealots of falsehoods and archaic practices. They believed Massis granted them lineage magic in exchange for performing ritualistic blood sacrifices with spell work. Spells were forgotten magic, rarely ever utilized in this age, and I'd never seen a heretical witch, nor seen evidence supporting the claim that they received lineage gifts. Banishment runes covered Bramberry Forest and kept them out, and the majority of heretics preferred hiding amongst the humans in the Slate Kingdom.

Like all religions, the abrupt silence from a god could cause panic that festered into desperation. Heretics truly believed the gods abandoned us because we were not devout enough, and their unanswered prayers swiftly turned into violence once illegal, long-forgotten spells were rediscovered.

"You are a *good* witch, my Dove. There is dark knowledge in this realm that is above your tier in this Coven. You deserved to know what happened to your mother, and I've told you what I can."

But why was she telling me this now? Unless...

"Was there another sacrifice –"

Maude growled, "We found the body on Carra's altar this morning, and before you ask, no – the identity is unknown. Neither Bramberry nor Rummerock reported any witches missing."

"Oh." I swallowed thickly.

Maude absentmindedly patted the bun of silvery hair secured at the nape of her neck. "I wanted to tell you so you could make smart decisions. That means staying *home* after sundown, and no wandering about alone in the dark. Do you understand?"

I choked down a sigh as I realized why Maude told me the brutal details surrounding my birth mother's death.

She worried about me.

Me and my *laughably lackluster magic.*

My eye twitched as I tried and failed to hide my scoff. "Are you not giving the same warning to the rest of the Coven?"

"Of course I am," Maude bristled, as if I offended her for even asking. "But I wanted my daughter to verbally *promise me* to not take unnecessary risks."

"So, you warned Polina, too?" It was a low blow. Irritation ignited in Maude's pure emerald eyes. "Because you're *so* worried about your daughters?"

"Polina may be the most stubborn witch I've ever met, my Dove, but she would *never* take unnecessary risks now that she has the boys to think of." Every word was carefully bitten out as Maude regarded me with haughtiness.

Definitely not the gut check I thought she'd take.

Maybe this isn't about my magic.

Maude straightened and flicked her wrist towards the door to her study. It swung open and banged against the wall. I winced at the noise. Switching to Terrian, the common language spoken throughout most of Terramere, Maude added, "Not to mention, Polina is the second strongest witch in the Coven. *You* ranked in the lowest tier, and that warranted more than a written missive shoved under your front door about a mandated curfew that you could easily feign ignorance on receiving."

Never mind, there is it.

I deflated, a bitter taste flooding my mouth. My frustrations over having a crap heritage gift didn't change the fact that I was grateful Maude admitted the truth of my birth mother and warned me of danger.

Even though the warning hit my insecurities dead on. With brutal accuracy.

"Good night, Mother," I said dully, rising from the chair.

"I love *and* adore you, my Dove." Maude settled down into her seat behind the desk, propping a thin pair of glasses onto the bridge of her nose. "Never forget that."

"Love and adore you most," I replied, repeating the saying we swapped every evening since I was a toddler, eliciting another one of those almost-smiles from my mother.

"Take the lit path back to town, please. I have witches patrolling the area and they're aware you're heading home."

I nodded. For all of Maude's icy exterior, she truly cared about every single witch and human in Bramberry. As her daughter, I guess it wasn't all that hard to understand her curt warnings came from a place in her heart of pure love.

Knowing Maude would be busy for the rest of the evening, I took my leave. As I headed down the hall, a tendril of silvery light snaked from Maude's study winding around my wrist before disappearing in a soft *woosh*.

Maude wasn't overtly affectionate, but her magical hug made me feel loved all the same.

A throaty croak ripped me into the present. Sitting on the carved balustrade, a large Moon Crow observed me with beady eyes. The white crescent moon on its head stood out against its deep black body. From the leather pouch strapped to it, it was here to deliver a message from another Coven.

"Hello," I said politely, bowing to the feathery messenger.

Ruffling its feathers, the Moon Crow cawed loudly, puffing out its chest and the leather messenger pouch embroidered with a sigil of three stacked triangles.

Before I could remove the letter from the pouch, a syrupy-sweet voice fluttered over to me. "I'll take that."

Juliette strolled through the doorway with a toss of her sandy brown hair and a smug smile. I tolerated the witch since she was five years my junior, though she never missed an opportunity to talk down to me in front of the high tier witches in our Coven.

Polina outright hated Juliette with a passion.

Well, Polina didn't like many people to begin with.

I gritted my teeth, keeping my tone pleasant, "Hi, Juliette."

Juliette barely spared me a glance as she stroked the Moon Crow's feathers and gingerly plucked the scroll of parchment from the beastie's pouch. "You should get back to your little townhouse before it gets too dark out, Dove. There's a curfew, you know, for the *low* tier witches."

I swallowed my rebuttal that the curfew was for *all* witches. Juliette would simply respond with another, equally cutting, insult dripping with fake concern.

Too mentally exhausted for a verbal sparring match, I squeezed past her to open the front door. "Glad you can handle delivering a letter."

Juliette squinted. "*Excuse* me?"

For a heartbeat, I debated the merits of stooping to her level, but if I did, she'd just get less vague and bitchier.

"Nothing," I muttered.

She smirked at my concession. "That's what I th-"

I shut the door in her face.

Standing on the porch, I grounded myself with the scent of petrichor before starting down the trail to town, waving in acknowledgement to the high tier witch stationed at the halfway mark. I didn't remember his name, though the silver magic humming across his knuckles alluded to him being one of Maude's high tier advisors. From the frown on his face, he wasn't thrilled at Maude's order to keep an eye on me. Frankly, I wasn't pleased with it either.

Frowny Asshole kept a respectful distance as I picked up my pace, bundling my skirts in my fist to arrive home faster and release him from his bodyguarding duty.

Once the edge of town came into view, he called out an *almost* polite good-bye before spinning on his heels and stomping back towards the Manor. The moment he disappeared around the bend, my shoulders relaxed. I slowed my steps and listened to the sounds of nightfall.

I loved identifying small noises – the distant hoot of an owl, rustling breezes through leaves, sifting soil as critters scavenged for a meal. The last moments of dusk were my favorite time to be outside, and I paused to soak in the activity around me. Maude's mandated curfew would put my exploring on hold for at *least* a month.

The second I started walking again, a hush blanketed the air. Skin prickling, I froze, straining my ears for indication of a threat.

One heartbeat.

Two.

And then a howl tore through the stillness – mournful and low. I pushed magic over me like a shield as another threaded through the air in response. Heart hammering in my chest, I shrank into the shadow of a tall oak, rallying pale blue magic to my palms.

Wolves traveled the outskirts of Bramberry Forest, but I wasn't afraid of a wolf loping out of the tree line.

I feared the demons that crept into our realm from Avamere when the veil was thin enough.

Volkhounds, a wolf-like demon that blinded their prey with shadows, rarely approached areas with a large population of witches. There hadn't been a volkhound sighting in Bramberry in centuries.

Unfortunately, that only made my panic worse.

Because volkhounds weren't a threat to Bramberry Forest – the grimm were.

Triple the size of a normal wolf, closer in comparison to a horse, a single grimm could wreak havoc on an entire town. Able to change form between corporeal and intangible, the grimm were rumored to hunt dying witches, herding their souls into Avamere for Massis's army instead of allowing them a peaceful afterlife in Minmere.

There were no reports of grimm being killed. They could only be weathered – like a tempest of teeth and dark fury.

There were *also* no reports of grimm in Terramere since the culmination of the Witch War. Volkhounds and other horrifying demon species still slipped into our realm, but some scholars speculated the grimm grew too powerful in Avamere and could no longer pass through the veil.

I firmly reminded my stuttering pulse of these facts as I choked down irrational fear. Maude's warning and the story of my birth mother's death had my nerves frazzled.

The howling was most likely wolves *miles* away.

A sharp hawk call overhead broke through my unease. Stepping out of the shadows, a grey squirrel chattered from a branch above me, and a cool breeze swirled down the path.

The forest was once again filled with noise. I kept a shield of magic up for protection – just in case.

Ten minutes later, I was scowling at the dark entryway over my door again. With a wave of my fingers, my shield peeled from my skin and shot into the iron lamp, the metal rattling as magic rooted into the glass bulb, illuminating the threshold as I entered my townhome and locked all four locks and the deadbolt behind me.

Sleep tonight wouldn't come easy.

Thankfully, I had a new book on an ancient fae language to read. My stove was a little wonky, but between a plea for it to work, a spark of magic, and a dash of luck, my kettle was soon whining.

Teacup in one hand and the heavy tome titled *Linguistics of Larimar* in the other, I collapsed onto my couch and flipped to the first page.

Books didn't care that I had weak heritage magic. They granted the same knowledge to every being who opened their thick covers – regardless of their gifts.

Chapter Three

DOVE

"What did Maude want last night?" Polina asked, interrupting my quiet brooding as she shuffled mushrooms around a saucepan.

I pulled a loaf of sourdough over to slice it. "Nothing much. I think she just wanted to complain about the witchlings under her roof."

It killed me to keep a secret from Polina – especially one that involved the truth about my birth mother. But Maude made me swear to keep our conversation private.

Polina snorted a laugh. "Any of them causing as much trouble as we did?"

"I don't believe it's possible to replicate that level of mayhem, dearies," Maude replied dryly, breezing into Polina's kitchen.

I whipped around to our Coven Mother, stunned that she'd be here after everything she told me yesterday.

"We weren't expecting you," Polina said, her tone mirroring the same amount of surprise. "What can we do for you, Mother?"

Maude jerked her chin towards me. "Dove, I need to speak to Polina for a moment – alone."

I nodded hesitantly, "I'll, um, go let Arthur and the children know dinner will be ready soon."

I glanced from Polina to Maude, and the confusion on my face must've been clear because Maude shot me a grim nod. "Thank you, my Dove, we'll be out in the garden shortly."

With that obvious dismissal, the silvery sheen of a soundproofing rune wove across the kitchen threshold behind me.

I huffed. Maude bestowed a secret upon me – and now one to Polina as well. Shoving that gnawing wave of unease from my mind, I opened the arched door that led to the garden.

Polina's husband, Arthur, barreled past me, running towards the back gate. Henir shrieked with glee atop Arthur's broad shoulders as his father made a show of spinning around abruptly, Henir letting out a high-pitched squeak of excitement. Elijah was close on their heels, chasing his father and brother across the grass.

I shouted Arthur's name, and he galloped over, Elijah headbutting his knees as they stopped in front of me. "Hey, Dove." Arthur grinned, his deep brown eyes crinkling as he slung Henir from his shoulder and deposited him onto the ground. With barely a heartbeat to righten himself, Henir cackled in his naughty baby voice and darted off on slightly unsteady legs to tackle Elijah.

"Maude asked for a moment alone with Polina. I came to let you know dinner will be ready soon." I kept my voice steady, though Arthur's lips pressed into a thin line, his gaze flicking into the house.

"She's in the kitchen talking to Polina," I added in a low voice as Elijah bolted past, tendrils of shadow pooling in his wake.

"Everything alright?"

I shrugged because I wasn't sure.

Arthur frowned, pushing his dark brown hair from his forehead. I adored Arthur for Polina, and though Arthur inherited no witch magic, he'd always been a cornerstone of Bramberry.

"Are you worried?"

I gave him a wicked smile. "Am I worried about them being together in the kitchen filled with knives? Course not, Arthur, they haven't had an argument in...a week?"

I laughed when he blanched, half expecting him to hurry into the house and double check that his stubborn-ass wife was playing nice, but just then, Maude and Polina appeared in the doorway.

"Arthur." Polina's face was drawn; color leeched from her cheeks.

"Watch the children for a few?" Maude asked, though her tone made any potential rebuttal moot.

Arthur took Polina's hand, and they followed Maude back into the house.

I wasn't strong enough to fight, but I *could* keep two rambunctious children busy for a few minutes.

"Okay!" I called, drawing the attention of the boys currently digging in the dirt for worms. "Who can find the creepiest bug?"

POLINA WAVED HER PALM, sending a pulse of white light over the table that swept up crumbs and deposited them into the trash on a magical breeze. In the living room, Arthur was telling a story of gods and beasties traveling on an epic, child-friendly, quest to Elijah and Henir, his deep baritone rising and lowering as he mimicked the voices of different characters while Maude and I helped Polina clean the kitchen.

After Maude spoke with Arthur and Polina, I wracked my brain, trying to come up with something that would make sense for Maude to tell them and not me – especially if it was about my birth mother or the body recently found in the temple.

I hadn't come up with anything. So, treading carefully, I prodded.

"Is everything alright?"

Polina and Maude exchanged silent conversation, and I shifted nervously. Polina and Maude rarely ever agreed on anything, so this shared concern had my hackles rising.

"You need to tell her," Polina snapped.

"My Polina, you're as hard-headed as –" Maude started with a sigh.

"Either you tell her, or I will."

Okay, there's the Polina and Maude I grew up with.

"There was a Moon Crow from the Royal Coven right after you left last night." Maude circled the dining room table, flicking her fingers at her copper brown coat that rose to life to wind around her shoulders. "The letter came with dire news on the King's health, and I made the decision to handle one crisis at a time. I'm getting old, you know."

I didn't tell Maude I'd seen the beastie as I left, nor that Juliette had taken the letter. "Is that a secret?"

"No, but since a body was just found in our temple, I'm cautious. The Crown announced it is unlikely King Velik will recover, and the King's Heir, Prince Theodoric, has been named Regent. Once his father passes, he'll be crowned King of the Jade Kingdom. But Prince Theodoric is personally visiting every Coven in the Jade Kingdom for a *diplomatic tou*r to meet his citizens."

"And that's...bad?" I questioned.

The Royal Coven may have been filled with pompous witches who boasted about their heritage magic and ran off any in their Coven that didn't hold a title, royal blood, or a strong level of power...but what did that have to do with the body in the temple?

A frown tugged at Maude's lips, and she all-out glared at Polina before turning to me. Behind her, Polina bared her teeth at Maude's back, reminding me of our years together in the Bramberry Manor.

Maude shook her head but addressed me all the same. "I flipped through my research today to see if I could find any similarities between the death of your mother, and the body of the witch in the temple two nights ago."

I glanced to Polina, wondering if she wished to learn about her birth parents, or if she knew what became of them.

"There were slight differences on the cuts and runes etched into the dead, but upon further scrutiny, there's one sigil that was repeated on both bodies that I originally dismissed almost three decades ago as either a rune that was no longer widely used, or a secret sigil that only held bearing to the witch that enacted the killing – like a personal signature." Maude flicked her hand, the tip of her finger glowing as she drew lines in the air.

The sigil took shape, revealing three triangles barely layered atop each other, a three-quarter circle surrounding them. The image shook something loose from my memory...I'd seen it before – or something similar.

But where? I pictured the books I read through last night, trying to marry the glowing illustration before me with a printed copy in a dusty tome. But that didn't seem right. I moved closer to the table, eyeing the design from all sides.

"The sigil is associated with a single witch in a single Coven, and I never in my years believed I would hold any type of animosity towards the Crown..."

My breath hitched as I pieced together where I'd seen that sigil before.

Last night – stamped onto the Moon Crow's pouch with a letter to Maude from the Palace.

"That's the symbol for the Royal Coven," I breathed, stunned at the thought that my birth mother's death could be linked, even loosely, to the Coven that ruled the Jade Kingdom.

"Not the Royal Coven," Maude corrected quietly. "There's only one witch who uses that sigil to signify who he is. It's the symbol for the King himself."

Chapter Four
DOVE

SMALL STICKS AND MOSS crunched under my boots as I trudged heavily through Bramberry Forest. I barely noticed Maude at my side, her steps near-silent as we headed back towards town.

I managed to say good-bye to Polina and her family after learning the King's personal sigil had been carved into my birth mother's body, though my tongue was thick, and hot tears collected at the corners of my eyes.

Had the King of the Jade Kingdom killed my birth mother almost thirty years ago? And if he did...why?

"You need to practice walking silently through the trees, Dove," Maude muttered, her silver hair glowing in the strands of moonlight breaking through the canopy.

I grunted in return, though I made a half-assed attempt to lighten my gate, rolling my feet in my boots and keeping my heels off the ground like Maude taught me years ago. I felt silly doing it, since the only reason Maude demanded I learn to slip through the forest like a wraith was due to my non-impressive magic. So that I could flee if I was confronted by a stronger witch.

Which, to be honest, was the majority of witches.

"Are you still practicing your self-defense?" Maude asked as we rounded the edge of the uninhabited part of the Bramberry Forest, the soft orange lamps from town glowing in the distance.

"Every day." My fingers twitched, hunting for the sheath I kept strapped around my ankle. It wasn't technically a lie. I did *most* of the exercises daily to keep my body in shape, though I'd never admit to my mother that sometimes I left the house and forgot to bring my dagger with me. I figured now wasn't the time to take that verbal lashing.

"And are you studying your languages?"

I paused.

"I...yes." I stopped walking, suddenly suspicious. "Why?"

Her slim hand latched under my elbow. Tugging me towards town, Maude blew past the turn she normally took to Bramberry Manor, leaving me with the embarrassing realization that I was being escorted home to my probably dark entryway by my mother.

Maude was silent until we turned onto my street. Every doorway was illuminated – except mine. Blush creeped over my face as I braced myself for Maude's hour-long tirade on safety that I knew I'd be on the receiving end of soon.

To my surprise, Maude merely quirked a disapproving brow before flicking her finger towards my shadowy porch, a ball of silver rattling against the iron casing and banishing the darkness from my door.

"In," she grumbled, shooing me up my threshold.

I groaned internally, unlocking the door and backing up with a small bow. Maude took no notice as she brushed past me and entered my little home, more magic bursting from her palms to light the assortment of lamps and candles I'd accumulated.

"A cup of tea would be lovely, thank you, Dove," Maude announced, though I hadn't offered. I couldn't help the soft chuckle that escaped my lips as I moved towards the stovetop and refilled my kettle.

Maude stooped over my kitchen table, shuffling through the pile of lesson plans and books I hadn't tidied up before going to Polina's house. Maude's presence in my home had me on edge, the power and grace radiating from her made my kitchen feel cramped and small.

I felt small.

"You've studied ancient runic languages on how many nations now?" Maude asked as she rooted through my notes.

"Four," I answered quietly, pulling two teacups from my cabinet. I didn't particularly want a cup of tea this late, but Maude would take offence if I didn't sit with her, and I doubted with the little sleep I got last night that I'd have any issues passing out tonight.

My academic brain loved learning, and the lesson plans Maude and the other teachers provided for the witchlings coming through Bramberry Manor were never enough for me to feel satiated. By the time I was ten, I was taking advanced linguistics classes and had fallen in love with the study of translation.

From then on, each year she'd push me to learn more, master another. I was fluent in two languages, could speak, read, and write well enough to get by in a couple more, and by the time my study material ran out of subject matter on those, she switched me to ancient and forgotten languages, an exciting challenge since most of them were written in runic symbols.

"Witch, Fae, *and* Gargoyle?" Maude prodded further, straightening and moving over to the rickety bookshelf in my living room.

"Yes, Mother. Fae from the Ruby Kingdom and the Larimar Islands, the Witch tribes that used to inhabit the Slate Kingdom, and one from a small sect of gargoyles that used to live in the Obsidian Kingdom."

My magic may be weak, but in a classroom setting, I found my power. It was one of the reasons I jumped at the chance to assist the other teachers in the Bramberry Manor after Maude announced my studies were complete.

Making lesson plans and training schedules, researching niche topics for a professor that didn't have time, organizing the student rosters as courses were completed...I may not have my own group of witchlings to teach, or my own topic of study to lecture on, but I reveled in my book-smarts. Being able to spout out information made me feel better when in close quarters with witches whose heritage magic ran circles around mine. Maude always told me *'play to your unique strengths.'* That mantra burrowed deep into me over the decades.

The kettle whined, and I poured the hot water slowly into each cup, thanking my lucky stars that my stovetop didn't put up a fight tonight. The last hit my pride needed was for my mother to pity-pour magic into fixing my home. I already figured the light she pushed into the lamp on my doorway wouldn't go out for at least a month.

"There was more in the letter from the Palace," Maude hedged as she took the cup and sat down on the edge of the armchair in my living room, her back perfectly straight and her ankles crossed beneath her.

I gritted my teeth, sliding past the bookshelf to perch on my lumpy grey couch. "More than them suggesting the King murdered my birth mother by sending us a wax seal with the same sigil you found the night before on another victim?"

I knew it was probably not true – anyone could've carved that royal mark into my mother's body to frame the King thirty years ago, but a part of me desperately needed to hear if Maude believed the Crown was lowering itself to blood sacrifices and murder.

Her responding scoff immediately lightened my mind. "My Dove, if I thought for a single second King Velik – who backs charities, feeds the homeless, and supports each Coven directly – was slithering through the darkness murdering innocent witches for some illicit ritual, I would already be calling a meeting with every Coven Mother to take him off the throne."

"And what *do* you think?" The question was daring – even for me.

Maude rolled her lips together with a smack, peering at the teacup in her hand. "I like these cups, my Dove. They hold a nice amount of tea."

I gave her a flat look. We both knew damn well those teacups had been stolen from Bramberry Manor by Polina two years ago.

Sensing my mounting anxiety was beginning to peak, Maude sighed, "I think that sigil was etched into the body post-mortem as a threat to the King. It could be a lower-level witch, or anyone with hatred for the Crown. The sigil is widely known. They are performing *blood sacrifices,* my Dove. Sane people don't perform blood sacrifices."

"And?"

"And King Velik has been indisposed and bedridden for a month. Not to mention, there's rumors that he is too sick to use magic. I'm more worried that whoever carved the King's sigil into the body is going to attack the Regent while he's in town."

"Oh."

Maude sniffed delicately, sipping the tea. "I have three of my most trusted witches scouting the forest for clues, but that's not the reason for my extended visit."

I figured as much, so I stayed silent, waiting for Maude to continue.

"The Prince Regent will be in Bramberry in about ten days– give or take the length of his stay in Rummerock. The message I received noted there is a renewed push to interpret the Vessel Book Prince Theodoric will receive upon his coronation – the Crown is once again looking for translators willing to study the Book of Carra."

My interest was piqued. The Book of Carra had been handed down from each King or Queen to their Heir since the Vessel Book was found in the Jade Kingdom after Queen Minerva took the throne.

But no one could read it – the god language so old and forgotten that only a few scholars were able to piece together a few words. When it had first been located, Queen Minerva declared it a symbol that witchkind would soon return to the gods' favor.

But after Queen Minerva's death, her Heir took over possession of the Book of Carra, and we were still as omnipotently ignored about as usual. Translators were bought in to try their luck at reading its pages – to find the key to the gods' blessings hidden in its depths.

And so, it went on. Kings and Queens got old, died, or handed the book down to their Heir, and each new ruler would send out a missive for anyone with experience translating ancient languages – or anyone who wanted a fool's shot at glory – to come to the Jade Palace and take a gander at interpreting the formidably confusing runic language.

At this point, thousands of years later, it seemed laughable, but every new ruler thought *they themselves* would be the one to sit the throne and find the secrets in Carra's story – to receive the god magic in its pages that no witch could siphon.

Many had tried.

"I'd like you to go. Travel to the Jade Palace and interpret the Book of Carra."

I took a deep breath, choked down a sip of tea, and shook my head in disbelief. "Why? No one's been able to translate the Vessel Book – why do you think I'd stand a chance against Elite Scholars who've studied the Book of Carra their *entire lives?*"

Maude sniffed delicately, as if I was being entirely unreasonable. "They aren't you."

"You're right – they *aren't me*. I haven't spent my life pouring over a single page of a Vessel Book."

"But you *have* spent decades learning a multitude of different languages," Maude said pointedly. "And you'd be in the Jade Palace studying the book with both shadow and light witches."

My breath hitched. Maude smiled victoriously.

Gods above and below.

I saw stars. I could go to the Royal Library, meet and learn from the Royal Scholars of the Jade Kingdom – one of only two Covens both shadow and light witches cohabitated. I could go under the pretense of helping to translate, but I'd be in the middle of the largest collection of books in all of the Jade Kingdom with *unrestricted access.*

"I could learn about shadow magic," I murmured, already mentally packing my meager belongings in a bag. "From some of the best teachers in the Kingdom. I could bring that knowledge back here to help train Elijah and become a teacher for both light and shadow witches..."

"Dove, you will never be a fighter in the physical sense." The words weren't spoken in an unkind way, though they made me wince. "But you are one of the brightest witches I've ever had the pleasure of teaching, you are well-behaved, gentle, and your thirst for knowledge is unquenchable."

Maude's words were kind, though they still left a lump in my throat. "Right now, I cannot, in good faith, allow you to train Elijah. He's too young, too impressionable, for an inexperienced teacher. He needs someone who can handle his level of power, and it would be a disservice to him to give him to a teacher who was still learning herself."

I cast my eyes down, though I knew Maude was right. Elijah deserved a teacher who could train his unique and powerful gift – not learn alongside him or teach on concept alone. It was the same reason I wasn't able to hold a class by myself.

I could teach the *content* of what witchlings needed to learn, but my magic held me back from showing students any visual technique.

"If you wanted to, you could go to the Jade Kingdom and give it a solid attempt at translating the Book of Carra, but you could learn *more* – learn anything you wanted. Play to your strengths."

"I'd study more advanced methods." The lesson plans that always seemed plain and outdated practically begging me to go. "Even if it's just from a conceptual manner with stronger witches who could implement my lessons for the actual magic. Maybe I'll find a topic I love and write a book on it..."

I trailed off, mind whirring at the possibilities. With a pleased hum, Maude nodded. "You could learn anything, Dove. Even though your gifts are limited, your mind is not. If you go to the Jade Kingdom for the Vessel Book, and spend your spare time learning everything you can, then, in a few months, we can revisit your ask to assist with Elijah's training or create a class on a topic you excel in."

I knew there'd be more planning to do, that I would most likely panic pack, second guess myself a hundred times, worry myself into a frenzy until I got sick, and ultimately beg Maude to let me stay here instead, but at that moment, a calming presence swept over me, and a small voice in the back of my head whispered, *"Go."*

CHAPTER FIVE
MERRICK

"He's waking up." A feminine voice with a thick accent cut through the haze clouding Merrick's mind.

Another female, more brusque than the first, answered stiffly, "I'll get Winnie."

Merrick didn't have the energy to open his eyes, let alone make any sense of his situation. He drifted back to sleep, his body too heavy, unresponsive, *aching*.

The lull of chirping songbirds and the rustle of a breeze through curtains permeated his dreams, but in them, he saw Sparrow's golden hair, tousled in the wind, heard her chiming laugh as she fed birds in her garden.

A lance of pain dug into his thoroughly broken heart, shoving him closer to consciousness as he grappled to stay with this version of Sparrow who looked up at him with love shining in her aquamarine eyes.

"Oi, bonehead!" A new voice jarred through him, chiding and sharp. It had his brows furrowing, unable to match the dream-Sparrow with that lilting accent – that odd name. A soft hand touched his forehead, but Sparrow was interlocking her fingers with his, tugging him along the rim of a waterfall. Merrick sank deeper into unconsciousness, praying reality would fuck off.

"He groaned in his sleep, your –"

"*Winnie.*"

"Right, um – Winnie. He...he was groaning in his sleep. His fever broke, so we pulled him off the sleeping draft."

"Alright. I'll take it from here."

Shuffling footsteps. The sound of a chair scraping across wood.

Merrick growled low, squeezing his lids shut.

The dream flickered around him, Sparrow's beautiful features morphing into Lenna's pale, panicked face, her eyes wide and tear streaked. *"Merrick,"* the dream-Lenna gasped, *"Merrick, I'm so sorry."*

A stabbing pain in his wing sent Merrick roaring into consciousness, force-feeding him that bitter reality he was so frantically avoiding.

He was a prisoner.

He was being tortured in a dingy, sandy cell in the Ruby Kingdom, two hulking guards laughing, slamming daggers through -

Fuck, his wings.

Merrick's eyes snapped open, and he lurched forward with murderous intent, hand shooting out towards the blurry silhouette leaning over him.

His fingers wrapped around the column of a delicate throat, and he snarled, the images of those fae guards blinding him with fury.

A strong force latched onto his wrist, peeling his fingers away and slamming his fist into the mattress.

Merrick thrashed, bellowing his rage through fuzzy vision, reality and panic mixing together until he sank into his basest instinct, rooting through his soul for that thread attached to his Sentry – the magic that could transform him from male to beast.

"Hey! Snap out of it, you big fucker!" That feminine voice yelled, cutting through his concentration.

Merrick blinked.

The fact that he could *see* sunlight, that he was in a *bed*, and could *hear* birds chirping made no sense. He'd passed out from torture in a dark cell, surrounded by the moans and shrieks of other prisoners the cruel King Eamon of the Ruby Kingdom kept in the dungeons. He thought he'd die *permanently* this time.

So, where the *fuck* was he now?

He stilled, easing the tension from his muscles, until his ragged breathing evened out and his vision focused. A pair of bright green and copper eyes filled his vision, curtained by short light brown hair. Merrick flashed his fangs, but those hazel eyes only narrowed with frustration. A sharp *tsk* his only response.

"Are you gonna chill out? Or do I have to keep holding you down?"

"You can try," Merrick sneered. "See how that goes for you."

A soft chuckle answered.

Those curious eyes were gone, allowing him a clear view out the large window with a wooden frame that overlooked a cheery afternoon. Fluffy clouds dotted the blue sky, leafy trees filled the landscape, and lush, rolling hills were visible in the distance. Merrick tried pushing himself up to sitting with no success.

Nothing made sense.

Where was the *sand?*

The endless, shitty sand that chafed his bare feet and stung his eyes.

But this didn't look like the Ruby Kingdom.

He was in... a bedroom? A circular table sat at the end of the bed, holding an assortment of oddly shaped bottles. Nothing was where he expected it to be – from the chipped, painted basin holding linens soaking in green-ish liquid, to the paisley curtains letting daylight in.

He was flat on his back, tucked into a white comforter, little clusters of delicate pink flowers stitched along the hem.

It was the type of comforter Sparrow would love.

Was Sparrow here?

He attempted to sit up again but couldn't get his wings to cooperate. His confusion intensified as they merely twitched and stayed where they were - spread out at his sides and half tucked under the blankets.

The sound of a chair squeaking had his heart banging painfully, but Merrick already knew Sparrow would be sitting there with her long, tanned legs, curtain of golden hair, and piercing, crystal-blue irises.

But it wasn't his rejected mate that his eyes landed on.

Instead, a petite female with chin length brunette hair, no wings, no horns, and no visible *acat*, appraised him silently, meeting his glare with her own.

She wore a beige tunic, the sleeves rolled to her elbows, and a pair of light brown breeches that matched her hair. Chestnut, knee-length boots tapped against the floor, confusing him further.

"Who're you?" Merrick grunted.

The female cocked her head, those sharp eyes flaring. For a beat, Merrick didn't think she'd answer, but then –

"Winnie," she said simply. "And you are?"

Merrick huffed, ignoring the sinking pit in his stomach that Sparrow wasn't in the room. "Where am I?"

"You didn't answer *my* question, bonehead. Who. Are. *You?*"

His jaw ticked as he regarded the female with a menacing glower that always served him well through the ranks of the Irridessen armies.

But the tiny spitfire simply snorted, leaning her forearms against her thighs, never breaking eye contact. "Are you a spy?" she asked plainly, tucking a strand of hair behind a perfectly *rounded* ear.

A human? Merrick clenched his jaw. He'd die before giving this stranger any information that could be detrimental to the Queens of Irridessen, or to Lenna.

Was he in Irridessen?

Did someone pull him from that cell? A – a diplomatic trade?

Had Queen Esmeray advocated on his behalf?

Or...Sparrow? Did they give King Eamon something in exchange for Merrick's life?

A wave of guilt crashed over him. He was a warrior. Had been since he was young, thrown into the training barracks in the Obsidian Kingdom and forced to either thrive in the harsh conditions or die trying.

And well, he did die – a century later – only to be bought back, to be resurrected and mated to the most beautiful fae female he'd ever seen.

Only for that to be taken away from him, too.

For that same female, with tears in her eyes, to confess their soul tie was false, that his true mate died before receiving her *acat*.

Sparrow kept *her* true mate, his best friend, Laurent, and left Merrick with a ghost soul tie.

He'd never again be able to receive the one gift he'd quietly desired his entire existence.

He didn't want pity, didn't want to be the burden of Irridessen, the stain on Esmeray's reign.

And he didn't blame Sparrow for her choice.

Winnie's boot heel tapped against the ground. Merrick avoided her steely gaze, opting to stare at one of the tiny, embroidered flowers on the comforter.

"I'm not a spy." Merrick ground out.

But well, he was...in a way. He'd left Irridessen to keep Lenna, the Oracle of Terramere, safe in enemy territory, and was sneaking around the Ruby Palace for information to send back to Esmeray.

He'd fucked that up, too.

"That's exactly what a spy would say," Winnie mused, her lips tipping up into a wicked smile. "Well, and exactly what someone who was *not a* spy would say. So, I guess we're at an impasse, gargoyle."

Merrick shrugged, his focus on the darkness covering the slate grey scales of his wing. He glanced over to the window again. With the angle of the sun...no. Shadows shouldn't be there.

"Tell me who you are, and why you were on our border, and I'll let you up."

In time with her statement, those shadows drifted across the flat expanse of his wings, feeling like the softest caress of fingers.

"You're doing this?" Merrick hissed, struggling again as the suffocation of imprisonment slammed invisible shackles around him once more. His pulse thundered, and he threw a seething, fangs-bared, dirty look to the female sitting, unaffected, in the chair next to the bed.

Winnie rolled her lips together, as if she was choosing her next words wisely. "You were found, barely alive, on the border of the Topaz and Jade Kingdoms. The healers among us wanted to help, though the warriors debated the merits of leaving you to die."

"Then why didn't you?" Merrick bit out, anger coiling in his gut. "Why didn't you leave me for the witches to butcher?"

The venom in his tone didn't affect Winnie as she assessed him with a cool, unimpressed expression. "There was a vote. The healers won out."

"I'm in the Topaz Kingdom."

"No."

The answer sank in slowly. Surveying the woods outside the window, Merrick swallowed. He'd been to the Topaz Kingdom before...and this landscape was *drastically* different.

Which meant –

"I'm in the Jade Kingdom."

"Obviously," Winnie chuckled, as if he'd cracked a damn good joke.

Suddenly, the shadows against his wings were a threat.

Witch.

Winnie was a *witch*.

This wasn't fae magic holding him against the mattress. It was stolen magic siphoned by a species so cruel Carra refused to give anyone with witch blood a soul tie.

A nagging voice in his head tried throwing him in that category, too, with his ghost soul tie.

"Let me up, *parasite*," he spat, the muscles in his arms bulging as he fought against the shadowy bonds slithering over his wrists and biceps.

"Not until you swear you won't eat us in our sleep, *bonehead*," Winnie hissed, her calm, unruffled demeanor slipping away.

It was the first true emotion she'd revealed.

And it was...*fear*?

Merrick flinched. The pure hatred he felt for witches reflected back at him through those hazel eyes.

And, *fuck*.

He didn't like that one bit.

"Gargoyles don't eat witches," he retorted halfheartedly, remembering with a pang of guilt how Lenna asked him the same thing when he first found her in the Doortan forest.

It was Winnie's turn to look bewildered. "Of course you do. That's why your teeth are so sharp."

"We don't eat human flesh," Merrick scoffed. "Our teeth are sharp – but not as sharp as fae, and those self-righteous bastards *definitely* don't eat other beings."

Winnie's nose scrunched.

"Forewarning – while you were unconscious, we gave you a potion that would kill you if you ate human flesh."

A rough breath was the only noise he could make.

Or maybe Winnie rendered him speechless.

There were fables that spoke of gargoyles as protectors of the gods, as beasts that devoured non-believers, but he thought those rumors were only in the Slate Kingdom, where most humans didn't know magic existed.

Lenna's old Manor depicted paintings of gargoyles whisking humans away for disavowing their faith, so for those tales to travel to a Kingdom where no gargoyles had lived for thousands of years *was* believable...but still.

The absolute bullshittery of the claim settled against Merrick's shoulders. He assessed the frowning witch seated near him, and let out a bark of laughter, making Winnie recoil, her chair legs screeching against the floor.

"You made a poison..." He choked between stifled chuckles, ache spearing through his ribs. "To *kill* me...if I ate a witch?"

He must be losing his mind.

He'd gone mad.

Delirious tears welled up behind his lids.

A witch was *scared* that he'd *eat her*. It was too much. He remembered Lenna's face, how she'd been thoroughly freaked out when he dropped from the trees – granted he'd been in his Sentry, but *still*.

"I – yeah," Winnie sniped, and Merrick saw right through her tough mask to the terrified little witch that found a half-dead gargoyle in the woods and nursed him back to health.

"Winnie, that's a fucking fable created by the humans in the Slate Kingdom. I don't even like my steaks rare."

His chuckles subsided, and he hiccupped, wishing he could use his hands to wipe the tears from his eyes, though whatever witch magic she had still kept his arms firmly stuck to his sides.

"That's what the Veilhaven Coven believes. It's not *just* the humans."

"I don't know where Veilhaven is," he replied bluntly. "Gargoyles don't associate with witches."

Winnie sighed loudly. "Just promise me."

"How do you want me to promise that I've never eaten a being before?" Merrick shook his head at the absolute insanity of this entire situation.

This would only ever happen to him.

The witch was silent for a moment. Then, she stood abruptly, hair swinging, and strode from the room, slamming the door behind her.

Low voices began conversing on the other side of the door, though as hard as he tried to hear what they were saying, he couldn't make out a word. There was a patter of multiple footsteps, before the door was thrown open once again, and Winnie returned, holding something in her fist.

"Do you know what this is?" She waved a rock in Merrick's face. Merrick quirked a brow. He'd either descended into a new level of madness that made him want to provoke the witch, or he truly didn't care what happened to him now.

But seeing this through was better than being tortured by those bumblefucks in the Ruby Palace.

"I'd say it's a rock," he deadpanned.

Two sets of nervous titters came from the doorway, drawing his eyes to the females on the threshold. They darted away, though he could still see them standing in the hallway of what appeared to be a simple stone cottage.

Winnie opened her fist, showcasing a rounded stone with a flat face, a pointy symbol carved into the surface.

"This is a truth rune. I had the strongest light witch in the village imbue it a few days ago. You hold it, I ask a question, and you answer. If you answer truthfully, the runestone won't react. But if you lie, it will burn your palm, and I will kill you."

"Delightful," Merrick replied dryly. "And I'm assuming you're going to ask the rock if I eat witches? Is this rock going to know the *truth* truth? Or will it only react to what the caster of the rune *believes* is the truth?"

After spending time with Esmeray, he'd learned how to negotiate with lunatics. It was a skill he picked up navigating court life under King Scottrell, but the current Queen of the Obsidian Kingdom really honed that talent for him since she was notorious for, well...being one of those lunatics.

Winnie opened and closed her mouth, eyes narrowing as if she couldn't tell if he was jesting or not.

"One second," she grumbled, sprinting out of the room with her weird rock.

The whispers of multiple females started up again in the hallway.

And with a sinking wave of sobering clarity, Merrick realized his life was currently held at the mercy of an angry little witch and a rock.

Carra's tits.

CHAPTER SIX
DOVE

TIPPING MY FACE TOWARDS the sky, feet surrounded by a ring of half-wilted flowers, I drank in the sunset drawing shadows across the meadow. A tingle of nervousness zipped through my blood, boiling in exhilaration.

The meadow was bustling with activity – witches and witchlings alike threading their fingers through patches of dancing wildflowers, siphoning raw power to fill their souls. A few bustled between withered areas, scattering seeds and imbuing growth runes into the soil for the next generation of flora to bloom.

I'd never left the Bramberry Forest before. And even though my soul was filled to the brim with power to support my heritage gift, and Maude's curfew was going into effect for the evening soon, I wanted a few moments alone in the meadow to revel in the autumnal breeze, the aroma of sweet wildflowers, and the full moon beginning to appear as the sun set.

According to Polina, Maude was already considering lifting the curfew since there'd been no signs of suspicious activity since the last body was discovered, but I'd definitely be home before night truly fell.

I grinned to myself as I thought over the three-month opportunity to consume knowledge straight from the coveted Royal Library.

I'd get to meet the Royal Coven, see the famous Vessel Book our Kingdom coveted, read and study any topics I desired. Maybe I'd make academically inclined friends.

Even the thought of traveling through a *veles* for the first time made me giddy.

Veles were ancient portals that never moved nor disappeared, though no one knew for sure who created them or when. Using a *veles* was a convenient way to move across the Kingdom, and I'd only ever read about the portals that shone with glass-like sheens. More than once, I wondered how it felt being whisked away by magic.

Was it nerve-wracking? Or boringly unassuming?

Did you hold your breath while stepping through? Was it like being underwater or breezing, carefree, through a field of summer grass?

I couldn't wait to find out.

The closest *veles* was a day's ride from Bramberry Coven's territory through the Quiet – the sole piece of the Jade Kingdom where no Coven held ownership.

I glanced around Bramberry Meadow. If I stayed the full three months, the next time I stepped foot in Bramberry, it would be winter, and I'd be bundled up in as many layers as possible, plodding through snow drifts and ice.

Though Maude protected the meadow with weather runes during the coldest months, it was still annoying to siphon while your fingers froze. Weather runes didn't protect against the temperature – only kept snow off the wildflowers while growth runes coaxed them to bloom.

Anticipation simmered through me. I was both anxious over leaving Bramberry's familiarity but *so* ready to travel somewhere new. No one knew exactly when Prince Theodoric Balabanov and his troupe would arrive, but Maude guessed he'd show up within the next day or two. A celebration feast in town square was being prepared, and the flurry of activity around town was beginning to overwhelm me.

Everything I needed for the Jade Palace as an official translator of the Bramberry Coven was packed into two very full trunks – courtesy of Polina's "*help*" – including a long, stunningly beautiful gown fit for a royal ball. It hung in the back of her closet for years. I argued it was completely unnecessary, but my sister wouldn't relent, and she was *not* by any definition a "*light packer*."

Looking around the now empty meadow, I wondered where the Royal Coven siphoned their magic from. Coming to a stop in the middle of the field and sinking to my knees, I folded my bare feet underneath me. My boots stayed home. I needed to feel the soft soil and thrum of nature underfoot, to be close to the heart of Bramberry Forest.

Laid out amongst the flowers, their heady scents mixed with petrichor and tickled my nose. Streaks of pink near the horizon melted into purples and blues, creating an ethereal backdrop for the full moon that grew brighter and bolder as stars flickered into view around it.

Brisk air rustled my hair and umber hued skirt as the temperature dropped. I pulled my hands into the sleeves of my cardigan, bunching the extra fabric in my fists while listening to the breeze whistle through foliage like a siren's song desperate to lull me to sleep.

My lids grew heavy as the full moon flooded the world with beams of silver.

"Hi, Carra," I whispered, my words directed to the goddess who chose to favor the fae instead of her devout witches. "We're all still here, waiting on you to tell us how to fix it – how to earn your love again."

I waited in silence for an answer I knew would never come.

And among the echoes of owls hooting in the darkness, the soothing croon of creaking tree branches, and the sifting of leaves in the gentle wind,

I relaxed deeper into the bed of flowers, content to listen to Bramberry Forest come alive with nighttime activity like I'd done so many nights before.

More to myself than to the silent goddess above me, I breathed, "What if I figure out your book, Carra? Will you be happy? I hope so – otherwise you and I need to have a *long* talk about your choices."

CHAPTER SEVEN
MERRICK

"The runestone will tell the *true* truth. Not just what the caster of the rune *believes* is the truth," Winnie announced, strolling back into his room hours later and picking up their conversation as if no time passed at all.

"Wonderful," Merrick monotoned, glaring through the window at the full moon rising above the trees.

His body was exhausted, but Merrick's mind couldn't rest. Since he could only move his head and neck, he'd spent most of his alone time studying the silky shadows binding him to the bed - unable to figure out how they were anchored.

And then the full moon rose, and he directed his rising ire towards that instead.

Winnie plopped into the chair next to his bed, shooting him a stern, '*don't fight me*' look. "I'll release one of your wrists so you can hold the runestone. And then I'll ask the questions."

"What if I don't *answer* your questions?" Merrick challenged, ripping his gaze from the pretentious moon to level the witch with a scathing expression.

"Then I'll kill you."

Merrick let out a sardonic gasp. "After you spent all that time healing me? If you ask me, that sounds like a waste of magic."

He didn't know what drove him to goad her, but something about the way those hazel eyes flashed with contempt was so satisfying he couldn't help it. As badly as he wanted to roar his frustrations at the shining orb taunting him from between hazy purple clouds, he couldn't do a damned thing while restrained to the bed.

"I *didn't* ask you."

Merrick rolled his eyes.

Winnie growled and leaned closer, bracing her forearms against the mattress. His mocking retort hung heavy in the air before she deigned to reply.

"*And*," Winnie added, a disdainful sneer curling her lip, "I'm not a healer. *My* vote for what to do with your sorry ass landed firmly in the *opposing* camp."

Fuck.

She was a warrior. A fucking witch warrior with some sort of smoke magic that he didn't know a single shit about.

"Duly noted," he muttered, the enticement of riling her up deflating with a dull *poof.* Staring at the beams along the ceiling, Merrick decided it may not be best to provoke her *too* much while he was her...captive?

"*Wonderful.*" Winnie echoed his earlier comment, though the way she said it sounded *much* more venomous. She trailed a sharp nail down his restrained forearm, scraping across the five thick, black bands of his *acat.* When she tapped his fist, Merrick unfurled his fingers begrudgingly.

The runestone dropped into his palm. Winnie pressed small, cool hands around his knuckles, wrapping the rock in his grasp.

The movement caused a strand of hair to swing in front of her face, engulfing him in a rush of her scent – supple leather and sage. It shot a bolt of heat through his blood – a sensation he hadn't felt since before the battle in the Opal Palace's throne room. Nostrils flaring, he whipped around, a low, warning rumble escaping from his chest.

His Sentry perked up, curious.

Or, *fuck*, was that his –

Winnie's plush lips parted slightly, her eyes widening as his focus snapped onto her. If the weight of his full attention intimidated the witch, she didn't show it. She simply tucked the strand behind her ear and leaned back in her chair, putting distance between them.

"Alright," Winnie said brightly, pulling away and crossing her ankles as if she hadn't just threatened his life and given him a godsdamned hard-on. "I think the shadow bindings should stay on for now. Remember – if you lie, you get burned, and then I kill you. And I'll be messy. And slow. Got it, bonehead?"

Biting back a groan, Merrick settled on keeping his face stony – hostile, willing his cock to chill out.

Gods, what was wrong with him?

This was serious.

But whatever she asked him, he wouldn't expose Irridessen.

He could survive torture. He'd take the burn, the pain, even death for his Kingdoms, for his friends that turned family, for –

"Do you think I'm pretty?"

He narrowed his brows, speechless. Winnie preened in her chair, a coy smile on her heart-shaped face, a wicked glint in her eyes.

"I'm mated," he snarled.

A searing burn against his hand caused him to drop the rock with a curse.

Though the pain was nothing compared to the agonizing, finite truth the runestone revealed.

His ghost soul tie was well and truly real.

At that crushing realization, he half-wanted Winnie to drive a sword through his gut or choke him with those iron-clad shadows.

Just to put him out of his misery.

"No, you aren't," she said quietly, as if somehow, she understood the weight of that burn on his palm, understood the gravity of the answer he gave.

But she didn't even know his name. She couldn't understand the significance of his answer.

A hollow feeling crept through his soul, the same darkness that threatened to consume him when he'd run like a coward from Sparrow. But now, the darkness seemed thicker, more suffocating.

And maybe it was in sheer desperation to banish that darkness that had Merrick confessing quietly, "Name's Merrick."

If she was surprised by his change of demeanor, Winnie didn't show it. Instead, she stuck out her hand and said firmly, confidently, "Well, *hello*, Merrick. It's a pleasure to formally meet you."

"So, GARGOYLES *DON'T* EAT beings, witches, or human flesh?"

"No, nope, and gross, no." Merrick shifted against the mattress, watching leaves rustle outside the window as he and Winnie continued their weird truth rock game.

She'd released his wings, shoulders, and arms from her magic, though the ones binding his thighs and ankles were still intact. But he was sitting up now, able to get a better look at the deep scars and still-packed poultices adorning his wings.

"Are you in the Jade Kingdom for any nefarious purposes?" Winnie asked from her chair, her bare feet now tucked underneath her thighs and boots sitting next to his bed.

"I went to the Ruby Kingdom to protect a friend. But shit went bad, and I was used as a bargaining chip to keep her in line. King Eamon tortured me for days, a week, maybe – I don't know. The last thing I remember is a sandy cell, passing out from blood loss, and waking up in this bed."

Their gazes swept to the truth rock in his palm. Aside from the first question, he'd collected no more burns.

The runestone lay flat, unassuming, in his palm, and Winnie nodded slowly, accepting his answer.

"The Ruby Kingdom is a thorn in our side," she said bitterly. "Their alliance with the Topaz Kingdom causes them to show up here from time to time, under the cover of 'securing their borders.' But it's a farce for them to get away with crossing *our* border and terrorizing our southern towns."

"I've gotten that gist from them. Do you know anything about the war King Eamon is threatening Irridessen with?"

He'd admitted to living in Irridessen, and Winnie seemed interested in hearing about his time in court, though she politely avoided asking anything considered *treason-adjacent*.

And somehow, over the hours of truth, a tentative understanding was being formed.

Merrick didn't know how to feel about that since he'd believed witches were nothing more than god-abandoned, soulless leeches for over a century.

"No. The Jade Kingdom was cut out completely from diplomatic meetings after the Witch War. We've stuck to our end of the treaty – more or less. But we've been isolated for thousands of years."

"You don't have spies lurking around?"

That caused Winnie to chuckle roughly, her fingers running through her short hair. "Not any sanctioned ones. The Jade Kingdom keeps to itself, and each Coven does its best to not stir up trouble. We aren't without our own radical sects that try to push the Jade Kingdom into action, but we typically tamp down that nonsense within our own borders."

Merrick mulled over the information provided. Winnie was either someone important to her Coven or a high-ranking warrior for the Jade Kingdom. She spoke well, but there was a wildness in her that didn't align with being a Lady of Court.

Not that Esmeray ever presented herself as anything other than a nightmare of bad manners and sass, but Merrick had learned Esmeray had her own reasons for doing things, and even her most insane plans garnered annoyingly solid results.

"If I give you freedom to get up, what will you do?"

"Go back to the Ruby Kingdom. Save my friend."

"So, head straight to your death? That's a boneheaded decision."

Silence.

Merrick wracked his brain for a reply, coming up short. Blowing out a rough breath, he scratched at his beard, the hair longer and coarser than he'd ever let it grow before.

Winnie let him brood.

He needed to go back to the Ruby Kingdom, smuggle Lenna home to Irridessen – but could he?

He'd be killed on sight if he was found in the Ruby Kingdom, and on the slim chance he *was* able to return Lenna to Irridessen, King Eamon would waste no time declaring war on Esmeray.

And Sparrow.

Sparrow was Queen of the Opal Kingdom. If they went to war against the two southern Kingdoms of Ingotheria, he'd be putting his rejected mate in danger, too.

A sinking pit of dread had his mouth tasting like ash.

Running through multiple plans where Lenna's safety was possible without the threat of war, the aching truth remained unyielding.

"Fuck," he spat, fingernails digging into his beard, scraping against his dry skin.

He couldn't return to the Ruby Kingdom to save Lenna without dying or causing more of a diplomatic nightmare. Lenna's rescue had to come from Irridessen – from beings other than himself.

Someone else – *once again* – needed to fix his mistake.

"You were a warrior for a long time, right?" Winnie asked thoughtfully, though he'd already said as much.

Merrick grunted in response, fisting the stupid truth rock. It dug painfully into his initial burn.

With a grimace, he cursed himself for being hard-headed, for taking his mind speak ring off. There'd been selfish relief in leaving it behind on the windowsill of the Obsidian Palace, but now, Lenna was alone, surrounded by enemies, and he couldn't get in contact with anyone. And Lenna's mind speak ring had self-destructed after being forcibly taken by a Ruby Kingdom guard under King Eamon's orders.

Merrick doubted Winnie would let him send a missive to the Obsidian Palace. Even if she agreed, the distance over the sea between Kingdoms was too great for a Moon Crow to fly.

Though the Oracle did have friends in the Ruby Palace – like the fiery fae female he'd met briefly. And Lenna had Hale, the half-fae baker and Lenna's partner, who wouldn't be harmed as long as Merrick was presumed dead.

It would only be a matter of time before Esmeray got suspicious as to why she couldn't reach Lenna through her ring. Once that happened, Merrick had no doubt Irridessen, and its Vessel Queens, would intervene on behalf of the Oracle's well-being.

Merrick had no clue exactly how many days passed since Winnie found him half-dead on the border. Maybe Esmeray already figured out what King Eamon was up to. Maybe Lenna was now back in Irridessen with Hale. It was a foolish hope, but one he wished to believe.

Winnie shifted in her chair, her chin propped against her fist, elbow braced above the leather sheath buckled around her thigh. She dragged her eyes to his. "If I asked you to help protect innocent beings from a terrible fate, what would you say?"

Meeting her gaze, Merrick was smacked with the awareness that his fear stemmed from being useless – unnecessary. In not having something to fight for, not having a purpose.

And with that, Merrick flicked his eyes to Winnie. The grim determination on her face burned with intensity, speaking to a pain he wasn't privy to, but understood in his soul all the same.

"I'd say, give me a weapon and unleash me on your nearest enemy."

He couldn't get to Lenna right now, but he *could* protect others.

Neither of them glanced at the dull runestone in his fist. The truth was evident enough in Merrick's tone, in the fire that ignited inside of him for the first time in months, chasing the darkness from his mind and bathing him in pure, purposeful light.

CHAPTER EIGHT
DOVE

"WAKE, DAUGHTER!"

The feminine voice, panicked and sharp, ripped through my subconscious a heartbeat before a heavy weight slammed against me.

My eyes flew open, a bolt of adrenaline lighting through my blood.

I sucked down air as I was dragged across the ground, and I must have screamed because a hand lurched out of the disorienting darkness to clasp around my throat. Thick fingers fisted in my hair, yanking me firmly into a hard body, my head bouncing painfully off the chest of the mysterious attacker as I was forced to my feet.

A jagged scratch across my collarbone had me struggling harder against the unyielding force holding onto me. The cut burned, telling me in no uncertain terms that I needed to fight back.

Awareness flooded my body, and all those years of self-defense training roared to life.

With a muffled shriek, I slammed the heel of my bare foot into my attacker's shin. Fury made blood boil in my veins as the hold on me barely loosened, so I switched tactics, going slack, pushing them off-balance, before throwing my skull back, hitting them in the chin.

Stars burst behind my eyelids at the impact, but I shook it off the moment their hold on me released.

I lurched forward, driving my elbow back, rewarded with the crunch of a broken nose. The assailant howled in pain, and I was off – sprinting towards the tree line.

Blue light sparked to life from my palms, settling against my skin and the soles of my feet like a shield as I dove into the dark forest.

I didn't chance a look behind me, focused on running as fast as I could.

To the Manor.

To Maude.

A blast of white light punched my shield with the force of a battering ram, causing me to stumble and lose precious momentum, but my magic held, blue sparks ricocheting in every direction as I leaped over downed branches in my path. From years of Maude's training, I could make a pretty solid protection barrier, knowing in a life-or-death situation, fleeing was solidly in my forte – fighting back was not.

"Over here!"

The command told me there was more than one witch in the moonlight-soaked meadow. A whimper of panic escaped between breathy pants.

Heavy footsteps to my right had me swerving around the trunk of an old birch, my hair whipping around as I changed direction, propelling myself through the outskirts of the forest and toward the thinner trees ringing the meadow. Forcing my breaths to slow, even, I adjusted my gait to the balls of my feet, silently thanking Maude for bitching at me to practice being fast without making noise.

I'd almost doubled back now, hoping they'd call out again and give me a sense of their position. Creeping along, I kept to the shadows, nearing the trail that led straight to the Manor.

My ears strained as I listened for any sounds of the attackers on my heels, but I only heard the rushing of my heartbeat as I picked my way to the shortest path that would take me to Maude.

Maybe they lost me. Maybe they –

A ball of pale blue light shot from the center of the meadow, straight at me. I flung myself out of the way. The magic crashed into an oak, splintering the bark.

With ragged breaths, I flat out sprinted the last fifty feet to the Manor's path, lungs seizing. Shouts rang out again, and this time, I heard bodies crashing through the brush.

Fighting back a sob, I burst through the ring of brambles separating me from the trail to the Manor, my terror causing a burn to flare at the base of my throat, pulsing with aching heat.

The Manor was a fifteen-minute walk away. At the pace I ran, I'd make it in half the time. A whizzing sound blew past, smashing into a tree right in front of me and exploding into a haze of sparks, causing a huge branch to crash down to earth.

I swallowed my scream. Dropping to the ground, I crawled under the fallen limb, pressing my palm against the branch. I'd ask Maude for forgiveness for siphoning the ancient tree once I was safe. But the moment I began siphoning the energy from the branch, a wave of nausea had me dry heaving so harshly black spots dotted my field of vision.

I shoved away from the limb like it burned me, my stomach rolling and plummeting as I gasped down lungfuls of brisk night air.

Magic from the ancient trees was off-limits.

Now I knew why. I'd *never* felt sick from siphoning before.

But I needed to keep my well of magic full. Just my shield alone was swiftly draining the power I siphoned from the meadow earlier.

And in my stress-packing, I'd chucked all my imbued runestones into my bag, not anticipating I'd need one before leaving for the Palace.

Stupid. Stupid. Stupid.

Fingers shaking, I quickly drew a detection rune into the ground.

Once the lines were connected, I slapped my hand against the cool soil, the rune sucking down magic at an alarming rate.

The rune glowed blue. I hopped to my feet, ignoring the screaming in my knees. The detection rune would alert me if an attacker was close.

My breathing reduced to short hisses as I rushed on, never allowing myself to sink into the pure dread that bleated in my head, the forest blurring as I veered down the narrow path, the view of the moonlit meadow flashing through the thin trunks whenever I ran too close to the edge of the forest.

One.

My detection rune alerted me that an assailant was heading my way. I corrected course, crashing further into the forest and changing directions at random, losing the trail to the Manor, hoping I could confuse them into losing *me*.

I knew these woods like the back of my hand. The Manor was seven minutes away – five if I ran faster.

Two.

"Fuck," I stuttered, sliding over a boulder and hitting the ground hard on my knees, my palms slamming into the soil, thankfully, my shield lessened the blow. I etched another detection rune into the soft dirt. Whoever was following me may find my first direction, but I doubted they'd anticipate me leaving the most common trail towards the Manor.

I knew these woods.

A patch of weeds grew tall in the crevice between trunks, and I grabbed a fistful as I bolted past, squeezing the long leaves in my hand and siphoning the scarce power from them. Pulling magic from the forbidden trees was too risky. I couldn't afford to get sick.

Five.

I choked back a wail of frustration when magic whispered there were now five assailants passing my new detection rune.

The terror threatened to reduce me to my knees, but I shoved down the panic and forced my legs to continue running.

But a sinking feeling began bogging me down, a solemn numbness slithering through my head. Heavy boots approached from behind.

Suddenly, it felt like I'd been herded *right* into a trap.

Who were they? Who was chasing me?

My limbs grew heavier, and though my mind was sharp a few minutes ago, it was now sluggish – slow.

I stumbled, saving my footing at the last second, my palm brushing and pushing off from the ground to propel me further into the dark.

A blue-ish sheen out of the corner of my eye blurred my vision. I recklessly crashed through the forest, scrambling over thorny brush, dried leaves crunching under my bare feet.

Wait.

They could hear that.

They could hear *me*.

I contemplated how long I'd stopped covering my tracks, how long I'd forgotten to muffle my footsteps, but couldn't come up with a solid answer.

Confusion settled around me like an icy, wet cloak, slick against my sweaty skin. The slice on my collar dribbled blood, thrumming in time with my heartbeat, fingers of pain like molten lava now digging into the nerves in my arms. Every step hurt, like I was walking across shattered glass.

Staggering, I rubbed my eyes, blinking furiously as my sight blurred and unfocused. The trees around me began dancing, my panic a rich, rhythmic tune.

Their usually rigid trunks distorted in time with my labored panting, growing and shrinking, warping with streaks of vivid color that left me winded and dizzy.

The Manor. I needed...I needed to get to the Manor.

I pumped my arms, but the more I fought to gain ground, the slower I became. A dull thudding began in my temples, spreading like wildfire until I could barely keep my eyes open against rolling waves of agony.

Gritting my teeth, I forced one foot in front of the other, my hands listless and swinging at my sides. Every muscle in my body trembled, my bare feet kicking up swirls of sparkly dirt that glimmered against my sticky skin.

And the sight of that shiny dust on my arm had my heartrate thundering and the blood chilling in my veins.

When did my shield fall?

Where was I?

I dropped to my knees, confusion tugging me into its comforting embrace as I stared blankly up at the sky above me, at the ever-changing colors of the branches twisting and writhing over each other.

The huge, brightly illuminated moon boldly peeked at me from between vivid orange and turquoise leaves that vibrated through the air.

"Hey Carra," I mumbled, my tongue thick as I hit the ground, sparkly dirt fluttering around me.

My eyelids drooped, and I got lost in my own mind where everything or nothing at all made any sort of sense.

Chapter Nine

DOVE

I was cold.

So insanely cold – like I was laying on a slab of ice.

My head pounded in agony, though with every thud of my heart, the pain radiating from my temples to my toes lessened.

A sharp slice of hurt on my thigh had my senses crashing and stumbling over each other, racing to be the first caught up to the present, and I moaned, trying and failing to sit up. Shivering, I slitted my lids – only to find my arms bound to my sides with cords of thick rope.

Deep, soul crushing fear sank in swiftly. I thrashed, unable to make out anything but the blur of a fire and a couple shadowed figures. A burn traveled up my leg. I let out a shriek at the unexpected sensation.

"She's awake," a voice croaked from above my head. I twisted, vision blurring.

That voice.

That voice was the assailant from the meadow.

They were chasing me.

And...they caught me.

My heart threatened to either stop beating altogether or ramp up in its attempt to flee while leaving the rest of my body behind. It was a knife's edge, a precipice.

Give in? Or fight.

It seemed as if my entire being wavered between finalities on opposing ends of the spectrum.

I forced my heart to stay with me at least a little longer while I figured out what was going on.

"Don't distract me. I need to make sure I get the blood runes right." A second voice, one lower in tone, replied from somewhere near the pain in my thigh.

Everything was slowly coming into focus, but I couldn't figure out where I was, my mind foggy and dazed.

A shuffling sounded. I opened my eyes to clearer vision.

Two black-cloaked figures huddled over my thigh. I couldn't see their faces. Full masks of gauzy cloth hid their identities completely.

They muttered something between themselves, their attention on my bare leg. I saw a flash of steel. And a shrilly echo screamed in my ears as the blade the second assailant held dug into my thigh. Or maybe that was me screaming because my blood was seeping out of a jagged gash and onto the...

Altar.

Hysteria flooded me.

I was shackled down to the altar in Carra's temple.

Those were blood runes being carved into my flesh.

I was the next sacrifice.

I screamed until my throat rubbed raw, bucking wildly against the bindings on my wrists and ankles as a churning wave of sick crashed over me.

The assailants paused, waited until I was still, and then cut again, ignoring me completely.

My breathing stayed shallow as I angled my chin enough to see what they were doing. The clothing I was wearing was gone, leaving me in my underthings, the thin, white material now grungy and spotted with blood.

A third figure appeared from the shadows, their gauze covered face peering at me before sweeping down to where the other two huddled around my leg.

"Should we gag her? I don't want the yelling to attract attention."

The second figure – the one with the dagger – shook his head. "No one's coming out this way."

I whimpered, finding my voice, hating that it was quiet and meek and filled with terror. "Please, let me go. Let me go. I won't tell anyone you kidnapped me."

A chuckle met my ear, before the third man scoffed, "*Let you go*? But you should be *thanking* us. Your divine purpose will help us find favor with our gods once again."

With a choked mewl, I begged my tongue to work, to argue, to tell them about my life and how I was needed and important, finding it dry and unwieldy in my mouth. A dizzying apprehension settled against my shoulders as one of them twisted my wrist against the binding to the point of pain.

"Don't speak to her," the man with the dagger growled before searing into my flesh again.

Hot blood wept forth. Too much blood.

A hiss from the third masked assailant.

"Not too deep. She needs to be alive for the ritual to begin."

"Shut up. I know."

My teeth chattered as the dagger cut in slow, precise strokes.

One of them hummed in appreciation, but I was too focused on not passing out to see who it was. "Massis will be happy with this one. You were right – a full moon will bring forth many of his horde."

"And you're sure the *veles* are open?"

"We'll find out soon enough."

I screamed as a fire-hot brand was pressed against my hip. A haze of black wafted from my skin, dissipating into the still air.

"The blood rune is activated and the *veles* are ready. It's time."

The three figures straightened, chanting in an odd language. *A spell.* I fought to slip my wrist out of its binding, afraid of being caught in their spell work's web. Spitting blood from a split lip through my teeth, my dry throat throbbed, and, fighting to stay conscious, I recalled Maude's curt voice in her self-defense class, "Don't ever give up. One second, one breath, one small action, can be the difference in you returning home or going to Minmere. Never give up. Never stop fighting."

I blocked out the radiating pain of my battered body, the smell of charred flesh, the soft sound of my blood *drip, drip,* dripping off the side of the altar and splattering onto the stone floor below.

I focused only on the binding on my wrist – the binding I would gladly break my thumb to escape from. I'd done it before – part of the training that seemed so asinine at the time but prepared me in its own fucked up way.

A soft glow bathed the altar in red light, tearing through my concentration.

I tried to make sense of it but...that light was coming from me. The assortment of crude blood runes carved into my flesh were glowing as their chanted spell became louder.

Waves of excruciating agony erupted.

My spine bowed off the cold altar, tremors wracked my limbs, my muscles seized.

Screeching ringing filled my ears.

I sucked in a rattling gasp.

And then...something *snapped*, and I was gone.

"You aren't supposed to be here."

A voice both ancient and new, wickedly cruel and achingly kind, blooming and withering, spoke from above me.

I rose on shaky legs, my bindings gone. I braced for that bite of pain, that cold sensation of my body on the altar, the heat of fire licking against my skin.

Nothing.

Even the twinge in my neck was gone, and I slowly raised my head, feeling disembodied and empty. A cry spilled from my lips as I recoiled.

Though the witches primarily prayed to Carra and Massis since they were the gods that bestowed blessings on witch kind in the past, the sight of the goddess before me had my knees hitting the black stone floor in utter reverence.

Because I stood before Phades, Goddess of Death, as she lounged upon her throne of bones.

"Am I dead?" I asked, my words quivering under the heavy gaze of the death goddess's empty eye sockets. With the skull of a ram, the body of a wraith, and black curled horns that sucked in any flickers of light that blazed through Minmere's halls, Phades regarded me silently. I shivered.

Minmere.

Where all souls – regardless of species or magic – came to rest after death's embrace.

I sucked in my breath, though once I did, there was no longer a need for me to draw air because –

"Not fully." *Phades clacked her jawbone as she leaned towards me.* "You, Witch, have much more of a story to write."

"What happened?" *I wracked my brain, remembering every chilling detail that led me to this result yet not understanding why my fate ended here.*

Phades sighed, the end punctuated by a growl that rattled existence itself. "You are currently connected to a source of magic that is as ancient and ageless as the god realms themselves. I did not call your soul here – it would seem you are traveling through god realms on your own accord."

"I'm dying on that altar," *I whispered, the words weird to say aloud, especially since no panic or terror accompanied them. I was...at peace.*

"Yes, Witch," *Phades nodded as a glimmer of purple shimmered out of the corner of my eye.* "But see to it that you don't give in to the finality of death. Fight back, tear open the confines of your magic. They are taking your life from you – take from them instead."

I took a breath – this one more of a necessity for my lungs - and I did as Phades directed. Screwing my eyes shut, I sank into my tiny well of magic. But with a pang of disappointment, I realized I had no power left.

"Deeper," *Phades urged, her voice a purr. I heard her bony fingers clack against the throne's armrest, and wondered if her sharp, onyx nails gouged lines into the bones she sat upon.* "Push through the connection you are holding to the god realms. It would be curious if you found magic there, wouldn't it? And even more curious to see what you'd do with it."

Her odd words made little sense to me, but I gritted my teeth, slamming my consciousness into the barren pit of my power, clawing through the bottom of the dry kernel of magic inside me where my heritage gift lay.

And when I hit a soft give in the bottom of that pit, I shoved through it.

I fell down, down, down, into my own soul, grappling at that connection and pulsing red light, the rush of ice-cold air and frothing current of magic whining with reckless power.

I careened into that power, vaguely knowing I was out of Minmere, but not entirely sure where my soul was traveling now.

My soul crashed back into my body. I shrieked in rage.

Drunk with power, and furious over not being strong enough to save myself, I attacked.

The three cloaked figures scrambled away as I curled my fingers into fists, connected to their ritual by the stream of red in my consciousness.

And with a roar that seemed to pause the air itself, I siphoned it, welcoming that volatile power into my soul, wrapping it around me in a cloak of my own destruction.

With a howl, I pushed every morsel of stolen magic to my palms.

And with a mighty *crack,* my bindings incinerated.

My freedom was met with shouts of fear, the figure with the dagger bellowing at his partners to contain me.

But I couldn't be contained.

Because I was *unleashed.*

With a swipe of my hand, the figure closest to me careened into the wall in a flash of red-tinged purple magic. I scrambled up, falling off the side of the altar.

Slapping my hand against the glowing blood rune on my hip, I siphoned the last drops of magic from their ritual.

As the red glow dimmed, a wispy tendril of black shadow shot through my fingers, curling around my wrist before darting away.

Staggering upright, I raised my free hand as another cloaked figure rushed me, the silver dagger raised and blue light magic sparking through his fingers. I regarded him for a mere heartbeat before shoving away from the altar towards the dazed body of his cohort, swiping my arm behind me as I went.

A wave of purple and red magic burst from my palm, whipping towards my attacker, who evaded my strike at the last second.

I couldn't help the wild laugh as he whirled around, dropped the dagger, and fled into the night.

Numbly, I pressed my palm into my side, a rush of healing magic intrinsically searching for the deepest injuries and healing those first.

My regular well of magic *never* allowed me to heal myself. I was accustomed to my soul being calm, my gift shallow and familiar.

Now, my power was a churning sea, strange and reckless. Before I could marvel at the heady rush, my control slipped, and the tempest of red wrenched free. I fought desperately to keep it, to bury it into my soul.

It may have been a desperate gamble, or a greedy, unspoken desire for a witch so used to rationing tiny morsels of power from a meadow of flowers, but a hollow grief engulfed me as that thrashing ocean of power receded from my grasp.

The swift disappearance of power made my legs shake. Pulling myself up using the lip of the altar, I fought to righten myself on unsteady feet as unconsciousness threatened.

I needed to breathe.

But before I could suck down more than a shaky gasp of air, a figure in my peripheral barreled towards me, hitting me in the stomach and sending me to my knees, the air I needed so desperately knocked from my lungs.

I collapsed into a heap of bloody, trembling limbs as two cloaked figures lurched forward simultaneously, sensing my demise and their chance at seizing control.

With a sob, I threw my hand out, but no magic rallied, my chance of escape ruined.

Their hands dug into my tender flesh. Yanking me from the ground forcefully, they worked in tandem to bind my wrists to my sides with a length of rough twine.

"Call him back," the one with the raspy voice bit out. "She's out of magic and we can get more from her."

The second figure wavered.

"Do it now," the one holding me snapped. "You don't want to anger *him,* and Massis won't grant you what you seek if you give up."

Without waiting on a response, I was shoved forward, crashing into the side of the altar with a quiet mewl. My stricken soul aware this fight was good and lost.

The figure tugged me up by the hair. Tears blurred my vision as I was shoved back atop the altar, falling painfully on my bound wrist.

I screamed, earning a slap across the face from the hands closest to me.

"Shut up," he grumbled. "I'll finish this myself. Grab that dagger and bring it here."

His partner didn't answer.

Then, a muffled *thump* ricocheted off the stone walls, the temperature in the chamber plummeting as an unearthly growl echoed through the chilled air.

The assailant sucked in a sharp breath, spinning away from me and towards the sound.

From the corner of the crumbling temple ruins, a thick tendril of inky black smoke reared up, growing and twisting, pooling against the rough floor.

The *shick* of claws dragging against stone pulled my attention to the shadows forming thicker and larger – until a solid black wolf with pointed ears and ruby red eyes stepped from the swirling darkness, its lips peeled back to reveal pearl white fangs.

"Massis," my captor wheezed, terror lacing his words. "I've been a loyal follower, bringing your demons earthside to assist you in claiming what you most desire. Please, banish your grimm from this temple, so I can bring your horde from Avamere with your blessing."

Grimm.

A grimm had come through the veil.

This night was going from terrible to awful to even worse. I swallowed my panic, focusing instead on shimmying myself towards the lip of the altar. I didn't want to be here when that demon-beast decided it was hungry.

A harsher snarl rang out, as in answer to my assailant's prayer.

I stayed perfectly frozen, wondering if grimm were similar at all to the wolves that ran through the forest, baying at the moon. If I pretended to not be here, maybe it would forgo eating me and focus on eating my attacker.

A beat of silence passed.

I scooted quietly toward the edge of the altar.

But the beast materialized right in front of me, red eyes pinned to my bleeding wounds.

I held my breath, heart hammering to the point of dizziness as every rational thought eddied out of my head. Fighting a healthy dose of fear, I locked eyes with the grimm.

And to my complete surprise, the beast huffed, bowing its snout to me.

Okay, what the fuck.

I pressed my lips together, wondering how delusional I was to consider this was real.

My lungs felt as if they were curling up inside me. The grimm inhaled my scent, ruffling strands of my hair that weren't sticky with blood.

I tried recalling anything I'd ever read about grimm from my well-worn copy of *Terramere's Beasts* by my favorite author, Neera Mellow, but with the giant wolf inches from my face, it seemed my brain fled, taking all knowledge with it in its haste.

Every muscle in my body tensed, waiting for that sharp row of teeth to send me straight back to Minmere – for good this time. I flinched.

Nothing happened.

I distinctly heard the click of claws retreating, and I cautiously opened my eyes as the grimm slunk around the corner of the altar, its fur so dark I could barely make out where the night ended and the beast began.

I glanced from the volkhound to the cloaked figure scooting against the wall in an attempt to run away. He was ten feet from a large crack in the temple where a slice of starlight pointed to a hidden escape route.

Hatred ignited through my blood. I scrambled up, my bound wrists and scraped knuckles dragging painfully against stone, the volkhound forgotten. Pure loathing consumed me, driving me to attack against better judgement.

But before I could form a plan in my mind, the grimm sprung from the dark – faster than an arrow. A blur of fur and shadow, the sickening sound of jaws closing around my assailant's throat, the tang of fresh blood.

He didn't even have time to scream before succumbing to death's teeth and fury.

As the body stiffened and fell still, the grimm turned to me, maw dripping crimson, and slipped into the shadows once more.

Chapter Ten

DOVE

I LURCHED TO MY side, puking up bile and blood, the sound of my gagging echoing off the stone walls of the temple. Chest heaving, I focused on sitting up without passing out. The metallic taste in my mouth had me shuddering, my throat raw.

In the corner, the fire was still crackling, throwing disorienting shadows around the bodies of two assailants, the gore and stench of death in the air making me woozy.

Better them than me.

I eased my stiff neck left and right, confirming the grimm wasn't lurking in the dark, waiting to finish me off. My wrists were still tied together, and my fingers were numb, but those two aches were *far* down on the list of things that hurt as radiating pain thrummed through me in time with my still-racing pulse.

At how narrowly I avoided death, I leaned over the altar, spitting out a mouthful of blood and bile.

Slowly, my mind pieced itself back together, tidying up a nice box of trauma to reveal later. I pushed myself up awkwardly, breath catching on a wheeze from broken ribs. Blood pooled in my mouth. I had internal injuries as deadly as the deep gashes on my skin.

I needed to siphon. Right now. Or I wouldn't make it to sunrise.

Which meant I had to get outside. In the ruins of Carra's stone temple, there was nothing to pull power from.

An icy muzzle nudged my bare shoulder. I almost fainted in fear.

The beast's giant paws made no sound against the blood covered altar. I didn't trust myself to look at the grimm, hoping I wouldn't wake up back in Minmere.

My muscles locked as that soft nose pushed into my palm with sureness, knife-sharp teeth grazing the veins in my wrist. Freezing breath fluttered over my sore flesh. Understanding flooded my veins. I'd traded one predator for another. The grimm could finish me off easily. I let out a cry of fear, as if that would save me from –

The rope bindings went slack.

With a twist, I yanked free of the rough twine, staring at the beastie in awe. As if it felt my attention on it, the grimm sat back on its haunches, its thick tail thudding against the altar, sending plumes of shadows wafting and curling into the air.

"Did you...untie me?" I asked dumbly.

It yipped proudly, body wriggling, that tail thumping faster against the altar – though no blood soaked into its fur.

I was reminded of the dog my neighbor played with in his front yard. The yips meant their pup was happy.

At least for a normal dog. I didn't know much about Avamere summoned entities of the apex demon variety.

I eased off the altar onto unsteady legs, my body trembling and bloody.

The grimm stayed where it was, head tilted – as if it knew I was reeling at the enormity of this situation.

Breathing through my nose and hissing the breath past my split lip, I aimed my feet towards the wall ten feet in front of me. With support, I could navigate to the mouth of the temple, and from there...

I'd *crawl* home if need be.

But I had to get away from the demon. One wrong move and it could attack.

I carefully placed one foot in front of the other, but the moment I tried to support my weight, my leg spasmed. Dropping off the altar, I fell hard to my already bruised knees.

The grimm huffed.

Hearing the beastie leap off the altar, I swallowed my scream, scrambling over to the stone wall. An unnatural rush of cool air surrounded me, chilling my bare skin as razor sharp claws clicked against the ground.

But as I fought to stand, using the wall as support, a demanding snout pushed into my side. The black hound squeezed me between itself and the wall – holding me upright.

Warily, I measured the massive demon leaning against me. Its back came up to my throat, and the beast's breath hit the top of my skull.

I slowly extended a hand towards the grimm. Our eyes locked, and a connection of something *familiar* soothed my panic.

Weaving trembling fingers through the scruff on its neck, the volkhound's thick muscles bunched and relaxed under my palm. Steadying myself, my raw throat burning, I fought to calm my nerves. The grimm took a hesitant step toward the mouth of the temple. Biting back a groan of pain, I tightened my fist in its fur.

I shoved away the impossibility of the situation, mentally flipping through the book by Neera Mellow on the beasts that – literature noted – only responded to Massis's commands. I could practically see the page in my mind, how neatly the dark ink was printed against yellowed parchment.

Grimm are the most elusive of Massis's horde of demons. Though no grimm have ever been captured for study, scholars confirmed grimm are blood-thirsty beasts whose powers align closely with the shadow magic Massis granted half his witches.

Able to travel long distances by melting into darkness around them, grimm were devastating in the Witch War, summoned by Massis's faithful followers to prepare the realm of the living for Massis. Gods help our damned souls if the grimm once again enter Terramere, because nothing can deter them from their hunt.

Resolving to find better books about the shadowy beast, I dismissed the idea of being eaten right this moment. Wincing as a twinge of pain lanced through me, my gaze wandered back towards the grimm that seemed perfectly content to brace the majority of my weight.

Two pointed ears perked up from its skull, twitching as we slowly made our way out of the stone temple and into the chilly night air. As I greedily inhaled a shaky breath that didn't smell like death, grass crunched under my bare feet. Those ruby eyes swiveled towards me, and a flame sparked through the irises. The grimm tensed.

A male voice rumbled out from the dark trees ringing the ruins, and a deep laugh answered. Two more assailants. Their tone was easy, carefree – not that of captors realizing their prisoner escaped, but terror slammed into me all the same.

My pulse skyrocketed. Dread pounded through my veins, dizzying, overwhelming dread.

There were more out there. They would find me again. They would –

My grip on the grimm loosened.

I collapsed, gasping for air, fighting for control over my quaking limbs.

With pure panic rushing through my veins, my feverish skin burned as I scrambled towards the closest tree – a slim birch with white bark peeling off its trunk. Siphoning magic from Bramberry Forest had made me awfully sick before – but I would much prefer being alive and nauseous over dead.

Taking the last few feet at a desperate lunge that scuffed my battered knees, I slammed my hands against the prickly bark, wracked with guilt at destroying this tree for my own personal gain.

The grimm's absence was like a phantom limb, the disappearance of cool fur in my hands spiking my fear.

Had it abandoned me?

Left me because I was a weak witch?

Was I not worth eating?

My palm ached as I offered hushed apologies to the birch. Starting at the leaves, my well of magic began to fill – bringing with it that now-familiar wave of nausea as each silver-gilded leaf curled and died.

The power settled into my well of magic, and I forced myself away before hitting my threshold, directing the trickle of energy to the cuts and burns along my flesh, feeling the soft sting of new, pinkish skin.

Like before, when I siphoned the Bramberry tree by the meadow, I felt sick, but that stomach-twisting, soul-retching vertigo wasn't as crippling as before.

But I was lukewarmly alive at best, so maybe the Bramberry Forest took pity on me.

I focused on easing the pain from my head, torn muscles, and broken ribs. The less deadly injuries would need to be healed later, but I was running out of time.

As healing magic flowed, my senses sharpened. I slipped into the pool of magic the birch held, hoping none of the attackers could see the birch's leaves withering, the bark turning from white to ashy grey.

A howl tore through the air, and the little hairs on the nape of my neck stood on end. Terrified screams went up a hundred yards away.

And...the night was quiet once more.

I huddled at the base of the now-dead tree, drawing a growth rune in the soil with cracked fingernails. Pressing my palm against the earth, I pushed a kernel of power into the rune. Hopefully, a new sapling would bloom in the springtime.

Self-defense was one thing – but I'd give back to the forest I grew up in, thanking the ancient entity in my own way.

The padding of paws drew my attention towards the dark forest. Ruby red eyes reflected back. Within a breath, the grimm stepped from the shadows once more, its gaze locked on mine.

As I gingerly rose from the ground, the grimm butted against my side once more, silky fur rubbing against my arm.

Though my ears strained and my eyes skimmed every corner of darkness, every tree, every clearing, no assailants appeared on our slow walk back towards my house. And when my bare feet finally touched the cobblestone street leading to my front door, I whimpered in relief.

Now that I no longer believed the giant beast would eat me, our connection grew into a comfortable hum that buzzed through my bones.

Going to the Manor crossed my mind, but I was exhausted, and the idea of recounting my terrifying ordeal at this very moment to Maude made me want to break down. I just wanted to curl up in bed and sleep.

The emotions slamming into me were escalating towards a full-on nervous breakdown. I'd prefer to do that alone in private.

Coming to a stop at the bottom of my entryway stairs, a lump lodged in my throat, I released my hold on the grimm, rallying magic from the birch tree to unlock my door. My clothes were gone, my key with them, leaving me in blood-stained undergarments with a fat dose of relief that none of my neighbors were outside in the middle of the night.

I extended my hand towards the rusty door lock, pulling magic to my fingertips.

Purple wisps shot from my fingers, darting through the keyhole and unlocking the deadbolt with a *click*.

I blinked.

Blinked again.

Again.

A roar started in my head as my mind went wholly blank. I stared down at my palm, where a very *not blue* light was slowly fading.

What the fuck?

My light magic always manifested as a cool, robin's egg hue of blue, another jarring fact that separated me from the higher-ranking witches in the Coven. *Their* magic was pure, brilliant light that came in hues of silver or white.

Witches with lesser heritage gifts manifested shades of blue, a dismal reminder of my inadequacies every time I used magic in front of others.

My head spun. I'd siphoned from the ritual, but all that power was used up in my attempt to escape. And even then – it had been a burst of deep, dark purple tinged red – not this...vibrant lavender glow cupped in my palm.

Was it the spell work? The ritual itself? Or did siphoning the forest's ancient magic warp my own gift temporarily? Was that why I'd gotten so sick?

It had to be the birch. A spell was short-term magic – another reason the practice had been abandoned in favor of runes.

Which meant my light magic would go back to its normal blue shade once I ran through the rest of the power from the birch that sat in my soul.

With a resolution to dig deeper into this tomorrow, and bone-deep weariness, I left all my confusingly unanswerable questions on my porch. I swung the front door open - only for a blur of fur to dart past with a joyful chirp, trotting into the house with its wispy tail held high.

"Are you...do you want to stay here?" I asked incredulously, as the grimm leapt onto my grey couch, the rickety frame squeaking under its considerable bulk. Without really expecting an answer from the beastie, I locked every lock and double checked each one obsessively before peering at the grimm in my living room.

It was now sprawled against the cushions, hind legs half dangled off the edge of the couch, licking its front paws.

My dry throat suddenly took precedence. Without stopping to grab a glass, I flipped on the sink, and stuck my mouth under the faucet, slurping lukewarm water straight from the tap. After the night I'd had, it was the best tasting water in the entire realm.

Gurgling a mouthful to get rid of the blood residue in my teeth, I spit into the basin and drank deep. I needed to bathe, get the feel of my assailant's hands off my skin, inspect my wounds, heal whatever still marred my body.

As I turned towards the grimm again, my academic mind scrambled for answers. *Why am I not getting eaten by a grimm right now? What do I feed my somewhat domestic volkhound? Can I keep a giant shadow wolf as a pet?*

The sight of the volkhound curled up atop the lumpy couch, tail curled over its long snout, made my heart squeeze. Especially as the deep rumbles of the grimm's breathing made it to my ears.

I smiled.

"Thank you," I whispered towards the sleeping grimm, emotion from my near-death experience choking the words at the end. Unsure if the beastie would be here when I returned, I backed up slowly, careful to avoid the creaky board by my bathroom. With tears brimming against my lids, I softly closed the door to take a much-needed bath.

CHAPTER ELEVEN
MERRICK

"WE'VE *BEEN* OVER THIS, Tallah," Winnie snapped. "The bonehead doesn't eat witches. Put the claws away."

Merrick frowned behind Winnie, watching the dark-skinned witch named Tallah warily. She'd been one of the two females in the cottage when he'd woken up – one of the witches who'd healed him. But now, the fact that he was out of bed, standing a foot taller than any of them and untethered by Winnie's shadows, it seemed the witch was having second thoughts regarding her approval of his presence.

The battle axe in her hand pulsing with light magic was a solid clue.

"Don't give him a weapon," Tallah warned as she surveyed Merrick with distaste.

"He's unarmed," Winnie growled, a challenge glinting in her hard eyes. Tallah straightened, lips pressed in a firm line.

In a show of good faith, Merrick lifted the hem of his shirt, revealing the empty waistband of the slightly-too-small trousers.

None of the witches were anywhere *close* to his size. But somehow, a couple pairs of simple, drawstring pants and long-sleeved tunics, altered to accommodate his wings, had shown up in his room that morning. The thoughtful gesture was confusing, but these witches didn't want to shuffle their prisoner around the Jade Kingdom nude.

Tallah huffed, lowering her axe slowly, as if his compliance irked her. Merrick dropped his shirt, tightening his wings to his back until a burn of pain sundered through them.

In Irridessen, he'd never gone *anywhere* without an array of weapons, and though Winnie told him she'd hand over a weapon once they arrived at their destination, traveling without a single dagger was...uncomfortable.

The fact that he couldn't Sentry wasn't helping, either.

Thinking about his wings felt like a punch to the gut. Winnie had quietly explained that delicate bones in his left wing were shattered, tendons were severed, and his right barely fared better. The healers did what they could, but where they were unsure how magic would affect the complex injuries, rudimentary methods were used instead. Though he could hold his wings off the ground, herb-packed poultices to ward off infection and rows of neat stitches along the thin membranes made it so he couldn't stretch them out to their full span.

Merrick had to admit the witches did their best. Even a fae healer specialized in gargoyle wings would've had a difficult time given the sheer amount of damage he'd been found with.

If he shifted now, every barely healed bone and tendon would simply snap again. And though he'd be able to Sentry once the stitches came out, if a gargoyle sustained major wing injuries, there was a chance flight in either form would become impossible.

An hour ago, Winnie told him they were leaving at nightfall. She'd tossed him an empty canvas bag and scampered back out of the room.

Dressing himself was difficult since he couldn't lift his arms without agony dancing down his back and wings. By the time he successfully got a tunic on and the buttons at the top fastened, he'd broken a sweat.

But as he gingerly tugged on the black trousers, grimacing with every slight movement, he silently made two vows.

The henchmen protecting King Eamon would meet death by his blade. He'd godsdamned fly again.

At least the fuckers hadn't sawed off his horns. That was the most disrespectful act one could do to a gargoyle – taking away the link to their lineage. Gargoyle horn patterns followed familial lines, though some half-fae, half-gargoyle beings – like Esmeray – inherited horns directly from the god that blessed them.

Merrick mindlessly rubbed his palm against one, the slate cool under his touch in the chill night air.

Around them, witches bustled about, focused on preparations, though they all gave Merrick a wide berth. All except Winnie - who stood next to him, barely reaching his sternum, though the petite spitfire appraised the scene with her arms crossed and a sharp gaze like the finest of commanders.

She allowed his freedom after he'd promised to help fight her enemies, though she hadn't gotten around to telling him who the enemies *were*.

He'd learned a lot about witchkind these last few days while his strength slowly returned. Surprisingly, Winnie kept him company, passing the time with card games and polite, non-intrusive, questions. The runestone she'd been so adamant about using had stayed on the windowsill, untouched. As he packed up his meager belongings, Merrick tossed the truth rock into the bottom of his canvas bag.

Now, they were moving out of this small village, heading towards one of the towns where Winnie received confirmation of a threat needing to be eradicated. A caravan of wagons was packed and ready to move, but Merrick's presence as he'd ducked from the stone cottage and strode towards Winnie with his rucksack caused a tiny uproar with the group they were traveling with.

Tallah was the only one brave enough to go on the offensive. Her wife, Emrin, seemed less than enthused about Merrick coming along, but she'd taken one look at him and shrugged – stating he was *definitely* big enough to be a warrior, and they could use all the help they could get.

Winnie's group consisted of three other light witches from the Royal Coven, plus Tallah and Emrin who were from the Coven in Shadymoss.

Tallah finally backed down when Emrin stepped between her and Winnie, leaning over to peck a kiss on her wife's cheek, whispering something in her ear that Merrick couldn't make out through the curtain of Emrin's long copper hair.

Witches followed the customs of marriage like the humans in the Slate Kingdom. He'd known beings in Irridessen who hadn't waited for a soul tie and married instead, but he never understood the appeal until now. He'd never receive a soul tie again. The thought stung, burning as painfully as his wings.

"We good?" Merrick ground out.

"It's fine," Winnie clipped, glancing away, ash brown hair swinging in her face.

"The Royal Coven is more accepting of you since you're um…gigantic. Obviously strong. A warrior. But Shadymoss has a long history of being dramatic over newcomers. I –" Winnie seemed to reconsider whatever she was about to say. Instead, she sighed deeply. "Emrin and Tallah are good people. They just worry."

Spinning on her heel, signifying the conversation was over, Winnie led him towards the row of carriages. The light witches illuminating the area weren't over here, and the dark pressed in on all sides. He couldn't see a damn thing.

With a deep breath, Merrick trailed a mental finger down the thread of his Sentry. Until recently, he'd never pulled the magic apart, never adapted just *one* sense to that of his beast. It wasn't a skill he'd ever cared to learn.

His Sentry was massive, with thick grey hide and scaled wings, a spiked tail, and razor-sharp fangs and talons. Lethal. Able to outfly the majority of other gargoyles.

There'd never been a need to take those pieces apart, to be anything *other*. But during the long, dull hours where he laid in bed, he'd practiced.

It was weird - morphing just his eyes to those of his Sentry, or his ears, or teeth. The difficulty alone of peeling that strand of power apart without accidentally losing his grip on it, going full-beast, and rebreaking his wing was enough to make his heart pound.

But already, the practice paid off. His gargoyle sight honed in on a half dozen trunks stacked atop each other next to a high sided cart. Without waiting to be asked, he stooped down, careful to lift with his legs, hauling them easily into the carriage. Winnie whistled appreciatively.

"Like I said – freaky strong." Lowering her voice, she continued, "The witches will come around. Just give them time. It's been an...adjustment for them as much as it's been for you. No one's ever seen a gargoyle before. Even fighting with Topaz, there's no gargoyles dispatched for border skirmishes. Only fae."

Merrick didn't know what to say so he grunted instead, taking in their surroundings with his enhanced vision. A cool breeze filled the air, alluding that winter wasn't far. A long snouted rodent shuffled through a mound of dirt, hunting for food. It was peaceful. The crunching of boots over golden leaves, the rustle of branches...the low murmur of witches talking amongst themselves...

He wondered if this Kingdom got snow, and he wondered if he'd be here long enough to see it.

He wondered what the weather was like right now in Irridessen. If Sparrow was preparing for her first winter solstice as Queen. If she even knew he was missing.

He wondered if Lenna was still safe in the Ruby Kingdom, if the frigid temperatures that befell the desert during the night were beginning to creep into the daytime, too.

And then he wondered what the *fuck* was pulling the carriage.

"What is that?" Merrick asked, jerking his horns toward the odd creature. Rounding the corner, he noticed a second hitched next to it.

They had bodies similar to a horse, with lean, muscular legs that feathered down into longer fur that draped over cloven hooves. But their hides were an assortment of stripes and spots, the color palette soft, deerlike.

To top it off, the second beastie sported a rack of antlers. Size-wise, they were a bit smaller than a horse, thinner, too, those lithe, sinewy muscles speaking to speed and agility.

"Those are forest kelpies," Winnie said, patting one between the ears. "Stronger than a draft horse, swift as a deer. We've been breeding them for centuries."

Merrick guessed it was female, since it had no antlers. The forest kelpie's large, brown eyes were depthless, outlined with thick black lashes and a sweet disposition. The beastie let out a low whistle, nuzzling further into Winnie's hand.

Merrick moved closer, the kelpie's back came up to his abdomen. The beastie side stepped at his approach, eyeing him with apprehension. Mutely, Merrick held out his palm, allowing the kelpie to sniff him and decide if he was worth her time.

"I talked to Emrin," Winnie added, her fingers grazing down the male kelpie's spiky, black tipped mane. "With your stitches still healing, you'll be in the cart for this trip.

"Out of sight out of mind," he stated flatly.

"Stop." Winnie moved in front of him, fire leaping into her irises. The firm expression on her face hushed his bitter mind. The witch waited until he met her eyes before poking his chest with a finger. "No *'woe is me'* shit here. Got it?"

"Got you," Merrick husked, raking a hand through his hair. He hadn't had a chance to cut it or shave his beard, and the length was starting to irritate him.

Around this many witches, he was totally out of his element, barely able to string together more than a few words at a time to respond to Winnie. More than once, he'd found his pulse jumping as witches siphoned a patch of vivid mushrooms growing near the cottage, waiting for one to turn and attack.

Winnie nodded to the covered carriage behind them. It wasn't much bigger, pulled by three kelpies, and looked only slightly more comfortable than the wagon he'd tossed the trunks into.

"That's your ride. We keep it as an infirmary, but you can sit in there. The kelpies are too small for you to ride. I'll ask around when we get to the Shadymoss Marsh and see if we can get you something more...um, gargoyle-sized."

Merrick gritted his teeth. Great – they were headed right for a Coven even *less* welcoming to newcomers.

Without replying, he stomped over to the covered carriage and hauled himself through the open door. Ducking his head, Merrick squeezed onto the flat bench that likely doubled as a bed for injured folk. A medley of open crates sat opposite him, and he considered moving them to the other cart so he could get more leg room.

But before he could summon the strength to clamber back out of the carriage, a whistle split the night, the carriage jolted into motion, and his hands shot out, bracing on either side of the cramped interior. Resigned to his fate in the tiny box on wheels, Merrick shifted as much as the space would allow, trying desperately to keep the jostling of his inflamed wings limited.

The hours dragged by – counted by Merrick's irritated observation of the waning moon arching through the sky. He'd barely been able to stretch out as they trundled slowly along the dirt road.

He tried settling his wings against the thin mattress he sat upon, and the carriage immediately hit some sort of bump or divot in the road. Merrick swallowed down more than one bark of fire-hot misery, not wanting the witches to think he was weak.

Winnie and her troupe rode next to the caravan, astride their beasties, talking amongst themselves. The waves of conversation were just over-lapped and muted enough that Merrick couldn't concentrate on holding his wings slightly aloft, keeping his neck lowered so his horns didn't punch through the canvas top of the carriage, and also listen in on what they were saying. He could adjust his ears to his Sentry, but didn't trust his focus while balancing so precariously.

He heard random strings of words here and there, but nothing that would be of any use to anyone in Irridessen. Which, he reasoned with himself, didn't actually count as spying.

It was *barely* eavesdropping.

The only time his attention piqued was when Winnie's voice rose among the group, her dry laugh and cheeky sarcasm the sole sounds he could peel from the melody with ease.

Yesterday, he asked who they'd be fighting. Winnie had gone quiet for a long moment, and when he repeated the question, she'd assured him in that clipped tone that he'd be filled in once they made it to their destination. And then she promptly left his room.

The awkward stares and wide berth the other witches resorted to barely registered to him. He'd been through worse. It was somewhat of his mantra these days, reminding himself that he'd survived a lot prior to this encounter with witches, and he'd survive this, too.

It was due to his internal battle of brooding and clenching every muscle in his body that Merrick barely registered the chatter and noise abating with a sharp inhale.

"Weapons!" Winnie roared.

Chapter Twelve
MERRICK

Merrick lurched forward on instinct, the upturned tips of his horns tearing through the roof of the carriage.

A hard jolt of the carriage had him careening backwards. He grunted in agony as his left wing pinched between his body and the wall.

Thundering hooves, shrill screams. Bursts of bright light.

Merrick threw open the door, half jumping, half falling to the ground. He could barely hear the witches crashing through brush as the forest kelpies harnessed to the carriage trumpeted in fear, struggling to free the wheel trapped between thick roots.

It was only when he reached for the dagger at his side that he remembered he was unarmed.

His stomach sank like a stone.

A feminine scream had Merrick throwing open the crates opposite the makeshift bed, rifling through their contents for any sort of knife. To his frustration, it was all medical supplies – herbs, gauze, a few books, sewing needles.

What if that was Winnie? What if she needed help?

A blast of white light lit up the trees, but the quick glimpse didn't reveal who was foe.

Though anyone threatening him while brandishing a weapon or magic was typically an enemy.

Except for Esmeray.

And sometimes Laurent.

A loose kelpie with small antlers galloped towards him, bellowing in terror, spittle frothing from its mouth. Without thinking, Merrick snatched the beast's reins in one hand, narrowly avoiding the sharp antler the kelpie flung out as he dragged the beastie to a halt.

"It's alright," Merrick soothed, using his bulk to hold the kelpie still. "You can get back to tearing through the trees in a second." Twisting the reins firmly in one hand, Merrick grappled along the underside of a slim saddlebag, the cool touch of steel met his fingertips.

A short sword. Huffing a breath of relief, he released the forest kelpie. The beastie shrieked and bolted into the night.

Weapon acquired, Merrick ran towards the fighting.

An uncanny gust of wind rattled through sparse trees, carrying a foul odor.

Merrick broke through the tree line; the short sword gripped in his hand. Sliding into his experience of being a King's Guard in Irridessen's force, scanning the shadows for enemies was instinct.

A masculine shout went up about fifty yards to his right, and Merrick adjusted his path, running as fast as he could towards the noise.

Where was Winnie?

A blast of light in his peripheral illuminated his path for a split second as he closed in on the sounds of a struggle.

The distance between the light magic and the keening whimpers of one of the male witches meant the fighting had spread out, that the enemy was separating their forces, trying to pick them off one by one.

That was dangerous.

Especially for witches who needed to siphon additional power.

Vaulting over a fallen tree, his eyes snagged to the crumpled figure on the ground.

Skidding to a halt, Merrick stooped over the man, recognizing him as one of Winnie's Royal Coven.

The stench of decay festered, growing closer. A figure skittered between two thick oaks twenty feet away.

It was all the warning he got before a bolt of purple magic speared from the dark, aiming right at him.

Merrick hurled behind the tree to his left, crouching low. The blast slammed into the middle of a tree to his right. The pine crashed backwards, its slim trunk decimated.

Fae?

Fae he could fight. He could tear into fae, no problem.

Fae with chaos magic?

That didn't bode well.

A rustling sounded to his right, followed by a wheezing rattle.

Merrick swiveled around the trunk, short sword raised, ready to lob the head off of an unsuspecting fae who traded their *acat* for Massis's destructive chaos magic.

But he was met, instead, with a nightmare.

The being was slightly shorter than himself, with a milky, hairless hide and grey-ish veins. It was somewhat humanoid – except for the disproportionate limbs, blacked out eyes, and bone horns jutting from its skull.

The creature hissed, its lipless mouth splitting to reveal a row of rotted black teeth. It charged, swiping out a gnarled hand tipped with claw-like fingernails.

Merrick bared his fangs, swiping the short sword out.

The blade went right through it.

Not in a *'cutting the asshole's hand off'* way – in a *'this is a fucking ghost'* way.

The creature peered down at its intact hand, flexing unnaturally spindly fingers.

For a beat, the creature looked at Merrick with confusion, cocked its horns.

And then its expression morphed into one of bloodlust.

It rose to its full height.

Purple magic sparked at its palms.

Merrick darted behind another pine tree a split second before chaos magic shot at him.

It didn't make sense. He could *see* veins through that hide.

Veins meant blood.

Blood meant the *thing* could bleed.

Bleeding *enough* meant dying.

Fumbling for some sort of clarity as to the ghost-like creature, he slipped soundlessly around the trunk. The grotesque creature was hunched protectively over the body on the ground again. But this time, it tilted its skull back, that nightmarish mouth parted, and a forked tongue flicked out, tasting the air.

Merrick held his breath.

The creature's nostrils flared.

Merrick held his breath, heartbeat pounding, not wanting to exhale a direct pinpoint of his location.

Seconds ticked by.

Or maybe it was a full minute.

Two.

Merrick's lungs ached with the desperation to be filled. He sank to his heels, hidden behind the tree trunk and a patch of brambles, his fingers trailing across the ground around him.

The creature turned back to the dead witch, picking up his forearm and curling over it. Those razor-sharp teeth jutted out, sinking slowly into the witch's veins at his wrist.

A rock came loose under Merrick's fingers.

Snatching it up, he chucked it towards the creature.

It passed right through, not even garnering the ghost's attention as it gulped down mouthfuls of blood.

"What the fuck," Merrick cursed under his breath, bracing himself in his hiding place.

An unnatural, purple glow emitted from the creature's mouth.

Dread curdled thick in Merrick's chest as the realization sank in. The creature wasn't out for blood – it was siphoning the dead witch's power, pulling it out one swallow at a time.

Chaos magic was unpredictable. But the fae in Florra had been flesh and blood – not this...ghost-like entity his blade couldn't penetrate.

A series of chirps sounded behind the creature, and Merrick watched, horrified, as two more slunk out of the shadows, their movements jerky as they crept forward on all fours.

They clustered around the body, yowling at each other as they jockeyed for position, each one trying to siphon magic from the dead witch.

With his eyes glued to the creatures, Merrick slowly retreated, backing up as quietly as he could manage without attracting their attention.

He was outmaneuvered, out of his element, and had no clue how to land a strike on a ghost – let alone how to kill one.

He needed to find Winnie. They needed to flee, regroup.

If anyone was alive.

Carra's tits.

And maybe the gods really, truly abandoned this kingdom because luck was definitely not on his side. His foot scraped the ground, right against a patch of autumn leaves that crunched under his boot.

In the quiet clearing, it sounded like cannon fire.

All three sets of black eyes snapped to him simultaneously.

The closest one dropped the dead witch's wrist, staring right at him with those blacked eyes.

Merrick refused to make peace with his death.

He raised his short sword with a fierce snarl. Gods, it wouldn't do any good, but he'd go down swinging through smoke before he rolled over and accepted his fate.

Phades couldn't have him before, and he'd be damned if she could have him now.

"Get down!" Winnie yelled, right as tendrils of black smoke ensnared two of the creatures like vines. The shadows coiled tighter, cutting off the creatures' shrill screeching.

Winnie's magic wound tighter and tighter, covering them completely. Then, on a phantom wind, it billowed away.

Leaving no trace of the ghost-like creatures behind.

Winnie jumped her kelpie over the downed pine, the beastie loosening a deep, trumpeting peal, brown fur speckled with red and black blood.

The third creature let out a high-pitched wail as shadow magic crashed through it, leaving only its echoing cry behind.

Temper boiling over, he fisted the short sword tighter and stormed towards the witch who just saved his gods-forsaken life.

Again.

But before he could open his mouth to cuss her out for not giving him a weapon or telling him what was going on, Winnie swung towards Merrick and pinned him in place with a furious scowl.

"What the *fuck*, bonehead? I told you to *stay in the carriage.*"

Chapter Thirteen

DOVE

The abrupt knock at the door jolted me awake before the masked assailant in my nightmare succeeded in capturing me as I bolted through a thicket of dancing tree trunks.

My eyes were dry, and probably bloodshot, based on the way my tears burned. I could still feel rough hands on my skin. The sharp dagger in my flesh.

A weight against my legs brought me back to reality, and with a soft, almost disbelieving exhale, I took in the mound of fur snoring away at the foot of my bed.

As if it sensed my consciousness, the volkhound raised its head.

"Good morning," I said quietly, my gaze roving over the beast as a wave of unnatural calm washed through my veins.

With a soft huff, the huge grimm shook its head, ears flapping, before rolling onto its back, stretching massive paws in the air.

The knock at the door came again, my skin breaking out into clammy sweat.

But with sunlight streaming through my bedroom window, the panic from the night before dimmed, and my analytical sense concluded if it truly *was* one of my assailants, they wouldn't be banging on my door in the middle of the day.

I kicked off my covers, tugging a robe on before hurrying towards the entryway. With trembling fingers, I peeked through the peephole. Polina and Henir came into view. Relief swept through me.

The shuffle of paws, though, had my anxiety spiking again. There was a *demon* in my *living room.*

Whirling towards the grimm, I hesitated, unsure how to ask it to hide, but it merely huffed, as if it knew what I was asking. With a *poof*, the grimm vanished before my eyes.

I clamped a palm over my mouth, stifling my squeak of surprise, as the couch cushions indented from the four freaking paws walking across it. The couch creaked; a large divot appeared.

Well, now the volkhound was *invisible* and laying on my couch.

Calm flooded my blood, as if the grimm was telling me it was no threat to anyone that wasn't a threat to me.

It was a weird instinct that made little sense, but I trusted it all the same.

Polina shouted my name again, and I smoothed sweaty palms down my robe, making sure no wounds showed on my visible skin.

I hadn't peered too closely at my still-healing injuries while bathing last night. Instead, I'd scrubbed quickly, lost my nerve, fled to the bedroom, and cried myself to sleep.

Whatever. I was exhausted, overwhelmed, had weird purple magic, and a grimm living in my house. My problems were far from over.

"You look like shit," Polina said conversationally as I opened the door. Henir perched on her hip, a wicked grin on his cherub-like face.

"Shit!" Henir crowed proudly, clapping his chubby hands together.

"Sir!" Polina snapped, as if it'd already been a long day. "I will wash your mouth out with soap; you do *not* cuss."

With a second curse – in Cravic this time – Polina stooped, depositing Henir to the floor.

"Cuss!" Henir screeched, giggling and toddling towards the couch, where the *invisible grimm* sat.

With a garbled string of excuses, I lurched towards him, only to freeze as the indent disappeared from the couch, a thin plume of smoke shooting into my bedroom.

"You okay?" Polina asked cautiously. "I can pick him back up if you don't want him tearing your house apart."

"No...No, he's fine," I answered quickly, flapping my hands. "I thought he was um...going to trip. The floor swelled with the rain, so there's a few boards that are-"

"Dove."

Polina quirked a brow at me, knowing something was amiss. I pushed down my frazzled nerves, letting a slow breath out from between my teeth. My fingers twitched, and I awkwardly patted down my hair just to do something with my hands.

Everything felt...different.

And I was trying to remember how to deal with normal.

"Good morning," I croaked, clearing my throat. Polina surveyed me with a sharp look.

I gave her an innocent smile in return.

"Morning?" Polina snorted, sweeping past me and into my kitchen, rustling through the drawers. "Did you stay up late reading or something? It's the middle of the day, Dove."

I had no idea when I'd made it home last night, but I'd slept hard until the nightmare woke me.

"I – yeah," I muttered sheepishly. "Are you searching for something?"

"Maude sent me to come get you." Polina pulled out a container of cooking oil. "We didn't see you at the feast yesterday, so I figured you were either buried in a boringly astute book, or obsessively double checking that you're all packed."

Wait. What?

"What do you mean – the feast was *yesterday*?"

With a bemused glance, Polina dug through my pantry, taking out a loaf of bread and two cheeses wrapped in wax paper.

"The Prince Regent is in Bramberry?"

Her eyes narrowed. She could tell I was hiding something - but was coming up short as to what it could be.

Thankfully, before she could drown me with questions that I wasn't answering, Henir toddled over, demanding his mother pick him up. Polina shushed him, holding out a few chunks of bread from the loaf. He took the offering with glee, crushing the soft bread in his fists and waddling back to the couch.

I pressed my lips together. I'd been asleep for longer than a single night.

As casually as I could, I craned my neck towards the clock on my mantle that showed the current moon phase. The symbol of the moon was shadowed with a sliver of black, signifying that it was waning, and that I'd slept through the night, day, night, and half of today.

What the fuck?

"I wasn't feeling well," I stammered. "I made some tea with sleeping herbs, chamomile, and lavender, but I guess they were stronger than I anticipated."

"Well, I didn't see you at the Manor this morning. Wanted to make sure you were okay."

"Thank you. I um…" Off-kilter, I was afraid to voice any of the questions in my head.

"Maude called everyone to the Manor this evening. Prince Theodoric wants to thank Bramberry for their hospitality, or whatever. It'll be long-winded and boring, but the Regent is *extremely* handsome, which helps. Oh – and you're leaving tomorrow morning for the Jade Kingdom."

I couldn't be more grateful for Polina's presence at this exact moment because it at least gave me a starting point to figure out what I missed.

"Was the feast nice?"

Polina shrugged, unhooking a large wicker basket from my wall and packing it with the food she was brazenly stealing from me. But I was leaving *tomorrow*, and would be gone for a couple months, so I'd rather Polina take my food than for it to go bad.

"The feast was fine. Everything went smoothly. Like I said, *most* importantly, Prince Theodoric is *very* handsome. You're going to enjoy traveling with him. Maybe try to rub elbows...*play nice*...if you know what I mean." Polina made a kissy noise and smirked.

I groaned.

"I'm not going to have time to seduce a *Prince*, Polina. I'll be studying."

"Well, you know, if it comes up, jump on it. And I mean that in the literal sense."

Covering my blushing cheeks with my hands, Polina laughed, the sound light and welcoming against my spinning mind.

"I need to get to the Manor." It was safer to change the subject far, *far* away from my sex life.

Polina chuckled again, neatly packing the last jar of jam into my basket. "Get ready and I'll choose an outfit for you from what isn't packed."

I nodded, scrambling to organize what I needed to do. Everything I was bringing to the Jade Palace was already at the Manor, since I was staying the night there to leave with the Prince's caravan in the morning.

But losing a full day to sleep threw me for a loop, and nothing could shake the disorientation of being off schedule.

I needed to talk to Maude about the horror I experienced. I had to warn her. I wasn't leaving Bramberry unguarded.

And there's a demon in my bedroom and my magic is weirdly purple.

"Help yourself to my pantry." I tore a piece of bread from the loaf Polina hadn't yet wrapped. *Gods*, within one bite, I realized how *ravenously* hungry I was, my stomach hollow and queasy.

"I was planning on it," Polina replied dramatically, as I headed towards the bathroom.

Gritting my jaw, I shut the bathroom door.

I took a shallow breath, then another, deeper one, turning my attention to the mirror above my sink as I removed my robe. In the reflection, my blue iris looked brighter than my brown one, and both were incredibly bloodshot. Grabbing a brush, I ran it through my tangled hair, succeeding in making it even frizzier.

With a sigh, I averted my eyes from the mirror – and my gaze snagged on a slice of puckered skin near my hip.

A choked gasp escaped at the sight of the thick, jagged rune scarred over with shiny skin.

My heart stuttered. Nausea swept through me at the thought of a permanent blood rune carved into my flesh.

It wasn't a rune I'd studied before – two diamonds linked with a straight line – though there was a small break in the middle line, confirming the rune couldn't draw any power from my soul.

With gentle fingers, I prodded the sigil, bile rising in my throat. I had no experience healing scar tissue, which meant I'd have to ask Maude.

I couldn't keep the lamp on above my front door.

Couldn't heal myself properly.

Lifting my palm, I desperately hoped, for the first time in my life, to see blue-hued light.

A bright orb of lavender appeared.

Fuck.

Polina was still in my kitchen rummaging through my pantry – standing between myself and the books on magic in my living room. Until she left, I wouldn't be able to skim through the pages for answers to the oddly colored magic that conjured easily from the confines of my soul.

Dropping heavily onto the rim of my bathtub, a rush of emotion hit. Blinking rapidly, I refused to let any tears fall, wrapping myself in a cocoon of pleasant thoughts to take the edge off the all-consuming panic clawing at me from the inside.

Once the pressure lifted from my chest, I gave a resolute glare to my reflection in the mirror. Snatching a crumpled, rose-colored headscarf from the shelf near the sink, I tied it with deft movements around my mane. The embroidered ends hung loose and long on the sides of my head. Within a few seconds, I'd woven a thick braid down my back, the scarf twined through the strands and keeping it secure, the wide band across my forehead keeping the frizz to a minimum.

It looked put together and – most importantly – I liked it. There would be time later to process my trauma. But...I was *alive.* And I wouldn't squander this incredible opportunity over surviving evil witches. Most of them were dead, anyway, thanks to the grimm.

Gods below knew you could turn around a shit day by dressing up. At the very least, I could be pretty while inevitably breaking down in Maude's study.

Polina interrupted my monologue of forcefully cheery thoughts. "I'm dropping this food at home before going to the Manor. Meet you there?"

I called back my agreement before staring at my reflection with determination.

One hour.

One hour to figure out why my magic was purple, throw on clothes, and meet with my mother.

The second Polina left, I rushed over to my bookshelf, shoving through the stack of thick books until my fingers latched around the brown leather spine of *Witch Magic and its History*.

I dropped to the wood floor, wrapping my robe tighter around myself. Blowing out a shaky breath, I pulled an ink pot off the shelf, dipping my fingers into the cool, black ink.

With quick, practiced strokes, I ran an ink-covered finger against the grain of the floor, painting a perfect square slightly larger than the size of the book, with bisecting sets of parallel lines.

With a wave of my hand, purple magic ignited each line of the sigil until I was staring at an activated seeker rune thrumming with more magic than I'd ever siphoned previously.

Swallowing my trepidation, I placed *Witch Magic and its History* into the center of the rune.

Though I'd seen Maude activate this rune a hundred times, I'd never been strong enough to cast one myself. Normally, I'd shuffle through indexes, tables of content, and flip through pages, reading snippets of paragraphs here and there until I found what I needed, but I had an *hour*, and I really hoped this rune used up the rest of the birch's power so my regular light magic would reappear.

I closed my eyes, sinking into my well of magic, finding it...much deeper than before. The caress of power pressed against me, as if the churning purple magic wanted me to explore it further.

I was tempted to dive deeper to see exactly how far –

Focus Dove.

Holding both my palms above the book and seeker rune, I rolled my shoulders back. A large part of me believed this wouldn't work.

"Purple Magic," I stated aloud, more confidently than I felt. Bending a slice of power through the rune, I ordered it to take me to any pages in the book that held mention of this weird hued power coursing through my veins.

Witch Magic and its History floated into the air, the cover opening with a snap, pages fluttering swiftly. The book stopped, dropping back to the floor with a rattle.

The rune dimmed, and I leaned closer, reading the paragraph on the open page.

Fae magic can take on an array of color that corresponds to the god/goddess that blessed the acat. Element wielders (fire, water, air, earth) rarely have a separate-colored battle magic. Normally, their magic takes on the appearance of the element they hold control over.

Common colors of fae battle magic are red, blue, or yellow, with purple, green, silver and gold being very rare and signifying a much higher power level than typical fae magic.

I skimmed the rest of the page, disappointed to find no other mention of wielding purple magic – fae or witch. The thrill of imbuing a seeker rune faded fast. Staring at the soft purple light weaving through the rune on the floor, there was no tug of warning telling me I was close to using up my supply of magic.

With a quick glance at the clock on the mantle, I sighed, the noise ending in a growl of frustration. *Was I just supposed to go to Maude and ask her to fix all my problems?*

The acrid tang of disappointment constricted my lungs. Burying my face in my hands, I held my breath until the urge to cry passed.

A cold nose on the side of my neck brought me face-to-snout with the grimm – now in its solid wolf form. It sat next to me, a keening type of knowledge in its eyes. My soul settled immediately seeing that the beast was still here.

"I wish you could talk," I murmured, stroking its thick fur. "You probably know *exactly* what I'm dealing with."

The grimm snorted as if it empathized with my struggle, before raising its foot to paw at the book in the rune with expectant red eyes.

"You want me to try again?"

A whine was my answer.

Checking the time, I acquiesced, "Okay, but then I need to get dressed and you need to go all...invisible so we can head to the Manor. Deal?"

The grimm cocked its head, and I wondered if it could understand what I was saying. Glancing to the bookshelf to find a different textbook on magic, the grimm barked, like it was telling me to stop. "I need to get another book, beastie."

The grimm snapped its jaws in the air, as if it was truly trying to speak, before nosing *Witch Magic and its History* away from the rune. It reached out a massive paw, patting me on the leg, an urgent expression on its face.

Pissing off a giant demon wolf, no matter how much I believed it liked me, was not in the best interest of my time management.

Maybe I was going mad.

The volkhound nudged my hands towards the seeker rune that held no book.

I complied, even though I knew it wouldn't work. The rune needed a book to seek. But, hovering my palms over the rune, I said, "Purple Magic."

Another, harder, knock on my shoulder had me breaking my loose connection with the foreign magic in my well. The grimm was now staring right into my eyes, silently urging me to do...to do *something*.

The magic inside my soul stirred and churned, rising inside me as if it was feeding off my mounting anxiety. The grimm's red eyes flared brighter, until they were glowing, bathing the hairs on its muzzle in eerie ruby light.

Oh.

"You want me to imbue more power to the seeker rune?"

The grimm bobbed its head in a way I was definitely taking as a *'yes.'*

I bit back the words on my tongue that wanted to tell the beastie the seeker rune only worked on one specific book at a time, that nothing was going to appear from an empty rune, but the intense look on the grimm's face made my magic well up further, frothing to be let out. I cleared my throat, easing power through my fingers.

Wielding this much magic was completely new to me – and it made me both giddy and terrified to accidentally lose the connection.

Reckless.

This magic – this rush. It was reckless.

Yes, this was a reckless abuse of ancient tree magic that I'd be begging for forgiveness for at some point. But I'd always been weak. Might as well use up the last of the birch's power for intellectual gain, right?

"Purple Magic."

But as I struggled to grip the funnel of power from my soul and ease it out through my hands, my inexperienced hold on it slipped.

Suddenly, instead of thin tendrils of purple weaving in the air between the seeker rune and myself, ice-cold power burst from my palm, hitting the rune with such force that I rocked backwards.

An echoing pulse of lavender erupted from the rune, rippling outwards with a *boom* that shook the house so hard books fell from their shelf.

A plate on the counter clattered to the floor, shattering instantly.

I scrambled upwards, clenching my fists to cut off the connection to the volatile power. Lavender light bathed my entire living room.

The high-pitched ringing in my ear told me I'd done something that...probably wasn't good.

"We're done," I announced to the grimm shakily, backing away from the smoldering sigil. I needed to wipe away the ink, break the rune. Then I'd dissect what the actual fuck happened.

Snatching up a kitchen towel, I dropped back to the seeker rune still emitting bright purple light.

Thankfully, the second the cloth smudged away a corner of the square, the rune went silent, and the light disappeared. Breathing rapidly, I frantically scrubbed the rest of the sigil away.

Once I was positive that every last drop of ink was gone, I leaned back on my heels, exchanging a glance with the giant wolf demon.

The grimm dipped its head at me, though its attention flicked towards the entryway.

A heavy thud smacked against the front door, causing me to shriek and scramble to my feet.

Magic sparked between my fingers. Creeping closer to the front door, the volkhound right on my heels, I rallied power to me, ready to unleash at whatever hit my door with that much force.

I called a glittering shield around me and the grimm, and before I could second guess how stupid my actions were, my fingers twisted the doorknob.

Ripping the door open, I braced, ready to take on the threat that appeared.

But no one was there.

Heart hammering against my ribs, I chanced a glance around.

A broken flowerpot and a cracked window across the street caught my eye, but the timer to get to Bramberry Manor was draining swiftly, and I didn't have time to investigate further.

Especially since the empty town signified everyone was already at the Manor for the Prince Regent's parting words.

I retreated into my house, magic cooling and shield disappearing, but my eyes drifted to the front step, landing on...*a book*?

Stunned, I snatched up the thin, olive-colored book, and scurried back into my home, locking every single bolt on the door.

It was only when I was securely back in the safety of my house did I flip the book over.

Somehow, the seeker rune worked – not in finding a paragraph or page, but an entire *book*.

The grimm moved in my peripherals, assessing me as I looked at the title. It was in an old language, painted in beautiful, swooping calligraphy, though time had warped the letters. The language was one I'd studied in the past. I knew the basics but wasn't fully fluent in it.

Sounding out each syllable, I whispered the translated title out loud, "*A Testimony to Massis and His Hidden Lineage Gift.*"

CHAPTER FOURTEEN
DOVE

STANDING A FEW FEET behind Arthur, Elijah, and Polina, I shifted Henir on my hip. The entirety of Bramberry was packed onto the front yard of the Manor – about five hundred witches and humans total - necks craning to catch a glimpse of the Prince Regent.

Since I pushed away the temptation to read the odd book summoned to my doorstep, I'd arrived to the Manor on time, wearing the jade skirt and cream-colored tunic Polina laid out for me.

Maude wouldn't be snappy at me for missing the feast, but being late to her gathering would've pissed her off. Thankfully, my mother hadn't appeared yet – nor had the Regent.

It wasn't common for the Crown to visit Bramberry Forest. So, with the Royal Coven's arrival, there was a heavy sense of anticipation in the air, mixing with threads of gossip about the King's illness and what would come of his children and Kingdom once he passed.

I wondered if Prince Theodoric brought either of his elusive siblings with him – or if his visit would spark wild rumors of their whereabouts. There'd been gossip about Prince Theodoric's brother refusing to attend any Royal events, and it was common knowledge the Princess disappeared two decades ago and hadn't been seen since.

Talk circulated, though it swiftly abated around Maude. If anyone was found criticizing the King's family, Maude would give them a verbal lashing and assign them to some awful chore – like oiling the wood paneled walls in the Manor with nothing but a slim paintbrush.

She was a fierce supporter of King Velik and spoke of him intimately – as if she was close, personal friends with the leader of our Kingdom. Though, to my knowledge, they'd only met a handful of times over the centuries.

While Henir babbled away in my arms, I listened to snippets of conversations around me, though overlapping voices made it hard to focus. My hearing honed in on someone discussing the Vessel Book. Attention piqued, I drew closer, curious.

For all of the terror I'd dealt with during the ritual, I was more than ready to embark on a journey that consisted of silent libraries, peace, and study. I'd throw myself into learning in order to get past the dread hovering around my mind.

The witches discussing the Book of Carra moved away. My shoulders slumped. No eavesdropping for me.

I smoothed Henir's curls from his forehead, telling him how much I'd miss him while traveling. The grimm was currently invisible, and though I couldn't see it, I could *feel* its presence – as if it noticed my panic and was telling me, in its own way, that it was here to stay.

As evening set in, darkening the yard and making it hard to recognize even the faces next to me, I reminded myself that I stood among my Coven, with a friendly demon at my back, and was sleeping under the same roof as Maude tonight.

Tightening Henir in my hold, I scooted closer to Polina and Arthur. I knew I was safe here.

My palms were still a little clammy, though.

Silence blanketed the crowd as Maude glided onto the porch, put together and powerful in a black silk suit. With a flick of her fingers, silvery light illuminated the yard.

"There is no need to *gossip* in the dark," Maude sniffed, earning a chuckle from the Bramberry residents.

"Thank you for being here *on time*." Maude gestured to the door behind her. "And thank you for welcoming Prince Regent Theodoric Balabanov, Heir to the Jade Kingdom, into our humble home." Maude's voice rang out amidst hearty cheers; I rose to my tiptoes to see better.

Two stocky guards marched out first, their heavy boots thudding across the Manor's porch. Fur lined caps covered their heads, and both wore tunics and trousers dyed a rich chestnut. Jade colored cloaks fluttered in the brisk air as they stomped to opposing sides of the steps leading up to the Manor's door, their stiff body language intimidating.

They wore an assortment of runestones hung on pendants, and I couldn't help but admire the fat emeralds set in delicate filigree backings that swung proudly from the ends of golden chains.

I knew the Royal Coven was strong.

Wealthy.

Imposing.

The guard on the left swept hard eyes over the crowd, his lips thinning as he took in the residents of Bramberry. He glared down his nose at the gaggle of witchlings barefoot and sitting cross-legged in the grass at the base of the steps. An ugly curl at the corners of his mouth formed as he all but sneered down at the young witches in disgust.

My throat dried out seeing superiority displayed so easily.

Did the entire Jade Palace consist of only arrogant, high-tier witches with haughty, self-important attitudes?

With a wince, I glanced at my mother.

That was a shitty, irrational, thought and Maude taught us from a young age to never be so quick to judge those we didn't know.

She told us each witch and human had their own unique skills that benefitted our Coven, and though I'd been bullied as a witchling when my light magic came in weak, and placated and pitied as an adult, the notion that everyone excelled in their own, special, way was a perspective I did my best to remember and emulate.

For Maude's rigid formality, she was a firm believer in giving others grace.

Maybe the guard was having a bad day. Or, I was paranoid from my ordeal and subconsciously overanalyzing normal behaviors – hunting for cruel intentions and ulterior motives.

But the swirling doubt vanished as Prince Theodoric appeared, and my gaze settled onto the most handsome man I'd ever seen.

Polina's coy forewarning didn't do him justice at all. Handsome wasn't a strong enough word. He was *stunningly* beautiful – as if the gods themselves chiseled every one of his features to utter perfection.

Prince Theodoric was only a few years older than myself, sporting a fur-trimmed tunic that emphasized his broad shoulders and lean waist. Silky golden hair framed a clean-shaven face, and a confident, self-assured gleam in his brilliantly blue eyes said he'd step seamlessly into the role of King with poise. I couldn't have turned away from him if I'd tried, drinking in every detail of his lithe stature as he strode towards Maude. Polina laughed, nudging me with her elbow as I gawked, completely speechless.

The residents of Bramberry roared their approval as the Prince Regent nodded politely to Maude before casting his eyes over the crowd.

It could've been purely my imagination, but I swore pinpricks of static charged the air the moment Prince Theodoric's piercing gaze hit mine. Instantly, the din fell into a muted drone of nothingness, as if the Prince and

I were the only ones here, that everything outside of us no longer mattered. Prince Theodoric straightened, lips parting slightly as he stared at me with intrigue. I took a step forward instinctively, following the warmth igniting through my core.

"I told you he's wonderful," Polina sighed dreamily, elbowing me again, this time in the rib. Her voice broke through the Prince's thrall, pulling me from that charged connection. "I'm almost sad I didn't learn a bunch of dead languages so I could study a dull book for a few months. It'd be worth it knowing that man is under the same roof."

"Hey!" Arthur exclaimed, fake indignation screwing his mouth into a dramatic frown. "You're married with *multiple* kids, you ass."

"Hmm?" Polina's lips tipped up as she fanned herself. "Oh, right. You."

Arthur snorted, murmuring something that had her giggling with delight. I was very glad Maude started talking so I could drown out their incessant, sappy, *adorable* flirting.

I glanced back up to the Manor, wanting to meet the Prince's eyes again, but the family in front of me moved, blocking my view. I sidled to the left – and slammed right into the person next to me.

The man grunted in surprise, his hands shooting out to steady me, one landing against Henir's back and one on my elbow. "So sorry," I whispered. Henir cooed something I couldn't decipher from my arms.

I turned towards the stranger who had so graciously stopped me from falling – only to come face-to-face with another wildly gorgeous man.

Gods below.

He was at least a foot taller than me, all broad chested and rugged, with thick biceps and a strong, square jaw peppered with the shadow of facial hair. Messy, dark brown hair fell above a set of hazel eyes.

Eyes that danced with wickedness as he pulled his hand from my elbow. My breath stuttered as his heated gaze slid down my body.

"Careful there, darling," he growled softly. "Those pretty doe-eyes will only get you in trouble with me."

With a squeak, I darted back towards Polina and Arthur. But they were still too wrapped up in flirting with each other to notice my misstep.

Henir wailed, reaching for his father, and I passed him over to Arthur, running my sweaty palms against my skirt as my heart raced, the man's words a sultry echo in my ears.

Sure, I'd messed around with a few of the men in Bramberry over the years, though nothing serious ever came from it.

And they *never* looked, or spoke, like *that*.

In a town where most everyone grew up together, the unfamiliarity of the Prince and the dark-haired stranger added to their appeal. I scolded myself as I tuned back into Maude's speech, though my focus kept dragging to the Prince Regent at her side.

As Maude bowed low to the Regent and finished her speech, Prince Theodoric placed his hand over his heart. "Thank you, Bramberry, for making me feel so welcome. I'm grateful to my father, King Velik, for his guidance, and I beg to the gods that his health returns to him."

A beat of reverent silence followed his words. Prince Theodoric shook his head sadly, pain flitting across his features. "But in his absence, I'm proud to take the reins of this great Kingdom, and rule with the same passion and patience my father displays so effortlessly."

Cheers broke out around me, and in the melee, I searched for the dark-haired stranger I'd bumped into, but he was gone.

SWALLOWING AGAINST THE DISCOMFORT, I stared at the ceiling in Maude's study, my skirt pushed down a few inches to reveal the rune on my flesh.

"Hmm." Maude traced the silvery scar with her finger. She muttered something in Cravic I didn't catch, though the lump in my throat made it impossible to ask her to repeat it.

Once Prince Theodoric and his guards headed back to their rooms to prepare for our departure, I'd pushed through the crowd, worried I wouldn't catch my mother before her evening rounds.

But Maude must've sensed the heaviness etched in my soul, because the moment the Prince cleared the edge of the hall, she'd called out my name and demanded I meet her in her study.

Most of the townsfolk were milling about out front, and some of the witchlings snuck away into the forest with mischief written all over their faces. That firmed up my resolve to tell Maude immediately.

If anything happened while I was gone, especially if it hurt a witchling, it would break my heart. My Coven needed to know something nefarious was happening in the woods.

I'd taken two steps over the threshold before breaking down into hysterics. Maude immediately shoved me into her study and shut the door while I sobbed and told her every detail of the sacrifice I could remember as frantic, uneven breaths squeezing my throat, as if the memory wanted to choke my words.

Now, I was flat on my back on Maude's couch while she peered at the carved blood rune on my body, wire-rimmed glasses perched on the edge of her pert nose.

She'd held me while I cried, saying nothing, stroking my hair and wrapping her arms around me tighter than ever before. And when my blubbering finally subsided to a cruel case of hiccups, she told me she was proud of me for fighting back, and that extra precautions would be taken to make sure no one was outside after sundown.

I hadn't yet told her about the grimm nor the weird purple magic, but she'd been insistent on seeing the scar once I mentioned it.

"This is an old rune," Maude said, speaking Terrian once more. "I think this is where you held onto that connection to whatever magic you siphoned. The skin scarred when that power channeled through you."

I argued hollowly. "But it felt like I *held* that power, *owned* the magic – not just served as a conduit for it to come through me. And all of the blood runes on my skin glowed that same red."

Maude clicked her tongue, shooting her hand out towards the bookshelf. A chunky tome floated over, and she snatched it out of the air, waving a hand over its cover. The book rattled, pages flipping quickly before settling on a chapter about halfway through.

"This is the sigil." Maude pushed the tome closer to me, her nail tapping the page. And there was the same symbol as the silver scar on my side – two diamonds linked together by a straight line.

"It's a blood rune that is extremely difficult to master, as well as highly illegal, since it connects a god realm to Terramere when the right spells are uttered. In this case, I believe whatever power the ritual *itself* held, you connected with the veil, and your subconscious slid down that connection." Her fingers traced the straight line of the sigil.

"That's how you ended up in Minmere, and when Phades advised you to tunnel into your magic, the goddess was guiding you through Avamere, to land back earthside."

I thought mentioning my encounter with the Goddess of Death would shake Maude, would shock her, but all I'd gotten in response was a grumble and something that sounded like a thinly veiled insult about Phades sticking her nose into witch-related-things that weren't her business.

"But the god realms are sealed. How was I able to slip through?"

"The god realms were sealed with *god magic* – not witch magic nor fae magic. Deities are not infallible, though if they ever bless us again, I'd appreciate you never telling them I said that." Maude looked pointedly down her nose at me, the thin lines around her eyes crinkling.

"So..." I trailed off, biting my lip between my teeth as I floundered to voice the hundreds of questions screaming through my mind. "Could it all be related to the heretics?"

Maude closed the tome and stood. "Don't worry about this, Dove. I'll research the similarities between your truth and the notes I have from the other rituals. But you *must* leave this to myself and the high-tier witches to figure out."

I flinched, stopping my frustrated rebuttal from passing my lips.

Don't worry.

Leave it to me.

I'll have stronger witches handling it.

It was Maude's way of protecting me, I knew that. And gods above and below knew that I didn't know much, couldn't help much, aside from giving Maude the details of what I'd seen and heard.

The academic side of myself relaxed at the thought of moving past this traumatic event, getting my feet back underneath me. It wanted to focus on healing and attempting to decipher the Book of Carra, to learn as much as possible while in the Jade Palace.

But for the first time in my life, burying myself into studying felt...like running away.

Maude wasn't waiting on me to answer her, so I sat up and straightened out my clothing, relieved the panicky dread was gone now that Maude was aware of what happened.

"Go get some rest, you have a long journey to the Quiet's *veles* tomorrow," my mother said offhandedly, her eyes taking on a glassiness I knew all too well.

I'd regurgitated a ton of details on a mystery that haunted Maude for decades. She'd be pouring through every note, tome, and scrap of information stacked ceiling-high in the shelves of books behind her desk until sunrise.

I bowed and rose from the couch, sensing Maude's silent dismissal.

"You're a good, gentle witch, my Dove." Maude patted my cheek on the way to her desk. "Never let anyone take that from you."

I bobbed my head again.

But a dark, restless thought wove through me as I stepped into the silent hall of Bramberry Manor.

What if I didn't want to be a 'good, gentle witch' any longer?

What if I wanted to be...more?

Chapter Fifteen
MERRICK

"Do you want to tell me what *the fuck* you were doing?" Winnie snarled.

Merrick hissed. The spitfire had dismounted her kelpie in one fluid movement and threw the reins to Tallah who was still astride her own steed with a frown on her lips.

Winnie jabbed her finger into Merrick's chest hard enough to bruise. "You decided to just scamper out of your *runed* carriage to get yourself killed by dukhmora? For what reason?"

"You didn't think to tell me any of this before we left?" Merrick snapped back, throwing his arms out wide. "I heard the sounds of a fight, figured you got ambushed and *did what I've been trained to do.* You asked me to fight. I went to do that."

"With a steel blade? Have you no common sense?"

Merrick threw the useless short sword to the ground, a sense of dangerous calm rolling through him. Winnie's temper roared hot – an out-of-control wildfire determined to reduce her surroundings to simmering ash.

He knew about that. His temper normally hit the exact same temperature.

But something had changed in the aftermath of his imprisonment in the Ruby Kingdom. That welcomed shot of burning adrenaline that always ignited his veins had been replaced with icy venom.

With it, his head felt clearer that it had in years.

Unfortunately, that meant he couldn't dismiss the reality of the nightmarish beast he'd seen with his own damn two eyes.

Now, as any good Captain would do, he demanded information. In a move he'd seen his commanding officer do hundreds of times during debriefs, Merrick rubbed his temples with his fingers, avoiding Winnie's simmering eye contact.

Finally, he ground out, "*What* the fuck is a dukhmora and, more importantly, *how* can it use chaos magic?"

It was Winnie's turn to act shocked, her bristled body language and furrowed brow instigating Merrick further. "You don't have dukhmora in Irridessen? And what the fuck is *chaos* magic? That's *heretic* magic. It's purple."

"No," Merrick bit out, "That's chaos magic. Not to be *that* asshole, but I have it on good authority from the *Goddess of Fucking Death*."

At the mention of Phades, her mouth dropped open.

With a scoff, Merrick leaned over, crowding her, their faces mere inches apart. "Actually, no. I'm going to be that asshole. That's *godsdamned* chaos magic. Plain and simple. Massis was bestowing it to fae in exchange for their *acatis* in Irridessen."

She went silent.

Merrick simmered in his own frustration.

Finally, Winnie's gaze darted to the dead witch on the ground behind them. Two witches were gently lifting the limp body, wrapping it in linen.

"You've spoken to Phades?" Winnie croaked, all the heat from her words gone.

"Not personally," Merrick growled low. "But my Queen's blessed by Phades. Queen Esmeray is the Vessel of Death. Phades had some *lovely* conversations with her. I was privy to them after the fact."

"Vessels are activating?" Winnie whispered, her legs wobbling as she swallowed. For once, Merrick saw her mask crumble, saw the indecision in her eyes. The fear.

It took the sting right out of his own tone. He nodded slowly, hating that he'd caused Winnie's panic. "Two of them in Irridessen. Queen Esmeray is the Vessel of Death. Queen...Sparrow...is the Vessel of Life. Bestowed by Faune."

"Life and Death. That leaves Destruction and Salvation." Winnie chewed her lip, helplessness in her eyes as she watched the body of the dead witch be taken from the clearing. He wondered how close Winnie had been to the witch who lost his life to those... dukhmora.

Death never got easier. In the frenzy of battle, it was different. Death didn't seem real. He'd fight, and kill, never giving thought to the dead until hours or days later, when their faces would interrupt his dreams.

That's when reality would settle heavily in his gut. As if he could feel it now, he rolled his shoulders, his wings rustling against his back. A sharp pain rumbled through his back.

"The dukhmora are a species of parasitic demon coming earthside from Avamere," Winnie sighed deep, as if she bore that same weight. In a clipped voice that trembled with nerves she continued, "From a ritualistic sacrifice Massis's loyal followers are enacting. Massis grants lineage magic to one witch who casts the spell during each ritual. Chant the spell, kill the sacrifice, complete the ritual – just to hope Massis chooses *you* over the other witches chanting that same spell. It takes a lot of power to pull off a spell of that magnitude, so only full-fledged witches with a manifested heritage gift can perform it for a chance to gain a lineage gift. And as the gods continue to forsake us, more witches are banding together to perform these horrific rituals. Dukhmora... they siphon power by drinking witch blood. And they're difficult to kill since they're intangible. Just a couple dukhmora could decimate a town if there's not enough strong witches to defend it."

"Gods above," Merrick ground out a rough curse, sitting on the trunk of the downed pine. That darkness at the edge of his mind wanted to incapacitate him now that the high of fighting had dissipated.

"I've been tasked by the Crown to hunt down and dispatch dukhmora back to Avamere."

He pushed the darkness away, gaze sliding over Winnie. Her declaration settled between them.

Emotion warred through her hazel eyes.

Regret.

Disappointment.

Guilt.

Those same emotions were what sent him down his own spiral of depression. Those were the pieces of the darkness that forced him to leave Florra after his soul tie clicked in place with Sparrow.

And gods above and below knew he needed support. Not that he hadn't had it. He'd found himself in too deep, when the wallowing already festered, the darkness already won.

It had taken Esmeray shoving a list of names into his hand and telling him to get his shit together that finally began peeling those layers of depression back one by one.

Only for that suffocating darkness to snap back shut around his mind, thicker than before, the moment Sparrow told him Briar's story.

He patted the spot next to him, the harsh knock of his hand slapping the wood jarring Winnie out of her haze. Winnie silently stepped closer, wavering for a moment before sitting gingerly, fixing her somber eyes to the patch of grass where bright red blood still shone against the dirt.

Tallah and the others had disappeared, most likely taking the body to be put to rest.

"You really don't have demons in Irridessen?" Winnie finally asked, her voice so soft Merrick almost missed it.

He grimaced and shook his head. "I knew they existed during the War, but I had no idea there was demon activity in Terramere currently. We've dealt with fae that have chaos magic, and we...burned the bodies after battle because we weren't sure if Massis could reanimate them with demon spirits using the bodies as a host."

The forest around them began reawakening. Cool temperatures brought about a wind that blustered through the trees, rustling the bright orange and yellow leaves. Crickets resumed their chirping, and the soft creak of limbs swaying filled the air.

Distantly, he heard the other witches singing in another language. It sounded like a burial hymn. An occasional sob broke the song, and his heart clenched as he thought of Lenna, how she'd cried and begged King Eamon to spare him.

"Phades said Massis is granting *chaos magic* – not heretic magic?" Winnie asked carefully, each word punctuated, as if she didn't want there to be a single speck of miscommunication, as if this was too important.

It felt like standing on the edge of a precipice, and whatever happened next would be a free-fall.

"I've never heard of heretic magic in Irridessen," Merrick answered truthfully. When Winnie didn't respond, he peered closer, bumping her shoulder with his to prompt her to answer.

All the color had drained from her face, and she stared blankly at the blood on the grass, her hands knitted together in her lap.

"Is that...does that change something for you here?" Merrick asked awkwardly, the rigid stillness of the witch next to him causing alarm bells to clang in his head.

Something was wrong.

Winnie finally loosened a long exhale, turning to face him directly.

There was dread in her eyes.

Dread and painful acceptance.

"It changes *everything*," she breathed.

Part Two

FORSAKEN

Chapter Sixteen

DOVE

THE MURMUR OF DEEP voices drew me from a fitful sleep. Squinting bleary-eyed towards the window, a muted glow peeking through the curtains told me it was not yet dawn, but night was officially over.

A *bump* from the hall outside made me stiffen, but the shadow-hued grimm standing next to the locked bedroom door was a deadly-yet-needed reminder that I was perfectly safe.

Which meant I could eavesdrop.

Careful to limit the noise I made, I slipped from the covers and padded over to the demon's side, my fingers instinctively threading into the fur at the nape of its neck. The grimm stood tall, steady breath fanning over the top of the headscarf I'd donned before bed, the icy sensation sending a shiver through my bones.

I eased my ear up to the door right as a harsh, masculine voice snapped, "I don't care what you *think*. I *know* there's a heretic in Bramberry. Do your job and smoke them out."

"How can you be so sure?" A second male voice, calmer than the first, replied smoothly.

A spat curse had me leaning harder against the door, holding my breath, not wanting to miss a single word. I pressed a hand over my wildly thumping heart.

How could a heretic get into Bramberry if Maude's runes kept them out?

"Your job is to find *them* – not question *me*. And keep it quiet. We don't want anyone aware of this yet."

The second man cursed in Cravic.

"Stop that – you know I don't understand what you're saying."

"Maybe you need to broaden your horizons." The amusement laced tone elicited another growled order from the first man, but I couldn't make it out as their bootsteps faded down the hall.

The grimm sniffed the air before letting out a huff of irritation, passing me and leaping back onto the bed, sprawling out on its back with its paws in the air.

It could've been anyone in that hallway – Bramberry Manor was filled with high-tier witches who reported to Maude. Maybe Maude already notified her trusted inner circle about what happened to me, and the voices I overheard were witches on assignment from our Coven Mother.

We weren't the type to question Maude's commands. If she said no one was allowed outside alone, then no one would be outside alone. If she notified a select few that there was a potential heretic in Bramberry, then they'd be on the hunt – no information trickled down to others unless absolutely necessary. But it sounded like Maude was taking this threat seriously, and that alone had my panic easing.

It would be at least an hour or two before I needed to get dressed, and waking up so abruptly had adrenaline flowing through my veins. Crossing the room, I dug through my trunk. I'd brought along a few books – the book that appeared on my doorstep amongst them – but it was the well-loved copy of *Terramere's Beasts* that I grabbed.

As I crawled back under the covers, propping myself against the smooth wood headboard, the grimm belly-crawled closer, resting its giant head on my thigh. I scratched between its pointed ears, holding the book open in my other hand.

"If you're going to travel with me, you need a name."

If the beastie was going to stick around, I definitely needed to call it something special. As if the grimm understood my words, which I was more and more sure it could as we spent time together, those ruby eyes locked with mine.

"Medvel?"

The grimm threw a paw over its snout, a move I was taking as a "*no.*"

"Hmmm... Volken?"

"*Hmmmph.*"

I was rewarded with a flat glare to accompany the dramatic huff before the beastie rolled onto its back. Wriggling and stretching while letting out a series of soft whines and chirps, our fun game of communication was leaving a lot to be desired.

But when I glanced down at the volkhound, clarity slammed into me, my lips popping into an "*O.*"

Gods above and below.

The grimm was very much telling me it did not like the *male* names.

The lack of bits and balls confirmed something I'd never really given thought to before.

"You're a *female*?" The very apparent fact mentally smacked me upside the head.

Rolling back onto *her* belly, the beastie huffed, as if my stupidity was thoroughly annoying.

"Of course you are," I cooed, tossing *Terramere's Beasts* onto the top of my duvet to use both hands to pet the grimm. As she let out a satisfied grunt, my eyes fell onto the book cover illustrated with varying animal paw prints tracking through a forest floor. But it was the name of the author that caught my eye. *Neera Mellow.*

"Neera," I said triumphantly. "It's the name of the author that wrote one of my favorite books. I was obsessed with learning everything about beasties when I was younger, and this was the first book I purchased after I moved out of the Manor. Do you like that name?"

With a much more enthusiastic snort, followed by a swipe of her ice-cold tongue on my cheek, I knew Neera was the perfect name.

We settled into content silence. Neera snoozed lightly with her paws crossed on my lap, while I flipped through the short chapter on grimm and volkhounds, before shuffling back through to my favorite passages on other beasts.

The sounds of witches and witchlings waking up and getting ready for their day began around us, but in this tiny room, with my book and my demon, I soaked in the relaxation until a loud knock at my door pulled me from a passage I was rereading on Forest Kelpies. Neera disappeared in front of my eyes, though I could still feel her weight against me.

"Coming!" I called out, giving the invisible beastie a few more seconds of love before swinging my legs from the bed.

"There are people coming up in twenty minutes to collect your bags." Juliette's chirpy voice wafted under my door, and I scowled at her since she couldn't see me.

"Thanks, Juliette." I kept the bite out of my tone, so she didn't find an excuse to test my patience this morning.

"Make sure you wear something pretty – it'll distract from your embarrassingly blue magic," Juliette sing-songed, her nasally voice fading with a laugh as she left, though it took all of my restraint to not throw open the door and throttle her.

With a deep, steeling breath, I reminded myself of the book-filled adventure to come. Neera reappeared, sitting on her haunches as I tugged on a pair of breeches and a light sweater. Even with Juliette's slight, I was giddy at the prospect of seeing more of the Jade Kingdom outside of Bramberry.

And my magic isn't blue at the moment – thank you very much.

Just to check, I flicked my fingers, and the bright glow of my still-odd magic bathed my palm in lavender light. Squeezing my hand into a fist, the magic winked out.

"Well, that's still one of many unanswered questions," I said to Neera. In response, she merely grumbled.

Though brisk, autumnal, weather awaited me outside the Manor, I wanted to feel out the crisp air before bundling up. The bathrooms on this floor were communal, and packing my drawstring bag with my brush and vials of beauty products reminded me of living here with Polina, of simpler times spent studying and growing up together, whispering about the big dreams we had for our futures under the cover of nightfall.

In a way, it was poetic that I'd spent the night in the Bramberry Manor before heading off on an adventure – as if the place I grew up in knew it would always be home, that it would always be here for me to return.

"You need to be invisible for a while - is that alright?"

Neera stretched her front legs out, her hulking form turning translucent. I waited until she was nothing but a shimmer of presence in my subconscious before opening the door to the guest room. A cool breeze ruffled through my sweater, Neera's way of telling me she would wait for me outside.

Smiling to myself, I hurried from the guest room, brimming with ideas of what to study once arriving at the Palace – the excitement tunneling my vision as I mentally recanted a list of topics to dive into first.

The allure of unrestricted access to the largest library in the Jade Kingdom had me so lost in my own head that I turned the corner and slammed right into a hard, muscular chest.

CHAPTER SEVENTEEN
DOVE

"ARE YOU ALRIGHT?"

A strangled gasp slipped from my lips as I stared up at Prince Theodoric.

He was incredibly handsome from afar, but up close, he was *breathtaking*.

His broad shoulders and considerable stature put him almost a foot taller than me. Golden hair framed his tanned face, accentuating thick lashes, sharp cheekbones, and perfectly sculpted lips. Dressed in a pair of dark blue linen pants that accentuated strong thighs, and a woolly black sweater that fit snug through the biceps and chest, all my thought processes halted.

There was genuine concern reflecting in his gaze, and this close, I could see his eyes weren't just blue – there was a silver starburst ringing them, as if even his irises knew he was royalty and crowned him as such.

Using his free hand to swing a heavy messenger pack around his body, his other palm clasped around my elbow, the warmth of his grasp soaking into my buzzing skin – heady and addicting.

But his touch jolted me back to reality.

"I-I'm so sorry, your Highness." I took a swift step backwards, remembering my manners and bowing low, a harsh blush flooding my cheeks until my face and neck were on fire.

A smarter woman would've curtsied, apologized, and darted off.

I, however, hesitated.

Prince Theodoric's thrumming presence wove through the empty hallway, causing my own gift to awaken in my soul. Shoving magic down, I swallowed against my dry throat.

Stupidly, I wanted to ask if he felt a *pull* towards me – if that moment we made eye contact on Maude's porch meant something to him, too.

Putting a few feet of distance between us didn't help.

He's the Regent of the Jade Kingdom.

Untouchable.

Unobtainable.

Probably engaged. Or at least betrothed. Most royals were.

I ducked my head in respect, staring at my old, ratty, boots that pivoted on their own accord.

Repeating my apologies for running into him, while fleeing, sounded like a great idea.

Prince Theodoric's hand shot out. "Wait – please."

The movement was so unexpected I reared back, our eyes meeting again. He stared at me with heated intrigue – as if he wanted every secret in my head and would judge me for naught.

With his attention fixated so directly, I shrank back.

"You're the translator for Bramberry, right? Dove Koroleva?" Prince Theodoric asked curiously, a slow smile spreading across his face as he uttered my name, revealing dazzling white teeth and a dimple.

Every gluttonous nerve in my body screeched with glee. My brain simply refused to process words.

He was the *Crown*.

I couldn't get my tongue to work. Everything was either moving way too fast or too slow.

Had it been two seconds since he'd asked me a question? Two minutes? *Gods, Dove, get it together. Just talk to the ridiculously handsome man.*

"That's me, your Highness. I've been studying languages and dialects for years."

If he asked me to translate a simple sentence into Cravic right now, I wouldn't be able to. That's how muddled my mind was standing so close to him.

"Please, first off, we'll be traveling and working closely on the Vessel Book together. I beg you to call me Theo." He chuckled, gesturing to himself. "I'm not big on parading titles around outside of official duties."

"Oh, yes, Theo." I nodded rapidly, the blush still painting my face bright red. "I...you can call me Dove. I um, don't have a title just...a name."

Stupid. Stupid. He knows your name already, you dolt.

"Then it's a pleasure, Dove." Theo took my hand in his and brought it to his lips, pressing a chaste kiss against the top of my fingers.

Swoon.

I curtsied, still holding my bag of toiletries, as I tried desperately to say something witty and brilliant and charming that would make Theo think of me again.

Unfortunately, what came out was – "The men's restroom is down the hall on the left if you...were looking."

Theo chuckled, squeezing my hand once before turning down the corridor towards the stairs.

The moment he was out of sight; I bolted towards the safety of the communal bathroom, struggling to get air into my lungs.

Why did I say that? That wasn't charming at all.

With a self-pitying groan, I pressed my back against the door, thankful the room was empty.

Tossing my bag onto the counter, I rubbed my eyes with the heels of my hands, replaying every second of that awkward encounter.

Mortified over telling the Regent where the *bathroom was*, I resolved to scamper to the carriage that would take me to the Jade Palace and lock myself inside with my books and my demon.

But as I secured the end of my long braid with a thick, paisley printed ribbon, a warm little thought burrowed through my mind.

Theo knew my name.

Could it be...that the Prince I couldn't get out of my head wondered who I was, too?

STILL FLUSHED FROM MY embarrassing encounter with Theo, I flopped onto the hard bench seat of the empty carriage, mentally berating myself for screwing up my chance to harmlessly flirt – just a *little* – with the Regent.

As I removed my traveling pack, two witches climbed in, chatting amongst themselves and taking the bench across from me. They nodded politely in my direction, and I smiled tightly in return, tugging the book on chaos magic out of my bag and tucking it into the cover of *Terramere's Beasts*. I didn't want any other translators noting the long-dead language on the cover and striking up a conversation for curiosity's sake.

Reading while the carriage rattled and the hours passed was difficult, and I gleaned as little from the witches sharing a ride with me as I did from *A Testimony to Massis and His Hidden Lineage Gift*.

Bron, the burly translator with a thick red beard and shaved head, was from Rummerock. He'd been invited to the Palace by Cordelia – the gorgeous witch next to him with brilliantly green eyes and warm, golden skin. She was in the Royal Coven, though I hadn't figured out what tier she was.

A particularly bone-jarring bump in the path had me shifting awkwardly, trying to rub life back into my aching hips. The bench was uncomfortable, though I was thankful to be out of the elements. Heavy clouds had gathered over the last hour, and fat raindrops were currently lashing against the sides of our carriage. The downpour showed no signs of lessening, but a rumble of distant thunder meant the storm was moving east – away from us.

Staring out the fogging window, a flash of red eyes confirmed Neera was trotting along with the caravan as we wove our way out of Bramberry and into the Quiet.

I wondered if the rain dampened her fur while she was invisible. I hoped not since we'd share a bed. I didn't enjoy the smell of wet dog – even though I was fond of the way she snuggled up to me.

I couldn't spy Theo through the rain, but I'd heard him politely refuse an offered carriage once the drizzle started. He was still on horseback, riding alongside witches from his Coven that I hadn't met.

There were two carriages between us, and one bringing up the rear. I'd glimpsed inside them out of curiosity. One was stuffed with trunks and supplies, the second resembled a healer's station, and the last carried a few elderly witches who'd accompanied Theo on his diplomatic tour but opted against being on horseback.

Chewing on my lip, I peered back at the paragraph testing my translating abilities. I understood the dead language enough to get by, but the fact it was *handwritten* was causing some grief. Shifting *Terramere's Beasts* in my grip so the hidden book wouldn't fall out, I squinted, sounding out the sentence structure in my head.

Once we arrived at the Jade Palace, I'd rewrite this book in Terrian. That would *really* impress Maude – especially if I also happened upon some glorious, long-kept god secret in the process.

And if I returned to Bramberry after successfully translating the Vessel Book, *too*?

I smiled to myself.

I could take my pick of teaching positions. Or create an entirely new class dedicated to translation. Maybe it would even win me respect from the high-tier witches in my Coven.

Before I could fall further into my daydream, the carriage came to an abrupt halt.

"Wonder why we stopped." Bron leaned forward, craning his neck to see out the window, his large frame taking up the entire window.

Cordelia tucked a strand of shiny, mahogany hair behind her ear. "Maybe Theo wants to rest the horses and dry off before we pass through the *veles*. They didn't use any weather runes to avoid getting wet." She sniffed, as if getting soaked when such a simple sigil could prevent it was absurd, but sometimes, you just needed the rain on your skin in order to feel alive.

A curt shout rang out over the misty rain. Bron shot Cordelia a cautious look, though she ignored him, flickers of pure silver light sparking to life as she shoved over to the window. I clasped my hands in my lap, hoping this didn't have anything to do with Neera.

Bron unearthed a short dagger from his bag. "You ladies stay here. I'll go investigate."

Cordelia reached under her pale yellow skirts, revealing a jagged blade with a bejeweled hilt – almost double the length of Bron's.

He gawked at her.

Rising from the bench, her light magic sank into the metal, making the weapon glow. "Mine's bigger, so just hold onto that little stick you got there. And don't get in my way."

I decided I liked her.

Bron stuttered, flicking his eyes to me.

Bending over, I unsheathed the plain, black hilt from the harness buckled around my ankle, and though my dagger wasn't as fancy or lethal as what Cordelia held, Bron raised his hands with a light chuckle. "Alright, *you* two check it out. I'll stay here."

Cordelia rolled her eyes, squeezing around him to open the door. "We're all going."

Without waiting for an answer, she gracefully hopped to the ground. Bron scrambled after her, navigating awkwardly through the cramped space while muttering under his breath about hard-headed women with weapons.

The contrast of Bron's passive personality to his hulking, brawny frame was enthrallingly entertaining – especially when his shoulder smacked against the rickety wooden doorframe, and he apologized to the carriage, a blush pinking his ears.

He was a gentle giant, and I had a feeling Cordelia would eat him alive.

Bron looked like he'd enjoy every second of it, though.

Our boots splashed through shallow puddles as we hurried towards the cluster of Royal Coven witches standing a hundred feet ahead of us.

The flat landscape of the Quiet was covered with sodden brown reed grass and scattered, gnarled trunks of trees barren of leaves - so unlike the lush forest in Bramberry. Without a canopy of dense foliage, I immediately felt too exposed to the sky looming above us.

My magic surged, seeking a way out, but I shoved it down, my eyes scouring the vast expanse of nothingness for any inkling of a threat. A cold breeze brushed reassuringly against my hand. Neera.

Knowing we hadn't stopped because someone noticed the grimm and raised the alarm had my shoulders relaxing a fraction.

Cordelia flicked her gaze to the fast-moving river on our left. "Don't fall in," she crowed, elbowing Bron in the side. "I'm not dragging your ass out again."

"It was *one time,*" Bron growled back, glaring down at Cordelia who batted her lashes back at him. "When you *pushed* me."

Cordelia smirked. I glanced at the dead trees to our right, their sparse branches twisting and reaching for the sky like bony fingers desperate to dig their way out of brittle, uninhabitable soil. Aside from our troupe, there was nothing and no one around.

No wind rustled the reed grass. Everything was so still.

An uneasy sensation tugged at my soul.

The Quiet was, well...*too* quiet.

Neera's presence hovered at my side as we approached Theo, still astride his pure white horse. Two Royal Guards stood protectively in front of the Regent, white light magic pulsing around their fists.

Ahead, I could make out the arched side of a bridge built from stone – the only way to pass over the river to the *veles* situated on the opposite bank.

A broad-shouldered man with dark hair stood in front of our troupe with his back to us. I couldn't see his face, but his wide stance and crossed arms made him appear imposing. In front of him, a group of haggard witches stood shoulder-to-shoulder.

"We have no quarrel with you, but if you don't move, you'll find yourself in a *very* different situation."

The man's statement held an undercurrent of wickedness, and the familiarity of it piqued my interest, though I couldn't place where I heard it before.

"What's the issue?" Cordelia murmured quietly, sidling closer to the Prince Regent.

Theo inclined his chin in solemn acknowledgement before placing white-knuckled hands at the base of his saddle horn. "These witches barricaded the bridge and refuse to move unless we pay their tithe."

At Theo's words, a wave of magic flooded my veins, causing me to stiffen at the sudden, off-kilter, sensation. Wrestling for control to push it back into my soul, Neera drifted forward, positioning herself next to the dark-haired man.

For a split second, while furiously wrestling thick strands of magic back into my well of power, I could've sworn he glanced down and startled, but it must've been my imagination. Neera was nothing more than a ripple of air. *No one* could see her.

Whatever connected us from the ritual was the only way *I* could tell where she stood. And right now, I was more worried about embarrassing myself, *again*, in front of Theo by letting my low-tier gift show.

It was going to be purple or blue - and neither of those was the pristine, silver hue of a witch worthy of flirting with the Regent of the Jade Kingdom.

Theo shuffled his horse closer to me, his features softening. "Go back to the carriage, Dove, in case this goes badly. I don't want anything to happen to you. These witches are desperate."

I opened my mouth to argue, to tell Theo I was strong enough to stand by him, when a witch lurking along the outskirts of the ragtag group caught my focus. The agitated way he moved struck me as unnatural, and when his dark, eerie gaze fixed on Theo, a sneer curled across his face.

"*Kill the Regent!*"

Before anyone could comprehend the threat, the twitchy man darted forward.

The guards pounced – but it was too late. In the span between seconds, the witch threw out his hands, a burst of magic erupting from his outstretched palms.

A burst of *purple* magic.

CHAPTER EIGHTEEN
DOVE

INSTINCT TOOK OVER, POWER flooding my body until every seam of my soul was interwoven with it.

Time slowed.

I called upon that reckless, ancient feeling magic, rallying it to my fingertips –

A wall of shadow crashed around Theo, Cordelia, Bron, and me – half a heartbeat before the attacking purple magic hit with a deafening *BOOM*. I ducked, covering my head with my arms protectively, power dissipating from my blood.

I screwed my eyes shut. A bright flare of lavender illuminated the black behind my lids. Cordelia shouted something, but I couldn't make it out over the shrill ringing in my ears.

"*Fuck.*"

The relief filling the curse had me tentatively opening my eyes, realizing the writhing mass of darkness absorbed the killing blow aimed at Theo – leaving the thick, black smoke of a *very* powerful shadow witch behind.

Cordelia whistled, impressed, tugging Bron up from the ground by the collar of his jacket. He'd taken the same defensive fetal position I had – which made me feel better.

The blood had drained from his face, making his beard more starkly orange than before.

I peered through the semi-translucent shadows. The man with the dark hair stared at me.

My breath stuttered.

He was the handsome man I'd stumbled into in front of Bramberry Manor during the Prince Regent's speech. And he was holding a palm towards us, inky shadows curling around his wrist. I'd never met a shadow witch before, aside from my sweet Elijah, but to see darkness wielded so effortlessly was brutally beautiful.

The mischief that played through his features at the Manor when he'd purred into my ear was long gone, replaced by an icy fury that only rivalled Theo. The Regent kicked his horse forward, roaring orders to attack.

Theo's guards released whips of light magic, coiling tightly around the witch who dared attack their Prince. The sharp crack of bone snapping, followed by a bellowing howl of pain, made me flinch.

Shadows erupted from the dark-haired man, taking the five remaining witches blocking our way to the ground swiftly.

Once the witches were incapacitated, the wall of shadows disappeared, curling like smoke towards the heavy clouds in the sky.

The witch with purple magic was closest to me, gnashing his teeth, spittle and blood spraying the dirt path. His body jerked against the magical restraints holding him down, but the Royal Guards' light magic was strong, not allowing the witch more than a few inches of movement.

Then he just...stopped.

Slowly the witch raised his face off the ground, his focus shifting...

To *me*.

I inhaled sharply.

His eyes were fully black – depthless voids of pitch darkness that held an echo of something far more ancient and deadly than simple hatred.

Settling that unnatural gaze on me, the witch's thin lips tipped up into a smirk.

Under my skin, magic slammed against the confines of my soul.

My throat went dry as I stumbled back a step, needing to put distance between me and...and...*this*.

The grip on my dagger was so tight I could feel my pulse in the tips of my fingers.

The rest of our troupe stayed back, eyes flicking between the captured witches and the Regent, as if waiting for justice to be served. There were two elderly witches and a handful of men in their mid-thirties – though every single one was either palming weapons or rallying silver-hued light that lit the path and banished away the gloom following after the receding thunderstorm.

Cordelia stood next to me, her lips pressed together in a firm line, the dagger in her hands still pulsing with magic.

"Justice must be served," she snarled. My heart pounded.

Would the Royal Coven murder a witch right here – in the middle of the Quiet – with no trial?

With a wince, I realized just how little of the realm I truly understood. How much I'd been sheltered under the peaceful canopy of Bramberry Forest.

That witch just attempted to assassinate the Regent.

Of course, a death sentence would be passed.

I swallowed, wishing I'd learned more of the world before embarking on this journey. Now, seeing what life was like outside the Bramberry Forest, my mind spun itself into knots.

Maude protected me from so much...

Part of me – a *small* part – now begrudgingly understood why. And I had to trust that Maude knew best.

Right?

Theo dismounted his horse, hands clenched at his sides as he stormed towards the witch with purple magic, hatred sharpening his lethal glare. "You crossed the Crown," Theo hissed. "But you won't live long enough to regret revealing your power, *heretic.*"

I blanched, every wistful thought of Bramberry misting from my mind, like an illusion being ripped away.

That voice...

The man in the hall – the one giving the order to hunt down a heretic witch in Bramberry.

It was Theo.

Chapter Nineteen

DOVE

Blood pounded so violently through my iced-over veins my hands shook.

"*Heretics* have purple magic?" I breathed quietly, desperate to catch Cordelia's attention.

She nodded once, barely inclining her head.

Shit, shit.

Did *I* have heretic magic?

How did I get *heretic* magic?

Was it the birch tree? Was that why it was illegal to siphon them?

The dizzying change of my power to purple now loomed like a burning pyre.

I must've caught Cordelia's attention a little *too* well, because she slid closer. "Heretics gain purple magic through *blood rituals*." She jerked her chin towards the shadow witch. "Finn's been hunting heretics for years. That's why he's been gone so long."

"I didn't know Finn was back at the Palace," Bron said, interrupting Cordelia and picking the *least* interesting part of her sentence to focus on.

Cordelia scoffed, "The prodigal son's return was fairly recent."

My gaze flicked to Finn, now standing next to Theo. I was smacked with another startling realization.

There'd been so much going on that I hadn't put two and two together until now.

Fuck.

Finn was actually Prince *Finneas* – King Velik's eldest son.

Bouncing my eyes from one brother to the other, they *did* have similar builds, though Finn was a few inches taller and bulkier than Theo. And where Theo's skin held a faint, sun-gold tan, Finn's was a much darker bronze.

But they had the same nose, the same prominent facial structure, slightly hooded eyes, and matching sneers on their full lips that sent a tingle down my spine.

And they both hunted heretics.

If Theo was the man I heard in the hallway, his brother had to be the second voice – the one tasked with *finding* the heretic in Bramberry.

Cordelia waved her hand, pouring magic over our group, providing more light for us in the aftermath of the skirmish. "The King's illness is serious, and since Velik can't use magic anymore, the healers said it won't be long before Velik is taken to Minmere. Finn showed up pretty soon after. The brothers seem to have rekindled a relationship after an... estranged few years."

I scooted closer, shelving the information on the brothers for a more direct line of concern, shivering in the night air that was cooling rapidly around us with the disappearance of the sun. "What sort of blood ritual?" I asked, wondering if playing dumb would get me more answers and less suspicion. If heretics were known to have purple magic...I glanced nervously between the three witches on the ground, mentally sizing them up against the men who attacked me just days ago.

Could these be my assailants?

"We aren't sure," Cordelia started, signifying her position in the Royal Coven was much higher than a standard witch. "But from our research, the blood ritual is part of a spell that warps a *veles* – connecting it to Avamere. In return for linking the realms, Massis is gifting lineage magic, giving heretic magic in place of light or shadow magic."

I shifted from one foot to the other, Cordelia's voice far-off and tinny.

"But Massis only grants heretic magic to one witch per ritual. Not to mention, most heretics would rather die than be taken by the Crown for questioning, so getting these fuckers to the Palace alive means we may be able to get solid answers before we dispose of them. Maybe even figure out the spell they're using.

Any witch found with heretic magic is immediately considered an enemy of the crown and sentenced to death. No trial."

The moment the words left her lips, two of the captured witches seized, foam frothing from their mouths, limbs stiffening.

A pair of Royal Coven witches rushed forward, healing magic billowing from their hands, but it was too late. Their bodies slumped, a trickle of blood seeping from their gaping lips.

And their eyes...their eyes were those same pupil-less pools of black, though now they stared through nothingness as death came swiftly, leaving four heretics alive.

Shadows pounced over the witch who attacked Theo, morphing into a dagger of darkness that sliced through the air with a sharp whistle, severing both of the heretic's hands at the wrist in one swipe.

The heretic let out a high-pitched shriek, his hands thumping listlessly onto the ground beside him. Blood gushed, puddling against the rain-soaked ground, though not a single witch in our troupe batted an eyelash – except for Bron, who looked as if he may pass out.

"Death runes," Cordelia sighed through her nose, shaking her head. "Such a pain in the ass."

I gaped at her informality as she squeezed past the healers and rolled the bodies of the dead onto their backs with a wave of her hand, revealing hidden blood runes etched into the ground pulsing with purple magic. Finn circled the prisoners still alive, shadows simmering in the wake of each booted footstep.

The Royal Coven descended into muttered conversation, breaking off into small huddles. All but Theo – who stood behind his guards, glaring at his brother.

Finn ignored him.

I forced myself towards the death rune, determined to see it for myself. Only a few hours outside of the Bramberry Forest, and so far, this adventure was much more nerve-wracking and eye-opening than I expected.

Surprisingly, the sigil was pretty simple for the amount of power it held – and the fact the circle with an "x" through the middle was drawn with blood. The heretics must've known their options came down to torture in the Palace, or death and unbeknownst to us, etched true blood runes into the dirt and imbued them after being caught by Finn's shadows.

Sure enough, Finn stooped over the heretic now missing both hands. The witch had passed out from blood loss, but Finn merely used his boot to roll him over, uncovering an incomplete rune.

Finn seemed lost to his mind for a moment, his eyes drawing from the captive over to where I could feel Neera's presence.

Can Finn tell Neera is here?

I dismissed the thought. There was no way he could see the grimm – she was completely invisible.

Right?

But, if I had heretic magic, a protective grimm at my side wasn't a bad thing to have. I let out a soft breath, hoping my magic wouldn't get me killed.

"Typical cowards," Theo growled.

Finn chuckled darkly, directing the healers to staunch the heretic's bleeding. The two older women huddled over the man, clasping their palms down on his wrist stumps. The flesh knit over the wounds; my stomach pitched at the sight of new skin growing over bone.

Theo turned his attention to the other three witches, who immediately began pleading their innocence. Disregarding them, he barked at his guards to secure their hands.

Thick shackles carved with runes pulsed with faint light, making quick work of securing each prisoner still bound with Finn's shadow.

"They nullify magic," Cordelia explained as she rallied a whip of light magic, breaking apart the death runes. The embers of purple disappeared, making the dirt path clear once more. "Makes it easier to transport prisoners. Though, I guess, Finn's way works too," she snorted, slashing me a smirk. "Bloodthirsty bastard he is. Nasty business."

A shiver slithered through my blood.

I took a long look at each captive as they were dragged away, forcing myself to dredge up painful memories of the assailants from my ordeal, but upon further scrutiny, none of these witches had been there on the night of my ritual.

They didn't fit the size description of the man that fled the temple. It both relieved me and made me anxious – knowing there were more witches out there desperately trying to gain favor with Massis for heretic magic.

And that there was a disturbing chance the purple magic I'd accidentally received was here to stay.

The three prisoners were secured to horses, the unconscious heretic thrown over the saddle like a sack of flour, his bronze shackles clanking hollowly from the juncture above his elbows since he no longer had hands.

"Dove," Theo reached for my elbow, concern on his face as he checked me up and down for any sign of injury. "I'm so sorry for this – are you alright?"

"I'm fine," I said softly, my heartrate accelerating as his fingers stroked my arm over my sweater.

Gods, getting involved with him in any capacity was such a bad idea.

For so many reasons.

But then the handsome Prince slashed me a quirked smile, that dimple popping up on his cheek, and all of my very practical concerns flew right out of my head.

Dammit.

Theo moved closer, his eyes searching mine for words unspoken.

My blood warmed in my veins as I met his gaze, felt the magic in his soul call to mine so musically it put me in a trance.

There was something here, between us – there *had* to be. It was the only reason I could come up with as to why we kept finding ourselves sucked into each other's orbits.

Finn cleared his throat dramatically behind us, aiming a particularly loathing look in my direction. "If you two are done, might I suggest we continue on our way? Unless, of course, you'd prefer to inconvenience everyone and arrive to the Palace well after nightfall."

The harshness in his tone startled me away from Theo. Theo stood there for a moment, as if he wanted to reach for me again, but everyone in our troupe *was* staring at us with a mixture of irritation and boredom.

It seemed the scuffle with the heretics only kept the Royal Coven entertained for so long.

Wrapping my arms around myself, I took a few steps back, putting space between us. Theo lingered, blue eyes desperate, as if he wavered between following his brother or staying by me, and while my heart crowed at the attention, my mind thrashed in panic.

"This may be forward, Dove, but I'd like to get to know you better," Theo murmured.

Without waiting for me to reply, he flashed me one more searing grin before turning towards his horse.

My breathing didn't restart until Theo was out of my immediate area, and I'd committed his desire-soaked gaze to memory.

But heavy fear screeched through my head the moment I realized I stood alone amongst a Coven that wasn't mine.

I couldn't leave and head back to Bramberry without Maude being disappointed in me for not going to the Palace. And returning home may be futile, anyway, with the runes surrounding Bramberry that kept out heretics...like me.

Since I left the protection of Maude's runes, would I be unable to reenter? Forever?

Panic welled up, squeezing my chest, but before overwhelming anxiety could take hold, I took a deep breath, reminding myself that there was no purpose in getting hysterical over mere speculation.

Maude would tell Polina and I that whenever intrusive thoughts invaded our heads.

I was also terrible with directions, so if I tried to trek back the way we came, it was much more likely I'd get so lost I'd end up in the Topaz Kingdom.

Finn remounted his horse, a giant black stallion that held just as much fire in his dark eyes as his rider did. He wheeled his horse around, scowling at the landscape surrounding us as if he was personally affronted by the thin, dead, trees.

The way Finn fought back, the wall of darkness that erupted out of him as a shield to protect me and his brother, the effortless way he controlled his magic...my academic mind slithered to the forefront, past the part of me quietly bleating in fear over potentially having heretic magic.

Unfortunately, if anyone could teach me about shadow magic, it was Prince Finneas.

Elijah needed a teacher. If I played my cards right, and came out of this with my head intact, I could bring much-needed knowledge of shadow magic back to Bramberry, help Elijah learn how to control his gift, and hopefully earn a teaching position in the Manor.

High risk, high reward...right?

Theo swung up onto his own steed, trotting towards his brother and the barricaded bridge. Thick bolts of shadows tore apart the cluster of rock and tree limbs that barred our way.

"C'mon," Cordelia huffed. "Time to move out. You don't want to land on Finn's bad side – he'll make what he did to those heretics look like a fucking tea party."

I forced my feet to move as the rest of the Royal Coven trailed after the Regent and Finn. A whisper of breeze darted past me, and I caught a glimpse of Neera's presence before she dove off through the sparse trees to run alongside the caravan.

It was only when I latched the carriage door shut, and the driver clicked his tongue to the horses pulling us, that I allowed myself to wallow in the newest and most urgent parts of my predicament.

The ritual in Carra's temple ended with me receiving Massis's power.

I was the heretic hiding in Bramberry.

Which meant I was being hunted.

By the Prince with desire etched on his face.
And his ruthless brother.

CHAPTER TWENTY

DOVE

I CHEWED ON MY lip, staring out at the landscape slowly morphing from barren trunks and reed grass to thin pines with branches full of evergreen and vibrant maple trees bursting with hues of reds and golds. With evening darkening the sky, it was a relief when the thicket of trees grew denser, even though the wooded area, broken up with random rock ledges and giant boulders, was still a far cry from the lushness of Bramberry.

This bank of the Quiet butted against the land the Royal Coven occupied, and the outskirts of Shadymoss took some purchase as well.

Bron was the first to break the stony silence permeating the carriage. "Your eyes are very unique – were you born with them? Or was it from an old injury?"

"You can't just ask a lady about her past," Cordelia chastised, cutting him a look that he brushed off as he leaned closer, his deep brown eyes surveying my uncommon ones.

"I'm not positive," I said, throwing Cordelia a small smile at the comradery. "My birth mother had light brown eyes, but I'm not sure where the dark blue came from. I was adopted by my Coven Mother as a babe."

I left out the part where she had been found dead after a blood ritual, her life forfeited for a cruel witch to gain heretical magic.

It made me wonder why Massis allowed these sacrifices to continue.

He was the one god who'd always been a protector of witches.

But now, he was promising witches lineage gifts in exchange for what?

Why was connecting a *veles* to Avamere so important?

"I don't ask to be nosy," Bron corrected with a grimace, running a hand through his beard. "On top of my studies as a scholar, I'm training to become a healer. Heterochromatic irises are a rare trait to be born with, and my focus is on healing the mind after traumatic events or blunt force trauma." After a beat he winced, "I'm sorry if you took offence."

"No offence taken." I looked from Bron to Cordelia. "I apologize for not being a chattier travel companion. This is my first time leaving Bramberry so it's...been different than what I expected."

"Heretic witch encounters included?" Cordelia asked playfully, as if this was any other day for her.

"*Especially* because of the heretic witch encounter. Our Coven Mother, Maude, rarely spoke to me about them. All these years, I thought they were nothing more than a sect of radical witches who felt the gods abandoned them. I never expected them to be...more. And I *never* imagined they truly had lineage gifts."

"Maude's always been vocal about protecting her Coven from heretics. I've sat in a few Royal Council meetings with her. She is a fierce protector of Bramberry. You must be proud."

I nodded, forcing a tight-lipped smile, hoping that it conveyed pride of my Coven and not the feeling that Maude lied to me for years. About heretics, about the rituals, about my birth mother's death. If she knew, all those decades ago, what Massis was granting witches who performed the blood sacrifices, why didn't she say anything?

Less than one full day out of Bramberry and I'd learned more about heretics than years spent asking my mother.

Was Maude protecting me?

Or hiding something?

The carriage bobbed and jostled as we sank back into silence, though my thoughts ran rampant. We probably had an hour of travel left before we reached the *veles* that would take us to the Palace. I'd use this time to needle Cordelia for more answers.

"I thought the god realms were sealed?"

Cordelia frowned, as if she chose her next words carefully. I kept my expression curious, friendly, hoping she wouldn't run to Theo and tell him I'd asked about Royal Coven business.

"The god realms *are* sealed," she started, "but that only stops the gods themselves from passing through realms. It keeps their physical beings in their specific realm."

I mulled this over, but it didn't really give me any new feedback.

"Massis has always been intrigued by our realm – because of the connection he can make to imbue a Vessel. Since he wasn't in the original quad of goddesses who came earthside, he wasn't a part of the Vessel Treaty and wouldn't be limited to imbuing one Vessel at a time. If Massis came to Terramere, he could imbue as many Vessels as he wanted with god magic."

"But *why* is Massis granting lineage magic to witches who kill other witches? Why the blood rituals and spell work?" I asked bluntly. "He's always protected us against the gods that favored the fae and gargoyles."

Cordelia grumbled under her breath about academically inclined witches and streams of '*why, why, why's.*'

I'd only just met Cordelia, but I could tell her temper ran hot quick, and from the few whiplash emotions I'd encountered from her already, I really wanted to stay on her good side permanently.

"It's an exchange – a bargain. The blood runes and spells link to the *veles* themselves, warping it from its normal trajectory to Avamere temporarily.

But the *veles* can only stay connected to Avamere for a short time – since spells don't last long – hence why blood runes are used to boost the spell itself." Cordelia blew out a rough breath, leaning closer. "Dukhmora are pouring through the *veles* during every ritual, decimating our southern towns. It's mostly confined to Shadymoss and lands south of the Palace, but dukhmora are nasty bastards to fight."

"Why..." Cordelia shook her head sadly. "All we can guess is that his desire to gift a new lineage magic is outweighing any past love for his original gifts, or he's angry with us, and the dukhmora are his version of a reckoning."

I glanced down at my rucksack, where *A Testimony to Massis and His Hidden Lineage Gift* was packed away. Resisting the urge to show it to Cordelia and Bron, I swallowed, holding my tongue.

If anything could explain my purple magic...

Something told me answers lay inside that handwritten book.

"The gods can be finicky," Bron added. "For example, Carra. We used to be bestowed soul ties like the fae, gargoyles, and humans. But now, no one in Jade, nor the Slate Kingdom, can receive a soul tie. It's like...every continent housing a large grouping of witches is cursed."

I wanted so badly to ask more, but Cordelia's face was getting more inquisitive and less friendly, so I switched tactics. "You grew up in the Royal Coven, Cordelia? I bet that's an incredible Coven to be part of."

The scrutiny disappeared from her face as she visibly relaxed, showing just how tense she'd been. Her plush lips curved. "It's amazing. I manifested light magic young, and it was bright silver immediately. I took my Coven vows after finishing school, and I've been working alongside King Velik's inner circle for two decades now."

"That's so great," I encouraged, relieved the investigative look in her eye disappeared.

Bron huffed, "Rummerock is cool too, you know."

The tension in the carriage disappeared as we spent the next hour chatting and laughing about our different upbringings. Bron came from a long line of scholars, though he was the sole witch in his Coven to take up the study of linguistics.

"So, you're a light witch too, right?" My palms grew clammy at Bron's innocent question.

"Sure am," I said brightly, balling the sleeves of my sweater in my fists, as the voice inside my head called me a *liar*.

I could've sworn a rumble trembled through the earth as the lie flitted past my teeth. "But I've never been a top tier witch. My magic was – *is* – light blue so I dedicated my studies towards teaching, and in my free time I study languages."

"You want to be a teacher?" Cordelia asked. I blew out a soft breath that neither of them picked up the slip of my tongue.

"Someday, yes. I hope to be able to teach both shadow and light witchlings."

"Did you always want to translate the Book of Carra?"

"I never really thought about it. Maude actually recommended I try. I love the art of translation, and if the years studying long-dead languages is helpful to the Jade Kingdom, then it was time well spent."

Bron rolled his shoulders back, stretching his neck from side to side. He was so tall that he had to lean with his forearms braced on his thighs so his shaved head wouldn't smack the top of the carriage. I could only imagine how hard riding in such a cramped space was for him. "I'm surprised Theodoric is opening the Book of Carra up so soon. Usually, new rulers wait until after their coronation before they decide what to do with the Vessel Book."

"I think it has something to do with the demon activity," Cordelia replied. Bron and I paused at that. I hoped she'd elaborate.

Thankfully, it was Bron who prodded. "What d'you mean?"

"The dukhmora attacks mean the gods are watching the Jade Kingdom, or at least Massis is. If there was ever a time where we needed Carra's god magic, now would be it." She stretched her legs out, peering through the window for a moment.

"I'm sure we'll all huddle over that book for months until the Regent is bored and over it. Then he'll send us home with no more clarity on Carra's ambiguous words than when we started." Bron's aloofness was lost against the brooding Cordelia smothered in next to him, but I, once again, changed the subject out of need for the tension to evaporate.

"How far are we from the *veles*?"

Cordelia chuckled lightly, a small tilt of her lips showing she was more amused than irritated. "We went through a few minutes ago. We'll be at the Palace shortly."

Scrambling forward, I squished my face against the window, desperate to lay eyes on the Palace I'd only ever *dreamed* of seeing in person, of studying in its famous library – I could almost see it now, me, walking through gilded halls with a stack of tomes to read under the shade of its ancient oaks.

Our carriage rolled along the interior of a crumbling stone wall, ropes of leafy ivy curling across jagged grooves and creeping along the edge like gnarled fingers. The canopy above us was similar to Bramberry, cutting off most of the dusk sky above us, though the ancientness that thrummed through the forest I'd grown up in was *nothing* like the short road up to the Jade Palace.

It was eerie here – as if one wrong breath would cause the surrounding flora to rear back and attack. Aside from the squeaks of the carriage and the soft clop of the horses ahead, there was only...stillness. No breeze in the air, no rustle of critters scavenging through trees, no distant hoots or howls from predators hunting under the cover of nightfall.

Instead, dense fog clung to the ground, pooling silver and thick over fat blankets of moss, though flashes of jade and gold tiles underneath spoke of a once great mosaic. Thick tree roots rose slowly through the earth, breaking through some of the tiles – as if the mighty oaks lining the drive were determined to take this area back for themselves.

Our wheels groaned, splashing through shallow puddles of dark water that shimmered like fallen stars when disturbed. I could tell this was once a renowned and prideful road leading to the Jade Palace, but now, weaving through the alcove of hauntingly alert trees, our mere presence seemed to stir an aura of tension into the too-still air.

Yet for all the hostility this place exuded, I was enthralled, giddiness causing gooseprickles to erupt down my arms. I turned toward Bron and Cordelia, awe shining on my face, only to be met with unimpressed expressions. Bron leaned down, loosening the laces on his boots. Cordelia shuffled through the bags at her feet, unaffected by our surroundings.

"Is there a mosaic under the moss?" I couldn't taper my sheer excitement. Just seeing the half-crumbled walls, the flickers of tiles – I wanted to know *everything*.

"Yeah." Cordelia secured the straps of her bag shut. "One of the first rulers after Queen Minerva had a mile long mosaic commissioned. She was a light witch who went mad during her rule but believed this would shift Faune's attention from the fae to witchkind – so this road was designed to entice Faune and regain her favor."

"Now it's a run-down landmark that we jostle along every time we head to the Palace from the *veles*. I've had carriages get stuck in the moss before, and there's nothing quite as irritating after days of travel than trekking the last half mile on foot, carrying all your shit." Bron tightened his hold on his rucksack, as if just the *thought* of getting out and walking pissed him off.

I slid my arms through my bags, awkwardly holding them against my body as the carriage slowed to a stop.

Bron sighed in relief. "We're here."

Adrenaline surged in my soul, mixing with my well of magic and creating a torrent of resolute clarity. Every answer I was so desperate to find could be behind these walls, buried in the Royal Library, calling for me to unearth them. The dread and fear in my chest since the heretics stopped us in the Quiet, since the ritual warped my magic, since I found out my birth mother was killed in a blood sacrifice, suddenly felt...*conquerable*.

I barely registered Cordelia following me out of the carriage as I got my first glimpse of the Jade Palace.

"Magnificent," I breathed, craning my neck to take in the Palace before me.

The Bramberry Manor could house a hundred witches. The Jade Palace could easily hold a *thousand*.

Giant ash trees bowed away from asymmetrical towers and pitched roofs that pointed towards an open, star-streaked sky. Arched windows spanned multiple floors, glowing with amber light that shadowed against those unnerving oak trees surrounding us like stoic warriors.

The entire structure mimicked a whimsical, overgrown cottage – complete with stone chimneys stuck at off-kilter angles, merrily churning out tendrils of smoke. Even the intricate filigree carved around the windows gave off a pleasant, charming warmth – a total contradiction to the eerie, mosaic-laid road.

Queen Minerva pulled inspiration from the Obsidian Palace to build this place, though the Palace was not as towering and spindly as the architecture carved from the Zircon mountains. Vines blanketed the stone walls and shrubs grew untamed around the perimeter.

As the Jade Kingdom grew, buildings were added onto the original structure, keeping the same peculiar structure while spanning out into the woods beyond.

It looked cozy, inviting, and a little haunted.

I loved it.

I knew the Jade Palace was the second smallest Palace in the Seven Kingdoms – narrowly beating out the Slate Palace on size. But still...laying eyes on it in all of its splendor, I had a difficult time imagining any of the other Palaces could be more incredible than this.

I'd gone silent, overcome with emotion, panic and thrill warring inside me as I took a single step towards the arched iron door.

"Stop." A gruff voice from behind had me whirling around, coming face-to-sternum with Finn. This close, his menacing aura had my magic shrinking back in my soul, so unlike the effect Theo had on it – where it strained to greet him, wanting to be let free to dance around.

But with all signs pointing to me accidentally receiving a lineage gift of forbidden power, I couldn't afford to let a single spark of lavender light escape.

I hadn't heard him approach, but his frown and crossed arms said he was either irritated at having to deal with me, or he remembered me as the clumsy witch outside of Bramberry Manor and was regretting showing me a sliver of interest.

Or he was still mad about that moment I had with his brother...

As if he could read my mind, Finn sneered, coating me in uncertainty. The flirty stranger from Bramberry Manor was gone. In its stead stood a glowering shadow witch with a threatening aura and what I assumed was a *very* thin thread of patience.

"Your *High-*...um, Lord Finneas, what can I do for you?"

I curtsied, mentally berating myself for not knowing how to address the half-brother of the Regent who was *technically* part of the Royal Family – even though his succession was revoked.

He snorted derisively but didn't correct me. "Come here."

Without waiting, he stormed off towards the corner of the Palace's entryway, where a large portion of the wall was fully destroyed and replaced with a wrought iron fence topped with sharp finials. It was also bathed in deep shadows.

I shot a worried glance at Cordelia and Bron, but they were too busy bickering over whose trunk needed to go where. Neither of them noticed the Regent's brother, nor that I was dragging my feet following the human embodiment of a thunder cloud into a dark, obscured corner.

Neera's presence brushed against my side. At least she was close.

The fog wove around my boots as I picked my way over to Finn, doing my best to avoid the puddles scattered across the odd mosaic. My magic fluttered nervously in response to the leap in my heartrate, but no incriminating purple glow leaked from my palms.

Finn stood rigid, glaring down at me as I slowly approached. A muscle ticked in his jaw. Wearing all black, he seemed at home surrounded by jagged shadows, and I half-wondered if this was darkness of his making, or if he took all of the new invitees to the Palace on such a...hostile jaunt.

Did he want me to say something?

Finn's calculating stare swept over me, his heavy gaze fraying my nerves. But before I could repeat myself and ask if he needed something, he grunted, "Stay away from Theo."

"Excuse me?"

"*Stay away* from my brother," Finn growled, glowering at something above my head as if this conversation was beneath him, yet he needed to get it rectified swiftly. "I saw how you looked at him in the Quiet."

I raised my brows, stunned at the venom punctuating his words.

Who did this man think he was?

With a dry scoff, he added, "If you know what's good for you, you'll prance back into that carriage and return to your Coven."

"You don't know me," I snapped.

"I know enough."

"I'm the translator from the Bramberry Coven. I'm here to *work*."

Fisting my hands, I drew up straighter. Fuck this. Finn had no power to send me back to Bramberry. And *why* would he wait until I *got* here to demand I go home?

Finn scowled pointedly to where Cordelia and Bron were still congregated around the carriage. "A young witch with a little bit of linguistic study sees an opportunity to seduce the Crown. Is that your deal?"

My magic reared up as my temper rose, flooding my veins like an inferno. I struggled to contain it – to not allow a single spark of purple to damn me further.

But for the first time, my magic fought back, careening inside me as if it wanted to break away and wreak havoc, using me as nothing more than the anchor to travel through.

A hundred retorts flooded my tongue, some biting, some nasty. Most containing a curse word or two.

Before I could tell him a single one, and to my complete bewilderment, he took half a stumbled step back, surprise flaring through his hazel eyes.

He opened his mouth and closed it.

Confusion danced across his dark features for a single heartbeat. But it was so brief, I could've imagined it.

The burning remarks faded on my tongue as our glares clashed. A high-pitched whistle filled my head. I bared my teeth at the arrogant asshole who looked like he was considering where to bury my body and if the repercussions would be worth it.

A few pulse-pounding heartbeats later, Finn broke the tension with a mirth-filled Cravic curse – as if he'd silently evaluated me and found me lacking. I would've normally been excited to find another witch who spoke Cravic, but unfortunately Finn was an utter asshole that I never wanted to speak to again.

"You know what? Do whatever you want. *But* I recommend you heed my advice, *darling*. This is your one – *and only* – chance." He lowered his head so our faces were mere inches apart. I refused to cower.

When it became clear I wasn't backing down, his rough voice deepened to a velvet purr. "If you step through that threshold, I'll do whatever *I* deem necessary to protect the Crown."

Shadows peeled back from the dark alcove, sweeping around Finn in a whirlwind. A beat later they disappeared, taking Finn with them.

"Fucking shadow magic," I seethed, hating the tinge of awe that diluted the heat in my words.

Finn could shadow walk, a similar gift to the fae's waning. Being able to command the darkness to transport you from one place to another was a skill only the highest-tiered shadow witches could wield.

Light witches could wane if they siphoned power directly from a fae – which, in our fae-less Kingdom, meant nil. I chewed my lip, wracking my brain for a reason why Finn left.

Thinking of his poor attitude and baseless threats made me irritated all over again. I chucked the asshole from my worries.

Maybe he wasn't used to anyone standing up to him.

I had bigger things to deal with, anyway.

As if it sensed my focus, my magic receded, scurrying back into my soul and quieting. I hadn't realized how close it came to the surface during my standoff with Prince Finneas.

With Finn's shadows pulled back from the dark corner, the small sheen of Neera became visible, the ripple of air telling me she was sitting on her haunches next to me. I marveled over the fact that she was taller than me in this stance.

I still wanted to research the grimm more. That would be the first topic I studied when I arrived to the Royal Library.

Well, that *and* the curious book sitting in my bag tantalizing me with its secrets.

I was here on my Coven Mother's blessing, Theo's proximity made my blood warm, and I'd already made a potential couple of friends.

If Finn wanted to start an unsanctioned fight with me, away from his dear brother's eyes, he'd have bigger problems.

Namely the massive grimm at my side that already killed witches on my behalf.

"Hey!" Cordelia shouted. Her voice sounded far away and tinny, blasting through my furious thoughts on Finn. "I'm taking you to your room so grab your bag and follow me. I sent your trunks up there already and now it's late, and I, for one, am *exhausted*."

Spinning on my heel and stomping through the puddles and moss back to the carriage, I reminded myself, again, not to let Finn mess with my head.

Cordelia popped a hip as I drew closer. "Look at you – already splashing through the muck like you own the place."

I laughed, Finn's smug face already forgotten. Linking arms, our bags jostling into each other's sides, Cordelia steered me up the wide steps and through the Palace's doorway.

CHAPTER TWENTY-ONE
DOVE

FUCK FINN. I CROSSED the threshold unscathed.

I told myself the reason I held my breath as I stepped into the Jade Palace's original, abandoned foyer was because the incredible architecture squeezed my lungs into a chokehold – not because part of me anticipated Finn leaping from the shadows to attack.

Slowing my steps, boots kicking up a fine layer of dust, I gaped at the deserted space. Nature had begun to win its war in here. Large, cracked tiles hid under layers of grime and dirt, more than one patch of grass shoving through the stained grout. An arched window stood, half-shattered, above what must've once been a grand staircase. A tree had grown through the space, blocking the entire right side of the stairs with thick limbs that curled around a carved balustrade.

Only our troupe, sans Theo and Finn, were in here, loudly talking and laughing with each other as they headed into a circular courtyard beyond a set of ornate doors. They didn't as much as spare a glance through the peculiar foyer – though the echoes of their voices lingered through the heavy air longer than normal.

A cold stone hearth in the corner held remnants of its last embers in little piles of soot. The mantle was askew – one strong gust of wind would send it clattering to the floor.

Little yellow and orange birds darted around dark wood beams. Nests of various sizes were strewn about – stuffed into holes of decaying wood, between cracks in the fireplace – even draped over the balustrade. And where nests couldn't be placed, cobwebs took up residence, stretching between the slats and reaching towards the pitched ceiling in thick sheets.

"This entrance is unused, nowadays," Cordelia said, almost apologetic, as I examined a mossy patch that seemed determined to swallow the feet of a busted armchair by the hearth. Not only was the moss intriguing, but the seat of the chair had been taken over by spores, shooting out fat mushrooms with vivid red caps. "We use it when we're traveling by caravan. Otherwise, we go through the side entrance. There's a row of rooms on the second floor, but they've been empty for almost a century. But if someone we don't like comes to visit, we spruce a room or two up just enough to be habitable. Which means fresh sheets, and we *shoo* out the majority of the bats."

She chuckled.

It didn't sound like she was kidding, though.

"Can't do anything about the squirrels, unfortunately. They don't fear anything."

At that, I let out a breathy laugh, imagining some snooty noblewoman screaming about critters in her room – the complaint ringing through the silent foyer and going noticeably unanswered.

"Your room is this way, c'mon," Cordelia announced, dragging me into a courtyard. Two beautiful weeping willows danced over marble benches, and a three-tiered fountain with murky green water sat in the center. Though no water moved through it, it was still a beautiful piece of architecture. Slabs of slate formed a walkway from the abandoned foyer, stretching across the courtyard to another set of doors. On both sides, a thick iron fence kept the forest at bay, though the night sky was hidden from view by the trees sporting autumn hued leaves.

Cordelia bustled to the brighter entrance, its glass doors thrown wide. We entered another building, busier than the one we'd arrived at, with a less dusty atmosphere. It opened into a lounge that mimicked the Manor in Bramberry – a large rectangular common area where a massive hearth with a merry fire took up a full wall, embracing us in warmth – so different than the chilled, silent foyer nature infiltrated.

An assortment of ornamental armchairs and couches littered the space, all in deep shades of olive and sage. Witches milled about, some sitting and reading, others using their magic to imbue rocks and etch sigils in the surface. At one of the long tables, a group of witches laughed and chatted amongst themselves, fashioning runestone necklaces with colorful wire and spools of thin chain.

The atmosphere was cozy, inviting. The tinge of magic and study coiled together beautifully, and my power bubbled excitedly, as if it too wanted to come out and play, and the danger of its purple hue was completely lost on it.

With a pang of disappointment, I smothered the urge. Before the ritual, I would've been embarrassed at the robin-egg blue of my light magic in the presence of top tier witches of the Royal Coven. Now, that embarrassment was pure fear.

If I *had* been gifted forbidden lineage magic, I needed to keep that to myself.

Cordelia ushered me past the common area to a wide staircase in the corner, pushing a silver key into my palm. "You're room thirteen on the left - third floor. I'll come collect you in the morning and take you to the library."

"Do I...just stay there?" I asked, gingerly taking the key from her, wishing I could explore more at my own pace.

She laughed. "You can wander wherever your scholarly heart takes you – just steer clear of the lake out back."

I wanted to ask *why* I needed to stay away from the lake, but I nodded instead, thanking her for the escort. Cordelia waved to someone behind me. "The library's in the next building after this one. If you follow the cobblestone path through the second courtyard, you'll see a bunch of old witches in robes hobbling along. Oh, and there's a dining area through the doors on the left. The cook drops off pastries and light meals this time of night for anyone still awake. Help yourself."

She hesitated a beat before hugging me. I squeezed her back, wondering if I'd already made a friend here.

"Thank you, Cordelia. I'll see you tomorrow."

She grinned and hustled past me, light magic sparking at her fingertips to open the door before she reached it. I allowed myself one more glimpse of the common room before resigning myself to the fact that I was *extremely* tired.

I'd been traveling all day, and it wasn't until I began climbing the steps up to the third floor that bone weary exhaustion hit.

I could explore tomorrow – after I got some rest and maybe a bath. Or...maybe after I washed up, I'd see what these pastries in the kitchen were all about.

Room thirteen stood at the end of a row of six, situated on a wide landing. I unlocked the door quickly, practically tipping into the room under the weight of the day and everything I'd learned.

It was small and sparsely furnished – with a narrow bed, a little desk, an empty bookshelf, and a cramped bathroom. A gorgeous stained-glass window in the corner shone with a soft prism of reds and oranges, filtered across the carpet from the lights of other rooms. Outside, I could make out the smattering of stars against a backdrop of inky black sky.

It was peaceful here, overlooking an alleyway and another tall stone wall that separated us from the forest.

Alone at last, I noted there were light fixtures suspended from the ceiling, though no buttons to turn them on.

Magic it is. I reached for my thick strand of magic. There was more than there'd been the day before – even though I hadn't siphoned anything since the birch tree.

"Oh, gods." The realization solidified in my mind.

I had Massis's *lineage* magic now. No longer would I need to siphon and scramble to fill my meager well up...now I had consistent magic brimming inside of me, replenishing itself easily as I burned through it.

The thought was sickening.

Thrilling.

Freeing.

Terrifying.

With the scrutiny around heretics, and the knowledge that the witches in this palace were well-versed in hunting them down, I had to keep my magic a secret.

I'd have to come clean to Maude to ever be allowed back into Bramberry, but if I could get a letter to my mother...would she still accept me with open arms?

Or would she turn me into the Royal Coven – protect herself from my illegal, confusingly-gained, magic?

Would anyone believe me when I said I was a victim?

My fingers shook.

With a careful hand, still unpracticed in controlling this much power, I wove a bite of magic between my hands until strands of purple slithered like moccasins through my fingers. I marveled at the magic's cool, silky texture, giddiness and dread mixing into a potent brew, shooting through my humming blood.

This level of power was incredible.

And it would get me killed.

I flicked my wrist towards the lamp hanging above the bed, a single thread settling into the glass bulb. The room glowed lavender for a single, nerve-wracking beat before dimming into amber light.

Neera appeared, her shadowy form slowly becoming more and more solid until I could run my hands through the scruff of fur on her neck.

"We're here," I whispered to the volkhound, jittery even through exhaustion, at the idea that tomorrow I'd see the library and begin trying to translate a Vessel Book.

Neera whined, wispy tail wagging faster, though her red eyes weren't trained on me.

They were focused on a cluster of unnatural shadows growing in the corner.

With a gasp, I scrambled backwards – but it was too late to tell the grimm to hide.

Finn strode into the room through the sheen of darkness, a sword with a black blade unsheathed and leveled at my throat. Playful cruelty reflected in his hazel eyes, flashing with triumph as he smirked.

"Hello, *heretic*," he crooned, "I distinctly remember telling you what would happen if you crossed the threshold. You made your move – now I'm making *mine*."

Chapter Twenty-Two

DOVE

Finn stalked closer, the black blade of his sword glimmering. There was no fury in his features, more...smug glee.

He'd wanted me gone. And now he had more than enough proof to make that a reality.

I backed up a step, my breathing sawing from my chest. "Wait – *please*. It's not what you think."

"A pity," Finn replied with a wry huff. "And here I was thinking you were the victim of a blood sacrifice gone wrong, leaving you as the only body able to receive the gift that our ancestors negotiated from Massis centuries ago."

I stopped breathing. Or maybe it just felt that way since all the air *wooshed* from my lungs as Finn's sword lowered, and he reached out to snatch my forearm, hauling me across the room and depositing me into the chair near the desk.

Neera merely evaluated the exchange with an uninterested air, her black tail full and fluffy, very visibly *here*. She stretched out and yawned, jumping onto the bed to settle atop the thin quilt.

Finn glanced at the grimm with a touch of wariness. But my fierce protector crossed her front paws with a bored chuff, ruby eyes half-lidded.

"How did you know?"

He'd hunted heretics for *decades* – of course he'd know.

He was the wild card I hadn't counted on.

"That you're a heretic? Or that you have a grimm following you?"

I paused. "Both?"

Finn chuckled roguishly, sheathing the sword at his side. His dark hair was swept out of his face with a leather band, though some of the strands had fallen to frame his face, contrasting sharply from his pressed black button up and pants.

"Do you know anything about heretics? Or volkhounds for that matter?"

I frowned. "I'm learning on the fly."

"Figured."

That pissed me off. I shot up from the chair, "You –"

Finn's hand landed on the top of my head, and he pushed me right back down.

It wasn't rough, but the audacity alone made purple spark at my fingers.

"There it is," he murmured, leaning over and curling his hands around the armrests, caging me against the chair. A vicious smile slashed across his full lips. "That's how I knew. Come here."

"*Oh*, so I can get up now?" I spat as he threw open the door to the bathroom.

"Don't be dramatic, darling. Go look at yourself in the mirror before you spit curses at me."

I bared my teeth at him. As much as I wanted to get up, my legs were wobbly, adrenaline and panic giving me a slim chance of standing without falling flat on my face.

Leaning against the doorframe, Finn jerked his chin towards the bathroom. "Your godsdamned eyes change color when you rally your magic."

What?

That got me up.

I rushed to the bathroom, gasping at my reflection.

Sure enough, my light brown eye was fully black, and my blue iris was now pure silver.

"What the fuck." I peered closer, my nails digging into the porcelain sink basin. I looked...terrifying.

"No one noticed," Finn said casually. As if that was enough reassurance. "Except me, of course. But that was more luck than anything. I figured someone in our caravan was close to death when I saw the grimm arrive, but then I noticed your blacked out eye in the Quiet when that witch tried attacking Theodoric."

"You can see grimm?"

He stepped into the bathroom with me, making the cramped space even more so as he met my gaze in the mirror. "I figured you were a heretic trying to get close to the Regent to kill him, yet when I pulled you aside outside the Palace, I could tell you were struggling to contain your magic. You rallied it again, and your eyes changed. But one turns silver. *That* isn't normal."

"You didn't answer my question," I mumbled stubbornly. "How can you see grimm?"

Finn moved towards Neera. I darted forward, placing myself between my beast and the shadow witch, throwing my hand in front of me in desperation. Lavender light bathed Finn's astonished face.

Flinching, I lowered my palms, though I didn't move aside. "You can't hurt her."

He rolled his eyes, as if I was being *entirely* unreasonable. "The amount of coddling you got in Bramberry is actually ridiculous. Were you a weak witchling or something before you got lineage magic?"

I reared back as if I'd been struck.

Finn must've known his statement hit too close to correct, and for whatever reason, he changed the subject.

"Massis created creatures after he was sealed into Avamere. His dukhmora mimic light witches, and his volkhounds, and the grimm, were made with the same essence as shadow witches. Since their magic is tied so closely with my own, I can see all volkhound, even when they're invisible."

"Oh," I whispered, slumping over, half sitting against the foot of the bed, my hand stroking Neera's soft fur. With a jolt I wondered –

"Were you always able to see them? Even as a witchling?"

Finn shook his head. "No. Not until I came into my full heritage gift at twenty-one."

I relaxed a fraction. If Elijah had seen Neera, I could only imagine he'd have said something, but it was still a new piece of information that I stowed away in my mind.

"Seeing her in the Quiet was the sole reason I regrettably decided *against* killing you outright. Grimm hitch rides on souls of the dead, using them as a connection to pass through the veil and land in our realm. But if the soul they traveled through returns to life, the grimm will follow that soul until their death, wreaking havoc wherever that soul travels until then. If a witch is followed by a grimm, it's said they'll live amidst death and destruction for the remainder of their time earthside."

Finn glanced sideways at Neera, asleep on the bed, not wreaking the slightest bit of havoc. He squinted, as if the sight of the some-what-domesticated grimm was puzzling. "Yet...she hasn't attacked any-one. When she appeared at my side, she came as a protector – not an aggressor. There was this..." he paused, placing his hand over his heart, "this calming presence in my soul when I noticed her in the Quiet."

I nodded. Neera projected that same thread of soothing magic into my veins – her way of telling us she wasn't here for nefarious purposes.

The fact that Finn intrinsically believed the grimm wasn't a threat was a relief, but he wasn't finished yet, and he was still pissing me off.

"So, I'm assuming, along the way, you died. And that beastie saw an opportunity to come through the veil. When you came back to life, the grimm was linked to you. Though I've never seen a volkhound so...friendly."

I swallowed. He'd really figured a lot of this out, but it still didn't explain why he'd threatened me. "With a little thinking and a lot of staring at you, I figured out a few things. One," He raised his fingers, flicking up one before inclining his head to Neera. "You bonded with the grimm because you were close to death, and your soul traveled through Minmere *and* Avamere before you returned to your body."

He ticked up another finger, waggling them in my face. "Two – everyone involved in your ritual died a very permanent death *somehow*," his eyes cut knowingly to Neera, "leaving you as the only living body for Massis to keep up his end of the bargain. Hence why *you* received the lineage magic."

A third finger joined the others. "And three, you trust no one with this secret of yours. The grimm stays invisible though it never leaves your side because you fear being found out as a heretic, and it can feel your dread through that connection you made during your d-...visit to Minmere."

I swallowed against the lump lodged in my throat, "You aren't going to kill me? Or hurt Neera?"

"I'll do you one better, darling." Finn crooned. I knew he'd have conditions. *Ass.* "I'll keep this secret of yours *if* you help me learn about this blood ritual. Spell work, blood runes, all of it. You tell me what happened, and I'll leave you and your beastie to the Book of Carra. Turns out, I'm pretty invested in seeing what happens when you get that Vessel Book in your hands."

There was more he wasn't admitting, and I was sick of surprises. "Why do you say that?"

Finn shrugged. "I've never seen a heretical witch with a silver eye. They always have two fully black ones when they rally magic. But if legend *is* to be believed, which is rarely ever, but bear with me, there's only one other goddess whose magic shifts eye color. And that would be Carra. Who, *coincidentally*, is illustrated in religious tomes with two silver eyes."

I didn't ask more about Carra since she'd abandoned witchkind so long ago, the bitter taste on my tongue having everything to do with being forsaken by the same goddess who swore to protect us.

"I doubt anything will happen..." Finn rubbed his beard. "But on the slim chance it did, it *would* be intriguing, wouldn't it?"

To even *think* I had any sort of connection to Carra was laughable.

"Why are you offering to keep my secret?"

Finn seemed...decent enough at the Bramberry Manor, but my perspective of him changed after arriving to the Palace.

He now appraised me with a less-than-kind-but-better-than-murderous curiosity, but I wasn't taking any chances tossing my survival into his hands.

"I know what it's like to have a brand of magic that's seen as less than. I'm the only shadow witch currently in the Jade Palace. The majority of them live in the Slate Kingdom, and while there are a few others in Jade keeping to themselves and laying low, the stigma around my magic hasn't granted me many favors in life."

He laughed, but it was a dry, ruthless sound, as if those memories were flaring and the taste of them burned.

"Did you know, when I was born, my father was overjoyed. He wanted to name me Heir even though I was born from his mistress – not the Queen. He didn't care. I'm the King's first-born son. He convinced the

Queen to claim me as her own. The original succession documents name me Heir."

I stayed quiet. Finn's demeanor changed again, a manic edge gleaming through his eyes, a sheen of fury and sour acceptance pulsing in the air.

"And then, my magic manifested when I was six. I accidentally siphoned, and in my panic, drowned the entire throne room in thick black shadow in the middle of the day. *That* was my downfall."

"My mother was a shadow witch. She was beautiful, and kind, and brilliant. But there were rumors of the King's involvement with her. After she died, before my magic came in, quiet conversations festered around the Palace – that my dark hair came from her, that my sister and I had her features. My slip up at six years old happened in front of the entire Royal Coven."

"And they changed the line of succession because you weren't a light witch," I concluded, a tug in my heartstrings feeding against the amount of pain reflected in Finn's expression.

"Right then and there." He nodded. "As a child, I thought there was something wrong with me. That my *magic* was wrong and it was all my fault."

Finn's rough voice steeled, and that cocky asshole attitude returned. "A lot has changed since then. When I was eighteen, I left. Over the next two decades, I traveled through the Covens, learned the truths of this world, and didn't step foot back into the Palace until Theodoric reached out and told me Velik was dying."

Finn ran his fingers through his hair and studied Neera as she slept. "That was a year ago. Before then, I was hunting heretics. But the reports were severely lacking. We didn't know anything about how they were gaining Massis's lineage magic – didn't know their true numbers."

His eyes flicked to mine. "We know now. The number of blood rituals and victims over the years has grown exponentially. Not to mention, we've been attacking this on three fronts – one fight against witches performing these rituals, one against heretics that already received a lineage gift, and one against the dukhmora slithering through the *veles*."

"We're spread thin. There aren't enough witches willing to help." Finn rasped through his teeth, shadows that had nothing to do with his magic darkening his features. "I can't blame them, either. I know what's out there. And it's enough to keep *me* up at night."

I shivered.

Haunted.

That was the way I'd describe the dead look in his eyes.

He'd seen too much of the evil in this world – and it left him haunted.

My heart ached. *Six years old*, and his entire world changed overnight. And he'd fled, seeking something to be proud of – only to stumble upon secrets, death, and carnage outside of the Palace walls.

"For the record, I don't like you, *nor* do I trust you. I need your help – and I'm not asking."

Any sympathetic feelings I'd had for Finn vanished.

"That's it then? You tell me you don't like me, yet ask for my help in the same breath?"

Finn stretched his legs out, crossing them at the ankles as he leaned back in the desk chair.

He was quiet for a moment.

"I could say, '*help me – or I'll sign your execution warrant myself.*' Does that sound *better* to you, darling?"

Gods. Such a shame. This man was so pretty until he opened his stupid mouth.

"Noted."

"Wonderful."

He stood, dusting his pants off as he headed towards the door. "You do your Vessel Book translations and study your little heretic heart out. I need to go handle something, but I'll be back, and when I return, we're going to go through every second of your ritual."

With his hand on the doorknob, he shot me a hard look. I glared right back, crossing my arms.

"If you're lying, withholding information, or avoiding me, I'll kill you myself. But if you tell me the truth, I'll keep your secret and leave you alone. I'll even let you return to Bramberry, unscathed, after Theodoric realizes the Vessel Book is a waste of time."

Finn gave me no room for negotiation. It was infuriating. Part of me wanted to break into a sobbing mess, beg him to give me time to process the trauma, to not recant the raw panic of being lashed down and ripped into atop that cold stone altar.

The other part wanted to break loose of the leash I wrapped myself in for my own safety.

That part craved vengeance.

Maude hadn't allowed me that retribution. She just pushed me to the side, to someplace coddled and soft, and told me stronger witches would handle it. Granted, I hadn't told her about my magic – a relief.

But I had lineage magic now. Didn't that make me...stronger than other witches? Wasn't *this* what Massis promised?

Unlimited, churning, replenishing power?

"Well?" Finn hedged.

"Why not demand I tell you everything now?"

A muscle jumped in Finn's jaw as he gritted out, "Because *right now* I'm pretending to hunt a heretic witch in the Bramberry Forest. Unfortunately for my brother, he'll receive a report in two days that says my search was unsuccessful and that I'm returning to the Jade Palace."

Oh. "You're covering for me."

Finn huffed a laugh lacking humor, as if the thought of his goodwill was sickening. "I'm a selfish person, darling. Theodoric tasked me with rooting out the heretic in Bramberry – and I did. I'll keep up appearances, but I want to be the only one to get the information locked in that pretty head of yours."

He had me in a noose, and the invisible threads were tightening around my throat.

"Just remember," Finn drawled, "if you're more trouble than you're worth, we haven't burned a heretic at the stake in months, and the Coven is getting...*antsy.*"

I pressed my lips together. Finn threw open my door, glancing at me over his shoulder.

"Do we have a deal?"

I locked eyes with Prince Finneas, wondering if I was gripping the quill and signing my own death warrant by saying – "You have a deal."

Chapter Twenty-Three
MERRICK

THE IMAGE OF THE still-smoking embers of the makeshift funeral pyre burned in Merrick's mind as they arrived at the small township.

Not a single word had been uttered during those last hours of traveling.

Before climbing back into his carriage, Merrick took in the haggard faces, the bloodstained cheeks streaked with shimmering tear tracks, the grief and exhaustion that hung heavily above their troupe, and his perspective shifted.

Witches weren't the cruel, bloodthirsty beings he'd believed them to be.

They were just as flawed and brave, as passionate and resilient, as any human, gargoyle or fae he'd met before.

It was more startling to him that the change in the way he viewed witchkind *wasn't* surprising.

If he was being honest with himself, that mindset had begun churning within him the moment Winnie asked if gargoyles ate humans. And now, in the aftermath of the dukhmora encounter, the barrier he'd mentally constructed between "*him*" and "*them*" had been smashed to bits, leaving not a single splinter of doubt behind.

Merrick was more similar to these witches than any other being. That didn't scare him, only needled at him incessantly. He'd be leaving the Jade Kingdom a forever changed male.

He'd made peace with the fact that he wouldn't be gifted a soul tie again and was begrudgingly tolerating the harsh truth that his wings may keep him grounded for potentially...*forever.*

And though he had enhanced speed and strength bestowed from Alke, it paled in comparison to the might of the heritage gifts the witches carried proudly.

Merrick felt...*different.*

As always, he kept his mind far away from Sparrow, but he mulled over the idea that the witches may be a worthy ally for Irridessen. Maybe he could ask Winnie if the King of the Jade Palace would let her travel to Irridessen to meet his Queen.

The thought of Esmeray and Winnie being in the same room terrified him – but only because he knew if the two of them could look past thousands of years of outdated and false beliefs, the pair would be causing gleeful mayhem together faster than he could warn Keerian.

He mindlessly stroked his thumb down the odd weapon Winnie shoved at him after they'd coaxed the panicked forest kelpies from the trees. She'd pressed the fragment of sharpened bone into his hands and told him since he had such a proclivity for running into fights he knew nothing about, he should, at the very least, have the option to make his boneheaded death honorable.

The crafted blade was pale grey with age, with carved sigils burned into its surface in an odd pattern that he didn't know a damn thing about. But, according to Winnie, it was the only weapon they could give him that would kill a dukhmora since he didn't have witch magic.

Once they began moving down the path again, he spent the hours sitting on an overturned wooden crate, brooding over the demon encounter and holding his aching wings off the ground. He now shared the tight carriage with an injured witch who spent the ride staring up at the ripped ceiling in a daze, too shell-shocked from blood loss and fear to do anything else.

The sun rose, and he'd barely noticed. But the moment the wheels squealed to a stop, he shoved out of the door, giving Emrin and Tallah a wide berth as they came to collect the wounded witch and take her somewhere with better healing supplies.

Winnie had disappeared already, and Merrick found himself standing on the outskirts of an oddly quiet little town with two Royal Coven witches who were too busy unloading their saddle bags to pay him any mind.

It took all of one minute before Merrick shuffled his feet, overwhelmingly antsy, and not at all interested in standing around doing nothing.

He appraised the caravan out of the corner of his eye, not sure if they were staying here, passing through, or if he was needed to help unpack and set anything up. When he took a few tentative steps to the side of the reed-edged road and no one stopped him, he allowed himself to consider other options.

Winnie mentioned the Shadymoss Coven was not very welcoming to outsiders, but from first glance, there wasn't a soul to be seen. They'd stopped a half mile outside of a rickety wooden fence that he guessed closed off the town itself, but aside from their group, everything was silent.

Too silent for Merrick's liking.

Thick, moss-draped cypress trees lined one side of a hard-packed road, the other sloped down into a pond of brackish water that reflected heavy clouds and a somber-hued sky promising another dumping of rain. A cluster of buildings in the distance were shadowed by a tall bluff jutting imposingly over the township, telling Merrick they'd traveled far east.

But without a map, he didn't know how close they were to the border, and he had a feeling Winnie wouldn't give him that information easily.

He casually slipped behind the cart, waiting for the witches to call him back. When they didn't, Merrick wandered into the tree line parallel to the road, his nostrils flaring with the taste of dense, earthy air tinged with rain. His slightly-too-small boots stomped over slick piles of gold and brown leaves scattered along the ground, muffling his footsteps as he headed for the structure up ahead.

A thatched roof cottage built from wood and mud bricks appeared, holding a somber stillness that seemed on par with the subdued aura permeating their own troupe. There was constant pressure in his chest, as if the weather was determined to make his time here dismal. Even though it was daytime, not a single sound came from the cottage, and as he strode closer, his Sentry perked up in his soul, putting his instincts on high alert.

An underlying scent of smoke mixed with the smell of soggy leaves and blooming algae.

No witches appeared as he slunk out from the cypress, picking his way past the first house and heading further down the road. A light fog slithered through the little town, dissipating under his quiet footsteps.

Winnie was nowhere to be seen.

A second cottage came into view, its roof half-caved in. He slowed his steps as he took in the damage, instinctively curling his hand around the bone dagger.

Long gouges slashed through the exterior siding, large pieces of hardened mud littered the path, and a concerning amount of splintered wood appeared burned at the edges. He hopped up onto a smashed pile of dull red bricks, teetering precariously for a beat before his wings remembered what counterbalancing was.

Ominous dread settled against his shoulders as Merrick stepped into the abandoned house.

Pottery lay smashed to bits, feathers from the mattresses and hand-made couches covered ornate rugs stained red with blood. He swallowed thickly as he rustled his wings, wondering if he'd be able to jump and glide over the crumbled wall to investigate more in the ransacked cottage.

Before he summoned up the courage to face the agony of spreading his wings to their full span, his attention caught on the opposing wall, where the front door leaned pitifully against one remaining hinge.

That would be the least painful option.

He hopped down from the bricks, narrowly avoiding shattered glass hidden in the pile.

His senses prickled as he slowly made his way around the wreckage, shifting his hearing to that of his Sentry to stay alert for any sign of danger. The bone dagger was in his hand as he cautiously toed open the door, the wood letting out a pained groan as it swung inwards.

A shift in the air had him darting backwards – just as the final hinge gave out completely, bringing the door and part of the supporting wall to the ground with a shuddering *ssshunk*.

Holding his breath, Merrick glanced around.

No one – witch or otherwise – came running towards the noise.

Raising the dagger, Merrick entered the cottage.

He swept his gaze over tangles of branches covering the living room, patches of thatch crunching underfoot as he moved towards the kitchen.

Bile rose in his throat.

The dining table still held evidence of a dinner for five beings, remnants of food and shards of plates telling him whatever attack occurred took the cottage's inhabitants by complete surprise. More cracked ceramic and chipped cups ringed the broken chairs, their contents reduced to sticky puddles and fast-growing green mold.

The stench of death had Merrick kicking aside debris to get to the rooms situated at the back of the cottage.

He braced himself, took a deep breath, and entered the room on the right.

It held a pair of small beds and a crib. Rubbing his palm over his heart, Merrick felt too vulnerable in here. There was immense relief over not finding bodies...though he had no idea where the beings were.

Children.

Witchlings – possibly.

But children. A *baby*.

They didn't deserve this.

He turned to leave.

A glimpse of something soft and slightly furry poking out from under the corner of the wooden crib leg caught his attention.

His jaw clenched as he knelt down, unearthing a stuffed bunny with mismatched blue button eyes and matted grey fur. It looked hand sewn and well-loved.

With a thick lump in his throat, Merrick tucked the little bunny in his belt.

A sense of urgency filled him.

Merrick crouched down, rooting through broken cabinets in a frenzy, bundling a few sets of usable child-sized garments, a couple more toys, and blankets that, thankfully, had no bloodstains.

When he found a cloth bag under a cabinet, he shoved the undamaged items into it before glancing around, searching through the remains of someone's home to find anything that could still be usable.

Picking his way out of the house, fury and hopelessness clashed within him. Whether this had been the dukhmora that waylaid them in the forest, or some other threat that had fallen over this town like a plague, the witches hadn't been prepared.

Merrick trudged into the next torn-apart house, and then the next, unearthing personal belongings that survived the brunt of the attack, packing them neatly into the sack.

His feet moved from cottage to cottage on their own accord. Merrick found another blanket, fashioned it into a rucksack, and kept going.

There was no presence of life *anywhere*. It was unnerving.

Worse than that, aside from pools of half-dried blood, he didn't stumble across a single body.

Stepping out of the last house on the row, now with three satchels tied and bulging with toys, clothing, and small trinkets that seemed like family heirlooms, he peered up at the sky. It was at least noon now, but a heaviness in the air spoke of rain blowing in.

He didn't know what exactly he was doing, but it wasn't *right* to leave those things behind. Merrick cut his eyes across the horizon, to the wall of rock that towered above the tree canopy, connecting to the mountain range slithered up against Ingotheria's spine.

Where was everyone?

"What are you doing?"

Merrick whirled around, hand flying to the leather handle of the bone dagger.

Winnie stormed out from a dense patch of darkness hovering at the base of a sprawling willow, tendrils of shadow billowing down the length of her forearms.

Merrick tipped his chin towards the damaged cottages. "What happened to the beings here?"

Winnie scowled, shadow magic weaving through her short hair, making the ends dance. "Seems the demons that found us, found them first."

With a heavy sigh, she flicked her gaze towards the last house on the row, its door blown clean off and laying in the center of what had once been a garden. "There weren't many witches here, most had gone deeper into the marsh to meet with their Coven Mother...unfortunately that meant the majority of beings attacked were human."

"Fuck," Merrick saw the carnage through new eyes.

Humans with no magic had been attacked by those...nightmares.

Gods above, he was a trained warrior with almost a century of fighting experience and even *he'd* been no match for a dukhmora.

Granted, with the bone dagger in his possession, he was very much ready for a rematch, though from the look on Winnie's face, he kept that to himself.

"Any survivors?"

It was almost clinical, the way he'd been taught to take after-battle assessments.

Emotionless.

But the weight of the personal belongings he carried made this painfully personal, as if he held lives instead of an assortment of toys and trinkets.

Winnie glared at him, her full lips tipping into a frown.

"Where were you going?"

Her tone deadened. And with it, a hint of accusation – of suspicion – thundered through the dense marsh air.

Shadows shifted from her wrists, slithering down and pooling at her feet.

Merrick's Sentry hissed inside his soul.

"What do you mean?" Merrick growled low, widening his own stance as the witch across from him on the mud packed road mirrored the move.

"You're carrying a shit ton of stolen stuff, sneaking around, as if you're planning to run. To *leave*."

Merrick bared his teeth, the only warning he'd give her.

Wordlessly, he dropped the three sacks to the ground, the edge of one tipping open to reveal the jumble of items from the cottages' ruins.

Winnie glanced at the bag. Her eyes darkened before flicking to Merrick's wing.

With his hands free, Merrick flexed his fingers, his muscles steeling into a defensive stance as he squared off against Winnie. He drew his wings tight to his back, knowing just how much of a target they were.

If she struck, she'd aim for them first – they were vulnerable.

His lips thinned.

It was exactly what he would've done, too.

She took a step closer, shadows rearing up around her shoulders like snakes, their faceless heads attuned to his every move. He sidestepped, keeping their distance, as they circled one another. He knew she was a strong witch, and he'd be damned if he got this far only to be attacked over a misunderstanding.

But the way she looked at him...

"Am I your prisoner?" Merrick asked, his voice gruff.

Winnie raised her chin. "No."

"So, I can leave."

She hesitated.

He saw the tiny, almost unnoticeable, flinch in her body language.

Her silence sharpened his understanding more than words ever could. He may not be a prisoner, but he also was not able to leave.

With a humorless laugh, Merrick crossed his arms, letting his defenses down, a move to tempt her into launching the first attack.

"Got it. So, I'm not your prisoner, but you sure as fuck aren't planning on letting me out of your claws."

"Were. You. Going. To. Leave?" Winnie asked again. The air hummed with power.

From his peripherals he saw the way her face hardened, but the emotion in her hazel eyes noted something else, something akin to desperation.

Merrick paused.

She wasn't going to fight back.

If she was preparing for him to walk away, she was bracing herself against that one, single word.

It almost seemed as if she asked if he was going to leave...*her.*

"No."

Winnie's shoulders slumped, shadows vanishing instantly. Her short brown hair was tousled; dirt and dried blood still clung to her skin. There was a rare vulnerability etched across her delicate features. Those plush lips parted ever so slightly, and a drumbeat began thumping through Merrick's blood.

She was beautiful.

They locked eyes, and he saw that same rawness, that same confusion and desire that flooded him simmering in her own gaze.

Silently, Merrick toed open the bag closest to her, though neither of them made a move closer.

"I hoped there were survivors hiding nearby. I found some things that seemed important, and I wanted to return them."

He pulled the stuffed bunny from his belt. Held it out to her.

Winnie sucked in a soft breath, her gaze flicking down to the bunny, and then the bag, where various other dolls, toys, and clothes peeked out of the canvas.

She stared at them for a long moment before swallowing, tears brimming against her lids. And for that moment, she didn't look like the powerful witch ordered by the Crown to hunt and dispatch demons back to Avamere, she looked like a terrified female, too proud to ask for help, too stubborn to admit how hard this all was hitting her.

A rush of panic swept over Merrick. He wanted to close the distance between them, collect the witch in his arms, *never let her go.*

Woah, where did that come from?

Merrick blew out a rough breath. He wasn't positive she'd allow him to rush over and hug her, or if she'd bury a dagger into his side the second he got within stabbing distance.

It wasn't the most favorable odds.

"C'mon, bonehead," Winnie finally whispered, breaking the tension between them, a razor edge with vastly different outcomes. She took a staggered step backwards.

Suddenly, the thought of her absence terrified him.

"Winnie." Merrick spoke quietly, every torturous promise and unspoken yearning punctuating that one word.

Her name.

She stiffened.

"What?" The flicker of desire he'd seen in her eyes was gone, replaced with a blank sort of wariness, as if she'd erected a wall around herself within mere seconds.

As if she'd realized that any attraction between them was simply out of the question.

Doubt fizzled up, that darkness beckoning from the edges of his mind.

Maybe Winnie wasn't attracted to him. Maybe it was all in his head, in the heat of the moment.

Merrick shook his head. "Nothing." Stooping down, he collected the bags of belongings he'd found.

She pressed her lips together as he trudged towards her.

As he approached, a blanket of shadow rose like steam into the air, morphing into a dark likeness of Laurent's fae-magicked portals.

Winnie jerked her chin, beckoning him over.

Pausing next to the writhing mass of shadow, her scent of leather and sage filled him, igniting the desire to touch her, and overriding the risk of a stab wound.

Tentatively, heart pounding so hard it made his horns rattle, he wrapped his rough hand around hers.

Winnie threaded her fingers through his, before tipping her head up, her heated gaze meeting his once more. His breath caught in his throat as she gazed up at him with wide eyed innocence, fracturing something aching and defensive inside of him.

With a playful smile she led him to the witch-magic-portal-thing she'd created. "I'll let you in on a little secret, bonehead."

Merrick knew without a sliver of doubt that he would've followed her into a raging wildfire if she'd asked – as long as she kept smiling at him like that.

Before they stepped into the swirling smoke, Winnie stood on her tip-toes, tugging him closer until she was pressed against his chest. Merrick braced her against him. Her spine arched under his hand. The gentle hitch in her breathing almost sent Merrick to his knees.

She sighed contently, relaxing into his touch, her lips curving into a wicked sneer. "If you *had* tried to leave me, I would've killed you."

And Merrick knew, without a shadow of a doubt, that he was well and truly fucked.

Chapter Twenty-Four
DOVE

THE HARDEST THING ABOUT processing trauma is the fact that it doesn't follow a linear pattern of healing. It isn't a clear-cut path with easily identified milestones to see how close you were to being "*okay.*"

Trauma lay buried underneath whatever was at the forefront of your mind until something shocked it into rearing its ugly head. Then it would force you to battle against your own emotions.

With Neera sprawled next to me, I stared out the stained-glass window at nothing. The fight was in my head, but with it came icy sweat followed by body chills, wracking sobs that had me burying my face into the pillow, and paralyzing numbness with the force of a white-capped wave, leaving me limp and shivering under the sheets. For hours, I scrambled to come up with solutions to my mounting problems.

But with flashbacks from the ritual in Carra's temple, it was one of those nights where no resolution appeared. Every time I closed my eyes, I could hear my assailants chanting that spell in a language I'd never heard before, feel the dagger burn my flesh, the phantom pain shattering through every nerve ending like lightning.

As the first rays of sunlight streamed into my room, I'd managed to exhaust myself enough to sleep.

A knock on the door jolted me awake.

I dragged myself from the sweat-soaked sheets, unsurprised to find Neera curled up on the floor. Giving her a quick scratch above the ears, she grumbled, curling tighter into a ball.

The knock came again.

Two hard raps in quick succession.

Neera glared at the door, yawned dramatically, and vanished. Somehow, even the slight shimmer as she disappeared had an attitude – as if my early morning rudely interrupted her illustrious sleep schedule.

"Coming!" I shouted, ruffling through the trunk of my clothes and unearthing a deep brown skirt and a cardigan knitted with different hues of green.

Cordelia made good on her promise to take me to the library.

I finished off my outfit by layering three necklaces against the soft sweater. Each chain hung past my breasts, holding a wire-wrapped rune-stone pendant. Now more than ever, I needed to keep up the appearance of being a regular, albeit weak, light witch who needed to siphon magic.

Hopefully, no one would realize the runestones didn't have a drop of power in them. I crinkled my nose. I'd need to figure out where the Royal Coven siphoned from and make sure I was seen there, too.

Gods. One day with lineage magic and I was already overwhelmed at hiding in plain sight.

Tossing a notebook and quill in my messenger bag, I hollered out a feeble apology from the bathroom to let Cordelia know I'd be ready in a minute.

Groaning at the aftermath of haphazard sleep, I rubbed my red-rimmed eyes, doing my best to forget the way they looked when I'd rallied my heretic magic. In the reflection of the mirror, I patted my bedhead, finger combing a few of the thickest strands behind my ear.

Nope. That wasn't going to work.

My hair was full of body - confirming it would be fruitless to try and tame it. Instead, I splashed some water on the ends, twisting it into a quick braid that trailed down to my waist.

A few swipes of blush and kohl liner made me appear slightly less tired, but knowing Cordelia was waiting for me, there was only so much I could do.

Stuffing my feet into boots, I hurried over to the door, profusely apologizing to Cordelia as I threw it open –

But it wasn't Cordelia who waited in the hall, holding a bouquet of pink and white flowers.

It was Theo.

Finn's growled warning wove through me as I stumbled back a step. "Your Highness, I'm so sorry to keep you waiting – I was expecting…Well, I wasn't expecting *you*."

Theo grinned. "I wanted to surprise you."

The Regent was dressed in black pants and a pressed, jade tunic embellished with gold thread. A slim crown lay against his brow, glinting in the morning rays coming through my window. I wondered what time he woke up to be *this* put together *this* early.

He extended the flowers. "These are for you. As a *thank you* for helping with the Vessel Book."

"Oh, Theo." I took the flowers, heart pounding to an energized beat.

Damn Finn. He wasn't here, anyway.

I'd *never* been gifted flowers before. Let alone caught the attention of a man who looked like the epitome of a golden god. All fatigue from my restless sleep disappeared.

"These are beautiful, thank you."

Theo winked, those silver starbursts in his heated gaze scorching. "Unfortunately, Dove, they pale in comparison to how beautiful *you* are."

Finn wanted me to stay away from his brother?

The brother with golden hair, and a Crown, and thick biceps, and, and *compliments*, and – Gods below, that *face?*

Yeah, fuck Finn.

I blushed wildly. "You can come in, if you'd like. I'll put these in water. I mean, of course you can come in– it's your Palace after all."

Oh good, I was rambling.

Theo laughed, and the sound was carefree and light, easing the frantically jumbled thoughts from my mind.

"I'd never infiltrate a lady's room without expressed permission," he chuckled as he stepped in behind me, "regardless of me owning the room or not."

Face flaming, I snatched the glass I'd used to rinse my mouth after brushing my teeth, filling it halfway with water from the faucet before placing the bouquet of stems in it.

"Incredibly beautiful," Theo murmured. He stood a few feet away, hands clasped behind his back as his gaze traveled over *me* – not the flowers in my hand.

"So, your morning duties for the Crown starts with hand delivering flowers to all the translators?" I joked lightly, comfortable in Theo's presence, though the weight of his gaze had my skin prickling with anticipation.

"Only the pretty ones," he confessed, taking my ribbing in stride. "I think the Royal Scholars would be a little nonplussed if I showed up at their door with a hand-picked bouquet and asked if I could escort them to the library."

I shoved Finn's glower from my mind.

In the bright light of morning, Finn's threats lost their strength. The sun banished away the edge of sharp terror he'd poured over me in the dark.

Plus, Theo found *me*.

That didn't count.

If I'd slammed the door in Theo's face, it could be seen as disrespecting the Crown.

"That's incredibly sweet." A small smile flitted across his face. "Cordelia promised to escort me, and I don't want to interrupt your... Regent duties?"

My justifying abilities definitely had something to do with the drop-dead handsome man standing in my room and the fact that I hadn't gotten laid in two years.

But more than that, there was a thread linking me to him. Witches weren't granted soul ties, but there *had* to be some sort of divine intervention at play that made Theo and I continue revolving around each other in a flirtatious orbit.

Theo plucked the makeshift vase from my hands and set it on the dresser. "What if I told you I ran into Cordelia and begged her to let me escort you this morning?"

A warm feeling wriggled in my belly, and it took all my focus to not fling myself into his arms and demand he ravish me. But before I could tamp down those wildly inappropriate daydreams, my stomach rumbled, reminding me that I hadn't eaten anything last night after Finn's unceremonious interruption and accommodating interrogation.

"To that, I'd say, does your escort include breakfast?"

"It would be my absolute pleasure to have breakfast delivered to you in the library. And if I may be so bold, ask you to have dinner with me tonight?"

"Will this be a purely professional dinner with the other translators in attendance as well?" I chanced a step closer, my eyes darting to Theo's *very* kissable mouth. Heat bloomed through my core.

Theo leaned in, pressing a broad hand to the small of my back. My breath hitched as our gazes locked. "Would it be improper if I said, '*absolutely not?*'"

His magic curled around me, my new lineage gift fluttering awake in response. Swiftly tamping it down, I gave Theo a bright smile.

"I think it would be *more* improper if I declined a request to have dinner with the next King of the Jade Kingdom."

As he guided me through the hall and down the staircase, I couldn't even spare a glance at my surroundings. His larger-than-life aura muted the color of everything around us, tunneled my vision to him and him alone.

We exchanged polite conversation as we wove through another, larger courtyard – though the simmering looks Theo threw my way were anything but.

Whisking me under an arched stone doorway, we entered an unlit corridor. The musty smell of mildewy earth was stronger here, and my pulse picked up before our steps activated orbs of amber light that flooded the hall. They clicked on as we approached and dimmed the further we headed into the maze. Uneasiness prickled my soul, magic alert in my veins.

I didn't like this eerie hall one bit.

But Theo, ever the gentleman, patted my hand and hustled us into an open common area hidden behind an unassuming wood door.

With three floor to ceiling windows overlooking the forest, there was no need for magical lamps to light our way.

My gaze traveled over stacked hardbacked chairs and desks pushed up against the walls. Massive rugs were rolled up, standing tall around the rim of the room.

It left more questions as to how much of the Palace was utilized and how many witches lived here.

Cobblestone walls rose high above us, and the scuffed wood floor echoed our footsteps as we moved deeper into the building. The air was thin and cool like the eerie hallway, but here...

There was an undercurrent of power – a tang of old magic that buzzed through my blood in a curious way.

Without seeing a single scrap of parchment, I knew we'd entered the Royal Library.

"I'll admit I took the longer route so I could spend a few more minutes in your presence." Theo slid my hand from his elbow to thread his fingers through mine.

I was trying to not outright ogle the Regent as we neared a massive door with elaborate copper handles fashioned into the likeness of a hawk in flight. In one smooth twist, Theo shifted between myself and the door to the library, gooseprickles erupting along my skin as his free hand slid up the side of my neck, cupping my cheek.

His palms were warm, smooth, and soft. I pressed into his touch as he tilted my face up to his. "I don't know what this is between us," Theo said, his eyes searching mine. "But I can't get you out of my head, Dove. Last night, I dreamed of you. It's like...from the moment I saw you, I knew how special you were."

"I feel it too." I arched my spine as he tugged our linked fingers to my back. My heartrate skittered as my back hit the stone wall next to the Royal Library's door. Our breaths came out in near-silent pants as we hovered on the precipice of either breaking apart or falling further together.

His brows scrunched, and a lock of golden hair fell over his eyes as we stood in this moment that had the power to change everything or nothing at all.

Theo's lips parted slightly, wanton desire darkening his blue eyes until the silver ringing his irises glowed.

This was everything I wanted – and everything Finn warned me *not* to do.

Really, this was everything *I knew* I should run from.

But...Theo had me locked in his presence, and even the illegal, forbidden magic in my heating blood couldn't convince me this wasn't a delightfully destructive idea.

And before I could persuade myself to go with the safer option and bolt through the library doors, Theo captured my lips with his in a chaste kiss.

A roar started in my head at the feel of his mouth on mine, but as soon as it started, it ended.

Theo pulled away. I squeezed my thighs together, though nothing relieved the ache that bloomed between them.

And Theo...there was wild reckless burning in his eyes. He inhaled a ragged breath, as if the barest kiss unraveled his composure.

Tipping his forehead to mine, he rasped, "I desire more, I desire everything you have, Dove."

"Then take it," I breathed, the words out before I could stop them.

Our gazes slammed together as his warm hand trailed down my face, my throat, his fingers toying with the runestones dangling tantalizingly close to my breasts.

Theo looked as if he wanted nothing more. Slowly twisting the three necklaces in his hand, using the chains to tug me flush to him, our lips met once more.

This time, there was nothing polite or proper in his manner as he slanted his mouth over mine to deepen the kiss. I moaned as he devoured me, as Theo's palm skated down my side, hitching the fabric of my skirt up past my knee.

Our tongues clashed, his cock thickening as he ground against me.

A sharp bark had us both slamming back into the present.

I startled, glancing around, sure that was Neera –

"What was that?" Theo released me, dark, unhinged desire written across his face as he surveyed the completely empty room.

Behind Theo's back, Neera's red eyes flashed for the briefest second.

Shooting the invisible beastie a flat look, the corner of my mouth twitched as a plume of smoke curled towards the ceiling and slipped through the wall.

It seemed even my beastie was saying, "*Stop kissing the handsome Regent and go do your job.*"

Stepping back, Theo cleared his throat, jerking his thumb towards the windows lining the room behind us. He was silent for a moment before he said gruffly, "Probably wolves in the forest. Nothing to be worried about."

I pursed my swollen lips together, still reeling from Theo's hands on my body.

Sure, wolves.

I was too turned on to care. As long as he didn't suspect Neera – I was good with wolves.

Theo nodded to himself, as if wolves were a completely viable reason for a single bark to ricochet through the empty chamber.

"It's the most reasonable explanation," I agreed, Theo's confusion allowing me to wrench my foggy brain from his thrall.

There were no scholarly books on the protocol for making out with the incredibly handsome Regent in front of the Royal Library. I was out of my element here.

I inclined my head towards the Royal Library's door. "I, um, should go in."

Theo spun back around, scrubbing his face with his palm. I hovered, fluffing my skirt and peering at him from under my lashes, waiting for him to say something or...dismiss me?

Did I have to bow? Curtsy?

Or...Could I...leave?

"Right, yes, of course," he said absentmindedly, though he didn't move, gaze bouncing around the still-very-empty room.

A smug sort of glee washed over me.

Theo seemed much more frazzled by our kiss than I was. He dragged a hand through his hair, straightened the crown on his brow, as if he was dazed.

Finally, tongue dipping out to wet his lips, he adjusted himself in his pants and stood straighter. I couldn't help it – my gaze darted down. As I quickly flicked my eyes back up, Theo threw me a lust-filled smirk at having caught my line of sight. "I'll accompany you in."

With a dramatic flourish that made me laugh, he reached over, opening one of the library doors.

The moment I stepped into the Royal Library, every bit of tension and stress held in my muscles relaxed. I let out a shaky breath as Theo quietly closed the door.

Cluttered bookshelves arranged in neat rows created shadowed alcoves filled with knowledge. For a moment, the thrill of laying eyes on the overwhelming amount of knowledge at my fingertips dimmed, my attention snapping to the architecture of the library itself.

It was, without a doubt, the most beautiful place I'd ever seen.

Along thick baseboards, an assortment of small critters carved in coppery-hued wood scampered through unbelievably detailed flower patches. Every stem of flora, every leaf, every feather was incredibly lifelike, and the little etched mice had thin whiskers tipped at the ends of their tiny noses.

I could've spent an entire day happily inspecting the architecture without opening a single book.

Grand pillars rimmed the entire space, their shafts sporting carvings of vines and moss. Craning my neck toward the pitched ceiling, hawks in various poses of flight were depicted into the thick capitals that towered high above us. As Theo ushered me along, I begrudgingly tore my awe away from the art to follow him.

The library was four stories high, with scalloped iron railing bordering each floor. Aside from the haphazard aisleways of the ground level, the second floor and up consisted of landings with built in shelves and rolling ladders.

The only outlier to the meticulously organized space was an incredibly detailed stained-glass window that dominated an entire wall spanning the second and third levels.

It was the sole wall not crammed with books – instead displaying a full spectrum of color that lit up the library with a cheery glow. I tried to back up enough to make out the detailing scene in the glass, but Theo veered down an alley of shelves, and I didn't want to get lost after already showing up late.

Ripping my eyes away was next to impossible, but a keening in my chest had me picking up the pace until I came upon the Regent and a cluster of witches surrounding a long table.

I slowed my steps as the group turned to me.

"This is Dove Koroleva, from Bramberry Forest," Theo introduced me warmly, if not a bit stiffly. "Coven Mother Maude highly recommended her."

"It's a pleasure, Dove." The eldest witch with a brilliant grey-white beard greeted. "Koroleva. Do you happen to be the Coven Mother's daughter? I've heard wonderful things about your magic. Manifesting a silver hue is quite commendable."

I winced internally. "That's my sister, Polina."

The mix-up happened every so often. It never got easier. No one ever asked if I was Maude's *weak* daughter.

Theo clapped his hands, not noticing the awkwardness now hovering over the table. One of the younger scholars sniffed, regarding me with lukewarm disdain now that my identity as Maude's *other* daughter had been confirmed. Between the scholars, the translators from Shadymoss sat with Bron, who gave me a sympathetic grimace.

Though it was unnerving to stand in the presence of the most brilliant scholars in the Kingdom, I was here because I *earned* the right to be – not to coddle the egos of men who had *decades* to crack the Vessel book yet came up with nothing.

With that, I steeled my spine and raised my chin, glaring right back at the pretentious scholar who'd gotten as far with the Vessel Book as I had.

"Where's the Book of Carra, Master Vole?" Theo raked his eyes over the bearded witch who, by the elaborate robes and fat emerald runestone hanging from a golden chain, must've been the Elite Scholar.

"It's in my study, your Highness – in the vault." Master Vole answered with surprise, his bushy brows scrunching together. "I thought we'd begin today by filling in the new translators on what we already know and have them share the languages they're fluent in before we bring the Vessel Book out."

"No," Theo clipped, waving his hand dismissively. "What is there to fill them in on? You know nothing – you haven't translated a single word."

"But, your Highness –"

"No, no, *no*. Go get it. I want the Book of Carra here *now*."

The nervous energy in the room rose as the scholars swapped expressions of concern. Master Vole, his face paling, pulled the black cap from his bald head. Twisting it between his hands he stammered, "If any of these translators are spies, bringing out the Book of Carra could be detrimental.

How do you know none of these witches are..." he lowered his voice to a strangled whisper, shuffling forward, "*heretics?*"

The Elite Scholar had a point. I mean, I *was* a heretic.

I think.

Theo's nostrils flared. "*Now*, Vole – or my coronation will include finding a new Elite Scholar."

The translators from Shadymoss, two men with umber skin and similar lanky builds, shrank lower in their chairs. I guessed they were brothers, or at least related, since the look that passed from one to the other said they were reconsidering their willingness to assist.

I slid into the empty seat next to Bron.

The Theo that brought flowers to my room and kissed me passionately in front of the library was a total contrast to the man who now seethed with boiling frustration while spitting out threats.

Master Vole hustled away, disappearing between bookshelves.

I had to remind myself that Theo was going to be King soon, and I knew nothing about the hierarchy inside the Royal Coven. Maybe Theo *needed* to use an iron fist to gain respect with the scholars – or Master Vole hadn't been helpful in the past?

Once Theo gained the crown, he'd be the new protector of the Vessel Book. It made sense that he see it whenever he wanted...*right?*

No one spoke a word.

This stand-off would result in me not getting breakfast delivered to the library. My hollow stomach gurgled at the thought.

Theo leveled a scowl at the other three scholars seated at the table. According to their matching black and grey robes, they were the leading authority on the Book of Carra's research.

A soft beat hammered in my ears as the tension in the room threatened to send me spiraling. Magic warmed my blood, and I bunched the ends of my sleeves into my fists, keeping my hands out of sight. I fought to keep my breathing even, to keep my heretic magic from rallying and changing the color of my eyes.

It occurred to me that Finn actually saved me from myself by telling me my eyes changed when I let magic swim too close to the surface. Now, as my power responded to the taught hostility smothering the room, I kept my head down, busying my attention with the hem of my sweater.

Taking a deep, centering breath through my nose and counting backwards in my head, my magic ebbed back into my soul.

Shuffling footsteps announced Master Vole's return, a thick iron box with sigils etched on every side gripped in his hands. Theo tutted as Master Vole hefted the box onto the table, a heavy *thud* echoing through the library. The Shadymoss translators shared another hesitant look with each other.

I held my breath – Bron paled.

"Open it." Theo crossed his arms. I could barely appreciate how his thick biceps strained against his tunic as I stared warily at the container emitting a silvery glow on the tabletop.

Master Vole, pink faced and sweating slightly, dabbed at his forehead with the fabric of his sleeve.

"What are those runes for?" one of the translators from Shadymoss asked.

Master Vole threw a pleading glance towards Theo before resting his palm protectively against the lid. "They're nullifying runes that keep the Book of Carra safe so no fae can track the Book's location by its personal thread of magic."

The translator scoffed, his dark brows narrowing in disbelief. "But no one can confirm the Vessel Book *has* god magic. For all we know, the Book's already been drained."

"Enough," Theo snarled, smalling his palms against the table. The translator swallowed thickly and leaned back in his chair, the momentary doubt on his face replaced with uneasiness. "Vole – get on with it."

With a frown, Master Vole tentatively placed two fingertips against the box. A thin film of silver swirled around his wrists as he siphoned the power from the nullifying runes.

As the sigils began fading, a ringing began in my ears.

I winced as the whistling grew louder. But the shrill noise made my limbs grow leaden, and a beat later, my hand dropping listlessly to my lap.

Bron's brows scrunched. I wavered in my chair, seeing his mouth move, but his voice seemed so...far away. I couldn't understand him – his words too muted and muffled.

Eyes widening, Bron shook my shoulder, mouth moving faster.

I tried to tell him that he needed to speak up so I could hear him over this archaic ringing, but my tongue was too thick and unwieldy in my mouth.

The library swayed around me as my veins iced over, sweat speckling my scrunched brow.

The screech rattling my bones refused to fade, and before I could assure Bron that I was fine, that I was just a little lightheaded and really needed to eat something, Master Vole threw the lid of the box housing the Book of Carra back, and my vision tunneled. The shrilly whistle turned into a bellow.

Fuzzing edges wriggled in my vision.

A tempest of nausea forced me to squeeze my eyes shut. The world teetered around me. Opening them again, I tried and failed to clear my hazing sight.

I caught a blurred glimpse of a pale grey leather book with silver symbols etched into the cover before everything went black.

Chapter Twenty-Five

DOVE

My lungs seized as I plummeted down, down, down through the nothingness.

Or maybe I was standing still while darkness rushed past so violently I couldn't draw breath into my lungs.

A disembodied voice hummed a single note, holding it until the ringing in my ears was replaced by a heavy drone, scattering my senses. I thrashed against the unyielding pressure in my chest, desperately clawing for air.

I couldn't make sense of my surroundings, couldn't tell where the dark began and ended, couldn't say if I was moving towards or away from something – or if I was moving at all.

The hum stopped abruptly.

In a whisper, I heard it.

A woman sobbing, soft and distressed, from somewhere in the nothingness.

Suddenly, the staggering pressure against me eased, and I gulped down lungful after lungful of air, aware of the woman's melodic voice getting closer, getting louder, demanding my attention. The wind roaring around me settled into a soft breeze, until I was floating along with the draft instead of fighting against it.

The crying stopped.

Then –

They killed the authors first.

I screamed – though no sound tore from my throat as the mysterious woman wailed, sounding so close to me I flinched back, though I couldn't see anything through the pressing darkness.

Then they murdered the scholars, before exterminating anyone who disagreed with their version of history. History has always, and will always, be written by the victors.

A manic laugh screeched from inside my head – or maybe it was right in front of me. I tried forcing my legs to move, but I was weightless, as disembodied as the cackling voice.

But there is a cruel, ruthless power that lurks in the truths of this *story. Power in truth.*

The cawing laugh faded as those three words repeated over and over, increasing into a chanted frenzy.

Like a tether snapping, my sense of self tumbled back into my body. I stumbled, blindly feeling my way around in the dark, my hands meeting no resistance as I stayed suspended in a never-ending midnight.

Power in truth. Power not so easily picked over and shuffled through.

Not so easily wiped away. The truth will come out, regardless of the repercussions.

History may be written by the victors, but history itself repeats – and if you don't make the same mistakes as your ancestors...you may reveal the truth this time.

Reveal the truth that was carelessly erased to stop the madness.

A gut-wrenching shriek had the hair rising on my arms and prickles erupting along the back of my neck.

The echoes of the unearthly cry ricocheted through my subconscious as I ran through the darkness, my hands stretched out in front of me, trying to find a wall. Though my footsteps met resistance, telling me there was at least a floor under me, my steps made no sound.

I tried to speak, tried to scream for help, but only managed a garbled husk. The message burned like a somber prophecy. I upped my speed.

There were no seers in the witch kingdom – that responsibility was bestowed upon those blessed by Moirai, the God who enjoyed rustling up panic through odd riddles. I knew that somewhere in the Seven Kingdoms there was a human saddled with the responsibility of being the Oracle, but this voice, this message, seemed more...rehearsed. Not personal, yet...desperate.

As if a story was buried within – waiting for someone to connect to it, to *feel* it.

Beware, Vessel.

Before I could comprehend the caution, my bare feet scraped against hard ground. I stumbled, catching myself with my palms.

My eyes watered, and I wiped away tears that ripped free during my fall. Standing slowly, every instinct in my soul begged me to flee.

Without warning, the darkness swept away, and a blazing white light flared, shining endlessly in every direction. I squinted against the glare, but aside from the smooth stone I stood upon, I couldn't make out a single thing.

Apprehensively, I took a step, a cool, silky texture flitted across my...bare feet?

I gasped.

I was dressed in a thin, gossamer robe, the billowy hem sifting and shimmering like mist.

"Hello?" I called, relieved to find my voice working again.

"Vessel."

I whipped around, searching for that crooning feminine voice - and found a very tall woman with ample curves and skin so pale it appeared almost blue-ish.

Her youthful face was frozen – expressionless.

But her eyes...

They glowed as if moonbeams were trapped behind her irises.

Silver hair draped past her knees, artfully covering her naked breasts, and a sheer piece of the same gossamer that covered me was wrapped around her hips, fluttering in a non-existent breeze. White feathery wings protruded from her back, extended and open, and though they didn't move, she hovered a few feet off the floor.

A diamond-studded diadem lay across her brow, the shapes of the stones making up some sort of pattern I couldn't decipher.

"Who are you?" I stumbled back a step, throwing my hands up to put some distance between us. "And where am I?"

"I am the Goddess of Salvation," she replied. Her lips didn't move with the words.

Those uncanny eyes tracked me with a wariness I knew reflected on my own face – as if neither of us were sure of this interaction. "And you, witch, are within the confines of your own mind, speaking with me through the god magic imbued in the Vessel Book."

"Carra," I breathed, my legs wobbling as the absurdity of this situation threatened to bring me to my knees.

Dark, devious reminders of the gods' injustice threaded through my mind. The shake in my legs faded. I stood taller.

"You do not bow before a goddess?" she asked haughtily. The words projected through the space, echoing like a sharp slap inside my head.

"You abandoned us." I rasped.

Carra ruffled her wings in indignation. The air around us shifted.

Her frustration roiled through the space between us, as palpable as a thundercloud. I sucked in a breath as the goddess stepped to the ground in front of me, tucking her wings to her sides.

Her hands formed fists.

Magic crackled in my veins.

I raised my chin, daring the goddess before me to strike.

In that moment, the weight of witchkind sat upon my shoulders.

One chance.

One chance to make the goddess in front of me see sense; to see how painful her absence had been on us.

"Why would I bow before an omnipotent power that has done nothing but forsake me? Forsake my kin?"

I couldn't help the harsh laugh as I threw my arms wide.

"*Why* should I grovel in the presence of a god who ignored every desperate prayer offered to the night? Who snubbed the same beings that built temples in her honor? And *why* should I give you any sliver of respect after you took away our ability to be soul tied?"

Anger mounted at the audacity of the goddess before me.

Even Phades, sitting on her throne of bones, had shown me compassion when she helped me find my way back to my body – and the Goddess of Death did nothing for witches until our souls passed into Minmere.

The air plummeted in temperature, though the rage in my veins warmed me from within. "You know nothing except false truths poured down your throat."

"But hear me now." Her voice lowered.

"Witchkind fought *against* me, *against* Aurramere, in the Witch War."

I'd never heard *that* before.

Carra seethed. "All because Massis claimed he'd reward those loyal to him with direct god magic if they helped bring him to Terramere. And they agreed."

"But he double-crossed them in the end, tying their blood to *him* so thoroughly that no other god could bless a descendant of his witches. And because of that, I'm unable to bestow soul ties to *anyone* with a drop of witch blood in their veins – regardless if they receive Massis's heritage magic or not."

My head spun at the implication.

I took a staggered step back, magic frothing in my soul.

Was this the hidden truth? That Massis isn't the benevolent god we believed him to be?

Massis was written in history as our savior – as the god who always guided and cared for witches.

What Carra was saying aligned more with my own inner thoughts that flickered in the wake of the ritual.

Had Massis tricked the witches once again by promising glory and power if lives were sacrificed to him?

Did this mean...

Pieces to a blasphemous puzzle clicked smoothly into place.

All this time...have we blindly followed a deceiving god?

I reared back as Carra stroked my cheek. Her fingers were oddly warm against my skin.

"Our only option to stop Massis was to lock him in Avamere. We were desperate. Massis took his chance and there was no way we could pass through the realms fast enough to head him off. By the time we realized he was gone, he'd already slipped from Aurramere, through Minmere, and was almost out of Avamere – thanks to the witches fooled by his false promises."

Carra sighed bitterly, "But Massis learned of our plot to imprison him inside Avamere and used our own power against us. With the last bit of channeled witch magic, he linked *all* the god realms together – ultimately sealing *every* realm and locking all of the gods behind the veil."

With a dry laugh, Carra's wings bristled, as if the memory of Massis's betrayal still stung. "We trapped *him* – but he trapped us, too."

I shivered away from her as her touch grew icy. A flame of molten silver ignited as she appraised me with a resentful look.

"*Massis* is to blame for witchkind's downfall. *He* lied to your people, offering them forgotten spells better left buried in the past, spinning webs of grandeur that cursed the very beings who swore undying loyalty to him."

There was a false sort of pity reflected on her ivory face, a cold acceptance that unnerved me more than anything else.

"From Aurramere, we watched in horror. There was nothing we could do to stop him as he added a single rune that, with the boosted magic from his witches, connected the realms together. He called our bluff, knowing if we reversed our magic and backed down, he was poised to enter Terramere."

"In our sacrifice to protect Terramere, we allowed the god realms to be sealed. But Massis, in his cunningly cruel way, had more planned. The moment the seal solidified, every witch soul that passed during the War was torn from Minmere and dragged to Massis in Avamere. He warped their souls into the beginnings of his demon horde."

"But Massis gifted other magics," I argued hollowly. "He blessed the fae – and *they* still receive soul ties."

"The fae only ever received his siphoning." Carra waved a hand. "The fae were his *first* experiment, until they saw through Massis's scheming and rebuked him, which ultimately saved their soul ties and lineage gifts. But the fae's refusal to help Massis come to Terramere is what set his sights on turning humans into witches. That's when he recreated his gift of siphoning into two different magics – light and shadow."

I pressed my lips together, wondering why so much of witch history had been erased so callously.

"Does that answer your questions, Vessel?" Carra's unmoving lips didn't stop her from letting out an irate huff in my mind.

But if I was truly irritating the goddess, I didn't care. According to Carra, *Massis* was the villain all along, blocking witch kind from receiving any other god blessings.

My problems were merely a drop into a churning sea of uncertainty that traced back *millennia*.

And as Carra's last comment sank through my skin, it seemed my problems were *far* from over.

Chapter Twenty-Six
DOVE

"You called me '*Vessel*,'" I croaked, the weight of that one word knife-sharp and heavy on my tongue.

"There are Vessels activated in Irridessen," Carra said flippantly, though a jealous gleam ignited in her eyes, making them glitter. She raised her fingers to stroke my cheek again. I jerked away.

Almost like she was talking to herself, her voice got softer, more melodic. "Phades seemed to believe it was necessary, and her empty-headed sister, Faune, followed along. Aella is as hot-headed as she is stubborn, so I doubt she will ever find a being worthy of the vestige, but I decided a long time ago that I would bestow my god magic once Phades did."

A faraway look that bled with contempt took over her emotionless face as Carra's wings rustled again. "Phades always scoffed at my power, calling me weak while coddling her useless sister in the same breath. I withstood her barbed comments, knowing that, one day, she'd activate her Vessel – and I would activate mine. Then, we would really see who, out of the two of us, is stronger."

Again, Carra huffed in my mind. "Of course, Phades believes she's noble – waiting until Massis started gaining strength, gaining loyalty again. But now... Activating a Vessel and seeing *which* Vessel can thwart Massis is the highest glory."

I gritted my teeth, keeping my expression neutral as I darted my gaze around, needing to escape my own mind. Something told me, no matter how much I quietly desired more power, I didn't want to pit myself against a being named the Vessel of Death.

Carra whipped around, as if she knew my unspoken urge to bolt. She drew up to her full height, wings out at her sides.

"And you, witch, will be *my* Vessel. I cannot grant lineage gifts, nor soul ties to your kind. But the magic it takes to create a Vessel works differently. I can imbue your soul with the power from my Vessel Book. And by gifting you god magic, I will prove to that boneheaded goddess that *my* power is *just* as formidable as hers."

Something akin to bloody retribution slithered through the air, threading the blindingly bright surroundings with something volatile and sinister. Carra glanced down, and said, almost as if it was an afterthought, "With my god magic, I'll give *you* the means to keep Massis trapped in Avamere."

She cocked her head, and that palpating instability that hung over her faded. Wherever I was trapped in my head, the Goddess of Salvation was warping the atmosphere. Now, a light, cheery feeling bloomed between us, and her smooth voice filled me once more. "Think of it as a...*gift*. I help your kind, and in exchange, you win me the glory I've been seeking since the God War."

"What if I refuse?" I dared ask.

Her pristine wings bristled as she straightened. "Why would you? I can teach you how to wield the power of salvation to keep the god realms sealed."

A threat lurked under those words.

Carra growled, "Massis *will* come, and even the gods dread the day he breaks free of his shackles. *If* he is able to escape Avamere, the gods sealed into Minmere and Aurramere will not be able to help Terramere fight him off."

"If you refuse, Massis *will* take over your realm, open Avamere, and allow his demon horde through to execute anyone of *any* species that does not bow. Massis is gaining strength, gaining supporters in high places that know the spells to bring him to Terramere under the pretense of receiving lineage magic, subverting the god magic that sealed him in Avamere."

"Is that why he's using ritualistic spell work to bring dukhmora through the *veles*?" I couldn't take my eyes off the goddess wreaking havoc on my academic mind word by word.

"Those silly sacrifices bring dukhmora through the veil like a trickle of water over a single rock. No, he needs a more powerful spell to unseal Avamere. But if his realm *is* ever unsealed, the horde will burst into Terramere with the force of a tidal wave."

"But then..." I paused to collect my thoughts. "*Why* is Massis granting heretic magic to witches performing the rituals?"

Carra laughed, the sound mocking and throaty. "*Heretic* magic? My dear Vessel, there is no magic named as such."

She reached out to touch my face again, and I was too stuck on her very obvious mistake to avoid it.

"No." I wondered how pissed off the goddess would be when I corrected her. "I have it. Heretic magic. There was a ritual. A – a spell was chanted, blood runes were carved on my skin. I was supposed to be the sacrifice, but –"

Carra hissed, snatching her hand away as she bared her teeth at me, rubbing her palm as if I'd burned her.

In response to her abrupt movement, magic burst through my soul in warning. The rush was so unexpected, I barely had time to restrain it before purple sparks shot from my fingers.

"There is *no* heretic magic," she screeched, quicksilver eyes blazing as she pointed an accusatory finger in my face. I winced.

"There is only *one* other magic Massis can bestow – a magic he's honed during his imprisonment in Avamere. If what you say is true, that you now have Massis's lineage magic...you've received *chaos magic*."

"Massis has hidden his chaos magic carefully – only appearing as a mirage into the minds of his cruelest followers to bestow it upon them. The millennia pass while he lurks, trapped in Avamere, growing more cunning and mad with every passing century."

Hidden.

Hidden Lineage Gift.

The book I accidentally summoned was titled *A Testimony to Massis and His Hidden Lineage Gift*. All this time... I'd held the answers to my staggering list of questions.

Carra looked disgusted. She fisted her hand, and the air vanished from my lungs. I clawed at my throat. I couldn't breathe. Heat waves shimmered at the edges of my vision.

"Any witch with chaos magic is no more than his *puppet*, the closest thing he can create to a Vessel, *an abomination*."

Everything I'd known...it was a lie. A pretty lie that dripped poison.

I thrashed, desperate to stay conscious.

My fingers twitched on their own accord.

Carra stilled, nostrils flaring as she appraised me with calculating ire.

Without warning, every muscle in my body seized up.

I couldn't even struggle as a dull drone hummed in my head, her power immobilized me, crushing me, until –

Carra cried out, her hold over me vanished.

I doubled over, sucking down breath after breath. Carra recoiled, lips parting into a snarl. "*You.*"

A purplish light surrounded me. With a strangled gasp, my eyes landed on the source – the carved sigil on my hip, my scar from the blood ritual, glowing through the thin gossamer.

The blood rune was *broken*. It shouldn't be able to channel power. But...the chaos magic...it hurt Carra. I pressed my palm against the sigil.

Embracing my lineage magic for the first time, a shiver traveled up my spine as chaos magic solidified against my skin like a shield.

I glared at the goddess floating above me. Massis tricked my ancestors. His followers almost succeeded in killing me. And now, the goddess who promised to gift me god magic to save my people sneered at me.

Carra flung her palm out. "I renounce you! You...you are an *abomination!*"

Her silver eyes were wide with fear, and in that moment, I understood why chaos magic was so destructive.

I faced the goddess; fists wreathed in purple magic. Carra swiped a hand out, white light slamming into my shield. Her god magic didn't even dent it.

My pulse thudded with the revelation.

"I know your secret." I advanced a step, magic sparking between us. "Tell me this, *Carra*. Is chaos magic so feared because it's the only lineage gift that can kill a god?"

Carra shrieked. "You *will not* be the Vessel of Salvation! You are tainted with *his power.* You will be the downfall of Terramere, and the gods will celebrate the sheer decimation of witchkind. *Begone!*"

Hatred and frustration slammed into me, and I flung out my hands, lavender light exploding from my palms –

But before it could strike Carra, the Goddess of Salvation disappeared in a blinding flash of white, and my subconscious careened back into unending darkness.

Though this time, I screamed the entire time I fell.

CHAPTER TWENTY-SEVEN
MERRICK

FROM THE CORNER OF the rocky cavern, Merrick watched witchlings tumble over each other, laughing and playing with the toys he'd found, completely oblivious to the somber atmosphere.

Winnie could shadow walk *through runes*. It didn't surprise him, but he'd been so tangled up in the clusterfuck she'd left in his head that when she tugged Merrick through the swirling black smoke with her, it had taken him a moment to realize how powerful she was as they stepped into a spacious cave.

Makeshift cots were set up in neat lines, a wooden table with long benches ran the length of one wall, and squat shelves packed with jars of food circled a small cooking area that sported a fire pit and iron pots hung from chains bolted into the rocks. As he dragged his eyes around the space in astonishment, at least fifty humans stared back at him with varying degrees of fear in their eyes.

He'd learned this cave was a safe house of sorts for the remote Shadymoss town. The bluff he'd seen held a carefully crafted sheen of magic, created specifically in case demons attacked the town.

Unfortunately, since there were no witches currently in Shadymoss, aside from the untrained witchlings, the town's residents were only able to *enter* the cavern.

They couldn't leave until the high-tier witches returned from their Coven Mother's gathering and dropped the barricades. It was a one-way-in system designed to make sure the witches could confirm the threat was gone while their families and children stayed safely hidden away.

Winnie had quickly and curtly introduced Merrick to a few of the humans that were responsible for the evacuation – and he was immediately in their good graces as he pulled bag after bag down from his shoulders, explaining quietly to the throng gathering around him that he had saved what he could from their decimated homes.

Toys were passed over to the children, both witchling and human, while heirlooms were returned to their rightful owners. More than once, Merrick had been thanked by teary-eyed beings, and once the items were distributed and the bags were empty, he spent an hour recanting everything he saw in town.

There was no division of species in the cool, softly lit cave – only survivors of a terrible attack.

He'd learned the casualties were minimal – that the few witches who stayed behind to protect the town fell during the fight – but their sacrifice allowed the humans to gather the younglings and run to the grotto.

The injured were being tended to by the healers in Winnie's Coven. The light witches, led by Emrin, were busy setting bones, mending cuts, and using their gifts on the assortment of burns and scrapes the townsfolk sustained during their plight.

Hollow eyes and sadness wafted through the cave. An ache started in his chest as a few Shadymoss residents cried, wrapped in embraces by their kin, or slumped against cots, staring brokenly at nothing.

Merrick averted his gaze, and once he finished his recollection of what he saw from town, he felt like he was intruding on a private moment. So, he banished himself to an empty corner to mull over everything he'd learned and collect himself.

As he brooded, a human child clutching the little stuffed bunny boldly asked to touch his horns. The sight of the bunny reunited with its boy was enough to choke Merrick up. He'd grunted in affirmation – and was immediately swarmed by the rest of the bright-eyed younglings.

He wasn't *great* with younglings – spending a century on battlefields and embedded in court politics didn't grant much interaction with these tiny creatures and their boundless energy.

But he did his best.

Merrick sat patiently as witchlings showed him their magic – which was really just sparks of blue light at their age, and then he answered all of their questions about being a gargoyle. Surprisingly, not a single youngling asked if he ate humans.

Their inquisitive nature and complete lack of fear confirmed the ways of the world were changing, that Terramere's future would be alright.

Merrick sighed, leaning against the cool stone wall, his sensitive hearing buzzing with the cheery shrieks of the untroubled children. Their attention had shifted, and the pack of younglings had migrated further away to play some sort of game that consisted of different colored rocks and what he thought might be animal bones.

He had no idea what time it was outside the cave, only guessing that, based on the time that passed since Winnie brought him here, it was around sunset.

Speaking of Winnie...

Since shadow walking them into the grotto, Winnie had kept her distance, though she kept shooting glances his way. Each time he caught her staring, she'd pointedly look away.

If he really wanted to be honest with himself, the only reason he knew she was watching *him* was because *he* couldn't keep his eyes off *her*.

Wings bristling, Merrick growled.

He wasn't in the mood to reflect on *why* he kept looking her way.

On their own accord, his thoughts drifted to another grotto, across the sea, where he learned his fated mate died before receiving her *acat*.

Physically, he knew none of it was Sparrow's fault. And Merrick was relieved she accepted the god magic from the Book of Faune. It would keep her safe. Make their enemies think twice about engaging in battle with a Vessel Queen.

Emotionally... Merrick could still hear her musical laugh, could picture her lively aquamarine eyes and her sunshine golden hair. During the long months of his self-imposed exile, if he *really* wanted to torment himself, he'd dredge up the memory of her scent, let ghosts haunt him from the darkness that seeped into every fissure of his shattered heart.

But somewhere along the way those ghosts began fading to nothing, and in their absence, he was grasping at the one thing he never believed he'd be granted.

Closure.

Instinctively, he turned towards Winnie. She was still dressed in her grimy riding leathers, her short hair tucked behind her ears and windswept, and a smattering of dirt visible against her cheeks. With a half-lidded gaze, Merrick scanned her for injuries, mentally noting a small cut on her lip and a bruise blooming on her sharp cheekbone.

Winnie was deep in conversation with a silver-haired crone, nodding solemnly along to whatever story the female was recanting animatedly.

The crone's spotted-with-age face split into a grin as she held up a silver and brass locket between gnarled fingers – an heirloom Merrick found half-buried under a pile of ash.

As if Winnie felt his attention, she flicked her eyes to him, her lips parting ever-so-slightly. Even with fifty feet of distance separating them, Merrick's stomach clenched as she offered him a coy smile. Tallah cut into the conversation, and the crone proudly showed off her locket.

But Winnie's focus stayed on him.

Merrick raised his chin, daring her to make the next move.

If they were any closer, sparks that had *nothing* to do with magic would probably crackle in the air as heated tension pulled taut between them.

He wasn't sure if she was insane, or if she was fucking with him.

One moment she was spitting venom, the next she was surveying him with interest from beneath her lashes. Yet he couldn't say with certainty that she had any sort of feelings for him. Maybe he was imagining it.

Gods, Winnie had him spun.

Suddenly, everything was too constricting.

He had to get out of this cave.

He needed fresh air.

Merrick already learned the sigils keeping the humans within the mountain didn't affect him – they hadn't been erected with gargoyle blood in mind.

Merrick strode towards the magic barricade, as inconspicuous as possible. Across the grotto, Winnie faced his direction, but if the worried crease between her arched brows was any indication, whatever she was discussing with Tallah was serious.

The barrier curled around his limbs, trailed across his wings, and deemed he wasn't a human, witch, *or* demon. And once the runes were thoroughly confused on where he was supposed to be, they gave up and spat him out into the night.

Within the shadow of the bluff, only a sliver of sky was visible. But thick, purple clouds hid the stars from view, and heavy pressure settled around his shoulders like a cold, wet blanket, alluding that storms had blown through the area recently.

Merrick blinked, his pupils shifting into the slitted form of his Sentry, adjusting his sight to the darkness.

Again, he wondered why he'd ever refused to learn this skill in the past.

He snorted sardonically.

Pride, probably.

Gargoyles operated on an *all or nothing* mentality. The world, to them, was black or white. Actions were right or wrong. You either shifted fully into your Sentry or not at all.

And sure, he'd *dabbled* in that vague middle ground on *occasion* in the past, but after dying on the floor of the Opal Palace's throne room, Merrick was really embracing the freedom that ambiguous grey area provided.

Hmm. Winnie might be right.

He paused, boots sinking into the sodden ground.

Maybe he *was* a little boneheaded.

Merrick let out a derisive huff. He would never admit that.

Ducking under sprawling cypress limbs, he stayed alert as he wove deeper into the slumbering marshland. Even though the air was heavy, stress melted from his muscles with each breath. Picking his way deeper through a grove of moss-laden trees, the spongy ground making his footsteps nearly silent, he decided to walk for a few more minutes before returning to the cavern and receiving an inevitable tongue lashing from Winnie for sneaking out.

Through blurring vision, Merrick tipped his face towards the sky. Hot tears welled up as a misting of rain prickled his cheeks.

The Jade Kingdom had changed him.

The next breath he took was less steady, and he half-sat, half-collapsed atop a boulder butted up against the base of the mountain range.

Breathing through the dull ache in his heart, he gave into one final wave of grief for his old life, one last pang of loss for the soul tie he'd never receive.

He let the tears fall then, balling his trembling hands into fists, each teeth-gritted sob pushing tracks of moisture down his face, wetting his too-long beard that he'd actually begun to like.

One rattling, unstable breath.

Two.

The moon hid behind smoky clouds, and Merrick let it all go.

Closure.

Healing.

With a clear head and a bruised-yet-mending heart, Merrick welcomed this new life into his soul.

Chapter Twenty-Eight
DOVE

THE MOMENT MY CONSCIOUSNESS slammed back to reality, panic turned to hysteria. I awoke in an unfamiliar room, sweat rapidly beading against my clammy skin. A soft weight pressed against my body, and memories of the altar in Carra's temple assaulted my mind. Hands shot from the shadows. I bucked and flailed, desperate for freedom.

Black tendrils of smoke wrapped snug around my wrists and ankles, holding me. I let out a blood-curling scream, faceless assailants haunting my vision. My whole body trembled, heavy sobs choking my cries. I flinched, dizzy and hyperventilating, waiting for the piercing sting of the silver dagger to slash runes into my flesh.

"*Carra's tits* – you're going to hurt yourself, *breathe*."

The restraining shadows stroked my fevered skin, and Finn's exasperated voice, followed with a stream of Cravic curses, made my muscles stiffen.

Every inch of my being felt like a stranger, as if I possessed a body that didn't quite fit. My soul writhed, stretching and fluctuating, magic pinging through my blood with the force of a battering ram.

"Just breathe."

His curt command somehow held a direct link to my panic. I involuntarily inhaled deep, heart hammering to an off-kilter beat.

"Do it again."

I stuttered through another breath.

Finally, the dread eased, my soul unwinding and fitting back perfectly.

Finn sighed heavily.

Even with my eyes screwed shut, I could *picture* his scowl.

I ground my teeth, trying to peel my lids apart, but they were so heavy it took all my effort to pry them open a few millimeters.

Amber light greeted me, assaulting my senses, clearing away the haze of confusion.

I was in my room, in bed, in the Jade Palace. A *very* grumpy Finn sat in the hard-backed chair next to my bedside, his arms crossed and – yep, that was a big, broody frown on his annoyingly handsome face.

Averting my eyes from his scrutiny, I found Neera, fully visible, lying on the floor next to him. I gave the grimm a smile, her presence soothing.

Neera whined, her plumed tail thudding against the floor.

My muscles unclenched one by one, and with it, the shadows holding me faded. I gingerly shimmied up to a sitting position, using the headboard as a back rest.

Finn regarded me carefully. The ribbons of shadow around my wrists and ankles were gone, but the red marks down my forearms said Finn's magic protected me from myself.

The source of the weight that threw me into a spiral was nothing but a thick, patchwork quilt tucked around me.

Our eyes locked. His gaze darkened, searching mine. Whatever he saw had a frown tugging the corners of his lips.

"How'd I get here?" I croaked, my throat scratchy and raw. It seemed screaming as I fell through nothingness had not been limited to the confines of my mind.

Theo had come to my room. Escorted me to the library.

Theo kissed me.

As if Finn was somehow privy to my racing thoughts, he frowned and pursed his lips. "You fainted in the library, and the healers couldn't bring you to consciousness. They took you to the infirmary. I moved you to your room."

This was all said simply, emotionlessly, though a muscle jumped in his jaw, saying there was more to the story he summarized through gritted teeth.

I squinted, piecing together the order of events, sorting them to a timeline.

Library. Vessel Book. Carra. Potentially dooming witchkind. Massis. *Chaos magic.*

Vessel.

The rest was blank.

I slumped against the headboard.

"And now you." I added the devastatingly handsome and really fucking irritating man to my list. "Of course. What better time to demand answers about the ritual that resulted in me *dying* than right now, right? While I'm vulnerable and dizzy?"

I would have loved to punctuate the words with more sarcasm, but my painfully raw throat allowed only a harsh rasp to pass my lips.

Finn snorted. "I didn't have much choice."

He inclined his chin towards Neera, who preened under his attention. "Your *pet* hunted me down in Bramberry. A grimm bursting from the shadows unexpectedly wasn't how I anticipated my day going. I normally enjoy living, so I followed her, and she shadow walked me here."

Neera's tail thumped faster against the floor, as if she was very pleased with Finn's story.

"Her name is Neera." I corrected Finn. "And she isn't my *pet*. She's my *friend*."

Finn let out a long-suffering sigh, scrubbing his stubble with his palm. "Duly noted, darling."

With a huff, Neera stretched and jumped onto the mattress, sprawling alongside my body. I buried my hands into her thick fur, murmuring hoarse praises that had Neera nudging my face with her icy nose, her frigid tongue sweeping over my chin.

"And *what* a good friend to have," Finn grumbled flatly, nodding politely to the grimm.

"And after Neera brought you here..." I trailed off. Neera realized I needed help and immediately ran...to Finn. Maybe because he had shadow magic? Or because he could see her?

Finn gestured wordlessly with his hand. "She turned into a...a glimmer?" I nodded. Neera hid herself from view but allowed Finn to see the outline of her presence.

"I followed her...glimmer straight to the library. By that point, you'd been taken to the infirmary. I found Bron, and he told me you fainted."

I kept quiet.

Finn leaned forward in the chair, threading his fingers together and resting them on his knees. "I went to the infirmary, and you were alone."

He swallowed tightly, pain flitting across his expression. "I moved you to your room. I've been here ever since."

"Theo wasn't there?"

"No, Bron and Cordelia came by earlier, but I haven't seen Theodoric. Why?" Something unsettling niggled in the back of my mind that I couldn't quite put a finger on.

"No reason," I muttered.

Finn looked as if he wanted me to elaborate, but, instead, he leaned back against the chair, crossing his arms. "Fine."

I glanced up at him, surprised he wasn't incessantly needling me for answers.

But he seemed lost in thought. I allowed myself to take him in, my eyes roving over his wrinkled black tunic that stretched across his broad chest, the sleeves rolled up to expose thick, tanned forearms. Next to the chair, his black-bladed sword was propped against the wall in its sheath, a small rucksack next to it.

His under eyes were rimmed in purple, and Finn's dark hair was unkempt, as if he'd run his hands through it a hundred times, as if he hadn't slept a wink since...

Wait.

"How long was I unconscious?"

"Two days."

My heart sank. *Two days.*

I'd missed dinner with Theo.

But he knew I'd fainted, and he probably had his own duties to attend to as Regent. He couldn't sit at my bedside and wait for me to wake up.

But Finn had. The little nagging voice in my head cooed. I had to know for sure.

"How long have you been sitting in that chair?"

Finn pinned me with a tired look. "A couple hours less than two days."

"Oh."

That sobered me. *Finn stayed by my bedside for two days. Why?*

More unanswered questions.

We lapsed into silence. Neera took that opportunity to wriggle closer, hunting for pets. I trailed my hand down her back mindlessly.

"What did you see?" Finn asked quietly, so quiet that, for a moment, I didn't think he'd spoken the words aloud.

Everything crashed through me again, and as desperately as I tried to block out Carra's shrill voice screaming that I'm an abomination, that my magic was not what it seemed, that I held chaos magic in my veins instead, it was a losing battle.

Tears pricked the corners of my eyes, and I tried wiping them away without Finn seeing, but it was no use.

"You connected to the Book of Carra," he guessed slowly.

I didn't want to explain that I'd spoken to the goddess herself, that I heard the warning in the Book of Carra. "I saw nothing." I hated lying, but the truth was worse. "I hadn't eaten. Got dizzy and fainted."

"Bullshit," Finn growled.

I dared him to call me out on it. The tentative truce that had slowly knit together between us over the last few minutes dissolved faster than his shadow bindings.

But I was exhausted from the whiplash of the last few days, and I just wanted to close my eyes and rest, wanted to hide away and lick my wounds in peace.

"I'm going back to sleep."

It was a dismissal.

Finn shot from the chair in one abrupt movement. Neera swung around, leveling Finn with a deadly stare, lip curled. A warning hiss reverberated through the room.

Slowly, Finn raised his hands. Tension and plumes of shadow coiled around Neera as she shifted her body to cover me.

"So, you'll collect me at your whim, but I can't get any closer to her now, huh?" Finn asked the grimm coolly.

Neera considered him a moment, until she finally huffed, lowering her head, though her pointed ears flattened to her skull, and red eyes tracked Finn's every move.

Much slower, Finn tipped his chin to me. His hulking stature standing over my bed had magic simmering in my veins – as on edge as the giant grimm. "You saw something. Admit it. The Book of Carra affected you."

I shook my head. "Like I said, I hadn't eaten dinner or breakfast, and I was lightheaded. I'm sorry Neera came to get you, but I'm absolutely fine. You can go back to doing...whatever you were doing."

His appearance in my room, for the second time, had me reeling. The Prince was hiding something from me. Something he didn't want me to know.

"*Whatever I was doing.*" Finn seethed, raking his hands through his hair. "Sure – I'll just fuck off back to Bramberry and continue pretending to hunt for you."

"Enjoy." I closed my eyes.

I heard Finn stomp to the door.

"If anyone *else* asks what happened with the Book of Carra, will you tell them the same bullshit story you told me?"

The threatening heaviness of a headache began digging into my temple. I had a feeling Finn's definition of "everyone else" pertained to only one person – his brother.

I cracked one eye open, peeking over at the door.

Was it jealousy?

Was Finn *jealous* of the fact Theo and I had a connection?

The idea that Finn desired me was laughable. I dismissed that insane notion the moment it popped into my mind.

I took him in as I debated the merit of answering truthfully.

His dark hair hung shaggy and tousled in his face, leaving the sharp slash of his cheekbone visible. With the sunset sending dusky hues through the window, his eyes were concealed in shadow, and every firm muscle in his back and arms was traced by the dim amber light.

Finn stood so still it looked as if he'd been carved lovingly out of stone, his brooding posture and devastatingly handsome features finishing off the chiseled portrayal of a vengeful god not used to not getting his way.

And since I was quite sick of the gods, I didn't reevaluate my answer in the slightest.

"There's no story to tell," I whispered.

Finn scoffed.

Waiting for his sharp-tongued retort, I held my breath and didn't release it until he left my room.

CHAPTER TWENTY-NINE
MERRICK

MERRICK SAT THERE, HIS soul slowly stitching itself together piece by piece, no longer determined to rip and tear himself to shreds on a path of self-destruction.

The soft chirping of crickets hidden in the long grass, the muted sound of slow-moving water trickling down the mountain, and deep croaks from whatever frogs squatted along the swampy banks healed him – recentered him.

Seconds, or minutes, or even an hour passed, but time no longer mattered as Merrick closed his eyes and prayed.

He'd heard that the gods didn't answer prayers in this Kingdom, but he said them anyway as his tears dried and the last shadows of his grief faded from his mind, leaving only the lessons they taught behind, sheathed in silver-linings.

Merrick wondered if Winnie knew he was gone. And then he wondered why his thoughts immediately pivoted to the spitfire witch.

And like a vengeful spirit, she appeared.

"Am I interrupting your grump time?"

Winnie crashed through the damp grove with the same grace as a boulder barreling down a mountain pass, shadows billowing around her.

Merrick pressed his lips together. *How could a witch who weighed so little make so much noise against sodden, spongy ground?*

"I don't *care*; I just figured your boneheaded sense of direction got you all lost," she added brightly, hopping over a puddle of mud with feline grace and coming to a stop in front of him.

"I don't get lost," Merrick corrected, crossing his arms. "The cave is right over there."

He jerked a horn towards the path back to the grotto. Winnie peered over her shoulder to where he gestured.

She shrugged. "Close enough, I guess."

It struck him then how close she was, how much smaller than him she stood even with him hunched over, sitting on the boulder.

Heat shot through his blood, and for a split second, Merrick wanted nothing more than to bend her over this flat rock and hear her beg him to fuck her.

He raked a hand through his hair in frustration.

He wasn't sure if she *tolerated* him.

Let alone liked him.

"Tell me something."

To his utter surprise, Winnie brazenly pushed into him, bracketing her body between his thighs. His hands wrapped around her hips on instinct. For an agonizingly long heartbeat, they stared at each other, her hands pressed against his upper thighs.

Merrick inhaled her scent, letting the witch who'd sent his entire headspace into a tailspin lead this interaction. Intrinsically, he knew Winnie was the catalyst of his healing process. He hadn't *wanted* to repair the scarred damage digging in his heart until his path crossed with this wicked female.

"What do you want to know?" Merrick asked.

He wanted nothing more than to drag his hands across every lithe curve of her body. Fighting against the urge, he kept them settled on her hips, waiting for Winnie to make the next move.

Battling a horde of dukhmora seemed less dangerous than having Winnie wedge her body against his. And the last thing he wanted to do was piss her off or do something stupid like read her intentions wrong.

Winnie leaned closer, her hair swinging against her neck, baring the smooth column of her throat. Her glittering hazel eyes narrowed into slits. "Why haven't you tried to kiss me?"

Merrick glared at her, his pulse thundering to life in his veins.

With a coy tilt of her head, Winnie looped her hands around the back of his neck. He knew damn well she could feel his cock harden between them. And with her breasts against his chest, the last few threads of his self-control slipped from his grasp like water.

"Why haven't *you* kissed me?" Merrick challenged back.

Winnie scoffed. "Because you're *insanely* tall, obviously. I can't reach."

"I'm still half-convinced you want to kill me," Merrick grunted, his grip on her hips tightening.

It took every ounce of waning restraint to not snatch her throat in his hand, to not feel her silky skin swallow against his palm, to *not* cross that line that they'd drawn in the dirt between them.

"I've only *threatened* to kill you. I've never actually *done* anything to you."

"I've only *thought* about kissing you," Merrick bit back, his cock straining against his slightly-too-small pants. "I've never actually *tried* since you look like you want to stab me."

Winnie let out a wry chuckle as his fingers dipped below the hem of her pants, finding soft skin broken out with gooseprickles.

"I like fighting with you," she admitted breathlessly. "Maybe I'd like to fight you *and* fuck you. No strings attached, no consequences. Just...here. Now."

Yes. Get this weird tension out of their systems.

And maybe, once they took care of this hazy lust that hummed over them, he'd find himself not as strung up around her.

Merrick slashed her a rakish grin, enjoying the dazed expression on her face. "You've got yourself a deal." Dragging his hand to the back of her neck, he fisted her hair. Winnie released a soft moan laced with desire. "Is that what you want?" Merrick teased, using his other hand to skate over her breast, feeling her nipple pebble beneath the thin leather corset. "For me to fuck you over this rock, and for us to walk back into that cavern like nothing happened?"

"*Yes,*" she breathed.

Merrick's last shred of self-control snapped.

He crashed his lips to hers.

Winnie's breath hitched – and then she was kissing him back fiercely.

And just like every interaction they'd ever had, it quickly turned into a battle for dominance.

Merrick angled her mouth to his. Then – she was straddling his lap, grinding down onto his cock, the sensation blasting through Merrick with the subtlety of a cannonball. In return, he palmed her ass, guiding her rolling hips harder and faster.

Fingernails dug into his neck.

They fell into a flurry of teeth and exploring hands. Merrick released her hair, wanting – *needing* to touch every inch of her. Winnie's back arched under his exploring hands, letting out a wanton whimper as he tugged loose the ties on her corset, pushing it down to give him access to her simple white tunic, the material sheer enough for him to admire the outline of her nipple.

Dipping down, Merrick ran the pad of his tongue over the visible peak, smirking at her moan, grazing the sensitive flesh with his fang.

Winnie threw her head back, pure bliss on her face as she wrapped her fingers around his horn, still undulating against his now throbbing cock.

Fuck. If she kept that up, Merrick was going to come in his pants.

With a guttural groan, he pulled away, bracketing her chin to steal another kiss, every nerve in his body erupting into blazing fire.

"Pants. Off," he demanded, unbuckling Winnie's belt, her bone dagger dropping to the rock and clattering off the side.

They broke the kiss long enough for Winnie to wriggle her tunic off, the corset still trapped around her waist, and for Merrick to undo the ties on his breeches. If he didn't get inside her in the next four seconds, he was going to lose his mind.

"You know I respect you – right?"

Her fingers stilled against the last knot of her breeches. Slowly, Winnie raised her gaze back to him, and she gave him the tiniest, briefest nod. "Yeah, I know."

Merrick bared his teeth, catching her throat in his hand, her pulse thrumming under his fingers. Her breath caught, fire igniting through her eyes until they were more copper than green.

As her uneven breaths fanned over him, Merrick growled, "Because in a moment, it's going to look like I don't."

Chapter Thirty
MERRICK

Winnie moaned, giving him access to her throat. Merrick raked his teeth across the smooth column, her heartbeat hammering under his teeth.

She tasted like freedom – a dew-covered morning and smoky campfires.

Within seconds, he had her bottoms down to her ankles, and, in turn, she'd freed his cock from the confines of his pants, the crisp, night air dotting her bronze dusted skin with tiny pinprickles.

The moment her hand touched the shaft of his cock, Merrick groaned, biting down on the side of her neck as he struggled to keep from coming right then and there.

With an appreciative hum, Winnie slid her palm down his thick length.

"Fuck, Win," Merrick blew out a rough breath. With just her *hand* he saw stars.

She shot him a dazed smirk before crawling off his lap, dipping lower, her tongue flicking out and swirling around the head of his cock.

"No," he snarled, his fingers shooting out and catching her chin. In one smooth maneuver, Merrick flipped her around until she was right where he wanted her – bent over the flat surface of the boulder with him behind her.

With his knee, he kicked her legs out wide, the leather breeches still cuffed around her ankles, baring her pretty pussy to him.

"My way," he ground out, running a finger up her wet center. Words were hard.

"Get to it then, bonehead," she panted as he lined up with her slick entrance. Notching the first inch inside, her rapid breathing turned to breathy moans, and every snarky remark in his head emptied out.

"Please," she gritted out, trying desperately to grind against him. "*Now.*"

Merrick didn't need to be told twice.

With a hard thrust, he seated himself fully, and Winnie spasmed beneath him, letting out a string of what he thought might be curses in another language.

"You okay?"

"Merrick, I swear to every god – if you don't fuck me right now, I'll leave you here with your dick out and go finish myself off."

He leaned over, his tongue licking up her spine before biting down on the juncture of her shoulder. "Say '*please.*'"

"*Please,* fucking gods, *now,*" Winnie whimpered, thrashing under him.

Merrick sneered, "What a good little witch."

And with that, he slammed into her again and again, their shared moans threading through the chilly night air. Gripping her waist in one hand, the other holding her firmly in place by the shoulder, he pounded into her, feeling her delicate inner muscles ripple around him.

She chanted his name between thrusts, her voice husky and raw. Pleasure zapped down every nerve in his body as Winnie came, body tightening, cries of pure, unfiltered euphoria ringing in his ears.

Not wanting this to be over yet, his teeth clenched so hard he wouldn't have been surprised if he cracked one, he fucked her through her orgasm until her muscles relaxed under his broad hands.

It took one, two more deep strokes for his release to shoot down his spine, and with a grunt, he pulled out of her, coming against her perfectly round ass.

Mind spinning with everything that just happened, Merrick admired the view of his cum sliding down her thigh, her swollen pussy glistening and puffy. He had the undeniable urge to slide one finger inside, but he knew he'd been rough, and if she was sore, he didn't want to hurt her.

Cupping his palm, he scooped as much cum off her as possible. Then, not really sure what to do with it because his brain was completely useless after the most intense orgasm of his life, he wiped it dumbly on the side of the boulder.

Winnie wriggled out from underneath him, swooping her breeches back up. With a dazzling grin, she retied the laces before shimmying her corset off, tucking it under her arm. "Thanks for that," she said with a raspy laugh, plucking her rumpled tunic off the ground as Merrick blinked at her, speechless.

Within seconds, she had her top on and her belt cinched back in place. Tossing her hair back, she side-stepped him easily, patting him on the cheek as she passed. "And you were worried I'd stab *you*."

Merrick, his entire axis tilted and his cock still out, could only stare stupidly at her retreating back as she deftly picked her way down the path towards the cavern's barrier without a care in the world.

And with his whole existence spun over her in tighter knots than before, Merrick, once again, realized just how utterly fucked he was.

CHAPTER THIRTY-ONE
DOVE

AFTER EXPLAINING TO A high-strung and red-faced Master Vole that my fainting spell was merely due to the fact I hadn't eaten in almost a full day, no one questioned my reaction to the Book of Carra or my return to the library.

It would've been easy to sink into a spiral of depression and dread, to replay the interaction with Carra over and over in my mind, to cry over her nasty words and her declaration that I'd be the downfall of witchkind.

I did feel a tiny sliver of relief that she hadn't imbued me with her direct power. It was difficult enough to hide chaos magic. I wasn't sure what I would've done if I'd also been granted god magic and made into a Vessel.

That responsibility would probably be passed to another witch – one more aligned with whatever high standards Carra desired.

Instead, I spent the hours after Finn stormed out of my room working on translating *A Testimony to Massis and His Hidden Lineage Gift*, reading by the beams of the half-moon creeping through the window and a tendril of chaos magic perched in the sole lamp.

By the time the sun rose, I'd confirmed the book was indeed written about chaos magic, and somehow, that solidified the revelation that I didn't give a fuck about what Carra thought of me.

With Neera nothing but a ripple of air at my side, I'd showered, dressed, and found my own way to the library. Even though I swore not to let anyone ever affect my mood again, dismissing Carra's proclamation as nonsense was easier than wondering why Theo never came to my room to check on me.

He was going to be crowned King sooner rather than later, and the analytical part of me knew he must be swamped in preparation for his coronation – on top of tending to his dying father and whatever else his soon-to-be-Kingly duties required.

But I kept replaying our kiss in my head. Strictly speaking, I kept my mind from wandering to the dinner we never got to have together, avoided wondering what it would be like to have hours alone with the incredibly handsome Regent.

I scrunched up my face, shuffling through papers for my notes under the sea of useless Vessel Book crap.

The scholars complained that the Book of Carra was too *delicate* for translators to rifle through, and requested that, instead, we work off a few pages of hand-written copies and begin by hunting for patterns hidden in the symbols.

Now, the Book of Carra stayed locked in its box covered with imbued nullifying runes, and about fifty pages of thick parchment was scattered across our table – each one an exact replica of the *actual* Book of Carra.

Bron was dutifully scribbling notes in a thick, leather-bound book that he'd been hunched over for the better part of eight hours, only stopping to crane his neck up whenever Cordelia asked him a question.

I wasn't sure exactly why Cordelia was here, since she wasn't a translator, but she showed up a couple hours ago announcing she was bored before plopping down on the chair across from Bron.

Not that I was complaining.

In Bramberry, all of the teachers were top tier witches, and they weren't ever interested in engaging in academic banter with me. No matter how masterful I was on the topic, if I engaged them in conversation, I got short, placating responses and their excuse to leave the room.

And Polina was my dearest friend, but she hated my long-winded tangents on niche, academic topics.

Being around brilliant witches like Bron and Cordelia was exhilarating. They saw me as an equal instead of as the weak light witch Maude adopted, and it was the closest thing to bliss I imagined you could find between packed bookshelves in the Royal Library.

Unbeknownst to the scholars, I'd bought the book on chaos magic with me, and half-hid it under a few of the pieces of parchment we were supposed to be translating.

There was a complex beauty to translation, a skill that, for a while, I believed would be my saving grace, my own crowning achievement. Unfortunately, I found out pretty quickly that not many people cared if you could understand a language that no one had spoken in over two thousand years.

I stuck my tongue between my teeth, struggling through a particularly chewy passage titled *Fae Magic Similarities*. Bron hadn't said a word when I pulled the tome out of my messenger bag and began painstakingly writing each word I translated into Terrian in my own notebook.

Though it was slow going, looking at the book from the viewpoint that I *had* chaos magic made it easier to muddle through. So far, I could tell the tome had been hand-written by someone else who'd received the purple hued lineage gift, though there was, so far, no mention as to how they received it.

I didn't want to consider the unknown author drove a knife between a witch's ribs while they were bound to an altar.

Curiously, though the language disappeared thousands of years ago, this book seemed fairly...recent. I'd tried dating it based on the ink and the book binding technique, but I was lackluster in both of those skills and was only able to guess the book had been written within the last couple of centuries. Whoever'd written this was either well into their life or dead. Either way, I didn't think they were missing it.

I mouthed each word in the paragraph I was working on, stumbling over a weird sentence that I couldn't quite complete the translation of.

Cordelia sighed loudly, snapping her romance book shut with a resounding *thump* that made Bron and I startle. "Let's go get something to eat."

"Gimme like...an hour," Bron replied distractedly, skimming over his notes again.

"Ten minutes," Cordelia countered with a sly pout, leaning across the table towards him, her long mahogany hair fanning across his strewn-about notes.

"Why don't you two ladies go eat without me?" Bron counteroffered, flipping the page over and scrawling slightly less intelligible cursive on it.

Cordelia narrowed her eyes at him before shooting me a glance that said *can you believe this ass?*

I rolled my eyes good-naturedly, stuffing the chaos magic book and my interpreted notes back in my bag. "Bron, you haven't eaten since breakfast," I tried. "Aren't you hungry?"

Bron muttered something under his breath, avoiding our stares.

Cordelia leaned back in her chair, rolling her neck and shoulders before nonchalantly flicking her wrist towards the table.

Every single page of Bron's notes, including the hand-written copies of the Book of Carra, burst into flames.

Bron let out a strangled shriek, pushing away from the flame covered table so fast his chair tipped over. Somewhere in the depths of the library, someone shushed him.

I stifled my laugh as Bron leaped to his feet, eyes wild, as the bonfire Cordelia casually started on the library table grew into a funnel of flame.

With a snort, I exchanged a smirk with Cordelia. *I* knew the fire wasn't real, since I stood a couple feet away from the flames and didn't feel any heat, but Bron wavered between shock and cussing Cordelia out with every curse he knew in *every* language.

The moment he bristled and opened his mouth, Cordelia closed her hand into a fist, and every lick of flame disappeared, leaving not a single scorch mark behind.

"You're a *crazy witch*." He threw himself on top of his precious papers, frantically checking each one for burns.

Cordelia chuckled as she stood and shouldered her pack. "Oh, you're fine. It was only the *mirage* of a fire. No harm done."

"What is going on over here?" Master Vole rounded the bookshelf that separated us from the rest of the library, heaving like he ran over as fast as his floor length robes would allow. "Someone said they saw fire!"

I kept my face neutral as I nodded to Bron, who still looked a little pale. "They probably just saw Bron's beard, sir," I surmised primly, trading a secret grin with Cordelia who rapidly agreed, her wide eyes the perfect picture of innocence.

We'd made similar jokes at Bron's expense over the last few hours. At first, I thought Cordelia was trying to pry into what happened to me by bonding with me – if anyone was shrewd enough to know a witch was hiding something it would be Cordelia – but she never questioned my brush with the Vessel Book.

I caught her surveying me with a quizzical expression once or twice, but after assuring her I was fine, she'd dropped the subject.

In hindsight, I was being paranoid.

Cordelia really wanted to be friends.

Master Vole's shoulders sagged as he gripped the back of the chair Cordelia abandoned, "Right," he wheezed, though his beady eyes jumped between the three of us with a hint of suspicion. "Alright, then."

Bron glared at us before giving Master Vole a sympathetic pat on the shoulder.

He added, albeit dryly, "I've been told my beard is *too* luscious and that, under certain light, people think my face is on fire because they cannot *believe* how immaculate the color is."

Cordelia and I struggled to contain our laughter. Master Vole gave Bron an incredulous look, blinking furiously before straightening from the chair. "Very well, Bron, my apologies."

"That's quite alright, sir." Bron shoved the last few papers into his bag with a little more aggression than usual before throwing the strap over his shoulder. "You never have to apologize for admiring my perfect facial hair."

Master Vole's bushy brows squeezed together in confusion, but after staring at Bron for a moment more, he shook his head and shuffled away.

Once the Elite Scholar was out of sight, Cordelia and I dissolved into a fit of giggles. I clapped my palm over my mouth to try and stifle the sound, but every time I looked over at Cordelia, we laughed harder.

Another round of shushes from the other people in the library made it harder to calm down. And when Cordelia let out a squeaky snort, we both lost it completely.

"Yeah, yeah," Bron grumbled, steering us to the main doors of the library. "You're welcome, by the way, Cordelia. If Master Vole caught you setting a fire in the library, mirage or not, you'd be kissing your library access good-bye."

Cordelia gasped through barely contained giggles, "Thank you *so much*, my little bearded hero!"

We cackled harder – especially as Bron's ears turned an adorable shade of pink.

Chapter Thirty-Two

DOVE

"You two are terrible, *terrible* pesters to the great name of linguistics," Bron snipped, though amusement twinkled in his eyes as he slung an arm around both our shoulders.

I was incredibly grateful for how fast friendship between the three of us bloomed.

"Bron, your work will still be important in the morning," I reminded him as we walked towards the dining hall, weaving through clusters of other witches heading in the same direction.

"Exactly," Cordelia quipped, flipping her glossy hair behind her shoulder. "Plus, I heard a rumor that the Royal Family is putting together a gala in honor of the King's legacy, so we absolutely need to eat dinner and decide what we're going to wear."

Bron looked at her as if she'd sprouted a second head. "They're celebrating his *legacy* while he's *still alive*?"

Cordelia shrugged. "Either it's epic or in poor taste, but either way, we're *going*. I found out from the kitchen staff, who heard it from the house matron's niece, who was told by the ladies-in-waiting. Queen Dahlia is personally planning it."

"When is it?" I asked, thinking about the beautiful dress Polina packed for me. I needed to buy her a gift if that dress got me laid, or at least, got me a dance with Theo.

"The full moon – *if* the rumors are to be believed." Cordelia shot me a secretive wink. "It would be nice if someone could confirm the gossip...you know? Maybe someone close to Theo?"

I *had* told Cordelia that Theo kissed me. Cheeks heating, I knew my face matched Bron's beard at that exact moment.

And as if I'd conjured the Regent with my thoughts alone, we rounded the corner, and there he was.

Theo's hands were clasped behind his back, and he was perfectly dashing in a jade green brocade with vines embroidered across the chest. His muscular legs were encased in tailored pants, and a slim crown of gold inlaid with emeralds sat against his brow, pushing his hair down while a few strands flipped up around the band.

Bron and Cordelia whirled towards me with mischief and glee written all over their expressions as the Regent strode towards us.

When Theo was within a few feet, he revealed his hands with a bashful smile, his gaze locked with mine. In one, he clasped a beautiful bouquet of red roses, the other, a slim black box with silver trim along the edges.

Stopping short of our trio, Theo nodded to Bron and Cordelia before addressing me. "Dove." Theo extended the flowers. "I'd be incredibly honored if you agreed to dine with me this evening."

As I took the bouquet, electricity sizzled as our fingers brushed. Blushing, I looked up into his handsome face, speechless.

"Dove will *absolutely* have dinner with you," Cordelia piped up conspiratorially, shoving me towards Theo as she linked arms with Bron and dragged the translator away with a swiftness.

Oh, my gods. I gave her an incredulous stare, though she blew me a cheeky kiss and disappeared around the corner.

This was really happening, wasn't it?

With an awkward cough, I tucked a few tendrils of hair that escaped my messy bun behind my ear, acutely aware I...well, I'd been hunched over a book all day in the library. This morning I'd dressed for comfort not appearance – never anticipating this turn of events.

Somewhere in my mane, there was a quill sticking out. And even though I wore a pretty bronze skirt with a cream sweater tucked into the waistband, next to Theo in his perfectly coifed garments, I was extremely underdressed.

"I would love to have dinner with you," I agreed firmly, hoping Theo understood how badly I wanted to spend time with him. "I just..." I gestured to my clothes. "I'm not really dressed for..."

Theo chuckled, holding up a hand. "You are beautiful, Dove. This will be a completely casual dinner. Me and you. Good food. Maybe wine?" He glanced at his own outfit and frowned. "I can change if you prefer."

My heart squeezed at the Prince's words. Even in the short time we'd known each other, I found him utterly charming, and in his royal finery he looked every inch the powerful ruler he was. "No, don't change." The words rushed out. "You look *very* handsome."

Theo held out his arm. "I'll at least ditch the crown."

I laughed, allowing him to guide me from the dining hall and through the courtyard filled with willow trees. The moment his attention shifted off me, I swiped the quill from my bun and stuffed it haphazardly in my messenger bag.

Reaching into my thread of magic for Neera, only a faint gleam of her presence shone through my soul. Before Theo could start a conversation,

I pulled from my connection with the grimm, sending her a wave of calm so she'd understand I was alright.

Her absence didn't worry me, though. With Finn's confirmation he'd stayed in my room for two days while I was unconscious, it was safe to assume Neera hadn't left my side during that time, either. The grimm probably was lurking through the forest hunting poor little furry critters and stretching her legs.

The crisp night air took the edge off my mounting nerves as we walked in silence. With a sideways glance to Theo, I caught a whiff of his cologne – spiced and subtle. The scent tickled my nose, reminding me of the cardamom plants that grew along the border of the meadow in Bramberry.

"Where do witches siphon here?" I asked, realizing I forgot to raise the question to Cordelia earlier.

"Hmm?" Confusion flitted across his features as he led me into an elegantly decorated corridor – empty aside from two broad-shouldered guards that stood imposingly in front of a closed door.

I touched my runestone necklace with the hand not tucked into Theo's elbow, holding it at the end of its chain. "I need to siphon," I explained, the lie falling effortlessly from my lips. "And I've been so busy with Vessel Book translations I haven't had time to siphon since arriving."

"Oh – anywhere, really." Theo said distractedly, passing the guards with a curt nod.

I followed his line of sight, noting the door sported a huge bronze padlock. The thick lock seemed so out of place amongst the rest of the elaborate décor, I slowed. At second glance, the padlock emitted an odd glow – like it was imbued with a rune similar to the ones on the box the Book of Carra was stored in.

"What's –"

"We don't have areas like Bramberry Forest," Theo interrupted, tugging me past the curiously protected door. "The Royal Coven is free to siphon anywhere outside the Palace walls. Growth runes are imbued after for new plants to flourish."

He didn't add anything else, though the muscles in his forearm relaxed the further we moved down the corridor. I upped my pace to match Theo's longer stride, dismissing the strange, locked door.

Even though Theo and I were spending time together, he *was* the Regent – responsible for the safety of the entire Kingdom. I was neither Royalty nor part of Theo's Coven. And the way he hustled me away from the guarded door told me the contents of *that* room were "*Royals only.*"

We sank into silence again, passing underneath brass chandeliers that threw amber light against gilded frames and life-sized portraits of past Kings and Queens that hung against stone walls and spoke to where we were. The Royal Wing.

It felt...different here. The air richer – more potent.

The most powerful witches in our history walked down this corridor.

And now, *me*.

Chaos magic sang proudly from the confines of my soul, responding to the startling realization that *I* was now in the highest tier of witchkind. The thought had me straightening my shoulders as we turned a corner into a narrow passage branching off the Royal Wing.

Theo squinted at me. "Are you alright?"

"Of course." I assured.

His brows pinched together, as if he wanted to say more, but a guard stepped through a wood door at the end of the hall, greeting the Regent and bowing low.

I sidled closer to Theo, pressing into his side as the guard ushered us through the door. At my touch, Theo tipped his face to mine, pressing a chaste kiss against my cheek.

"I'm so glad you agreed to dinner," he murmured as we entered a dark, and definitely private, alcove. Short grass crunched under my boots, and I gasped, stepping from the Palace into the most ethereal garden.

A tall trellis covered in vines hung along three high stone walls bordering and enclosing the area. Little white flowers crawled along it, perfuming the night with a subtle fragrance. Strings of bulbs zigzagged between the trellis and the Palace itself, creating a cozy ambiance.

Theo gripped my hand in his, walking me down a cobblestone path and a table set for two draped in crisp, white linens. A pair of crystal wine glasses, porcelain plates, and armchairs lined with plush pillows finished off the scene.

My eyes widened. "You did all this for me?"

The corners of his eyes crinkled as he captured my lips with his own. "Of course." He deepened the kiss. I melted in his arms.

That spark in my core hummed, but before it could be coaxed to ignite, a butler with white hair and icy skin swept through a hidden door behind the trellis, bowing to Theo before offering to take the bouquet I was holding.

With a flourish, he placed the roses into an empty vase sitting in the middle of the table, the thick stalks spreading and settling into the water. Theo waved him off with the order for wine, which had the butler bunching up the hem of his muted green robes and hurrying back the way he came.

"Please, let me." Theo said, pulling my chair out.

"Theo this is incredible," I breathed as he sat opposite me. The lush scenery, the dashing Prince, the gorgeous glasses...it was perfect. I'd never had a man put so much effort into me before – and Theo had, once again, blown my expectations out of the water.

"Well, half of it is because I wanted to have dinner with you," Theo reached across the table to intertwine our fingers together. "and the other half is my apology that I couldn't be there for you when you fainted. I'm so sorry, Dove. My father had another health scare right after you were taken to the infirmary, and Queen Dahlia demanded my presence immediately."

"Theo, please, there's nothing to apologize for. Even the healers said I was perfectly fine. If anything, it was my fault for skipping dinner."

The wine was delivered, and our conversation ebbed as the butler filled our cups with red wine. I picked up the glass, marveling at its weight. Taking a tentative sip, my mouth flooded with warm cranberries and something spiced – cinnamon, maybe?

I wasn't very knowledgeable about wine. Usually, I purchased whatever came in the biggest, cheapest bottle whenever Polina invited me over to have drinks and gossip.

Theo stared at me with wolfish, hungry desire illuminated in his hooded gaze, and my skin tingled as I met his eyes.

"And you're sure you fainted because you hadn't eaten?" His voice lowered, husky and velvet.

I nodded slowly, squeezing my thighs together. "It was just lightheadedness. My own fault for skipping dinner the night before."

Well, I missed dinner because his asshole of a brother crashed into my room and called me a heretic – but I left that part out.

Theo grunted, his lips tipping into a smirk. I drank another mouthful of wine, exchanging flirty glances with the handsome Regent. Swallowing, heat bloomed through my blood, and it made me wonder...what if I told *Theo* everything?

What if I confessed that I *had* connected to the Book of Carra?

And if I told him about the sacrifice, about my birth mother, about how my soul traveled through Minmere and Avamere...

What *if* I admitted I had chaos magic?

"You're deep in thought," Theo crooned, swiping his thumb over the back of my hand. "Is there something you want to talk about?"

I gritted my teeth to hold my tongue, hoping to still come off as pleasant. "Just thinking about you."

That *was* the truth.

If I told him everything...would he haul me to the dungeon himself?

Or would he realize that, with me at his side, we'd be the most powerful couple to rule the Jade Kingdom...in *history*?

"Hopefully all good things." Theo gave me a dashing smile, raising his glass. "To us."

I echoed the statement, clinking my cup against his, the weight of holding the crystal filled with wine aloft causing the glass to shake in my grasp.

The silver rimming his irises seemed extra bright tonight as he pinned me with his full, unyielding attention. I coyly hid behind the rim of my wine.

Theo was bold, and I had a feeling this dinner was going to end with me in his bed – especially if we finished off more than one bottle of wine.

I hoped we did.

The butler brought out the first course, a delicious salad with roasted walnuts, slices of creamy cheese, and water chestnuts.

I placed my half-empty glass on the tabletop, and Theo wasted no time topping it off. For a moment we gazed at each other, that connection between us taught.

"You know, you can tell me anything, Dove." Theo said, taking my hand in his again. "I always want us to be truthful with each other."

His sincerity made me relax. I picked up my drink, sipped it.

Why was I so worried about what he'd think? The way he looked at me – with desire and longing – assuaged all my fears.

Theo would understand.

There was no doubt in my mind.

"I want to tell you everything," I decided breathlessly.

Theo took a small sip of wine before setting his glass down, leaning forward in his seat and propping his forearms on the linen tablecloth. "I know you do, Dove. So, could I ask you something?"

The air around us shifted.

"Of course, Theo."

Was he going to profess his love for me?

It was so *soon*.

But he *was* going to be King. *Did he want me to be his Queen?*

Woah. Hold on.

A sheen of fog blurred my vision.

We'd barely kissed. He definitely wasn't going to make me Queen after a kiss.

Right?

The insanity of that notion made me side eye the strong wine that was, once again, in my hand. I swallowed the sip in my mouth, though I didn't remember taking it. Gods, I didn't even remember picking the glass back up.

But my mind was so fuzzy and giddy I couldn't focus on anything except Theo.

"This may be a touchy subject." He winced. "We received reports of a heretic witch in Bramberry. Do you know anything about that?"

This was my *chance.*

The entire sordid story bubbled up to my lips – every bit of the truth – how I was captured and tied to the altar, how heretic magic was actually chaos magic, but that there was nothing to fear from it – nothing to fear from me. I didn't want to hurt Theo.

I wanted to rule beside him as his Queen.

Gods below, where did that come from?

Why did I keep thinking of being Queen?

I wasn't thinking straight – was I?

This wine was stronger than I'd anticipated. I wasn't a big drinker to begin with. Blowing out a deep breath, I set my glass down, my vision wavering.

Once I let go of the glass, magic flooded my veins. I tamped it down, shoving it back into my well. I wanted to tell Theo on *my* terms – not because my eyes changed color.

Theo added, "When we arrived in Bramberry, the morning *after* the last full moon, I spoke with your Coven Mother, and she said there was *no* heretical activity in Bramberry Forest."

I picked up my fork with shaky fingers, magic battering against the confines of my soul.

Food. I needed to eat something.

Only half-listening to Theo, I struggled to control my lineage gift as I speared a bite of salad onto my fork.

Theo cleared his throat delicately, glancing at my fork hovering in the air with contempt. I paused. He flicked his gaze down to his own plate – he hadn't started eating yet.

With a grimace, I set my fork down and fisted my hands in my lap. *Fuck.* I forgot the customs surrounding the Crown – no one ate before the Royals took their first bite.

Once my attention refocused to Theo, he continued. "Sources confirmed a body was found recently – a witch butchered inside Carra's temple. That for *years* ritualistic sacrifices and forbidden spell work have haunted the Bramberry Forest." Theo leveled a stern look at me, and I bit my tongue to stop myself from spilling everything I knew. He'd tell me what he thought – and *then* I'd tell him everything.

His approval. That's what I wanted.

"It made me wonder if your Coven Mother's protection is as strong as she insists. *Or* if something sinister is going on in Bramberry Forest – something Maude's involved in."

I stared at Theo in bewilderment.

He couldn't...did he think Maude *performed blood sacrifices?*

I picked up my wine and took another gulp. That foggy haze threw Theo in stark clarity as every other color in the garden dimmed, making it seem as if he radiated gold.

"I can help you. I can *save* you. Do you understand? I *need* the truth, Dove. *Everything.*"

His voice was a soothing rumble, our connection urging me on.

I needed to tell him the truth. Especially if the Royal Coven was investigating *Maude*...gods. Bramberry needed Maude. I had to protect her.

A cool breeze rustled the strands of hair tucked behind my ear.

It's me – I'm the one you're looking for.

With a shiver at the dropping temperature, I reached for the last bit of wine – needing the confidence, desperate to reveal everything.

I touched the glass, and the crystal exploded.

Shiny, shattered fragments burst over the table. I screamed. Theo jumped up with a shout, eyes wide. Through dazed senses, a sharp stab of pain ignited across my palm.

Blood ran down my wrist.

Had I done that? Did my magic *do that?*

"Sorry to interrupt," Finn announced loudly as he stalked from the shadows, two yellow wine glasses dangling between his fingers. Dragging a hard-backed chair behind him, his lips curled into a wicked grin. "But I *really* couldn't miss this."

Chapter Thirty-Three
MERRICK

By the time Merrick collected himself, cursing gorgeous shadow witches with evil tongues and tight cunts the entire time, his mood turned from grouchy to lethal. Wings half-splayed, he stomped through the night dark forest, not caring how much noise he made.

If anything decided now was a good time to attack, he'd tear it in two with his bare hands.

Soon enough, and without incident, he stood at the barrier separating him from the grotto and that wicked little witch. Half of him debated the merit of sleeping on the ground outside the runes just to spare himself from being in the same cave as Winnie.

The other half of him, the dumb, traitorous half, wondered if Winnie would be interested in sharing one of those snug sleeping bags, curious to see if she could stay quiet while he rutted between her thighs again.

Shaking his horns to clear his lust-addled brain, Merrick hissed out a rough breath, raking his hand through his beard.

Gods, he smelled her all over him, the enticing scent of her arousal covering his hand and now his face. And that stupid part of himself took over, filling his mind with the idea of burying his head between –

Carra's tits.

He had to get it together.

Steeling himself, Merrick grunted one last curse and shoved through the magic barricade.

Only, he got stuck halfway, the magic sensing the essence of witch on him, debating if he truly was something *else,* or if he was allowed to pass through.

Completely flustered and furious, his hand morphed to the claw of his Sentry, swiping at the belligerent witch magic, before the barrier rudely spat him out onto the cavern floor.

Merrick straightened with a growl, dusting off his pants, his wings ruffling with indignation. On instinct, his gaze pinged across the grotto, to where Winnie drew a mug of what smelled like lavender tea from her lips, a diabolical smirk twisting across her face like a sword to the gut.

He thought fucking her would clear his head.

Merrick was woefully wrong.

All it did was wind him up tighter. Especially since she'd hopped off that rock like she'd taken a *lovely* restorative nap while he stood there, cunt drunk and stupid.

He glared at her.

Winnie winked.

Merrick saw *red.*

And then Emrin darted in front of his path, her bright hazel eyes shining.

"There you are," she said cheerily, completely oblivious to Merrick's foul demeanor. "I need to see you over in the medic area."

"Why?" Merrick seethed, staring over Emrin's head to Winnie, who blew him a kiss before twisting her hand around to flip him off.

Emrin craned her chin up, copper hair spilling around her shoulders as she gave him a confused look. "So, I can remove the last stitches from your wings," she said slowly, brows drawing together as she fumbled with the necklaces layered against her riding leathers. "I finished tending to the injured humans and still have magic left to heal the last few wounds on your wings. I..." Picking up on the brewing tension, she winced. "Winnie said she was going to let you know."

Merrick gritted his teeth, ripping his eyes away from the mean-ass shadow witch who definitely did *not* tell him that.

Under his weighted focus, Emrin paled before collecting herself, nodding towards a narrow cot, zipping a wire-wrapped runestone along the bronze chain, the etched sigil on the rock glowing as she siphoned. "Um, just sit...there."

The cot was made with the thinnest sticks possible and Merrick awkwardly balanced his weight evenly against the rickety contraption. Thankfully, making sure he didn't tip over and flatten sweet Emrin pulled his focus from the vindictive little witch lazily sipping tea.

Emrin patterned her fingers against the boning of his left wing. "I think if you work on building back muscle here, there's a good chance you'll fly again."

He let out a nervous breath as she ran a hand over the stitches where one of the Ruby Kingdom assholes severed a tendon. "And my Sentry?"

"Once the stitches are out, I'd say it's safe to shift – just don't fly as a Sentry until you've confirmed you can in your..." She trailed off, gesturing at his face, white-hued magic glowing in her palms.

"My humanoid form?" Merrick guessed.

Emrin crinkled her pert nose. "You really need a better name for that. It doesn't roll off the tongue as nicely."

That caused Merrick to chuckle. "Well, gargoyles aren't known for being a creative bunch."

Emrin smiled, pouring healing magic against the stitches.

"I appreciate it, Emrin," Merrick said truthfully, lowering his voice. "If it wasn't for you, I don't believe I'd have even a slim chance to fly again."

"It's what we do," she replied simply. "Healers heal."

The humans and witchlings had all migrated over to the sleeping bags and the other cots, some already falling into slumber while others sat amongst the soft piles of bedding, conversing in soft voices as to not wake those sleeping.

Tallah wove over to where Winnie sat, plunking down onto the bench next to her. The witches hugged briefly before Tallah launched into what looked like a serious discussion, causing Winnie's eyes to somber.

"We're staying here for a while." Magic flashed as Emrin worked down another set of stitches. "Tallah and I. Shadymoss is our home, and this may be one small village that makes up our Coven, but we want to help rebuild." She inclined her chin. "Tallah is telling Winnie now."

Merrick didn't know what to say, but Emrin didn't seem to be waiting on a response.

Her palm brushed over scars peppered along the interior of his wing, dissolving the bulk of scar tissue.

"Winnie's a good witch, you know."

In a much meeker voice, Emrin flicked large, hazel eyes to Merrick. "I know she's stubborn, and way too reckless for her own good, but she's had a hard go at life."

"Haven't we all," Merrick said dryly.

Emrin gave him a nudge with her elbow. "Be gentle with her. She doesn't love easily, and she doesn't let her guard down for just anyone. I think..." Her quietly spoken words wavered. "If you're able to break down her defenses, I think you'd be good for her."

"Winnie seems to be doing fine."

"Then you don't know her as well as I'd hoped," Emrin sniped with the sharpest expression he'd ever seen the soft-spoken witch make.

"Winnie is *gutted* by the devastation that happened here. She's shouldering this entire situation as if it's solely her burden to bear. I know she puts up this unaffected, flippant act, but deep down, she's *aching* to make it right. Even if it means having to deal with her family, she's promised the Crown will personally pay for everything –"

Merrick's mind snagged on that particular part of Emrin's confession. "How can Winnie promise the *Crown* will pay for the town to be repaired? Who *is* she to the Royal Coven?"

Emrin smushed her lips together. "Did I say that?"

He knew deflection when he encountered it, and the innocence that filled Emrin's cherub face told him all he needed to know.

Whoever Winnie was, she was definitely *not* "just another warrior" of the Royal Coven.

She was something else...something either elite in their Coven's rankings... or someone from the assembled court? Someone with a title?

He pieced together what he knew about the Jade Kingdom's Royal Line and how the Covens worked. Unfortunately, the *"out of sight, out of mind"* mentality that beings in Irridessen held for the Kingdom of witches began early, and none of his positions in court ever included encounters with the Jade Royals.

Aside from the fact he knew there was a King and a Queen, and that the Heir was male, he couldn't spout off any *real* substance about the witches that held power in this land. He knew there were two other children, offspring from an affair the King had, that weren't considered in the line of succession, but that was...really all he knew.

Emrin clicked her tongue, tapping his wing. "Can you spread your wings out for me? I want to see if there's any more scarring to remove."

With a deep breath, Merrick extended his wings to their full span, waiting for that burn of agony to lance down his back.

It never came.

Sucking in a disbelieving breath, he gave his wings a tentative flap – leagues more than he'd dared move them in almost a month.

There wasn't even trace soreness.

"Gods above," Merrick marveled, peering at the slate grey hide. Aside from some light scarring, his wings looked utterly normal.

Emrin beamed as Merrick let out a low huff of elation, snapping his wings to his sides and throwing them open.

"They feel better than ever."

With a delighted squeal, Emrin clapped her hands together, bouncing on the balls of her feet. "Really? I mean, gargoyle wings...*gods below*. I've never experienced *anything* like that in my training. You have *so many* little bones in there, and even a small amount of scar tissue can make them unbalanced, but I really do think, if you take it one day at a time, you'll be skyborne sooner rather than later."

Merrick scooped the witch into a hug, lifting her off the floor. "Thank you," he said gruffly, stricken with emotion that warmed his entire being. "You've done more for me than I could ever repay."

Emrin squeaked as he embraced her, and yeah, he may have hugged her a tad *too* tightly, but she awkwardly patted his cheek, her warm eyes brimming with tears. "I'm really glad we found you, Merrick," she admitted, glancing over to Tallah and Winnie sat. "Just swear you'll look after Winnie for us."

Merrick nodded, following Emrin's line of sight. A lump formed in his throat as Winnie appraised him with a tentative grin twitching along the corners of her lips, something akin to relief showing on her face as he extended his wings again, every muscle working the way they were supposed to. Merrick held Winnie's gaze, feeling all the tension slip from his body as she saluted him with her mug.

"I swear," he whispered, and though the words were for Emrin, he knew the sentiment went far beyond that single, simple vow.

CHAPTER THIRTY-FOUR
DOVE

FINN DISREGARDED THE PURE loathing on Theo's face, plunking the mismatched chair between us.

With heaving breaths, I slid my palm-sized mirror from the waistband of my skirt, squeezing my other hand to staunch the bleeding. Thankfully, Theo was too busy glaring daggers into his older brother to notice my irises fading from black and silver back to their normal hues.

"Finneas," Theo sneered. "What the *fuck* are you doing here?"

Keeping my head down, I waited anxiously for my reflection to show me I was in the clear.

Finn wasn't the least bit perturbed by Theo's irritation as he placed his wine glasses on the table and sat, lazily tipping up the front legs of his seat to recline backwards.

If I wasn't so focused on making sure my eyes went back to blue and brown, I would've kicked the chair out from under him.

It took only seconds, but the wait was agonizing – knowing if Theo found out I was hiding a lineage gift, I wouldn't be able to steer the conversation in my favor.

Finally, the last embers of rallied chaos magic dimmed, taking the haze of wine with it. With my head clear and my irises back to their regular coloring, I cut my attention to the table, firmly locking my power behind *reinforced* mental barricades.

Finn glanced sideways at me, running fingers through his dark beard. From the way his gaze flitted to me, I could tell he was also checking the color of my irises.

Asshole.

I gave him a flat look.

Sure, he pointed out my eyes change – but did he believe I was too dumb to keep my own gift hidden now?

"Theodoric, are you planning on healing Dove's hand for her?" Finn asked with false concern, reaching across the table to snatch the wine bottle, pouring a half-glass into each yellow cup.

And though the eldest son of King Velik sounded carefree – *bored* even, the raging fire in his expression told me, in no uncertain terms, that if I wanted to pick a fight with him, it should *not* be over this.

A muscle feathered along Theo's jaw.

"I'm fine," I said loudly. "I can heal myself."

Silently, Finn placed a new glass in front of me. I refused to meet his eyes.

Instead, I surveyed the wine with wariness. It affected me so strongly before, and I wasn't sure I wanted to drink anymore tonight.

Or at all.

Ever again.

And now that I wasn't befuddled by alcohol, the desire to tell Theo everything faded, leaving a slimy feeling of guilt behind.

I'd been so sure I wanted to admit to Theo that I had chaos magic.

Until Finn showed up.

Relief settled through me. My secret was still mine.

Well, and Finn's.

And with that sobering thought, I turned to Theo, "I'm so sorry about the glass. I swear I don't know how it broke like that."

"*Luckily*, I brought a second glass," Finn said coolly, tipping his own to his lips.

"I had another one for her," Theo growled.

Finn chuckled dryly, pointedly brushing shards of glass off the table with his hand. "I'm sure you did, Theodoric."

The tension hovering between them gave me the notion that Finn and Theo hadn't repaired their brotherly relationship as thoroughly as their Coven believed.

I fisted my stinging hand under the table, directing a single kernel of chaos magic to the cut.

Pride wriggled through me as neither a subtle lavender glow *nor* a single spark of purple appeared under the table as the slice knitted over, leaving a pinkish line behind.

And chaos magic cleared away the effects of alcohol?

Aside from the fact it was *completely* illegal to have, this forbidden lineage gift was really saving my ass here.

From under my lashes, I watched the brothers appraise each other. Theo's handsome face was twisted into a leer, directed at Finn, sitting between us while radiating smug satisfaction.

One looked like a golden, beloved god, dressed in resplendent garments, the picturesque vision of what a King should be.

And Finn, wearing all black – from his tunic with the sleeves rolled up to his elbows, exposing corded forearms and a deep tan, to the leather pants that hugged his broad thighs – looked like a vengeful, rakish...*ass*.

Tension pounded through the garden like a war drum.

And the longer they haughtily assessed each other, the longer I'd have to wait to eat.

Gods. I was starving. Which is why I stupidly said –

"I heard there's a gala for King Velik in two weeks?"

Theo and Finn whipped towards me simultaneously, and under the weight of their combined glowers, I shrank back in my seat.

Why did I say that? Read the room, Dove.

Theo exhaled, nostrils flaring. "That's correct. It's to celebrate our Father's incredible legacy."

Finn slid Theo's untouched salad closer, picking a couple walnuts out with his fingers and popping them in his mouth.

"That's *wonderful*, Theo." I poured excitement into my voice, hoping I could shake my date out of his plummeting mood.

Finn let out a wry cough.

My exuberance deadened as Theo's attention ripped right back to him.

I pursed my lips, reconsidering the cheery yellow wine glass Finn gave me.

The Dove that quit drinking alcohol a few moments ago was a stupid bitch. If I was going to sit through four more courses with these idiots, I was absolutely *not* going to be sober.

Picking up the glass, I swallowed a mouthful, anticipating the fog that veiled my senses once more.

I frowned.

Peered closer at the wine.

Took another, longer, drink.

And not only did that hazy buzz never come, but the cinnamon-y aftertaste was missing, too. *Was this the same bottle?*

I flicked my eyes up, confirming it was.

A sinking pit of dread settled in my gut. I couldn't pinpoint what exactly was wrong, but *something* felt...off.

"You weren't invited to dinner," Theo clipped stiffly to Finn.

"And yet, here I am," Finn deadpanned, popping another fat walnut into his mouth.

Gods.

Ignoring the foreboding hovering heavily over me, I drained the remaining wine in three gulps.

The moment I placed my empty glass down, Theo and Finn *both* lunged for the bottle.

Exchanging scowls, Theo yanked it from Finn's fingers, baring his teeth at his brother. Aggressively pouring me another full drink, wine sloshed over the rim, rivulets seeping down the thin stem and staining the white tablecloth a deep, bloody, crimson.

"I was having dinner with Dove. *Alone.*"

Finn rolled his eyes.

The butler took that moment to shuffle out with two dome covered platters. Noticing Finn joined our party, he paled, questioning eyes darting to Theo.

"Have the chef make me a plate please, Irvin," Finn ordered. "I'm staying for the remaining courses."

Nodding rapidly, Irvin averted his eyes as he set plates in front of Theo and me.

Theo sighed roughly, the sound turning to a hiss at the end.

Irvin looked mere seconds from anguish as Theo waved him away with a sour grimace that had my insides fidgeting and Irvin fleeing back behind the trellis.

No one uttered a word.

The tension grew thicker, suffocating the pretty garden and completely killing my appetite.

Finn's dinner came out a moment later, and he dove into the platter of smoked meat and golden potatoes with zest. I forced myself to chew small bites of steak, my annoyance festering as I glared at the man who crashed my dinner date. And a sullen Theo pushed food around his plate and stewed in silence.

Even though this evening was officially ruined, I kept waiting for Theo to bring up the heretic in Bramberry again.

He never did.

CHAPTER THIRTY-FIVE
MERRICK

MERRICK FELT LIGHTER THAN he had in a year – really since his commander, and best friend, became soul tied to the most powerful being in Terramere. That fateful night ignited a dramatic series of events, but it took Merrick almost losing his wings to realize how much he'd taken for granted.

And as he stood among witches, in a Kingdom he never believed he'd step foot in, a glimmer of hope looped through his soul.

"I knew Emrin could do it," Winnie said proudly, holding out a mug of tea for him.

Splaying his wings wide, Merrick appreciated the lavender and lemon aroma before tipping the drink to his lips.

"Bet you can get into some interesting positions in midair."

Merrick choked, coughing up the equivalent of spicy, boiling water.

"Anyway," Winnie drawled, clinking her mug against his as Merrick heaved and sputtered the scorching liquid from his lungs. "Grab your bag. We're leaving."

For the second time in mere hours, tears ran down Merrick's beard, though these were due to the dirty-mouthed witch and her viper's cup of white-hot venom.

Between hacking coughs, Merrick wheezed, "Go. *Where?*"

"Ten minutes!" Winnie sashayed away, radiating smugness.

Merrick stomped over to his bag leaned against the craggy wall. Snatching it up, he found Winnie across the grotto with the old crone, the locket Merrick returned to her still clasped in her gnarled fingers.

"Ah, the warrior who returned pieces of lives to the witches of Shadymoss, and the gargoyle mending the divide between our species," the female crooned as he approached.

Merrick bowed politely, "I'm sorry about your town. I wish I could do more to help."

"Bah, *this* town, *that* town." The crone gestured dismissively. "You're destined for greater things, gargoyle. A second chance at life shouldn't be wasted in penance for things you couldn't stop."

Merrick blinked.

Did Winnie tell her he'd been resurrected?

Cutting a glance at Winnie, she looked as surprised as him.

The crone pinned him with a knowing gleam in her grey eyes.

Swallowing against the lump in his throat that had nothing to do with choking on tea, he silently appraised the female before him. There was something familiar yet eerie about her...Merrick couldn't place it.

"Have we met before?" Merrick asked slowly.

Her thin lips tipped into a wry smile. "Maybe."

"What's your name?"

"I'm Lillian Merle."

Merrick widened his stance unconsciously as a wave of immense power emitted from the seemingly frail elder with twisted fingers and leathery skin.

At the shift in his demeanor, Lillian smirked, something reckless and wicked slithering through her pewter grey eyes for just a moment – merely the stutter between seconds before she dipped her chin in a curt nod. "You will always have friends in the Shadymoss Coven, gargoyle. Now, *shoo*. Your future beckons."

At a complete loss for words, Merrick tracked Lillian as she shuffled away, her fingers never leaving the locket clasped around her neck.

Winnie followed Merrick's line of sight. "I didn't tell her anything," she said in a low voice.

Eyebrows shot to his hairline. "Then how did she…"

With a shrug, Winnie loosened a breath from between clenched teeth. "Sometimes, I wonder if witches really are forsaken, or if we've locked the door to our own cage and forgotten, over the millennia, that we hold the key to get out."

"It is *much* too late for you to be spouting ambiguously eerie prophecy shit," Merrick grumbled, though chill bumps broke out along his skin at Winnie's words.

"Then you're going to *hate* where we're headed."

Fucking witches.

Merrick opened his mouth, ready to demand answers, but Winnie stopped abruptly in front of the other two witches who traveled with them, exchanging hugs and words in another language that Merrick didn't understand.

"Isn't the rest of your troupe coming?" Merrick asked hesitantly, glancing back over to the Royal Coven witches while Winnie tugged him closer to the barricade.

"Nope," Winnie said brightly, as if she'd been *dying* for Merrick to ask that stupid question *just* so she could give him that bullshit non-answer.

"So, where are *we* going?" Merrick growled.

With a wave of her hand, they passed through the barrier with no issue, and the moment they stepped outside, shadows pooled across the ground, stretching and rising into the air.

Winnie fluttered her lashes innocently as shadows wove and knitted together, building taller and darker before them. "*Us*? I'm *so* glad you asked. We really have a full agenda."

Merrick glared at her as they stood at the threshold of a swirling, ink-hued portal.

"Well, first on the schedule is a lovely nature retreat, and then we're visiting home, *sweet* home."

Her grin turned diabolical. "I hope you've brushed up on your court etiquette and sharpened your best dagger, bonehead. You're going to need it."

And before Merrick had a chance to spit out a single curse, Winnie pulled them into the swirling mass of darkness.

CHAPTER THIRTY-SIX
DOVE

ANOTHER COURSE CAME AND went without a single word spoken. I fumed while Finn and Theo regarded each other from behind mismatched wine glasses.

The only one enjoying himself was Finn, who kept throwing cryptic and haughty glances at his brother while devouring every bit of food placed in front of him. Across from me, Theo's face reddened, and I wondered how much more he'd endure before he snapped.

Unsurprisingly, it wasn't long.

Exactly two minutes later, as I picked apart a lovely sponge cake that, under any other circumstance I'd enjoy, Theo adjusted the lapels of his jacket.

Sat up straighter.

And, louder than what was considered polite for casual dinner conversation, announced, "Mother spoke with the council, and though *I'm* willing to wait until Father passes, we need a strong ruler now. The day after the ball, I'm to be crowned King."

His declaration sank into the grass at our feet, mixing with the sharp shards of broken glass and carrying the same effect. I couldn't even dredge up happiness for Theo – all I could see was Finn and the flicker of emotions crossing his dark features in rapid succession.

Stunned surprise.

Fury.

Bitterness.

And then...nothing.

Like a wall slammed down around him, Finn donned a blank mask, picking up his wine glass and dangling it between his fingers as if this entire conversation didn't bother him in the slightest.

"It's in poor taste to accept the crown before Father passes."

"The Jade Kingdom needs a strong ruler during these dark times," Theo shot back.

"Right. A *strong* ruler." Finn leaned back in his chair, lips curling up in a sneer. "So, why'd they decide on you?"

Cool hatred was the only way I could describe Theo's expression. In a low voice, the Regent snarled, "I have the Crown, which means I'm the strongest witch of our generation."

Finn swirled the dregs of wine around his cup. Flicked his hazel eyes to his brother. That icy indifference almost fooled me – but the set of his square jaw, the ripple of muscle that fluttered under the shadow of his beard said differently. "Crown or not, you aren't even the strongest witch at this *table*."

Theo stood from his chair so fast it tipped over and landed in the grass. I flinched as pure venom coated his words. "Finneas, do you believe *you're* stronger than *me*?"

Finn adjusted his glass to fit perfectly over a stain blooming against the white linen.

"You are *nothing*," Theo seethed. "The succession doesn't include you and it *never will*. Your title is a fucking *joke*, and if it wasn't for *me*, you'd be slumming through the Shadymoss marshes rolling in shit-filled bogs with your bitch of a sister."

I reared back, lips popping open. I'd never heard Theo be so rude. My stunned gaze darted to Finn.

Finn released a dark chuckle, appraised Theo with calculating cunning. "Must you stroke your own ego, brother? Do you have no one to do it for you?"

Theo's hands fisted at his sides.

"And I never specified *who* at this table is stronger than you." Finn dipped his chin to me.

I paled.

Asshole. Why was he goading his brother about my *level of magic?*

If Finn got me arrested, I'd *kill* him.

I shoved my hands in my lap. But just as quickly as Theo gave me a quizzical look, his gaze shuttered, and he turned away.

Did he dismiss *me?*

Wait, does Theo really believe I couldn't *be stronger than him?*

With the way Theo acted, I was glad I hadn't revealed anything about chaos magic. There was a hidden, darker side to the Regent that didn't mesh with the Theo that kissed me, that put together this dinner, that I *connected* to.

My temper sparked.

Finn cleared his throat loudly before I could do something foolish – like cuss out the Regent.

"My point, *Theodoric*, is that your statement was showy, and biased, and improper. As Heir, your position demands grace and poise."

"Don't you dare –"

Finn hissed, hazel eyes flashing. "*You know* what's out there. Outside your fancy Palace walls. Who's to say one of these *heretics* isn't leagues above you in power?"

Theo stilled.

And for the first time tonight, a thread of uncertainty crossed the Regent's face.

Shifting forward to lean his elbows against the table, Finn crooned, "You didn't manifest a *most wondrous* heritage gift, even if you did it would *still* pale in comparison to any witch with lineage magic. What are you going to do if they storm the Palace? Throw your illustrious crown at them?"

Pressing my lips together, I swallowed thickly, the little food I'd gotten down rumbling uncomfortably in my stomach.

"You're so obsessed with my throne that you can't just be *happy* for me, can you?" Theo yelled.

The air stalled around us.

Finn blinked, like he hadn't expected that to come out of Theo's mouth.

I wished Neera was here. Even if she was invisible at my side. But she was still absent, the link between us untouched, as if she *felt* me calling but wouldn't come.

"That's what I thought," Theo snipped. "You sit here, holding a grudge against *me* for being Heir, though *you* outed *yourself* as unfit to rule."

I sucked in a sharp breath. Finn had gone perfectly, utterly still.

With a wry bark of laughter, Theo continued. "I mean, we would've found out at *some* point before the crown hit your head, but once you manifested that same gift as your whore of a Mother –"

"I suggest you shut the *fuck* up about my mother, before you no longer have a head to crown," Finn thundered, shooting up from his own chair, shadows flaring to life around his wrists.

Covering my gasp by clamping my palm over my mouth, I sat, stunned. This was *cruel*. *Theo* was being cruel.

The brothers were inches from each other now, broad chests puffed, fists clenched at their sides. I scooted my chair back, wondering if they'd notice I left.

"If there's one thing I know about you, Finneas, it's that every day of your miserable existence, you *wish* you were me."

Finn's chin dipped, his teeth bared as they towered over me, pulses of invisible power crackling like static between them. "I've *been* you, and don't think for a *single second* that I'm jealous of your farce of a life. Go ahead, Theodoric, *do it* – rally your stellar heritage magic."

Theo gritted his teeth, struggling to contain his magic. Even if he was holding back, showing restraint, I wasn't a fool. Sooner rather than later, this was going to get physical.

My magic frothed inside me.

I tightened my hands in my lap, begging my power to dissipate, but it was too high-strung, teetering dangerously on the precipice that would reveal everything I'd carefully hidden away.

Without a doubt in my mind, I had *seconds* to get out of here before purple sparks erupted from my palms in response to the heated argument between Theo and Finn.

And like every other time in my life where confrontation became too much for me, I did the thing I did best – I bolted.

"I'm leaving," I mumbled, shoving my chair back. I grabbed my bag and ran out the garden door, leaving the Regent and the forsaken Heir behind.

No one stopped me as I ran down the corridor of the Royal Wing, past the locked door and the leery guards, through the circular courtyard, and into the Royal Library. This time of night, only witches studying late for lessons, and scholars cleaning up from the day would be here. No one would bother me – thinking I was just another academically in-clined witch.

Falling into the chair I'd vacated hours before; tears of frustration boiled over the edge of my lashes. Burying my face in my palms, I sucked down deep breaths until the events of the night faded, and the rush of magic that escaped my mental barrier dulled.

Finn ruined my night with the Regent – *why*?

Knowing him, he'd corner me in my room later with some sorry excuse for his behavior and skew this entire ordeal into another pitiful reason as to why I should stay away from Theo.

Was Finn mad at me for not telling him about the ritual?

Did he know I was lying about the Book of Carra?

He was so *adamant* that I had to avoid Theo...

But after seeing them interact tonight, Finn acted like he didn't care about his brother at all.

The laughable thought that Finn wanted me wound unbidden, once again, through my endless questions. And like last time, I dismissed it with a cynical snort.

And Theo – he was so kind, so attuned to me – until Finn appeared and riled him up. One minute, the handsome Regent was charming and sweet, the next he was threatening his brother while lobbing increasingly harsh insults across the table.

A soft weight bumped my thigh. Neera, mostly visible, lay on the ground next to the table. Her ruby eyes were filled with worry, and with a low whine, she pawed at my leg. Her presence sent a soothing roll of calm through my inner turmoil, and I relented, running my fingers through her smoky fur.

"You should be invisible," I chastised lightly, earning a grunt in return.

There were only two witches in the library, sitting on the other side of the room. We were situated under the second-floor landing, a maze of shelves hiding us from view.

Neera sat on her haunches as I slumped over in my chair, leaning my elbow against the table and resting my cheek on my palm.

I sighed, "Men are idiots."

Neera *harrumphed* as if she agreed.

"You're right." I nodded solemnly. "I should swear off handsome men with pretty eyes, thick, dumb biceps and stupid, rugged jawlines. *Nothing* but trouble."

Dropping my face in the crook of my arm I groaned.

Easier said than done.

Theo was dashing and charming. Our connection kept pulling us together, and I wanted more. If only we had a chance to spend time with each other alone.

I wasn't hunting for anything serious – and I wasn't deluding myself with the idea that Theo was. He would be King. I was here temporarily to translate a mean-ass book. Soon, I'd return to Bramberry and...then what?

"*Carra's tits.*"

Normally, I prided myself on the structured plans for my future. My routine. My quiet dreams of potentially becoming a linguistics scholar – or a teacher for both shadow and light witches.

But those carefully constructed visions were blurring thanks to a Regent vying for my attention and his brother's threats.

No matter how frustratingly handsome he was, Finn had a bad attitude and a shitty personality. I squeezed my eyes shut, willing my irritation to fade.

Did I find Finn attractive?

Yes – I wasn't *blind*.

But that was the only thing working in his arrogant, broody, dick-headed favor.

Pulling the book on chaos magic out of my bag, I settled in to finish translations on the chapter titled *Fae Magic Similarities*. After the dinner disaster and bolt of adrenaline from running, there was no way I'd catch a wink of sleep tonight.

Flipping my notebook open to the page I was currently translating, I forced myself to banish all Theo and Finn dramatics out of my head.

In a few months, Neera and I would return to Bramberry and go back to a quiet existence hidden amongst my home Coven.

Well, I'd have to beg Maude to take her runes down so I *could* get into Bramberry again, but after Theo admitted there was a chance Maude's barriers weren't as strong as she believed...

I straightened.

Gods below. Maude put *banishment* runes up to keep *heretics* out.

Heretics – who were given lineage gifts from Massis *in exchange for warping a veles.*

With a sharp breath, I shoved my notebook to a blank page, scribbling down what I remembered from Carra's bitchy monologue and Theo's lackluster dinner conversation.

Heretic witches were made by Massis.

Massis appeared into the minds of each witch, and *that* is what changed their magic while he stayed trapped in Avamere.

But...

I pressed my fingers into my side, against the scarred blood rune.

Pieces of a very complex puzzle snapped into place.

Massis hadn't given me *anything.*

When Phades urged me to travel back to my body, I siphoned the connection between the god realms and the ritual itself, ultimately changing my heritage gift of light magic into the lineage gift of chaos magic.

Which meant I'd *taken* chaos magic.

"Fuck," I whispered to the grimm.

According to Carra, Massis bestowed chaos magic onto a witch who *enacted* the ritual, who spoke the spells to warp the *veles*.

My breath hitched with the sobering clarity.

Even though I accidentally stole chaos magic, to keep up his end of the deal, Massis still needed to grant one witch a lineage gift.

My gaze shot to Neera.

She'd killed two of the assailants that chanted the spell and started the sacrifice.

But there'd been a third – the witch that ran into the forest once I came back from the dead.

Which meant...there *was* a heretic witch in Bramberry.

And it sure as fuck wasn't me.

CHAPTER THIRTY-SEVEN
MERRICK

WINNIE SHADOW WALKED THEM into a thicket of long reed grass.

"Over a distance, that's terrible," Merrick groaned, doubling over as his insides pitched and rolled. He willed the meager contents of his stomach to stay down.

"Oh, poor, *poor* gargoyle. *Such* a tough life." Winnie pressed her lips into pout, completely unsympathetic to his suffering.

The glow of orange across the horizon line hinted that dawn wasn't far off.

Which made the disorienting sensation of his organs turning to mush while being squeezed in a vice grip worse with the knowledge they'd been awake all night.

"Am I detecting...*sarcasm*?" Merrick asked scathingly, straightening with a wince and rubbing his chest with his palm until the world stopped swimming.

"I'd hope so," Winnie replied dryly, picking her way across the field. "I'm laying it on pretty thick."

Merrick snorted, appraising their destination with a wary eye.

Spanning miles around them, the first rays of light were beginning to expand his vision of the rolling hills covered in reed grass – but he had no doubt their journey headed towards the eerie ruins of some ancient, crudely built stone structure that jutted from the ground like the jagged teeth of a long slumbering beast.

"This is your home?" Merrick asked with feigned shock. "It's so...you."

"Bonehead," Winne scoffed.

"Parasite," Merrick shot back, though neither insult stung anymore. Now, Winnie gave him a smug, all-knowing smile as she upped her pace towards the dark, probably-a-terrible-idea-to-enter ruins.

"You couldn't've shadow walked us *closer*?" Merrick stomped after her, flicking his vision to that of his Sentry to expand his sightline. After everything he'd seen of the Jade Kingdom so far, there was absolutely no way he wouldn't utilize every skill in his arsenal.

"Nope." Winnie inclined her chin toward the ruins. "First off, shadow walking takes a *ton* of power, especially when I carry someone with me. And also, there's banishment runes embedded in the area from when shadow witches were considered enemies of the crown. To this day, no one with my heritage gift can get in unless we're completely tapped out. Only then do the sigils let us through."

"So, you have no defenses? You think that makes this idea any better?"

"I'm not defenseless, silly." Winnie batted her lashes at him. "I have a big, mean gargoyle to protect me."

Merrick huffed, eyeing the hauntingly unwelcoming entrance. He twined through the thread of magic that connected to his Sentry, ready to shift at the first sign of danger.

Unless there was dukhmora activity. Then, he'd have to fight in this form with the bone dagger. He touched the hilt reassuringly. "Of course, I have no qualms about heading into... what exactly are we heading into?"

"This is one of the temples where demon summoning rituals happen. I figured we could poke around, see if anything is worth seeing. If heretic magic is actually chaos magic, I want to explore the temple for clues to *what* Massis is preparing for. If he's gifting something so powerful to witches enacting blood sacrifices with spell work, then I'm worried."

"You never told me why chaos magic changes anything."

Winnie paused. "Do I actually know more than you?"

"I'd guess you know a lot of things I don't." Merrick concluded wryly, causing the witch to grin.

"Do you know *why* chaos magic is deemed the most powerful lineage gift?"

Merrick thought back to the reports he analyzed from Calcity – where Esmeray and Keerian fought against five hundred fae with chaos magic. "I know chaos magic can create desiccating smoke. And..." He wracked his brain. "Fae with chaos magic aren't easy to kill."

"That's a start," Winnie said slowly, "But the *very* illegal book I've read hints at something more terrifying."

At the mention of an illegal book, Merrick's blood iced over. He cut hard eyes to Winnie. "Any chance there's a well of magic in it? Because those are actually –"

"Vessel Books." She waved him off. "Those aren't illegal. Our Vessel Book is revered, we –"

Merrick gaped at her. "Wait. The *Jade Kingdom* has a Vessel Book?"

Winnie slammed her lips together, glaring at him like it was *his* fault *she* mentioned that.

"You know where the Book of Carra is?"

"I'm not confirming nor denying anything, bonehead."

The Book of Carra was in this Kingdom.

And Winnie knew where it was.

Lenna was being forced to search the Prism for the Book of Carra. If Merrick found it first...could he bargain with the cruel King to let Lenna go in exchange for the Vessel Book? The odds of the Vessel of Salvation being in the Ruby Kingdom were slim to none, so would it really be such a terrible thing to hand the Vessel Book over?

Winnie must have noticed how stiff Merrick went because she blurted out –

"Chaos magic is the *only* lineage gift that can kill a god."

Merrick sucked in a sharp breath. Texts published after the God War noted that only a god could kill another god. But if chaos magic could, too, then *fuck,* that really did change everything.

"Why would Massis grant anyone a gift that can kill him?"

Winnie shook her head. "Why would a being granted that sort of power ever betray him? They're receiving chaos magic from initiating rituals with illegal blood runes and forbidden spell work, which means the witches getting chaos magic are evil and *insanely* loyal to him."

That was a solid point. Merrick growled low, scolding himself again for not having his mind speak ring. This was information Irridessen needed.

"Think of this...if Massis gets out of Avamere, and any of the other god realms open, his chaos witches are able to help him fight the *gods.* It's the next best thing to creating a Vessel. Since Massis hasn't stepped into Terramere, he can't imbue a Vessel with god magic, so weaponizing a different lineage gift is the only thing he can do from his realm."

Which led Merrick to another, mind-bending thought. "*Vessels* can kill gods?"

Winnie nodded.

His wings tightened to his sides at the idea of Esmeray or Sparrow fighting a *god.* With a shudder, he knew Esmeray would love it. But Sparrow...she'd never shown an interest in training. Any fights she'd been in, Esmeray was with her.

The mouth of the temple loomed, and Merrick instantly felt as if he was being pulled in too many directions at once. Here, with Winnie. Irridessen – where two Vessel Queens stood with the power to kill a god and no idea they even could. The Ruby Palace, and the Oracle of Terramere.

If he could get Winnie to reveal where the Book of Carra was, he could steal it, go to the Ruby Kingdom, and check if Lenna was still there. If she wasn't, he could bring the Vessel Book back to Irridessen.

A bitter taste in his mouth had him grimacing.

The plan was good, but it would mean betraying Winnie and potentially destroying any hope of an alliance with the Jade Kingdom.

But if it came down to Jade having to choose sides in a war...

He took a long, slow, inhale, keeping his face neutral.

If it came down to choosing a side, Jade would have to ally with Irridessen because the rest of Ingotheria would rather exterminate witchkind than ever partner with them.

Either way, it was shitty. But maybe, if he explained to Winnie...

He swallowed. That was a wild card. He needed to feel her out more. If she was this protective of the Vessel Book, he doubted strongly she'd willingly hand it over to him.

"Are you coming?"

Merrick nodded, rattled over this new information.

"Let's make this quick." Winnie unsheathed her dagger, taking a tentative step past the ring of crumbled stone half wall surrounding the temple.

Even more on edge than before, Merrick followed her. There was no grass or plant life leading up to the temple entrance, nothing but dust and dirt. The wall of rock was the threshold. Now, Winnie had no magic. And with all this extremely important information in his head that needed to get to Irridessen? Merrick gritted his teeth. It would help no one if he died in this stupid, eerie temple. "And why aren't we going to the Palace *first* and coming back here with, I dunno...back up? Light witches who can use magic past the runes?

"Because that's boring?" Winnie unsheathed her bone dagger as she crept past shattered pillars.

"Win, what if chaos witches happen to be holed up in here waiting for someone to waltz in?" They were both whispering now.

"Then, *again*, it's a good thing I'm bringing a burly bonehead who has experience fighting against chaos magic, right?"

Merrick slowed his steps, something in his mind nudging him to ask – "Is it *legal* to walk into an old god temple in the Jade Kingdom?"

"Nope," Winnie muttered, setting her sights on the darkened entry arch. "That's another, *totally* valid reason why it would be a dumb idea to ask the Crown for permission to explore an abandoned temple that somehow opens the veil to Avamere."

"Obviously." Merrick snagged her by the waist, pushing her behind him with a pointed glare. He'd go first. Unsurprisingly, Winnie bared her teeth in return. Surprisingly, she allowed him to lead.

Begrudgingly.

They slunk around the rim of the temple, aiming for the wall with the arched entrance, keeping to the shadows as the sun rose slowly.

Right on his heels, Winnie hissed, "Do you smell that?"

Merrick let his Sentry roll through him. His nostrils flared, morphing into the narrowed, slightly scaled ridge of his beast, the rest of his face holding its regular appearance.

At first, there was only the musty aroma of dry grass and the slightly sweet smell of fertile soil from the field on the other side of the banishment runes.

But when he took an animalistic snuff towards the temple –

Blood.

Chapter Thirty-Eight

DOVE

At some point, the words in the book on chaos magic became blurry, and I don't remember exactly when sleep took me – only that I woke up hours later, rays of early morning sun glowing through the stained-glass window, and my face pressed against pages of notes with half-dried ink that stuck to my cheek when I bolted upright.

Neera was no longer at my side, but when I flung my consciousness down our connection, she sent a soothing pulse back, telling me she would return soon.

I stretched gingerly, a crick in my neck from falling asleep in a hard chair. The library was quiet, only an hour or so past dawn. I folded up my notes, stuffing them and *A Testimony to Massis and His Hidden Lineage Gift* into my bag.

That tricky passage on the similarities of chaos magic and fae magic still eluded my translations, though I was on the verge of a breakthrough with the work I'd gotten done last night. Once I changed, washed up, and ate something I'd go back to the library and continue working on it.

Exiting the library, I pondered what would make sense in the context of the translation. During my overnight study, I confirmed another oddity hidden amongst the handwritten pages... the *words* were from a dead, runic language, but the sentence structure was built like it had been written in Terrian.

As I climbed the stairs to my room, a trickle of witches began appearing, heading towards the kitchens for breakfast. My stomach growled at the aroma of freshly baked biscuits and bacon, reminding me of the woeful dinner with Theo and Finn, and the fact I barely ate.

Keeping my mind away from the Regent, I tossed around what I knew about fae battle magic. It was similar to a light witch's gift, and chaos magic seemed to work the same way – as a blast of power that could be molded into different attack forms.

Light witches could power sigils, and I knew I could too, thanks to my seeker rune experiment that bought me the book in the first place. Which meant chaos magic could power complex runes, and I bet blood runes were easy for me now, too.

I shivered at the notion of cruel chaos witches finding themselves with the ability to imbue the vilest of blood runes with sinister spells, though, illegal spell work aside, I wondered what *other* things blood runes could do. I had the power...shouldn't I experiment?

Snapping out of my quiet musings in front of my door, I blew out a heavy breath, forcing myself from the temptation to research true blood runes on my return to the library. True blood runes were forbidden, but I bet the Royal Library had books on the practice somewhere amongst the vast shelves.

With my hand on the knob, I paused, hoping there wasn't a pissed off Finn sulking on the other side. But, still annoyed that he crashed my date, if Finneas *was* lurking in my room, I'd cuss his ass out in Cravic.

Thankfully, when I cracked open my door and peered inside, it was blissfully, silently, empty.

That alone heightened my good mood, and I took a beat to breathe in the crisp, cool smell of fresh linens.

I made quick work of stripping off my clothes from yesterday, throwing them in the corner of my room to deal with later. Rubbing the sleep out of my eyes and loosening my bun from the tangled band determined to live in my mess of knotted hair, I washed the ink off my face, brushed my hair until it was a huge, fluffy entity of its own, and then spent a solid ten minutes fighting it into a braid that started at the crown of my head and trailed all the way down my back.

Tugging on a pair of flouncy, black pants that cinched at the ankles, I paired a simple sweater with it that draped off one shoulder, before shoving my feet back into my pitiful pair of boots that were long past their expected lifetime. But they were so comfy, perfectly molded to my feet, that I knew I wouldn't replace them until I'd worn holes through the bottoms.

My runestone necklaces still hung around my neck, and I reminded myself that I needed to loudly ask Cordelia where I, just another light witch, could siphon power. Maybe she'd be in the common room eating breakfast and I could ask surrounded by an audience.

I snorted, glancing at my reflection in the water-flecked mirror. As much as I was beginning to enjoy my lineage magic and the Palace, I looked forward to returning to Bramberry where I didn't have to keep up this farce constantly. It would be nice to not be constantly surrounded by witches trained to spot quote-unquote *heretics*.

And maybe it was the jolt of waking up in the library so abruptly, or that I was slowly coming to terms with the fact that I was a chaos witch, but I felt wired, *energized*. There was a certain thrill that came with power, and it brought with it the realization that I *was* the strongest witch in the Palace.

Spinning in place, I hummed to myself for the first time in ages, allowing my gift a reprieve from being cooped up in my well of magic. It trickled down my arms until bright purple sparked harmlessly to life between my fingers and my eyes changed.

But now... staring into the mirror, I tilted my head.

There was a beauty to the fully blacked out iris I hadn't really noticed before. It gleamed like the night sky, deep and endless, reflecting the light from the amber bulb hanging from the bathroom ceiling.

And the hue of my other iris resembled molten silver, glittering brighter than any jewel worn by a royal. I smirked. Theo could weigh himself down with all his gemstones and gold, yet I still shone brighter.

I'd barely had a chance to explore my chaos magic since receiving it. Scooping up my bag, I willed my eyes to revert to normal while thinking about what to get done today, starting with the translation on whatever similar gift to the fae I might have.

With chaos magic warming my blood, I wondered if there were any other books in the library that mentioned my gift. I *did* need practice on keeping it in check without locking it so tightly behind the barricades I erected in my soul –

With a *woosh,* I landed smack dab in the middle of the Royal Library.

For a split second, I stared, slack-jawed at my new surroundings, off-kilter and completely stunned. Then, darting behind the first bookshelf, I doubled over, adrenaline combining with chaos magic, the heady mixture spiking through my blood. A *flutter* against my lids told me my irises changed.

Carra's tits.

With my back against a bookcase, I buried my face in my hands until the world stopped spinning and my brain caught up from where I left it.

Up in my bedroom, apparently.

And by the amount of time it took for me to process what happened, my mind must've taken the damn stairs and the long way through the vacant corridor before settling itself between my ringing ears once more.

Waning *could* be done by a light witch who siphoned power from a fae, but chaos magic allowed me to wane *without a drop of fae power*.

Gulping down lungful after lungful of musty library air, I pulled the small mirror from my pocket with trembling fingers, the glass shaking in my grip. Shoving chaos magic back into my soul, I stared into it until my irises adjusted and I could walk without collapsing.

Well, it was safe to say I figured out the gift similar to fae magic, though I definitely didn't think it would make me so nauseous.

Focusing on the sounds around me, I stayed where I was, every muscle locked, listening for confirmation that someone saw me wane. But the library was, thankfully, not very busy this early in the morning, and everyone carried on like normal, none the wiser to the magic I'd revealed accidentally.

The deep murmurs coming from a table tucked behind the next row of shelves sounded like the witch brothers from Shadymoss, and I could barely hear Master Vole's shuffling footsteps behind the closed door of his study across the room.

I took a breath. Another.

Then I strode purposefully over to the table I'd slept at, pulled out the book on chaos magic and confidently fit the word "*wane*" into the passage I'd been struggling to translate for days now.

Scanning the paragraph quickly, a wide smile broke across my face.

I did it. I fucking did it.

In my notebook, I neatly wrote the passage on *Fae Magic Similarities* in Terrian.

Similar to the fae, witches who receive chaos magic as a lineage gift may also be able to wane. Though not all witches with chaos magic are granted enough of Massis's power to wane a great distance, if at all, a couple witches passionately insisted they received this ability, though their bland testimonials and refusal to demonstrate left a lot to be desired.

I sat back, shimmying my shoulders in excitement. *I could wane.*

Though the unnamed author appeared dubious that waning was truly a gift that came with chaos magic, I was willing to make an educated guess that whoever the author was, they hadn't received enough of Massis's gift to wane.

Another ill-fitting piece of the puzzle, but another piece all the same, confirmed whatever amount of power I took during the ritual, it was more than Massis would give to uphold his end of the bargain.

"Hey, Dovie." Bron appeared from between bookshelves, carrying a plate with three delicious pastries that smelled like apples in one hand, and two steaming mugs of tea by the handle in the other.

"I knocked on your door to see if you wanted to head down here together, but you'd already left."

"I couldn't sleep. Figured I'd get an early start." Taking the mug offered, I took a small sip, sighing contentedly at the notes of cinnamon. "You always pick the best tea flavors."

"You say that like there's flavors aside from cinnamon that pair with pastila."

Bron chuckled at his own joke as he maneuvered his large frame into the seat next to mine. The moment he put the plate on the table, I snatched a pastila, shoving a huge bite into my mouth.

We lapsed into a comfortable silence, translating the secrets hidden in our respective mysteries. About an hour passed before Bron sighed, scrubbing his fingers through his fire-orange beard with a forlorn look. "Can I ask your opinion on something?"

"Sure," I said, unenthusiastically. After Theo's *questions* last night, I wasn't keen on answering anything that made Bron so...nervous.

"D'you think Cordelia would say *'yes'* if I asked her to be my date for the Royal Ball?"

Not what I expected.

"Bronnie," I teased, mimicking his nickname for me. "Do you have a *crush* on Cordelia?"

Bron grumbled under his breath.

"I think you should ask her." I leaned closer, the most romantic idea forming. "And when you *do* ask her you should –"

"Cordelia!" Bron shot from his chair, half-shouting and scaring Cordelia out of her wits as she appeared with a romance book tucked under her arm and a mug of cider in her hands. Bron's booming voice was followed by more than one clipped, *'shut up'* from library residents at tables hidden amongst the shelves by us. "Will you be my date for the ball?"

I stifled my laugh as Cordelia gave Bron a bewildered look. "– Ask her in a romantic setting...like under the willow tree in the courtyard," I finished, though no one heard *me* since Cordelia shrieked with glee and threw her arms around Bron's neck, practically climbing up him and spilling her drink all over the floor in the process.

"Yes!" Cordelia pressed a smacking kiss against Bron's cheek. "I thought you'd never ask!"

"*Never ask*? Cordelia, you told us about the Ball *yesterday*."

"Still." Cordelia gave Bron a sultry wink as she clambered off him. "An entire day is ample time to muster the nerve."

I tuned them out while they bickered or flirted. The heated glances and soft giggles coming from Cordelia insinuated it was the latter, though I couldn't always tell with them.

By the time they realized I was still sitting at the table with them, I'd gotten a few pages of the chaos book translated. Whoever this author was, I suspected they were not as old as I originally believed. There were sentences that translated oddly, with incorrect grammar, as if the writer was fluent in the letters and symbols but hadn't mastered the dead language's complex wording structure.

It read more like...the book was written in code, and the key to the code was the dead language's runic lettering.

"Dove, have you gotten a date to the ball?" Cordelia asked, her bright hazel eyes shining. "Potentially with...the Regent?"

I threw her a withering glare that held no heat, causing her to groan in understanding that it didn't go as well as expected.

Then, as one does with friends, I poured out the debacle of my dinner with Theo, keeping the more sordid details to myself, focusing on Finn's rude interruption, and my escape to the library where I fell asleep.

"So, in conclusion, my only option is to swear off men, in general, for a few weeks. Maybe forever."

Cordelia let out a strangled squeak as I finished my tale with the flourish of an academic scholar. "Dove! *No!*"

Waving her hands erratically, she narrowly missed knocking Bron's ink pot over. He quickly snatched it, moving the spillable target out of range. He'd listened to exactly ten seconds of my story before going back to translate the pages in the Book of Carra, announcing he'd leave the gossiping to his Royal Ball date.

"What you need to do," Cordelia said mysteriously, tipping her chair forward and bracing herself against the edge of the table, "is be perfectly aloof until he comes crawling back."

I snorted, resting my elbows on the table and burying my face in my hands. "He's going to be crowned King, Cordelia, it's not like he has time to pursue me."

"Theo *likes you*. He doesn't invite women to private dinners. He's making his intentions clear."

"But he didn't make *any* intentions clear," I argued.

"Because Finn crashed it," Bron surmised stoically, his focus never leaving his notes.

Cordelia and I gave him a dirty look, but he was too enamored in translating to notice.

"Well, ignore them *both*. Let Theo come to you." Cordelia leaned back in her chair, the legs that were hovering precariously, hitting the ground with a dull *thunk*. "I'm serious – steer clear and watch Theo *fall* to his knees for you."

I considered her advice as I absentmindedly flipped through *A Testimony to Massis and His Hidden Lineage Gift*. The handwriting became more erratic and less structured as I neared the end, piquing my interest immediately.

"Fine." I wouldn't be able to peacefully translate a single word unless Cordelia got my reply. "Consider Theo ignored on the off chance that he comes crawling back to me, and *definitely* consider Finn ignored because he's a pompous asshole."

Cordelia preened, giving me a proud grin before turning her innate gift of interruption to Bron, bombarding him with questions on what he was wearing to the ball.

Their conversation quickly turned into a volley of whispered debate as Cordelia nixed every idea Bron came up with, and I flipped to the end of the book, backtracking until I identified the clear divide between the two handwritings.

The academic testimonials on chaos magic were written in neat lines, the symbols perfectly spaced and evenly inked. But the ending...

I squinted at the first line, where the runic lettering was written with a shakier hand.

After spending so much time reading this book, I could tell it was the same author, though these pages sported small droplets of ink peppered onto the parchment, and the symbols were slanted, as if penned in a rush.

I blew out a harsh breath.

There was a date.

In the middle of the first hastily written page.

I originally missed it because it was so small, slanted over the last words of neat, academic penmanship.

Gods below.

The transition led into a journal entry of the author's life, dating back two years ago – springtime.

I soundlessly mouthed the first line. My heartbeat sped over what I'd stumbled upon.

If anyone finds this book, and is able to translate my code, know I am already dead. They know.

I covered my mouth with my palm, taking a moment to wrap my head around this insane discovery. *Who was the writer? What happened to them?*

Rifling through the book, more and more journal entries greeted me, filling up the last ten pages. My own hands shook as I returned to the first entry, flipping to a clean piece of paper in my notebook.

And then I began the painstaking process of uncovering the secrets of a dead witch who inked hidden messages into a book they wrote on forbidden magic.

Chapter Thirty-Nine
MERRICK

The metallic tang flooded his mouth, causing Merrick to grit his teeth and palm the leather wrapped handle of the bone dagger. Positioning the weapon over his heart, sharp edge facing outward, he readied himself for a fight.

"Stay behind me," he warned, relieved Emrin and her healing magic allowed his wings to spread to block Winnie from darting past him.

"Don't be bossy," Winnie chided. "It's unbecoming."

"Duly noted and thoroughly ignored," Merrick growled as they slipped from the exterior wall now gilded in bright morning light and over the dark, unwelcoming threshold of the temple.

Nothing jumped out as his boots silently met with a raised stone floor. He switched his vision to his Sentry, reptilian pupils blowing wide to assess the interior. The space was empty, but the other half of the ruins were concealed from view by smashed pillars of carved, grey-green stone. He huffed.

Of course, the scent of blood would be coming from there.

"I've been King's Guard, a Captain and elite warrior for both thrones of Irridessen, trained entire squads of gargoyles on agility and flight maneuvers, and fought in countless battles over the last ninety years. Either you listen to me and do *exactly* what I say, or I'll throw you over my shoulder and we'll leave."

Winnie peered around the edge of his wing. "Damn, how old *are* you?"

He inhaled again, though this breath was to steady himself as he prayed for any god or goddess to grant him patience to deal with Winnie.

She nudged him in the ribs. "How old are you?"

"Is that really –"

He stopped himself.

Exhaled.

Winnie wouldn't drop it. There was no point in trying. "One hundred and thirteen," Merrick ground out, surveying the hidden corners of the room and the pile of rubble that formed a bottleneck leading into the other half of the temple.

"I've always had a thing for older men," Winnie stated, crouching lower into a defensive stance as she trailed behind him, the pair keeping their backs to the wall. "Didn't know I was into horns and wings, though. *What* a surprise."

"Are you flirting with me?" Merrick muttered. "Right this moment?"

"I think so."

"Can we shelf that for now? At least until we've confirmed there's no demons or chaos witches hiding in the shadows?"

"I mean, I *guess*." Winnie sighed dramatically as they neared the crevice between smashed pillars. Merrick's eyes, ears, and nose hummed with the gifts of his Sentry form.

A sliver of sunlight filtered in from the cracks where the pillars had once stood, and Merrick felt a bit better knowing she could see, too.

The shift in the air told him there was something on the other side of the crevice, and he paused, pressing back against the stone wall until he could stand over Winnie. Because he couldn't help himself, he pulled her against his chest and bent down, his lips featherlight over the shell of her ear.

"Either I lead, or I toss you over my shoulder, Win," he crooned, trailing his hand up her back, loving the feel of her spine arching into his touch. "And, personally, I'm completely okay with spanking you for not following orders."

"Your trainees must've *hated* getting on your bad side if you're so thrilled to dole out that sort of punishment." Winnie purred back, her palm skating over the bulge in his pants and his now-hard cock.

With a curse, he released her, holding her closer to the wall.

"You're trouble." He glared at her, the minimal light gilding her face in an ethereal, haunting glow. Gods, she was beautiful. All lithe muscle, with a sharp tongue and a wicked sense of humor.

Winnie cocked her head, giving him that charmed little smile. "I'm starting to believe you *like* troub–"

A rustling noise, picked up by his enhanced senses, had Merrick clapping his palm over Winnie's mouth, pressing her roughly against the stone, angling his body against hers protectively.

With hand gestures understood between warriors, he told her to stay still, quiet, and get ready for a fight.

Her eyes widened as his hand covered the lower half of her face, but she nodded, adjusting the carved bone blade in her hand to prepare for an offensive launch.

Merrick waited a beat longer, ears straining, until that noise came again – a soft snuffling from the other side of the pillars.

Heavy boots thumped against stone, loud enough for Winnie to hear. The witch crouched lower, her instincts honed and directed towards their silently agreed upon surprise attack.

Tightening his wings to his sides to keep his body streamlined and his newly-healed wings protected, Merrick snuck through the crevice leading towards the noise; Winnie close on his heels – the two of them moving in perfect sync with each other.

The second they stepped silently into the chamber on the other side of the pillars, the majority of sunlight disappeared, and a menacing snarl tore through the dead air.

It was all the warning they got.

Merrick hunted the shadows for the source.

A pair of ruby red eyes blinked into existence directly in front of him, and he was immediately taken to the floor in a flurry of snapping teeth and thick, black fur.

CHAPTER FORTY
DOVE

THEY ARE STARTING TO realize that I am different now - that something isn't right.

I've hidden my chaos magic, pretending nothing is amiss, but they are beginning to pull away, to question my leadership. I fear they will revolt against me, that their anger will grow a serpent's head, flicking out a forked tongue hissing for my exile or death.

All I can do is act indifferent, innocent. Hopefully they grow bored of their hunt, and all will go back to normal.

I never wanted this.

I never wanted more power.

My physical body was a million miles away. I stared at the unraveled words in my notebook, a chill skittering up my spine.

Whoever wrote this wasn't a witch who received chaos magic in exchange for chanting a spell in a sacrificial ritual – I knew that intrinsically, somehow.

Which made me wonder if the author found herself in a situation like mine, or if there was another way to receive chaos magic – ways lost to time, ways that didn't involve sacrifice.

The sun had finally risen completely, and Cordelia and Bron left a few minutes ago to refill their tea and stretch their legs.

Neither chastised me for spending time *not* working on translating the Book of Carra, and I was grateful they didn't badger me as to why. After I finished the journal entries, I swore to myself I'd work on the Vessel Book, but the mystery of the chaos witch's secrets was too enticing.

Also, Carra's words waited to be translated for thousands of years. They could wait a little longer.

Serves her right for being a bitch.

I stretched my arms above my head, rolling my neck and shoulders, feeling the tight muscles from my nap in the hard chair.

Gods, I really needed to go to bed.

Neera still wasn't around – I could feel her distance through the connection we shared but couldn't tell where exactly she was. But I knew she'd be back soon enough. She probably knew Cordelia and Bron would return, and I'd find her in my room in a couple hours when I went to take a nap.

I yawned, tears burning my dry eyes as I blinked up to the flickers of amber light dancing across the carvings decorating the wall.

Even though it was late in the morning, almost noon, it was quiet. The soft shuffling of books and parchment a lullaby to my mind. Yawning again, I shook life back to my fingers.

One more journal entry.

I'd translate one more and then go upstairs and take a long nap.

As I worked on the next journal entry – written a few weeks after the first – the door of the library opened, and strong, purposeful footsteps stomped inside.

"Dove?"

I froze.

Theo.

His voice rose out from somewhere near the entrance, much louder than appropriate for a library, but after all, it was *his* library. And no one would dare *shush* the Regent.

He called my name again, and I wavered for a moment as a rush of giddiness flooded me. The handsome Regent was searching for *me*.

He probably wanted to apologize for his poor attitude last night.

Cordelia's advice wriggled around in my mind. Her "*ignore Theo until the ball*" plan wasn't going to work if a couple hours after agreeing I jumped right back into his arms.

Frowning, I remembered how he acted at dinner, how he *dismissed me* when Finn hinted that I could be stronger than him.

In response, magic bubbled up in my soul, curious to the simmering frustration warming me from the inside out, as if it wanted to be involved in the decision making.

I'd *left*.

I left Theo in the garden and *now* he came to find me? He probably assumed I'd be with Cordelia and Bron, that I wouldn't cause a scene if others were around.

I bristled. The old Dove would scurry from the shelves, accept his apology and justify his actions.

But the old Dove wasn't here. And I was exhausted and grumpy.

Anger and loneliness wafted up inside me, and for the first time since I'd arrived at the Jade Palace, I truly missed Bramberry.

I mourned for the quiet of the ancient trees with the little town nestled between the thick trunks. The meadow of wildflowers that always grew towards the bright sun, no matter how many witches came and siphoned their energy. My home with its rickety furniture and creaky floors.

Homesick and annoyed, I stuffed my notes and the chaos book into my pack.

Well, this seemed like a wonderful opportunity to work on my waning.

Was it technically running away if I justified it as playing hard to get? Or was I, once again, fleeing from my problems?

I held my breath until I heard his footsteps fade, though his tone got sharper, more urgent, the further away he got. I darted my eyes around, not seeing any other witches.

Chaos magic soared through my veins.

And with a *woosh,* I waned from the library, a victorious smile flitting across my face. If Theo was this desperate to talk to me *now*, how desperate would he be in two weeks?

It was out of character for me to entertain these thoughts, but with the arrival of my chaos magic and the subsequent events that followed, I was changing.

It was too early to decide if I was changing for the better, growing into my own and becoming confident in my newfound power – or for worse. Would I wake up one day finding no familiarity reflected in the mirror?

Ultimately, I knew one thing: the witch who desperately scrambled through Bramberry Forest to escape cruel, power-hungry assailants, died on that cold altar in the ruins of Carra's temple.

And the witch reborn from blood and sacrifice wasn't about to trot out of the bookshelves when called upon like a well-trained dog.

CHAPTER FORTY-ONE
MERRICK

MERRICK ROCKED BACKWARDS, DODGING knife-sharp fangs snapping for his throat.

Across the chamber, Winnie screamed his name, causing the massive beast to pivot, pinning the shadow witch in its sights, instead.

His Sentry screeched, thrashing against the confines of his soul. But the few seconds it would take to sink into that bronze thread and shift left Winnie defenseless.

She had no magic.

Merrick couldn't take the chance.

Winnie stood with her back against the wall; bone dagger in her fist and fear in her eyes. The beast circled, hackles raised.

With a roar, Merrick lunged, slashed his dagger – but before the blade could sink into black fur, the beast just...*vanished*.

Steadying himself, adrenaline ripping through his veins, he scanned the pooling shadows, muscles braced for an incoming sneak attack.

Grimm.

The grimm was *nothing* like the dukhmora. The rabid, power sucking spirits he encountered on the road to Shadymoss paled in comparison to the threat they faced now. Grimm were in a category of legend all on their own. Cunning. Calculating. *Intelligent.*

An ice-cold breeze flitted through the air as the beast reappeared, pearl teeth bared in a silent snarl.

Merrick flared his wings out, pressing Winnie at his back. Thankfully, she didn't fight him. Baring his fangs at the grimm, sidestepping slowly towards the crevice they'd climbed through.

The grimm mirrored their steps with smoke-like fluidity, tendrils of shadow curling around claw-tipped paws.

It *looked* like a wolf, though it was three times the size. With pointed ears pinned flat to its skull, the grimm's head still reached Merrick's sternum.

If they could make it back outside...his strategic mind spun.

Outside the runes, Winnie could siphon. And once she could hold her own, Merrick could shift.

His Sentry was larger than the grimm. Not by *much* – but hopefully a powerful witch and a pissed off Sentry would be enough to deter the grimm.

Ten feet from the crevice, the grimm paused, ruby eyes flashing with eerie, otherworldly power.

The temple chamber flooded with dense waves of shadow.

This was it.

Merrick raised his dagger –

"What the – *Finneas*? You *fucking asshole!*"

From the vast curtain of darkness stepped a well-dressed male.

Winnie loosened a stream of words Merrick didn't understand – though he guessed they were curses.

The stranger addressed the grimm quietly, "I'm fine. Go back to Dove."

With that odd command, the grimm disappeared.

Merrick glared at the mysterious male who merely appraised him with a bored expression in return.

He was tall – though a few inches shorter than Merrick, with a broad, muscular frame and thick, dark hair. The shadows coating the floor billowed around him, keeping the majority of his face hidden. But Merrick made out the glint of a sword hilt strapped to his back.

It didn't seem like their problems were over just yet.

Merrick raised the dagger –

"Stand down." Winnie placed a hand on his bicep. Her order was a mere whisper, muttered under her breath. "And don't say a word."

Shooting her a look of confusion, she gave him a small, almost unnoticeable shake of her head. His lips pressed into a frown as he straightened, lowered his dagger – though he kept it in his fist.

Who was this male?

Tension hovered in the air – taught and volatile. Releasing the connection to his Sentry, his features shifted to their normal form.

With a snort, the stranger flicked his gaze to Winnie. "New pet? I've never met a gargoyle before."

"You have got to be *kidding* me," Winnie sneered.

And Merrick was completely floored when Winnie stormed across the temple, hands balled into fists at her side. As she approached, a glint of hope and relief crossed the male's face.

"Winona –"

Winnie reared back.

Swung.

And punched him right in the face.

The male staggered back. Winnie slammed her palms into his chest before he recovered from the first blow.

"Twenty fucking *years*, Finneas! And not a single word from you? I have to find out you went back to the Palace through *gossip?*"

Winnie's fist cocked back again.

"Gods below," Finneas caught Winnie's wrist in one hand as the other rubbed his chin. "Good to know you haven't lost a single ounce of your temper."

Winnie kicked Finneas in the shin. "I'll show *you* temper, asshole." He grunted and released her, black shadows dragging her away.

"Can you give me a godsdamned minute to explain?" Finneas shouted as Winnie thrashed against his magic.

The shadows shoved Winnie into Merrick, and he grabbed her shoulder to steady her, the grip on his weapon slackening. She shrugged away, snatched Merrick's dagger, and gestured to Finneas with the point of the stolen weapon.

Oh, good. Now she had two daggers.

His focus cut to Finneas.

"Explain how you're using your shadows right now, and *then* I'll decide if you're worth my time."

Whoever this Finneas guy was, Winnie was *not* happy. And he'd learned the hard way that if she wasn't happy, it was in Merrick's best interest to not be as well.

Finneas scoffed. "Sure. If you tell me why you have a *gargoyle.*"

Merrick narrowed his eyes.

Who was this ass? And why was Finneas looking at Winnie with relief, while she looked ready to beat the fuck out of him?

Well, that *was* the same look Winnie gave *him*.

Merrick inhaled sharply.

Gods.

Did Winnie –

"Finneas, this is Merrick. Merrick, this is my brother, Finneas. There. Introductions done. You can leave now," she said pointedly, waving her hand, and the dagger, at her *brother*.

Merrick felt the remaining aggression in his blood evaporate in a rush.

Brother – just her brother.

Thank the gods.

"I dropped the banishment runes a few years ago," Finneas admitted with a shake of his head. "If you hadn't drained your gift, you would've noticed they were gone."

"Why?" Winnie asked flatly.

Merrick glanced from one to the other, able to make out similarities now that Finneas closed some of the distance between them, and the mass of shadows faded enough for sunlight to beam through the gaping holes along the temple roof. Finneas and Winnie had the same tan skin, identical hazel eyes, and matching irritation scrunching their brows together.

But Winnie's hair was much lighter than the dark, almost black, hair of her brother. And she was a lot shorter.

"Because I had a feeling that someday my adrenaline-seeking, hot-headed sister would get the *dumb* idea to come investigate, and I didn't want her to be powerless when she did so," Finneas growled.

"Wow, thanks for letting me know ahead of time – *oh wait.* You didn't tell me anything." Winnie threw her arms out, and Merrick watched in awe as the darkness surrounding her undulated. "Why don't you fuck off back to your illustrious job of being Theo's bitch and leave me alone? I'm perfectly fine without you."

Merrick had never seen Winnie siphon before, but as the natural shadows in the temple seeped towards her, he saw her magic for what it truly was – *unlimited.*

A river of black slipped up her fingers, her arms, coiling around her elbows, sinking into her skin.

No matter what, there was always darkness shying away from the sun, and as long as Winnie could find a shadowy place untouched by daylight, she could replenish her well of power. Forgotten corners of a shelf, the unused space behind a door, the night itself – it was all hers to control, to absorb – to weaponize.

"We need to talk, Winona." Finneas started.

"That's not my name anymore," Winnie snapped back, dark warning hidden in the words uttered.

"Whatever you're calling yourself these days doesn't matter. What *does* matter is that I need your help. Father is dying, and the Royal Coven's having a ball in two weeks – on the night of the full moon. I need you in case my suspicions about Theo's...current infatuation...are correct."

"I don't care," Winnie hissed. "And how *dare* you use father's sickness against me, you selfish asshole."

"I've never been selfish a day in my life."

"You absolutely have!" Winnie cried. "You *left* the second you could, leaving me behind in that pit of snakes for another five years!"

"It wasn't my choice."

"Everything you've done is a choice! It's always been about *poor, misunderstood* Finneas!"

Finneas bared his teeth. "You don't know what I've been through."

Winnie let out a hysterical bark of laughter, a half-demented gleam in her eyes. "I don't give a fuck what you've been through – just like you don't actually care about me! If you had, then you would've taken me with you. But instead, you took the coward's way. You left. Alone. Without saying good-bye."

"You only have one side of the story."

"How was I supposed to get *your* side of the story when you *disappeared from my life for twenty years*?"

Merrick's eyes pinged from one to the other as they volleyed insults back and forth.

"I thought you'd have some faith in me." Finneas spat.

"Turns out my *faith in you* had a nineteen-year limit." Winnie retorted.

"Don't be fucking shitty." Finneas dragged his hard gaze from his sister to Merrick. "We all keep secrets. Don't crucify me for not sharing mine. Have you told the gargoyle who you *really* are? Or are you demanding my secrets while keeping yours tucked away?"

Winnie threw the two daggers to the ground. They clattered noisily against stone as she flung her palm out, shadows shooting towards Finneas.

But he dodged the attack smoothly, dissipating her magic with an easy flick of his fingers. Shadows wound around the legs of both witches defensively.

If the tension had been heavy before, now it was suffocating.

"Stop!" Merrick yelled, advancing on the pair, finally at his wits end with this family reunion. Winnie and Finneas were the same amount of stubborn.

"Stay out of it," They shouted back in sync.

Merrick winced, holding up his hands in mock surrender. "All I'm saying is everyone keeps secrets. That's totally fine if Winnie doesn't want to share them with me."

Finneas chuckled flatly. "If Winona hasn't told you already, it's because she's either embarrassed, or continuing to hold a grudge against her *dying father.* Why don't you ask her why she refused to give you her true name? Don't you want to know *why* she's been hiding in the woods with a rag-tag group of witches? Do you believe that was her *choice*? Or could it be...something else?"

"You don't have to tell me anything, Winnie," Merrick said quietly.

Winnie gritted out between clenched teeth, "Don't be a dick." A tinge of pleading laced her threat.

But Finneas ignored her, striding purposefully to Merrick, hand outstretched. "I'd like to reintroduce myself. My name's Finneas Voronin, eldest son of King Velik, Prince of the Jade Kingdom."

Merrick whirled towards Winnie in astonishment, disregarding the offered handshake.

Finneas chuckled darkly, shoving his hand into the pocket of his black pants. "That's right, gargoyle." He jerked his chin towards Winnie as she seethed with silent rage. "My sweet little *liar* of a sister is none other than Winona Voronin, *Princess* of the Jade Kingdom."

Chapter Forty-Two
MERRICK

MERRICK TURNED SLOWLY TO Winnie. She paled. Though her eyes still held pure, white-hot wrath, there was something else hidden in the depths of those wide hazel eyes.

Fear.

Uncertainty.

And above all...

A guarded, acidic sort of acceptance that had Merrick's heart squeezing.

"I don't care," Merrick replied bluntly, his gaze locked on Winnie.

She blinked, bafflement replacing the swirling angst across her face.

Even Finneas seemed surprised, though he hid it better than his sister. "You don't care that you're harboring a witch the Crown has been searching for? You *don't care* that *you* are now an accomplice to her long list of transgressions against the Royal Coven?"

At that, Merrick let out a rough laugh. "It wouldn't be the first time I allied with someone wanted by a Crown for some crime or another."

Merrick tugged her into his side, throwing an arm around her shoulder. "And I'm *actually*...her prisoner."

Finneas frowned. Shadows darkened around his feet. "Winona, I need you back at the Palace immediately. We don't have time to argue, nor are we bringing your pet."

"I'd prefer to be *prisoner* over *pet*." Merrick growled.

The Voronin siblings ignored him.

"We *were* going to the Palace." With a sly grin, Winnie shrugged. "I'm *shifting* my decision. If you'd be so kind to fuck off, we'll be on our way." The darkness she'd siphoned slithered to her palms, curling around her wrists.

She widened her eyes slightly as she gave Merrick a *look* he couldn't decipher. Squinting, he wracked his brain for what she could possibly be telling him. "*Right*? Bonehead?"

Gods, mind speak rings would come in handy right now.

Finneas raised a hand. "I can't take '*no*' as an answer."

Shadows denser than Winnie's curled from the floor. And Merrick immediately understood what Winnie was saying.

Winnie couldn't shadow walk. She drained her gift before walking into the temple, which meant she needed Merrick to get them out of here.

Shift.

He knew exactly how they were going to get away from her brother.

He only hoped it worked.

Winnie and Finneas stared each other down, magic rallied, daring the other to strike first. Merrick trailed through that bronze thread in his soul, banishing the worry that this would irrevocably damage his newly healed wings. For her, he'd risk it.

His plan hinged on guessing which Voronin sibling would make the first move, and he really hoped he'd chosen correctly since it took a couple seconds to Sentry.

Which meant he needed Finneas distracted.

"Win," Merrick said smoothly. "I'm ready to leave when you are, baby."

Finneas broke eye contact with Winnie to glare at Merrick. "*Ba-*"

Winnie lashed a band of shadows at her brother, just like Merrick anticipated.

And, as Finneas blocked the attack, Merrick's Sentry exploded from his soul.

He hadn't shifted in ages – gods, since before Faune's grotto. And it wasn't until his bones lengthened, his wings grew with reinforced muscle, and ridged, stone-like scales thickened along his slate hued hide that Merrick realized how much he missed being in this form.

Landing heavily on four talon-tipped paws, Merrick fanned his wings wide, snaked his maw towards Finneas, and bellowed so viciously that rubble shook from the precariously cracking ceiling. Finneas ducked as a shower of dust and dirt rained down around him.

Winnie scrambled over to Merrick, clambering onto his back. "Go! *Go*!" Her voice was pitched and filled with urgency as she wrapped her fingers around the short spike at the base of Merrick's neck.

Finneas cursed, wiping dirt from his streaming eyes. Under his command, tendrils of black reared up, morphing into disembodied hands that whipped towards Winnie.

If those shadow hands grabbed her, Merrick had no doubt Finneas would yank Winnie to him and shadow walk her to the Palace.

Whipping around, Winnie shrieking with the sudden movement, Merrick lashed out his spiked tail, effortlessly tearing through the shadows. The disembodied hands turned into harmless smoke.

Finneas *hadn't* accounted for Merrick – and Merrick was more than ready to get out of here.

Before he could strike again, Merrick tucked his wings tight against Winnie, shielding her, as he dove through the crevice, smashing through the pillars with stone horns that swept over his Sentry's skull.

Winnie screamed again, covering her head, though Merrick's wings protected her from the debris. The moment they burst into the entry chamber, Merrick swept his tail, smashing the crumbling stone with one solid hit. The pillars caved in, the booming crash echoing in his Sentry's sensitive ears, though it was worth it – now, Finneas couldn't follow them easily.

Because this next part of Merrick's plan was definitely something he wasn't *positive* he could pull off.

He barreled towards the exit, apprehension and thrill ripping along his churning blood, heavy paws thundering loudly over the stone floor. Lowering his horns, he tucked his wings around Winnie again, crashing through the narrow threshold with enough of an impact that the rock wall shattered behind them.

Sunlight flooded his senses. Winnie leaned forward, wrapping her arms around his Sentry's thick neck. She ducked her face into the crook of her arm – Merrick only knew because her panting breath fanned along his hide, shooting resolute determination through his blood.

He wouldn't fail her.

With a roar that was as much a prayer as it was a battle cry, Merrick flung his wings out wide, kicking up plumes of dirt as he galloped towards the iron gate, picking up speed.

The heavy months spent agonizing, worrying, and finally accepting a bitter truth were the last, weighty doubts he threw from his mind, leaving them behind among the tangle of reed grasses and ruins.

And Merrick *flew.*

CHAPTER FORTY-THREE

DOVE

I WAS GETTING REALLY good at waning.

Landing on the pitch of the roof, spreading my arms wide to counterbalance the blustery wind blowing leaves across the shingles, their mottled brown hues swirling around my boots.

The beam was wide enough to place one foot in front of the other. I turned towards the grey tinged horizon, inhaling the crackle of winter in the air. Dark thoughts drifted with the gust rattling windowpanes below my perch, bringing a sharp stab of homesickness.

Bramberry was my home, but the longer I stayed in the Palace, the more my heart tore between two very different paths.

After Theo's abrupt arrival to the library, after hearing the strain in his voice as he shouted for me through the bookshelves, I couldn't stop thinking about staying here longer.

With him.

But did he want me the way I wanted him?

I raised my eyes to the overcast sky. Everything was moving too quickly yet too slowly at the same time. In two weeks, my self-imposed avoidance of Theo would come to an end. Which meant I had a fortnight to decide if I wanted to pursue something more serious with the handsome Regent.

Was his interest just to take me to bed? Or was he wanting more...finite companionship? Marriage? Love?

Stop thinking about it, Dove.

I didn't believe he'd make me Queen when he took the crown. But before Finn interrupted our dinner, thoughts of a future at Theo's side made me second-guess all my careful and safe plans.

Maybe it was under the haze of wine and the fact Cordelia said Theo never pursued women, but if Theo *wanted* a serious relationship, and we courted for a while, no matter what, he'd be King and I'd be...

I shook my head, wiping clammy palms against my breeches.

Would I have to give up on my dreams to, instead, be duty-bound to Theo?

I wanted to teach, study linguistics, train both shadow and light witches. I could encourage a destigmatization of chaos magic – separate chaos witches from heretics. What I had wasn't the ruthless gift Massis granted his cruel followers. It was different.

Which opens up an entire dialogue about how you know this, and witches may not believe you when you say Massis doesn't have good intentions.

Everything felt heavy and complicated. But as much as I tried not to think about it, the unknown surrounding my future kept bubbling up in my head.

If Theo wanted me to stay after closing the Vessel Book from sordid attempts to translate – would I want to live here? Would courting each other set me up for a life catering to him? To the Crown and the Royal Coven? Or was this connection we shared a piece of a bigger picture guiding me towards a final, larger dream?

Gods below! What happened to not thinking about it – Dove!

"One day at a time." I chided myself amidst a flurry of wind toying with the end of my braid. "No point getting ahead of yourself."

From my vantage point over the circular courtyard below, I watched a witch bundled in furs hurry between sprawling buildings. Another sat along the path lined with weeping willows, reading under swaying branches. There was even a couple snuggled up on a thick quilt, a pile of small rocks between them, etching runic sigils onto the flat faces to create runestones. Even though there were other witches and humans here, the sheer amount of unused space was glaringly apparent. The Jade Palace could house a thousand witches – yet only a third of that seemed to be staying here.

With a shiver, chaos magic flowed under my skin, warming me against the chill of the changing seasons. Counting down the minutes, I kept my gaze trained on the courtyard until a head of golden-brown hair stalked down the pebbled path.

Theo had knocked on my door a few minutes ago, calling out to me again. My knees weakened at his gruff, manly tone – but I held off on throwing the door open and wrapping my legs around him. Instead, I waned here for the chilled sting of head-clearing air.

By the way he stomped across the courtyard, ignoring witches who attempted to speak with him, it seemed he was as gloomy as I was.

I shifted. Maybe I was being too hard on him.

The thought was uncomfortable. I cursed, shifting my weight from one foot to the other. Gods, maybe I should just forgive him. Theo seemed as edgy and anxious as I was.

Only when he disappeared into the hall leading towards the Royal Wing did I imagine my soft bed a few floors below, the warm comforter that I wanted to slide under.

And with a flash of purple, I waned.

I appeared in the middle of my bed, flopping down against the pillows for a beat to collect myself before rolling off the side and beelining to the bathroom. I'd change and head to the dining hall for dinner, spend a few hours in the spacious lounge, translating the next journal entries from the chaos magic book.

Stomach grumbling, I tossed on a heavier sweater, the material warming the chill in my bones. I tugged on a pair of fleece-lined breeches, following them up with my heaviest pair of socks.

As much as I liked the seasonal changes, the fresh smell of pine wafting from the forest, and the constant tang of burning firewood in the air, my physical body *hated* the cold.

Neera appeared as I grabbed my bag. I let out a happy squeal. In return, she whined enthusiastically, barreling towards me. I knelt before she succeeded in knocking me over.

Rubbing against me, her whole body vibrated with excitement as I ruffled her fur and murmured how beautiful she was. Tail wagging, plumes of smoke streaming and fading up to the ceiling, I kissed the spot between her ears. No matter the events leading us to each other, my heart was filled with love for my grimm.

"Are you coming to eat with me?" I asked playfully, straightening and moving towards the door. Just her appearance had my anxiety disappearing. Placing my hand on the doorknob, I waited for the grimm.

The moment I touched the handle, Neera cocked her head, cautiously creeping closer and nudging my bag with her snout. Then – with rapid, curious huffs that sent bursts of frigid air through the room, her lip peeled up, her sense of smell catching something that had her complete attention.

"What are you sensing?" I asked, standing still as her tracking instincts honed on an unknown scent. She sniffed the air again, following a trail from where my bag had hung on the back of the desk chair, to the door.

I pressed my ear to the door, not hearing any movement on the other side of it. Neera whimpered again, more urgently this time, her bulk shoving against me as she dug at the threshold where the door met the floor, her sharp nails gouging large splinters of wood from both.

"Okay, *okay,*" I admonished, shooing her away, my nerves frazzled from her strange behavior. Turning the knob quietly, I poked my head into the hallway. A thin box sat on the floor in front of me - with a note tucked under a bow of white ribbon.

My eyebrows scrunched together again as I glanced around the area – not seeing anyone or anything out of the ordinary. Tentatively, I picked up the box, bringing it into my room and shutting the door behind me.

"Is this what you scented?"

I held out the box. Neera recoiled, growling low in her throat.

I flicked my eyes from her to the present gripped in my hand, uncertainty simmering in my veins. But after a moment, Neera jumped onto the bed with a disgruntled – yet disinterested – huff.

Whatever smell put her on high alert must have faded when I opened the door.

Shifting my bag behind my hips, I peeled the folded paper from the top of the box, my wariness at the arrival of the strange package evaporating as I read the note once, twice hurriedly – and then a third time slower – a grin spreading across my cheeks as the words sank in.

Dove,

I've realized that your avoidance of me is entirely my fault, and I am sick with worry that you may write me off and return to Bramberry while there is so much left to explore between us.

I am so incredibly sorry for how I acted during our dinner date – my brother can be stubborn and protective – especially as he believes I'm lost to the cravings I feel for you.

This gift was supposed to be given to you during dessert, but I acted like an utmost fool and that pushed you away. Please accept this token as a sign of my deep desire for you. If you still hold any sort of affection for me, it would be an honor to see you wearing this to my Father's ball.

And if you have dismissed me completely, keep this anyway as a reminder of the time you spent in the Jade Palace, and as a memento of the Prince whose heart you so beautifully and viciously stole from his aching chest.

-Theodoric

P.S. Don't open this box until you're dressed for the ball. I want my necklace to be the last thing you put on because, if I have my way, it will be the only thing you are wearing come midnight.

I gaped at the note one more time, heart thudding loudly in my ears, imagining Theo undoing the ties of my gown, sweeping my hair from my throat, peppering kisses against my neck as his hands trailed down my skin.

With one last look filled with longing at the wrapped black box, I groaned. My patience was being tested. I wanted to open it *right now*. But if this was a way to let Theo know I wanted him, too, then I'd play along.

Spinning on my toes, I half-heartedly shoved the box in the drawer of my desk so it wouldn't tempt me to open it early. With thoughts of Theo worshipping every inch of my body, I glided across the room, making kissy noises to Neera until she cracked open one eye. I promised to bring her a treat back from the dining hall, hoisting my bag higher on my shoulder. Neera loosened a guttural sigh of contentment, stretching out until her hulking form took up the majority of the bed.

I practically floated down the stairs, Theo's note on my mind, humming a song both joyfully waltz-y and perfectly royal.

Sashaying through the line of witches waiting on food, I chose a plate stacked with leafy veggies and a cut of venison covered in a hearty smelling sauce before heading through the courtyard and into the common area. This time of evening, the communal tables were mostly empty, and a warm fire sizzled merrily in the grand hearth built into the stone wall.

A handful of witches hung around the lounge as I danced down the aisle between two tables towards an empty section of seats close to the fireplace. The smile on my face grew as I swung my bag onto the table. Cozying up on a plush chair, I dug into the vegetables on my plate, swiping them through the gravy to make each bite perfectly savory.

As I chewed, I unfastened the buckles holding my bag closed, the jaunty sounds of Bramberry musicians playing on a loop in my head.

I rooted into the pocket where I'd stuck the book on chaos magic and the notes I'd translated into Terrian, grasping at...nothing.

The music in my mind came to a screeching halt

Yanking the bag into my lap, I scrambled through the contents for the ratty journal.

When that search came up empty, I dumped everything out, frantically spreading the contents of my bag across the tabletop.

Library books, quills, half-filled ink pots, parchment, notebooks.

A chill that had nothing to do with the oncoming winter wracked through my bones as I stood over the table, staring hollowly into my now-empty bag.

After leaving the library yesterday, I'd stuck it into the side pocket and hadn't taken it out again. *A Testimony to Massis and His Hidden Lineage Gift,* and all my translation notes, had sat in my bag, in my *locked room,* since yesterday.

But someone must've known what secrets hid amongst the pages.

And they stole it.

CHAPTER FORTY-FOUR
MERRICK

FROM THEIR VANTAGE POINT in the sky, the Jade Kingdom stretched for miles in every direction, showcasing autumnal hues of reds and orange. With Winnie on his back, Merrick flew as close to the tree canopies as he dared, his Sentry loosening a bellowing huff of relief once they cleared the vast expanse of rolling hills and open fields.

They'd flown for an hour, and Merrick, both unused to flying in general and *definitely* not used to having someone on his back while doing so, didn't want to push their luck. Already, his muscles screamed at him to land, though it wasn't from pain but sheer exhaustion.

He dipped lower, losing altitude swiftly. Winnie squeezed her thighs tighter against his flank, ducking her head as they sank closer to a patch of sparse mangroves, the unique roots arching from the dark earth telling him they'd returned to the Shadymoss Coven.

Nostrils flaring, he glided towards what smelled like a river – hearing the rush and gurgle of water over rocks before spying the source itself. Wheeling around, Merrick touched down on the bank with a grunt, cantering along sodden ground until his momentum slowed and he could safely tuck in his wings.

The babbling water turned out to be more of a thin, stone-filled brook, but with the distance they'd covered, he doubted Finn could find them here.

Unless –

He halted, shaking his horns as Winnie scrambled off his back less gracefully than he'd seen her dismount a forest kelpie.

"Finneas can't track magic, right?"

Winnie shrieked, startling a flock of spirit magpies from the trees. Indignant screeches and glinting, dark-silver feathers filled the air, refracting rays of afternoon sunlight as the beasties took flight, fleeing for quieter groves. Clamping a palm over her mouth, Winnie yelped, "You can *talk* in that form?"

Merrick grinned, though in his Sentry, the expression was closer to him simply baring rows of sharp fangs at her. Settling back on his haunches, his spiked tail flicked, curling around him. "Of course I can."

Watching Winnie through slitted pupils, he was reminded of another time he'd Sentried, surprising Lenna with the fact he could speak. Well, Lenna hadn't known gargoyles *existed*, so her screams had been warranted – but still.

Thinking of the Oracle made his chest hurt, and he shot a prayer skyward that his friend was already safely back in Irridessen. If he got his hands on the Book of Carra, he'd check for himself, but he had to bide his time – not give Winnie a reason to distrust him. If she believed Merrick was up to something, she wouldn't tell him where the Vessel Book was hidden.

The idea of betraying her had his heart panging with more agony. He shuddered, shifting back into his humanoid form.

Winnie appraised him with wariness as he stretched out his wings and rolled his shoulders back, dusting dirt from his pants. Gods, flying felt *so* satisfying, though he was definitely out of shape.

"So...Finneas can't track us, right?"

With a snort, Winnie crossed her arms. "I don't know what type of fancy magic shit you're used to in Irridessen, but unless my brother had the foresight to find a light witch, have the light witch imbue a tracking runestone, and somehow snuck it into my pocket without me knowing...no."

Merrick gestured wordlessly to her clothes.

She glared at him. "You want me to check my pockets, don't you?"

"Oh, Princess, very much so," Merrick replied dryly.

With a frown, Winnie patted her pockets, finding no runestones in them. She checked slowly, telling Merrick she *also* wasn't thrilled that her brother revealed her secret.

"You aren't freaked out?" Winnie asked in a low voice, peering up at him from the corner of her eye. "That I'm a Princess?"

Merrick snorted, moving closer to the bank to sit down and catch his breath. "I figured you were connected closely to the Royal family, but I was more worried you'd tell me you're betrothed to someone who wouldn't take kindly to me fucking their fiancée over a rock."

"I'm not betrothed," she said quietly. "And it was a *boulder*."

It was Merrick's turn to glare at her, though it held no heat as his lips tipped up. Patting the ground next to him, he offered her his hand. "I don't care if you're a Princess, an exiled witch, or betrothed to some asshole with a fancy title. It makes no difference to me."

"Why?" Winnie hovered just out of reach, eyeing him with apprehension. "You find out I've lied to you since the first day we met, and you aren't angry?"

Merrick sighed heavily. "You're allowed to have secrets, Win. I'm in no position to judge you for them."

He dropped his hand, staring across the brook where a pair of vivid green birds perched on the exposed root of a mangrove, their long beaks pointed to the water as they waited for insects to buzz by.

Secrets. He had enough of those to last a lifetime.

Though the pain of losing Sparrow had worn off, and he'd healed from the gutting realization of having a ghost soul tie, it was still difficult to organize his past into a new narrative – one that wasn't bitter – simply peaceful.

Accepting.

The time had come. Really, he'd known he had to tell Winnie since they left the cavern and ventured out on their own. But...if he wanted Winnie to truly understand why her Royal title didn't bother him, then he needed to share this part of himself now.

Merrick dipped his chin, wings drooping low to his back as he glanced at Winnie. Steeled himself. "I'd like to tell you a secret of mine," he started. "A story."

Winnie, arms wrapped around herself, scrutinized him with beautifully cunning hazel eyes.

Patting the spot next to him, he waited until she closed the distance and lowered herself to sit beside him.

Clasping his hands together, Merrick gazed across the brook, though his mind was far away, standing in a grotto across the sea. "It's a story about two sisters who loved each other very much, and the gargoyle that was never meant to love either of them."

Chapter Forty-Five
MERRICK

Winnie stared at him, eyes glassy, as Merrick finished recanting the sordid tale of his ghost soul tie.

"There's nothing in the world I would've done differently," Merrick grunted. The first of Winnie's tears slipped down her cheek. Without thinking, he cupped her face in his palm, using his thumb to brush it away.

They sat in silence for a long while, side by side. Winnie laid her head against Merrick's chest, his arm slung around her narrow shoulders, holding her to him as they gazed out to the slow-moving water, both lost to memories of their own mourning.

He didn't push her to admit anything to him, but when the sky began to fade into thick streaks of pink and yellow Winnie cleared her throat, saying softly, "I left the Jade Palace when I was eighteen. If I stayed, I would've killed my brother."

"Finneas does seem like an asshole," Merrick muttered.

Winnie shook her head, "No – not Finneas. I mean, *yeah*, he can be a total ass, but no. I meant my other brother. My half-brother, Theodoric."

"Theodoric is a year older than I am. Finneas is the oldest, but Theodoric will take the throne once my father passes. Finneas and I..." Winnie sighed. "Our mother, Vanessa, was the King's mistress. Queen Dahlia hated her for many reasons – but the biggest was that Vanessa bore a son first. And my father *did* name Finneas Heir until *Dahlia* ruined that, too."

Winnie let out a colorful string of curses in another language before meeting Merrick's eyes. "I tried to be a good daughter, a good Princess, really. But it was an uphill battle from the moment I came earthside. My mother died giving birth to me, and my father never forgave me for taking Vanessa away from him."

It was Merrick's turn to utter a few choice words. "It wasn't your fault –"

She held up a hand, stopping Merrick. "I know that, now," she said firmly. "My mother was gravely ill while pregnant with me."

"But Velik pushed me away. He wouldn't hold me as a baby, wouldn't seek me out when I was a child, and aside from duties that put me in the same room as him, he avoided me completely."

Winnie scowled, plucking a pebble from the bank and chucking it into the brook. "I was a well-behaved witchling."

"That's...surprising," Merrick commented.

Winnie's eyes sparkled with wickedness. This close, Merrick could see the thick ring of copper breaking up the deep green of her iris.

"No, really." Her breathy laugh made Merrick grit his teeth against the rush of blood to his cock. "I studied hard, spent most of my time in the library, did everything asked of me, and never stirred up trouble. I didn't have a lot of friends, but I *always* had Finneas."

Winnie flicked her gaze down to the bulge in his pants, and Merrick grinned as a slow smirk flitted across her full lips. "Story first, Princess," he murmured.

She rolled her eyes.

"My magic came in when I was six. Finneas taught me everything he knew since we were the only shadow witches in the Coven. And by the time I turned ten and Finneas was fifteen, I rivalled him in power. And he was *proud* of that."

Winnie chuckled darkly. "Finneas tolerated Theodoric, but in my opinion, Theodoric was nothing more than a spoiled, coddled Princeling. And, of course, everything went to *shit* when Theodoric manifested light magic at fourteen."

A cool breeze blustered past them, carrying the promise of rain. Merrick glanced through the trees where purple clouds gathered, splashing dark colors across the sinking sun and golden horizon. He prayed the storm would fuck off. This was the first time they'd been so...open with each other and he didn't want it to end so soon.

In the back of his mind, Merrick knew sharing these pieces of themselves would make it harder for him to betray her and steal the Vessel Book. But, for right now, he let himself enjoy this moment, pretend this was his reality. A reality where he had a partner, companionship. Where he wasn't so...alone.

"Finneas and I are leagues stronger than the other high-tier witches in the Royal Coven. But, to everyone's surprise, Theodoric's heritage gift came in really weak. Instead of pure white light like my Father's gift, Theodoric's is blue – a sign the bloodline's heritage magic is rapidly fading."

"Velik wasn't thrilled that the son he named Heir received a crap gift. But Dahlia was *livid*. She'd never taken on any sort of motherly role with Finneas or me, but once Theodoric revealed lackluster magic, her icy avoidance turned into white-hot loathing. She wanted us out of the Coven and away from her *precious son* immediately – believing we'd kill Theodoric and take the throne."

In the distance, a rumble of thunder rolled through the sky. "Dahlia and Finneas got into a huge argument a few weeks after Theodoric's magic

came in, and that was the catalyst to Finneas leaving the Jade Palace."
Winnie frowned, pulling her lip between her teeth. Merrick leaned his chin
on top of her head, finding solace in her presence.

Winnie shivered as the temperature dropped with the setting sun. Merrick tugged her closer, banding his arms around her to keep her protected
from the gusts of wind picking up intensity. "When Finneas left, it crushed
me. And, overnight, everything changed. I was alone, and I hadn't realized
how much Finneas protected me until he was no longer there."

Merrick hated the tinge of sadness weaving through Winnie's words.
"Dahlia and Theodoric were determined to make my life as miserable as
possible. The way they saw it, Finneas leaving was not simply a departure
from the Palace, but a revocation of his title as Prince. To them, it was 'one
down, one to go.' Theodoric would throw insults at me, goad me, poke at
me until I snapped, and then he'd tell Dahlia and my father that I attacked
him." Winnie snorted derisively. "I mean, I definitely wanted to by that
point, but I never did."

"So, Theodoric's worse than Finneas," Merrick huffed. "And I don't like
Finneas, which says a lot."

With a soft laugh, Winnie reached up and patted his cheek. Her fingers
felt like ice. Merrick caught her wrist, enveloping her small hands in his big
warm ones. "We need to get you someplace warm, Princess."

"Then keep me warm, bonehead. I'm not done with my story."

Merrick wrapped her against him. She hummed in contentment, snuggling into his lap.

"My Father got sicker after Finneas left. He'd have momentary lapses in
judgement where he'd tell me I looked like Vanessa, ask who I was – ask if I
knew her. It broke my heart to see him so confused. Sometimes, he would
get so agitated, begging for Vanessa, that the healers would have to restrain
him, carry him back to his room. And as his health grew worse, he was

confined to the bed, drifting in and out of consciousness most days. Once he was no longer able to siphon or use magic, I wasn't allowed to see him."

"It sounds like Velik really loved your mother," Merrick said quietly.

Her eyes darkened as she stared at the other bank of the water. "I forgave Velik for the indifference he showed me when I was a witchling and tried to forge some sort of relationship with him. For months, we went for walks around the Palace when his health allowed, and he'd tell me beautiful stories of how he met Vanessa, the adventures they used to go on – their love."

"He was trying to make up for time lost between us," she whispered. "I really believe that." The sorrow on her face had Merrick tightening his hold on her.

"I'm here," Merrick promised. "Take the time you need."

They sat in silence as night fell around them. A light drizzle of misty rain started, and since Winnie made no move to get up, Merrick wrapped his wings around them, keeping Winnie dry.

Cradled in his arms, Winnie continued, "The day I turned eighteen, Velik asked to see me privately. Theodoric found out and lied to Dahlia, saying I threatened to kill him, and that I was forcing my father to change the succession to me. I had no idea any of this was being said behind my back. And, later that afternoon, when I headed to meet with Velik, Dahlia intervened, arrested me for treason, and chucked me in the dungeon."

Merrick gaped at her.

Winnie laughed. "It's funny in hindsight because Dahlia isn't as cunning as she thinks she is. By the time she finished bitching me out for threatening her sweet Theodoric, it was nighttime, and I shadow walked out of the dungeon in front of her."

"Gods above," Merrick grumbled, "talk about family drama."

"Oh, absolutely," Winnie replied breezily. "After I shadow walked outside the Palace walls, I decided I was done dealing with Theodoric and Dahlia, and if I ever wanted to return to the Palace, I needed to convince Finneas to come back with me. Unfortunately, he was hard to track down, and, instead, I ended up in the Shadymoss Coven. That's where I learned a royal decree had gone out telling the other Covens I was wanted for treason and that I attempted to kill Theodoric. I spent the next five years with Emrin and Tallah, on the run, never staying in one place too long."

"So, you *are* exiled?" Merrick hedged, trying to make sense of whatever Winnie was alluding to.

Winnie chuckled again, "Not at the moment, I think. Velik eventually found out, sent a personal letter to every Coven Mother saying I was *not* a fugitive on the run for treason and that I could come back whenever I was ready."

Even though her tone sounded carefree, Merrick heard the underlying bitterness there. Especially as she added, "After five years of being on the run, I didn't want to go back to the Palace. Emrin and Tallah had introduced me to the delightful wonders of dukhmora hunting, and we spent another decade and a half traveling together – building our own unofficial Coven and kicking demon ass when needed."

"Therapeutic."

Winnie brightened. "Extremely. Emrin, Tallah and our own Coven of misfits began unraveling the secrets of Massis's heretic...um, *chaos* magic, and that's really just kept me too busy to go home." She said the last part flippantly, which Merrick picked up on immediately. Ducking her head, Winnie inspected her nails.

Merrick snorted. "Too busy for twenty years?"

Winnie let out a laugh filled with spite and irritation. "Time flies when you're having fun getting into dangerous fights with demons."

He opened his mouth to call her out, but she squirmed from his arms, turning to straddle him. With their lips now only inches apart, her body rubbing his in a way that had every thought eddying from his mind, Merrick loosened a hiss.

"And now, the story's over," she breathed, slanting her mouth to his.

Winnie looped her arms around his neck, pressing herself against his growing erection and rolling her hips. Instinctively, Merrick gripped her waist, grinding her against the length of his cock with a heated growl.

It was a distraction. He knew it as much as she did, but as his fingers dug into her hips, eliciting a moan of want from her, he was exactly where he needed to be.

Chapter Forty-Six
MERRICK

MERRICK YAWNED, BLEARY-EYED AGAINST the early morning sun streaming through the curtains. He pushed the white sheets from his torso with a grimace, easing slowly out of the much-too-small bed as to not wake up the witch sprawled out and buried under the mountain of covers next to him.

Careful as to how much noise he made, he slunk into the kitchen, avoiding the floorboards that squeaked if he stepped on them, making his way to the water pitcher sitting next to the stove.

Two weeks had passed since they escaped Finneas and swapped increasingly traumatic stories of their past. The storm finally broke, chasing them from the bank of the brook, and Winnie directed him here. They'd flown before forks of lightning illuminated the night sky, but Merrick was forced to gallop the last few miles once gusts of wind and lashing rain made it near impossible to tell where they were headed.

When the stone cottage Merrick first met Winnie finally came into view, Merrick had been too exhausted to shift back, forced to catch his breath under the eve of the rickety porch, wings drooping against the wood planks and tail tucked up to his heaving snout. Winnie refused to go into the house without him. Instead, she stayed curled up between his flank and the cottage, trailing shaky, ice-cold fingers down each of his spikes and talons until Merrick was able to shift back to his humanoid form and demand she get her ass inside before she caught a cold.

They were only supposed to stay for a few nights to rest – a week tops – but they'd slept for three full days, and spent the next four alternating between sex, hunting in the surrounding woods for food, sleeping, and more sex.

Winnie found the little house abandoned when she was twenty and claimed it for her Coven of misfits as a headquarters for them to store supplies and rest between dukhmora hunts.

Winnie's heritage gifts were replenishing slowly. Once the sun sank below the horizon, she'd wander out into the woods, pulling rich, deep power from the night. Merrick always accompanied her, making sure the witch was protected while she refilled the deep well of her soul, the length of time it took testament in itself to how powerful her gift was.

She could only siphon for an hour or two before she'd get winded, a side-effect of having a heritage gift instead of lineage magic, and though Winnie said she could take out any threat once half of her well was filled, Merrick refused to even consider leaving until she returned to full strength.

Birds chirped and flew past the cottage as Merrick carried a glass of water to the front porch. After waking up from their three-day nap, they'd dragged two chairs and a small table out here, squished between the exterior wall and the thin wood railing separating them from the real world.

From his seat, he could barely make out a faint line of unnatural shadow curling in the air – a smokescreen Winnie erected to keep any demons and witches that weren't in her misfit Coven from stumbling onto their whereabouts. It encompassed the cottage a hundred feet in every direction, throwing a haze against the dense foliage.

"You're up early," Winnie grumbled, shuffling through the front door. Wrapped in a thick blanket and squinting against the morning light, she glanced up to the bright sky and hissed at the audacity of the sun to dare shine down on her.

"And you're not a morning person." Merrick raised an eyebrow as she stumbled towards him, hair mussed and tangled from the amount of times Merrick fisted the short, silky strands in his fingers last night. Once she'd finished siphoning, Winnie rode him again and again, teasing him with languid movements and breathy moans before he flipped her onto her stomach and pounded into her from behind.

"I'm a morning person," she snarled half-heartedly as she flopped into his lap. "Just not when morning comes around *this early*."

Merrick snorted, "Baby."

"Now is *not* the time to try out cute nicknames on me, bonehead."

"I was insulting you, actually," Merrick clarified, propping his chin on the top of her head as she curled into him like a cat. "You're *being* a baby. A whiny, grumpy –"

"Oh, *fuck* all the way off. That's like the pot calling the kettle a dickbag."

Merrick chuckled. Winnie let out a hoarse giggle, swiping his glass of water and chugging the remainder before sighing, her muscles relaxing into him. Merrick wrapped his arms around her, falling into silence as the new day began. Piles of leaves clumped along the ground, their amber and yellow hues browning. Between the changing foliage and the bite of chill in the air, winter was almost upon them.

Winnie peered up at him, a savage twinkle in her eyes. "We should go to the Jade Palace."

Merrick figured this was going to happen. They couldn't hide here forever, and he'd been counting the days down to the Royal Ball since Finneas mentioned it to Winnie. It was tonight. On the full moon.

Full moons no longer made him spiral into depression or brace for a wave of nightmares and anxious frustration, though he wasn't too proud to admit he wasn't thrilled to leave the slice of tranquility they'd created over the past fortnight.

"Do you have a plan?"

"I figured no plan is better. That way it can't get screwed up," Winnie said.

Merrick growled. Gods, this witch tested every single ounce of his patience. He'd strategized battle plans for almost a century. Without one, he felt completely off-kilter. "And what *exactly* will we be doing once we get to the palace?"

Winnie looked up at him with those big, bright hazel eyes, a feigned innocence in them that did nothing to downplay the smirk toying across her face. "You know the Ball is tonight. For my *dying* father. I figured we could go and, you know...*dance*."

Merrick glared at her.

"You *can* dance, right?"

Merrick ran a hand through his thick beard. "Yes, Princess, I can dance."

"Don't sound so gloomy," Winnie said with mock annoyance. It was *possibly* real annoyance – he sometimes struggled to interpret if she was flirting with him or readying to argue.

"Don't be bratty," Merrick countered, catching her pouty bottom lip in his teeth.

Winnie moaned breathlessly.

Definitely fake annoyance.

Batting her eyelashes, she hopped off his lap, tugging him up with her. "After a dance, or two, maybe I'll call Theo out on his shit - *or* maybe I'll have a few glasses of strong champagne and fuck you in the throne room. It's pretty up in the air."

Merrick groaned.

With a cheery smile that simmered with an undercurrent of wickedness, Winnie batted her lashes at him over her shoulder. Her mussed hair shimmered under the sunlight, and Merrick had to physically bite his tongue to stop the word bubbling on his tongue.

Divine.

Excruciatingly beautiful.

The morning light haloed her against a pool of gilded gold. It took his breath away. Merrick parted his lips, letting out a shaky exhale.

A much different sort of tension flickered to life between them.

This wasn't pure lust, not anymore.

This was –

"You're going to need to shift before we leave. I have a lovely idea that I think you'll agree is utterly brilliant."

Winnie rose on her tiptoes, pressing a kiss against his bare chest.

With a curse that Winnie chuckled at, Merrick allowed the gorgeous-yet-insane witch to drag him into the cottage, knowing, somehow, some way, he was getting in a fight tonight.

CHAPTER FORTY-SEVEN

DOVE

I WHEEZED AS CORDELIA dug her slim fingers through the laces of the corset, yanking each inch of satin ribbon as taught as a bowstring. The gown was *gorgeous* – dark green with large gold flowers embroidered along the skirt – which made the fact my internal organs were rearranging themselves bearable.

"One more inch," Cordelia promised, deftly slipping her thumb under the last eyelet.

Bracing against Cordelia's strong pull, I mentally patted myself on the back when she announced she was finished. We'd been holed up in my bedroom for the better part of the day, helping each other get ready.

Earlier, Cordelia arranged my wild hair with precision, turning the wavy strands into voluptuous curls before using two small combs to pin the curls away from my face, letting the length trail down my back to my waist. In return, I'd braided her silky hair into a coronet that wrapped around her head like a crown, wriggling gem-encrusted pins along the braid for extra sparkle.

Admiring ourselves in the mirror, we made eye contact through the reflection and grinned like fiends. Cordelia wore a deep blue gown that plunged scandalously low between her breasts, with long, sheer sleeves that looped around her middle fingers. Her skirts fluffed at ankle length, held off the floor by multiple layers of tulle. Combined with her golden skin and bright green eyes, Bron was going to fall to his knees in awe when he finally got a glimpse of her.

"We look amazing." I bumped Cordelia with my hip. She slashed me a gleaming smile in return.

"I had no doubt we would," she chuckled, turning this way and that in the mirror we'd propped against my bed, skirts spinning and pooling around her like hypnotizing waves rolling across a rocky shore.

Two long weeks had dragged by. With the chaos magic journal missing, I stared at pages of the Book of Carra and spent time with Master Vole, reorganizing dusty tomes and asking the Elite Scholar about the eight decades he spent as a professor.

He was enthusiastic to impart knowledge, making the arduous hours hovering over copied pages of the Vessel Book worth it. After a few days, I'd worked up the nerve to ask Vole for a book on blood runes. He'd hesitated for a beat before gently explaining that those tomes were restricted, though he did offer one that I eagerly started that night, only to find the information vague and repetitive, learning nothing new.

Bron and I made no progress with translations – unsurprising, yet frustratingly disheartening. The brothers from Shadymoss were also unsuccessful, and last I heard, they were returning home after Theo's coronation.

Last week, restless and bored, I'd holed up in my window-less bathroom and inked a seeker rune on the floor in an attempt to summon *A Testimony to Massis and His Hidden Lineage Gift* back. Neera squeezed into the small space with me, though after numerous tries, and her forlorn expression glowing in the wash of purple light, I gave up, more annoyed than when I started.

And to top it off, I hadn't seen Theo at all. He'd disappeared from the Palace, and though his absence *did* mean Finn was *also* gone, I impatiently counted down the days to the Regent's return.

Now, I was flushed with giddiness. The Ball was tonight, and I couldn't wait to dance, spend time with Cordelia and Bron, drink expensive wine, and *hopefully* explore the connection between Theo and me. Privately. With our clothes off.

Cordelia hovered over my shoulder as I eagerly retrieved Theo's gift. The moment I retrieved the thin box from my desk drawer, a shiver rolled up my spine the same way it did whenever Theo was close.

"I bet it's gold," she said dreamily. "Gods, or a jade runestone for you to hold your magic? Or...*oh*, a family heirloom." We paused, lapsing into silence to stare at the wrapping. Her guesses had my knees wobbling.

The way she spoke made Theo's token of affection seem...*monumental*. Unable to wait a second longer, I tore into the gift with trembling hands. We both gasped at the necklace laying in the velvet-lined box.

"*Diamonds?*" Cordelia shrieked as my jaw dropped, gaping at the elaborate gift from Theo.

Four diamonds the size of my fingernail hung from a thick, silver chain like raindrops on either side of a huge, flat-backed jade that appeared almost black in the low light of my bedroom.

The jade sat in the middle, against the chain itself, inset into a filigree of silver. I shifted wide-eyed disbelief to Cordelia.

"He gave me *diamonds,*" I whispered.

"*Huge* diamonds," Cordelia echoed. "And the fattest jade I've ever seen. Gods, it must weigh at *least* a pound, right? Go on, pick it up."

With shaky hands, I lifted the necklace from the box, marveling at its solid heft. Cordelia made quick work of sweeping my hair away from my neck to clasp the fastener.

We both giggled nervously as I stared into the mirror, fingertips stroking the jade. The necklace sat high, diamonds brushing the tips of my collarbone while the jade pressed against the hollow at the base of my throat.

"I fear this is the most romantic gesture I've ever seen," Cordelia sniffed dramatically.

"This has to cost more than my house in Bramberry," I said thickly. "Probably more than the entire *row* of townhouses I live in."

"You don't give a girl diamonds *just* to sleep with you."

I glanced at Cordelia, her solemn composure not hiding the pure glee twinkling in her eyes at all. Her lips, painted the same mahogany shade as her hair, twitched with barely suppressed excitement. "That's the type of gift you give a woman you want to *marry*."

Gooseprickles erupted down my arms at her words, and I swallowed thickly, the jade against my throat heavier with that perception. "That's...no." With a shake of my head, I touched the necklace again. "That's crazy, Cordelia. I'm vowed to a different Coven, and he's going to be King in less than two days."

"If Theo proposed, I'm sure your Coven Mother would understand," she said sympathetically. "After all, the Royal Coven is at the top of the hierarchy, right under the Crown itself."

"But I don't know if I *want* something serious out of this," I replied, a tremor shaking through my soft confession. "As much as I'm attracted to Theo, everything's moving too fast..."

I trailed off. I liked Theo, but as strong as our connection *felt*, we barely knew each other. And I *wanted* to get to know him, to spend time together, see if this connection was truly something special or if it was purely lust and intrigue wrapped in a confusing package.

Cordelia hummed, taking my hand in hers. "You need to do what's best for you. Not what's best for a man – no matter *who* he is. Whatever you decide, you know I'll support you."

"And Dove," she hesitated for a moment before adding, "when you do see Theo, don't apologize for ignoring him. Instead, *thank* him for respecting the fact that you needed time. Apologizing means you've done something wrong. And you didn't do *anything* wrong."

I blinked slowly. "I hadn't thought of that."

With a knowing glance, Cordelia said, "We haven't known each other for very long, but I've seen you flourish here. The Jade Palace is better off now that you've passed through its doors. You're kind, insanely smart, *and* wickedly gorgeous. The whole package, really." We both let out a soft chuckle. Crinkling her nose, she added, "I...as your friend, I don't want you to feel obligated to soothe Theo's feelings for him. *He* fucked up, right?"

She paused, gestured to me.

"Right." I remembered the way he'd acted at dinner. Part of me hoped his behavior could be explained away by nerves and frustration over Finn interrupting us, but since then, something niggled in the back of my mind – something telling me to pay attention.

"Exactly." Cordelia propped her hands on her hips. "So let *him* do the apologizing. Don't shrink yourself down to fit into his life."

She was right – we'd only known each other for a short time, yet I couldn't imagine life without her in it. I hoped she'd visit after I returned to Bramberry. Cordelia sighed dramatically. "With all these self-important boys running around, us girls stick together, right?"

That made me laugh, thanking my lucky stars for Cordelia's friendship. "Absolutely."

"I'm sorry I got carried away thinking of you and Theo together long-term," Cordelia said quietly.

With a dry snort and a raised eyebrow, I deadpanned, "*You*? Get carried away? No way."

Cordelia fanned her face with her hands. "I'm *sorry*," she whined, "but gods – I *love* love."

"*Well* aware." I groaned. "I've *seen* the books you read in the library."

She'd given me a list of her favorite romance novels last week, and I'd already finished two of them. And sure, they were centered *around* love stories, but they were *also* filled with scorching hot sex scenes that made my thighs squeeze together as I imagined Theo doing those delicious things to me.

With the mood in the bedroom light and full of anticipation, I took the deepest breath I could manage with this corset on. Tonight, I wouldn't overanalyze everything. I'd allow my instincts to guide me. If Theo believed I was wrong for ignoring him, then that would be my clue to break this off before it ever turned into something.

Cordelia was right. I'd set a boundary with Theo, and no matter how powerful his title made him, it didn't excuse his behavior.

There was still the matter of my chaos magic, but until Theo and I knew each other better, hiding my lineage gift was the safest option.

I stroked the jade necklace again, the gem cool under my fingertip. Maybe the necklace *was* merely a pretty gift doubling as an apology, and I was being paranoid for no reason.

Outside the window, stars began flickering to life across the night sky, surrounding the full moon that glowed silver.

"It's time to go," Cordelia sang, hurrying towards my door as I ripped my eyes from the entrancing moon, letting out a squeal of excitement that Cordelia echoed enthusiastically.

Tonight, I'd feel Theo out, see if there was even a *slight* chance that admitting I had chaos magic wouldn't end with my head detached from my burning body.

Tomorrow I'd figure out well...everything else.

Chapter Forty-Eight

DOVE

THE THRONE ROOM WAS stunning.

Dark cobblestone walls were lined with stained-glass windows, portraying individualized images of the twelve gods that couldn't bless witchkind through distinctive colors and motifs. The glass mosaics were ethereal, *powerful*, stretching larger-than-life towards the beamed ceiling.

Cordelia steered me left, mumbling under her breath about Bron being late. I, however, was completely fascinated by the moonbeams shining through colorful glass, gilding the floor with streaks of muted color. I could only imagine the throne room when sunlight burst against the mosaics, and gods, I wanted to see it.

There was Beyos, with his long, white beard, hovering imposingly above a churning sea with his hands raised. Faune – holding a vivid orange flower, her serene face and golden hair backdropped by a field of tall grass.

And...Phades, depicted in the window next to the Goddess of Life, sitting on her throne of bones, pitless eye sockets aimed at the dais.

The uncanny resemblance between the artwork and the *actual* Goddess of Death caused a chill to shoot down my spine. I turned away, glancing towards the end of the aisle to the three stepped dais.

"Oh," I whispered. An even larger stained-glass window rose above the rough-hewn throne currently sitting empty. This time though, the restricting sensation had nothing to do with my corset.

An ode to Massis took up the entire wall, the glass making it appear as if the god loomed over the room. After everything I'd learned, seeing the witch god's window caused my skin to break out in cold sweat. To the other witches in the room, the art was an innocent tribute to the god who granted us gifts.

But to me...it was threatening. As if Massis stared down those who assembled, hunting for his next sacrifice.

Unlike the other portrayals, where the gods were easily distinguishable, Massis's features were hidden under a black cloak or...or maybe it was a sheen of shadow. The color palette of the mosaic was almost entirely greyscale, creating an image that appeared dull and matte, the details hard to decipher when illuminated solely by torchlight and the full moon.

Only one part of the mosaic stood out.

I inhaled sharply.

Peering out from underneath the edge of his dark hood, Massis's eyes were visible.

And they were ruby red.

"Creepy, isn't it?" Cordelia said breezily, catching my focus.

Swallowing a curse, I willed my heart to calm. "It's very...menacing."

With a smack of mahogany painted lips, Cordelia started, "The artist –"

"Gods below, Cordelia," Bron interrupted, bowing as he strolled up to us, three thin flutes of sparkling wine held in one giant hand. "You are the most *beautiful* witch in this entire throne room."

Cordelia's face went from screwing up to snarl at Bron – either for interrupting her, or for being late – to full-on preening. Coyly she batted her lashes at him. "Thank you, Bron. And you – *wow*. Incredibly handsome."

"Don't mind me," I said loudly, "I'll just stand here as, what, the *second* prettiest witch in the room?"

Bron rolled his eyes, clapping me on the shoulder. "You're not the one I'm trying to win over, Dovie." The gesture was sweet, though with his gigantic palm and stature, his affection about knocked me off balance. "And, after spending so much time with you in the library, I'm starting to see you as a bossy little sister."

"I'm *older* than you," I protested in mock exasperation.

Bron chuckled lightly, smoothing down the sleeve of his dark grey tunic. "Little as in *little*. Tiny. *Short*."

"Bah," I waved him away. Bron conceded, passing us glasses of wine.

"Fine, you're second prettiest."

I squinted up at him, crinkling my nose. "Actually, coming from you, that does sound weird. Never mind."

A motley of musicians sat in the corner of the room, playing an up-tempo beat as witches danced, some in the arms of partners, others alone. The rest of the Royal Coven milled about, greeting friends, grabbing drinks from the butlers standing around the room, or claiming seats at the remaining tables. Everyone was dressed in finery, the array of colors and fabrics, sparkling runestone jewelry and intricate hairstyles a reminder that I was amongst the richest witches in Terramere.

I drank it all in, committing every detail of the Ball to memory. Once I was back home, I wanted to tell Polina everything. She'd love it here.

We just snagged an empty table near the entrance when Bron announced gruffly, "I'm going to get a drink." His glass was full. As was ours. Bron ducked his head, cleared his throat awkwardly. "Cordelia, would you *please* accompany me over, um...anywhere else?"

"Sure," Cordelia squeaked, throwing me a wink before gripping Bron's elbow and allowing him to scurry her away.

I stared after them, bewildered. *Where were they –*

"Dove."

My breath hitched, warmth zinging through my heart. I knew that voice – had dreamed of it for two weeks now.

And I found the man who infiltrated my dreams standing before me. With his staggering height, Bron must've spied him walking over – hence the quick getaway to give me privacy.

I curtsied politely, dragging my gaze down the handsome Regent. Theo wore a dark green doublet accentuated with velvety hems, matching pants, and a gleaming silver circlet that sat across his brow, holding back slicked, golden-brown tresses. The rest of the party melted away, reduced to nothing but wisps of muted color and sound.

I rose, a blush creeping across my cheeks as I met Theo's piercing blue eyes, the silver starburst around them darker than I recalled.

Forcing him to give me space for two weeks was...harsh. A lump formed in my throat.

What had I been so angry about?

I took a step closer, needing him to know I was sorry - that I *did* want him.

Wholly and completely.

Theo grinned as he noticed the necklace shining around my throat. He'd shaved since the last time I saw him, making his cheekbones appear sharper and dimples more pronounced. "You are absolutely ravishing, Dove."

"I'm sorry, Theo," I said quietly, owning up to my silly mistake quickly.

Theo raised a hand, granting me another, broader smile. "No apology necessary. I came on strong, and you needed time to understand how deeply I want this. But I was raised with the belief that if you *want* something, *go get it.*"

He slid a hand around my waist as he spoke. A simmering heat rolled through my veins, though it didn't flare with the passion I expected. Theo added, "I've dreamed of this. And the moment I first saw you, I *knew*."

I tipped my chin back to gaze into his eyes, my heart beating wildly. At his admittance, I arched against him, willing that spark to ignite. "You've wanted me since you saw me – *at a distance* – from Maude's porch?"

In response, his eyes darkened with desire, and my magic billowed to life, humming through my soul. I shoved it away before it could ruin my chance with the dashing, soon-to-be-King. "What can I say," Theo drawled, glancing away. "I knew you were special immediately."

Theo stiffened, the palm pressing into my lower back twitched. For a second, I wondered if I'd said the wrong thing, before realizing I hadn't said anything at all.

A trumpet blasted from the doorway, signaling a Royal arrival, alerting the party to pause their revelry and show respect.

The herald, a squat witch with strikingly green eyes puffed up dramatically and boomed, "All rise for her Majesty, Queen Dahlia of the Jade Kingdom, Mother of the Royal Coven."

"Come." Theo didn't give me a chance to argue as he towed me towards the procession.

The trumpet blew a final quivering note as Queen Dahlia swept into the throne room, flanked by her ladies-in-waiting. My anxiety spiked in sync with the hush that followed as witches lowered their eyes, sank into bows and curtsies.

The Queen of the Jade Kingdom was the most imposing witch I'd ever seen. She was tall, with ample curves and sharp, birdlike, facial features set in an uninterested scowl.

She had the same lightly tanned coloring as Theo, the same golden streaked hair and bright blue eyes, but where Theo was personable and charismatic, Dahlia was haughty – aloof. Her plum-colored gown was embellished with jewels, the layers of tight fabric draping suggestively over wide hips, finished off with a leather corset trimmed in gold that pushed her full chest up to her chin.

Fine lines cracked the thick makeup she'd caked around the corners of her eyes and lips. It was common knowledge the Queen hadn't conceived Theo until she was over two hundred, but with the amount of cream and powder on her face, it appeared she wasn't keen on displaying her true age.

To my mortification, Theo stepped confidently in front of the Queen's procession – *interrupted it* was more precise. My face flamed. I didn't dare check if everyone stared at us. The heavy silence told me they were.

Theo wanted me to meet the Queen right now?

"Mother," Theo announced proudly, jerking me forward. I smothered a yelp as he deposited me directly in front of the Queen who appraised me with lukewarm regard, magenta hued lips puckering in annoyance. "This is Dove Koroleva, from the *Bramberry* Coven."

I curtsied low, corset digging into my ribs, wishing time would speed up and whisk me away from this awkward encounter.

"The Coven Mother's youngest daughter." Dahlia mused, though her curt tone said she wasn't thrilled with our interaction. "Rise, Koroleva, I absolutely *must* get a look at the girl who is *so* interested in my *only* son."

I straightened, respectfully averting my eyes from the most powerful woman in the Kingdom as my pulse pounded with nervous energy. With a derisive snort, Dahlia hooked a sharp fingernail under my chin, tugging my face up to hers. The action was so unexpected I sucked in a bewildered breath, lips parting in surprise. Dahlia ignored me, sweeping a shrewd gaze from my off-colored irises, down my body, and back up again like I was nothing more than a pretty painting she considered hanging in her room.

"Maude's daughter. The one said to be so...*unspectacular* with magic."

I flinched like it was a physical slap.

And then Dahlia *tsk*-ed.

The sound was cannon fire to my fraying sanity – only made worse as a lady-in-waiting released a nervous titter behind her.

That doesn't bode well.

After an eternity, she flicked narrowed eyes to Theo.

Waiting for her judgement felt like walking towards the pyre.

Queen Dahlia scrunched her nose, disgust deepening on her face. I braced, defending my heart from what I knew would be cutting, dismissive words.

But she never got a chance to utter a single one.

A shrill trumpet blast broke the silence, and the royal herald shouted, his voice ending in a sputter. "All rise for her Highness, Princess Winona Voronin and...good gods, a *gargoyle?*"

CHAPTER FORTY-NINE
MERRICK

WINGS DRAWN HIGH AGAINST his back, Merrick glared down at the stumpy male who held a trumpet with shaking fingers and openly gawked at him.

Next to him, her small hand daintily looped through his elbow, Winnie sniffed dramatically. "A *gargoyle*? What gave it away? The wings? His *horns*? Or the fact that he's *so* tall?"

Few ideas were dumber than this.

Not many, and *definitely* not any that he'd ever be so cunt-drunk to agree to again.

Most likely.

"We're going to walk right in." Winnie snickered last night when he dumbly asked how they could infiltrate the Jade Palace. *"I'm the Princess. Which means I can entertain foreign dignitaries as I see fit. And you, bone-head, are* most *entertaining."*

Not waiting for the herald to respond, Winnie strolled into the throne room of the Jade Palace like she'd never left, chin held high and a savage gleam twinkling in her eyes.

Merrick had exactly one second to steel himself before the evil little Princess was commanding the attention slamming over them. "Don't worry everyone!" Winnie called out cheerfully, "Gargoyles *don't* eat flesh! I tested him with a truth rock."

It, unsurprisingly, didn't put a single one of the hundred witches at ease. Merrick's Sentry bristled, hovering right below his skin.

But then an old crone hobbled towards them, grey robes shuffling against the stone floor. Merrick guessed the male had to be at least eight hundred – if not older. But the crone's voice was strong and clear as he addressed the room. "The Princess is correct – I've had the pleasure of meeting many gargoyles over my lifetime." The male nodded to Merrick. "Welcome, good sir, to the Jade Palace. I am Master Vole, Elite Scholar of the Royal Coven."

That, surprisingly, *did* put most witches at ease, especially as Merrick bowed in thanks to the wizened male and shook his hand. Though wariness still came his way, no one challenged the Elite Scholar's truth.

Gods above, what did he have to do to banish that weird belief for good? Give up meat? Only eat greens for the rest of his damn life?

The room quieted, witches disregarded him completely. He almost asked Winnie what her *not plan* was when Winnie gasped loudly and ran towards a female witch with mahogany hair and bright green eyes waving enthusiastically at her, multiple layers of poofy blue dress bobbing around her ankles.

Merrick followed, shoving his hands into the pockets of his black pants.

The two witches threw their arms wide, colliding in an overly exuberant embrace, squealing with glee and rapidly speaking in another language, neither seemingly taking a breath while talking too fast for Merrick to pick up a single word. But the hands gesturing his way told him *what* the topic of their conversation was.

Him.

A hulking male witch stood next to the females, holding three glasses of sparkling wine. Merrick and the witch sized each other up. The male was just as tall and broad as Merrick, with a burly orange beard that was almost long enough to touch the base of his neck. Thick bronze chains swung over his dark grey tunic, each one sporting what Merrick now knew were runestones.

A light witch, then.

Neither male spoke, though Merrick dipped his chin in acknowledgement. After a beat, the male witch mirrored the greeting politely, though his body language said he'd do anything to protect the short, mahogany-haired female chatting with Winnie.

Merrick raised a brow, inclining his head towards Winnie. He'd keep the Princess safe. No matter what. Sensing his intentions, the male witch relaxed, a knowing smile toying at the corners of his mouth. He gave Merrick a single, curt nod.

Enough said.

Finally, Winnie laughed, squeezing the female witch's shoulder affectionately. The mahogany-haired witch danced away, the giant witch right behind her, glaring at anyone standing in her way. As he lumbered through the crowd, other witches quickly scurried out of the female's path.

"See? I told you it would work. No plan is the *best* plan."

"What language were you speaking?" Merrick asked, cutting his gaze back to Winnie. He was curious, sure, but the lilting accent and almost-guttural sounding words falling from her plush lips enchanted him.

"Oh," Winnie looked up at him brightly, "It's Nonna'vyoor."

"Nonna'vyoor?" He pronounced it slowly. Had he heard that language mentioned before?

Merrick wished he'd paid closer attention to Lenna's jovial partner during the long-winded tirades the half-fae was notorious for getting on about translating...stuff.

"Yep. From a cute little region called *None. Of. Your. Business.*" Winnie tossed her hair back and cackled like a crow as Merrick growled.

Her mischievous, sparkling eyes and never-relenting snark both irritated and turned him on simultaneously. *Gods.*

His traitorous lips tipped into a smirk as she beamed at him, utterly pleased with herself for the joke.

Neither of them were dressed for the elaborately fancy occasion. With the limited clothing options they had living in the woods for a fortnight, their options were either slightly wrinkled black tunics and pants, or black tunics and pants with an assortment of gore sunk into the fabric.

They chose the wrinkled option.

Winnie snagged two glasses of wine from a butler, passing one to Merrick before leaning into him and sighing contently. He banded an arm around her shoulders. "How do you feel being back here?" Merrick ducked his horns, murmuring the question into her ear.

"I'm alright," Winnie exhaled. "Seeing Cordelia helped."

The stir their arrival caused had abated, and the musicians near the dance floor played the first notes of a slow ballad. A violin wail trembled through the room, haunting and morose. It seemed like a better fit for a funeral – not a celebration of a King's legacy.

A King who was still very much alive.

Merrick was about to ask Winnie if she thought the same when a male witch in a green doublet stalked through the crowd, making a beeline for them.

"Who's this?" Merrick grunted.

"Theodoric," Winnie hissed, her words hidden behind the rim of her glass. Merrick's lips peeled back, exposing his elongated canines. A warning rumbled from his chest. Theo paused. Winnie flicked her eyes to Merrick. "Let me handle him."

Merrick released Winnie in case he needed to punch the light magic out of the Regent's ass.

"Winona." Theo nodded stiffly, voice clipped, as if this interaction pained him tremendously. The Regent ignored Merrick and his loathing completely. "What a surprise. What's it been? Ten years since you've been home?"

With a viper's smile, Winnie crooned, "Something like that, Theodoric."

Merrick kept silent, though internally he shouted, *Twenty years, asshole, you drove her from her home for twenty years.*

Neither sibling made a move to continue the conversation. Their seething stares clashed – held. Winnie raised her chin, expression bored. Theo kept his features impassive, though Merrick felt distaste and irritation swirling through the air between them.

"You weren't invited, Winona," Theo chastised quietly, never breaking eye contact with his youngest sister.

"I wasn't?" Winnie shrugged. "That's odd, I received my invitation *weeks* ago."

Did Finneas invite Winnie without Theodoric's permission? Merrick's mind whirled.

"Are you planning on staying to witness my coronation?" Theo frowned, a calculated coolness shifting over his face that immediately put Merrick on high alert.

Winnie hummed evasively, surveying her brother with contempt as she sipped her champagne. "I've come to witness *something*."

A muscle jumped in Theo's jaw, his hands clenching into fists at his side. Merrick widened his stance. If he had to intervene, he would in a heartbeat. There was something...*off* about the Regent. Something unnerving that had his Sentry pacing restlessly through his soul.

There seemed to be more here than a childhood rivalry, more than an Heir's paranoid that a stronger sibling was coming for their succession claim.

A foreboding sensation screeched at him to *look,* to *listen.*

Winnie all but dismissed the Regent to address Merrick sweetly, "Would you like to ask me to dance?"

"Why are you here?" Theo snapped, crowding closer to Winnie. Merrick bared his fangs at the Regent in warning.

"I'd be honored to ask for a dance with you, Winnie," Merrick confirmed gruffly.

"It was *wonderful* catching up, Theodoric," Winnie simpered, as Merrick flared his wings, forcing the Regent to take a stumbling step back to avoid getting hit. "But I'd rather gouge my own eyes out than think about you wearing my Father's crown."

Merrick wrapped his arm around the petite witch's shoulder, steering her away from her *other* asshole of a brother and towards the dance floor where, to his relief, the band had begun a slightly-less-morose tune.

Winnie twirled gracefully, taking his hand as Merrick ambled through the crowd of witches, barely noticing the fact half of them dove out of his way, and the other half simply gaped at him, intrigued.

His hooded gaze was focused on Winnie – the way she moved effortlessly, how her hips swayed seductively in rhythm with the low thump of a drum. She bit her lip, met his eyes with a mischievous smile.

With their height difference, Merrick stooped slightly for Winnie to wrap her arms around his neck, but once she did, she jumped, wrapping her legs around his waist and crushing her lips to his. His body reacted on instinct, fingers digging into the backs of her thighs, deepening the kiss.

"You really know how to make an entrance," he drawled against her mouth. Winnie gifted him a lazy grin soaked in desire as he rocked to the music, holding her against him.

Arching her back, Winnie chuckled lightly, her slim fingers playing with the hair at the base of his neck. She tightened her thighs around him. Blood rushed to his cock. "I've decided how we can make this party more fun," she whispered conspiratorially.

"You're right, I should fuck you in the first broom closet we find."

She laughed, "*Obviously*. I meant *after* that."

"What do you have in mind, you heathen?" Merrick grumbled, pressing a kiss to the side of her neck. Winie let out a soft moan, tilting her head back to give him better access to her throat. The couple dancing respectfully next to them shot Merrick a very pretentious glower.

Merrick flashed the male witch a single fang and the idiot practically ran off the dance floor.

"You're a fantastic dancer." Merrick nipped her silky throat, cock aching with the need to be inside her.

The Princess in his arms preened, as if it was the most wonderful compliment she'd ever received before catching his mouth with hers.

Between passionate kisses, Winnie breathed, "We're going to steal a Vessel Book."

Fuck.

Chapter Fifty

DOVE

I FOUND CORDELIA AT a round table in the corner of the throne room, focus glued to the entrance where guests trickled in. Lords and Ladies were announced by trumpeting squawks that made me flinch.

Was the herald supposed to blow the instrument as loud as possible? Or did he not know how to play the damned thing?

Cordelia sat alone, elbow propped against the white tablecloth and chin cupped in her palm, a dreamy expression on her face – only broken with a wince whenever the herald strangled another honk from his poor trumpet.

"You look like Bron just kissed you," I teased, trying to take Theo's stinging absence lightly. Once the Princess arrived, he'd bolted away with a harried excuse. The only good thing to his abruptness was that Queen Dahlia lost interest in me immediately, stomping past with a snooty *humph*.

"Not yet." Cordelia said mischievously. "But he will before the end of the night."

I wiped my clammy palms on my skirt, still shaky from meeting the Queen. "Why don't you kiss *him*?"

Cordelia grinned wickedly. "That's my alternate plan."

With a groan, I sank into my seat and accepted the wine Cordelia held out to me, taking a greedy swallow. Suddenly, I was *parched*.

Bubbles of fizzy wine burst on my tongue, the crisp taste shooting languid ease through every muscle. It took all my willpower not to chug it and grab another.

"Where'd Theo run off to? I swear, the way that man looks at you..." Cordelia pressed the back of her hand to her forehead and pretended to faint. "He acts like he wants to eat you *and* love you. It makes me *swoon*."

"He went to talk with his sister." I said distractedly, lifting my hair away from my sweaty neck and glancing in the direction Theo disappeared.

I wished Neera could be here. But the grimm had vanished with a disgruntled chuff two hours after sunrise when Cordelia banged loudly on my bedroom door and wailed that we needed to begin preparing for the Ball *now*. Knowing Neera, she was most likely in the woods or snoozing peacefully in my bed.

Once we returned to Bramberry, I'd reveal her presence to Maude, along with my magic, so Neera and I didn't have to hide forever. I hoped Maude accepted both of us, and hopefully my Coven did, too. But gods, I was *exhausted* from the amount of work it took to keep my chaos magic out of sight.

"Winona's the best." Cordelia's voice pulled me back to reality. "And don't worry about Theo, he'll show back up." She rose from her seat, waving over Bron – who was wandering around the dance floor carrying three glasses of wine. "Maybe Theo had to handle some royal thing."

I appreciated the reassurance, but my nerves were frazzled. And it didn't help that the next sip of wine I took tasted flat. Lips scrunching, I swallowed with difficulty, throat dryer than before.

Was it hot in here?

In answer, my skin broke out in heavy perspiration.

Bron plopped down in the chair next to Cordelia with wide eyes. "The gargoyle's *kissing* Princess Winona."

"At least *someone's* getting kissed," Cordelia muttered, glancing sidelong at her date as he handed us new drinks and drained half of his in one sip.

Bron hiccupped, oblivious to Cordelia's not-subtle-at-all comment. "Gods, this is potent." He smacked his lips together. "I know we're supposed to frolic through the wilderness during a full moon, but drinking on the Kingdom's coin isn't an opportunity I can pass up."

Fanning myself more furiously, my entire body prickled with cold sweat, my throat inflamed and raw. Instinctively, I swallowed, cringing against the scratchy burn. *Was I seriously getting sick? Right now?*

Frustration wound through me. If I came down with the flu *hours* before Theo and I planned to spend alone time together, I was going to scream.

Cordelia smiled coyly at Bron. "Is that a Rummerock tradition? Romping under a full moon like feral, siphon-drunk witchlings?"

Quirking a ginger brow, Bron slashed her a heated glance. "Of course, sweets. You can't beat the feel of moonlight on your naked skin." He loosened a deep growl. Cordelia's vivid green eyes flared. If I hadn't felt like shit, I would've teased them mercilessly.

"It's important to uphold tradition," Cordelia bit her lip suggestively.

Bron leaned closer to her, stroking a hand down his beard, the other disappearing under the table. A second later, Cordelia jumped, rattling the glasses on the table. Her dilated pupils cut swiftly to Bron.

Could they be more obvious?

Gods, I did not want to know what they were doing under the table.

I cupped my forehead in my hands, ignoring the heavy petting going on between my friends. Sure – I was *thrilled* they were caving after years of built-up sexual tension, but could they go somewhere else?

And *why* were they having a *full-blown* conversation during it?

Bron's focus never left Cordelia. "Even when we were in Bramberry, the moon called to me. I got busted by Coven Mother Maude leaving the Manor to go walk the woods. Granted I didn't know Bramberry had a *curfew* but –"

My attention snagged. "Wait, Bron – you were *in* Bramberry for the last full moon?"

Cordelia and Bron snapped their heads towards me in guilty surprise. Had they forgotten I was sitting here? It would've been comical if my pulse wasn't pounding over Bron's reveal.

Bron withdrew his hand from – *Nope, not thinking about that.* He nodded slowly, brows scrunching together. "Yeah, we arrived before sundown, well before the full moon rose."

I inhaled sharply.

Theo told me his caravan hadn't arrived to Bramberry until the day *after* the full moon.

Why would Theo lie?

Rising from my seat, I skimmed the area for Theo, but in the packed throne room, it was impossible to locate him.

Maybe he'd simply forgotten the day he arrived?

A bitter taste filled my mouth. I snatched my drink from the table and tossed it back, hissing as the bubbly liquid irritated my throat.

Cordelia frowned in concern, sliding her chair closer to me. "Dove, are you –"

Another trumpet blast yelped over the party. I grimaced as the horrid screech echoed.

"All rise for his Majesty, King Velik Balabanov of the Jade Kingdom, and Prince Finneas Voronin."

Murmurs of disbelief turned to boisterous cheers as the King shuffled over the threshold. Witches jostled against each other for a better view of the aisle.

Finn supported Velik's weight with an arm banded around his father's shoulder. The broody shadow witch wore a black jacket with jade buttons, sleeves rolled to expose his golden, corded forearms. Finn's spinel sword hung ceremoniously at his waist in a jeweled sheath, and with dark trousers hugging his broad thighs and a stony expression glowering from under his rakish beard, I hated to admit he exuded pure, delightful sin.

"Carra's *tits*," Bron whooped, shooting to his feet, joining the Royal Coven in enthusiastic applause. Every clap pierced my skull like arrows as a nasty migraine sunk its claws deep. My sight blurred. Over the din, Bron shouted, "This is *incredible*, King Velik hasn't been to an event in –"

"– over fifteen years," Cordelia finished, beaming proudly at her King, wiping happy tears from her eyes.

I staggered to my feet, grey-ish spots popping across my vision.

Teeth gritted against a particularly agonizing flash of hip pain, I exhaled shallowly. Even though standing made me nauseous, it couldn't dissipate the awe of seeing the King in person for the first time.

Deep lines crinkled merrily at the corners of King Velik's eyes as he gave his Coven a warm smile. Atop his head sat a simple gold crown, and his grey hair brushed the tops of his hunched shoulders. A curve down his spine spoke to the debilitating sickness that stripped away the majority of his mobility, his magic, and kept him bedridden for decades. That illness left the King so frail his sage-colored robe swallowed his bony frame.

Finn practically carried his father up the steps of the dais, steadying Velik as the King grasped the throne's arm rests and gathered his bearings. There was so much angst written across Finn's tight jaw, reflected in his solemn gaze, that an ache burrowed into my racing heart.

Velik lowered himself into his throne, eliciting another round of celebration from his Coven – so exuberant the windows quaked, and dizziness threatened to drop me to my knees.

Finn stood rigidly at his father's side, hands clasped behind his back. The sight of him –the rugged panes of his face, those dark hazel eyes, his menacing stature, all broad and muscular, even the thick tendons in his neck...

I shook my head, desperate for relief from the combination of fevered skin and woozy head. *Was I seriously ogling Finn?*

The Coven lapsed into deafening silence. I fought to stay upright, legs trembling with the effort.

Finn dipped his head, Velik spoke quietly in his ear.

After a moment, Finn dipped his chin and returned to his position next to the throne, glancing across the eager crowd. To my sheer surprise, his eyes settled on *me*.

Our gazes clashed. He jerked forward. Stopped himself, brow furrowing in concern. I panted, heat tearing across my flesh.

Finn's features blurred.

As much as I tried to deny it, I was sick and overheating.

After Finn spoke, I'd head upstairs. Maybe if I slept for an hour, I'd wake up refreshed and catch Theo before midnight. The brazen promise in his note had a blush rising to my cheeks that had nothing to do with my fever.

I want my necklace to be the last thing you put on because, if I have my way, it will be the only thing you are wearing come midnight.

Cordelia would let Theo know I left if he came searching for me.

"Thank you for being here," Finn husked, eyes never leaving mine. "King Velik wishes to speak to you himself, but for the sake of his strength, I urged him to allow me to repeat his words on his behalf. He's reminded me that his voice may be soft, but his heart continues to thump with the lifeblood of this great Kingdom."

Velik mumbled something, and Finn tore his gaze from mine. I glanced around, looking for Theo among the masses. Maybe I could catch his attention, let him know I was returning to my room to rest.

After a sweeping survey from wall to wall, my confusion grew. Neither Theo *nor* Dahlia was here. Princess Winona was missing, too, along with the gargoyle.

Applause rang out as Finn straightened.

Once again, his eyes found me, though this time, a flicker of...of *agitation* cracked through the mask of stoicism he brandished like a weapon.

I swayed.

Finn started speaking again, his voice rough.

"King Velik understands the worry he's no longer fit to rule. My father was informed by the Royal Council that Prince Theodoric Balabanov, Regent of the Jade Kingdom, will be crowned King tomorrow evening."

A single witch applauded.

Someone coughed.

The clapping stopped.

King Velik feebly called Finn. Finn dutifully leaned down to receive more of the King's message. I squinted, scanning the Coven again.

Still no sign of Theo or the Queen.

Still no gargoyle wings – no Princess.

I settled my tilting vision back to the dais.

Just in time to catch Finn tense and stare incredulously at his father.

King Velik nodded – once. Finn shook his head vehemently, arguing *against* his father's message, his features tightening into something akin to torment.

From the nervous rumbles breaking across the throne room, no one could hear Finn, though his mouth moved furiously as he countered whatever the King decreed, blood leeching from his face.

"What d'you think the King's said?" Bron asked worriedly.

Cordelia frowned, fiddling anxiously with the silver ring on her finger. "Whatever it is, I don't think Finn was aware until this exact moment."

Icy sweat dripped down my neck. I wouldn't have been surprised if my breath plumed in the air like it did in Bramberry Forest after snow fell.

Parting my lips, I wheezed, forcing my vision to the dais.

Just a few more minutes, and then I could lay in bed. Hopefully Neera was up there and ready to snuggle. The grimm's presence always made me feel better.

Shuffling steps and whispered conversation floated through the air as the witches grew antsy.

Something big was happening, though what – no one knew.

King Velik waved Finn away, mouthing an order and gesturing for Finn to address the Coven.

Finn staggered back, scrubbing his beard roughly, hands shaking as bad as my own.

I braced myself against the back of my chair, a startling sensation curling through my chest. Not in pain – recognition.

It bathed Finn in a new light – one that had me second-guessing every interaction we'd ever shared. Finn acted icy, arrogant, calculating.

Acted.

But this...*this* was Finn. The *real* Finn.

It was the rawest and most vulnerable I'd ever seen him.

He stared at his father for another long moment, trepidation in his haunted eyes. Finn's throat bobbed, lips parting ever so slightly.

King Velik leaned back in the throne and nodded encouragingly to his son.

Finn took one step forward.

Two.

Closed his eyes.

And like a flame guttered by a single breath, when Finn opened them again, every desperate emotion was firmly concealed behind that blank mask.

"My father, King Velik, of sound mind and failing body, has declared an immediate change to the line of succession." Gasps shot up throughout the Royal Coven. I pressed my hand over my heart, trying and failing to stifle my own shock.

"The throne will no longer fall to Prince Theodoric." Finn steeled himself with a rough breath. His tormented eyes flicked up – met mine.

"It falls to *me*, Crown Prince Finneas Voronin, *Heir* to the Jade Kingdom."

Chapter Fifty-One

DOVE

"What is going on, Finneas?" Queen Dahlia snapped, storming into the throne room with a sneer twisting her overly lined lips.

The herald, still slack-jawed from Finn's announcement, scrambled to raise his trumpet and announce the Queen. Before the instrument touched his lips, Theo shoved past, knocking the trumpet out of the squat witch's hands as he strode across the threshold on Dahlia's heels.

From the absolute wrath churning across Theo's furious expression, it was safe to assume he'd heard the decree.

Theo was supposed to be crowned tomorrow.

"King Velik requested to speak with *his* Coven," Finn growled, standing protectively between his father and the Queen as she fisted her skirts in a white-knuckled hand, approaching the steps of the dais. My vision spotted.

"*I* am Coven Mother," Dahlia screeched. "Royal decrees go through *me*. He is *sick*, Finneas! How dare you get this poor man out of bed and parade him about. Velik should be *resting*!"

Velik said something, though his words were too soft to hear.

Master Vole hustled forward, intercepting the Queen before she reached the steps. Before Dahlia could knock the Elite Scholar aside, he flung his arms out wide, white light magic sparking at his fingertips.

The Queen recoiled.

That small glint of magic might as well have been a sword pointed directly at Dahlia's throat.

Even though a healthy dose of fear wavered his voice, Vole raised his chin in defiance. "Your Majesty, King Velik announced a change in succession to the Coven as a *whole*. I cannot, in good faith, disregard my King's ruling."

Theo's face fell flat.

He paused, scanned the room.

"*The King is not in his right mind,*" Queen Dahlia shrieked, jabbing a sharp fingernail into Vole's shoulder. "There will be *no* changes to succession. Prince Theodoric Balabanov will be crowned tomorrow night as the *Council* approved."

Finn leveled a glare at Dahlia, crossed his arms. "Then call a council meeting. Now."

"No," Dahlia hissed.

One word, and the heaviness in the room thrummed with the promise of violence.

Another sharp slice of pain shot through my head. Through slitted eyes, I scanned the throne room.

Where was –

Theo wasn't standing in the aisle anymore.

He was ducking through the crowd under the mosaic of Faune, head bowed, neck muscles strained and corded, as if he fought the urge to scream. Even with my skin breaking out in cold sweat and every muscle aching, I wanted to take that anguish off his shoulders.

Tonight was supposed to be a celebration of Velik's legacy, the exciting beginning of Theo's reign. I tracked him from the corner of my eye, wishing I could alleviate the insurmountable pain he undoubtedly felt.

But I didn't know what to say.

And...I was conflicted.

Taking my affection for Theo out of the equation, I weighed facts only. If Theo was crowned against the King's wishes, it was treason.

Yet, if Dahlia convinced the Royal Coven that Velik wasn't in his right mind, Finn's claim to the throne would be void. Which went against what Velik decreed.

Finn and Dahlia squared off, Master Vole between them. Dahlia drew herself up, gesturing at a royal guard stationed near the base of the dais. "Escort King Velik back to his room immediately."

The guard shrank back.

Velik smirked.

"Queen Dahlia, please – we must bring this before the Council," Vole argued. "The King *publicly* renounced Prince Theodoric's claim *with sound mind*. Not only has the entire Royal Coven heard the King's decree, but the majority of the Council is in the Palace, *right now.*"

Cordelia shifted next to me, magic illuminating her palm. Her sharp gaze was pinned on Finn, but the mahogany-painted lip trapped between her teeth spoke to her own indecisiveness.

Clearly, I wasn't the only one uncertain.

Another bout of dizziness slammed into me. I grappled for the back of my chair, catching myself before I collapsed. Gods, this was the absolute *worst* time to get sick.

Finn dropped his arms, fingers flexing at his sides. Shadows slithered around his feet, insinuating a volatile escalation to an already delicate situation. "Either you call the Council, or I will."

Dahlia's birdlike features pinched as Finn's magic spread. "You'd dare attack the *Queen* of the Jade Kingdom?"

Finn's face hardened, and the utter loathing in his eyes answered that question for her.

In response, light magic bathed Dahlia's angular face.

Vole braced himself.

Dahlia raised a glowing palm –

A whorl of darkness erupted from the floor to the right of the throne, drawing everyone's attention.

Princess Winona shadow walked onto the dais, followed by the hulking gargoyle, a dagger in his massive fist. Tendrils of shadow danced between Winona's fingers as she bared her teeth at the Queen. "I'd think long and hard about my next move if I were you, Dahlia. Finneas is *much* more refined than I am."

"Wonderful," Dahlia sniffed, though her hand lowered. "The King's *illegitimate* children finally return home when he is at his weakest and most confused – just to bully him into changing the succession from his *rightful* Heir."

More sparks of magic flickered to life around the throne room.

Velik seemed completely at ease, merely watching the scene unfold before him with his elbow propped against the throne's arm rest, chin in hand.

But the King appeared relaxed. Around the room, witches edged closer, magic rallied.

Were they defending the King, Finn, and Winona?

Or were they siding with their Coven Mother? Ready to protect their Queen?

Master Vole trembled like a leaf, but to his credit, stayed rooted to the floor, guarding the foot of the dais.

Rivulets of sweat slid down my scorching flesh as my head throbbed. I pressed my lips together, a whole new host of problems rearing up.

This wasn't my fight if it was considered Coven-related. I was vowed to Bramberry – technically speaking, I wasn't *allowed* to get involved.

But it *was* my fight, as a citizen of the Jade Kingdom, if the throne was at risk.

It didn't matter, though, overall. I couldn't defend *either* side with *forbidden fucking chaos magic* – not without revealing my secret to every witch in this room while I was already at the disadvantage of being sick and weak.

I glanced to the door.

If fighting did break out, I could wane. Granted, it would create a purple flash, but if everyone was distracted, no one should realize it was me – or they'd chalk it up to a weird trick of the light seeing as we were surrounded by colorful stained glass.

But the idea of running left a sour taste in my dry mouth. I cared for witches in this room, and if I ran, I'd be leaving my friends unprotected.

The Coven at the Queen's back tittered nervously, torn between allegiances. Lovers side-eyed each other with suspicion, easing apart to put distance between them. Others exchanged grim nods, intertwining glowing palms together.

I took the deepest breath I could manage. My migraine *pounded*.

I was going to throw up.

A hand grabbed my shoulder. I whirled around, biting down a shrill scream.

Screwing my eyes shut, I opened them to Theo, hand extended, with pleading eyes. "Come with me – it isn't safe for you here."

His hair was mussed and limp, sticking up around the rim of his crown as if he'd run his fingers through it a hundred times over the last few minutes. A reckless, panicked mania burned through his eyes. I hesitated, my gaze slipping to Finn on the dais.

Theo cursed as he tracked my sightline to his brother. I grimaced, swallowed against my raw, burning throat. Before I could say anything, Theo snatched my wrist and roughly yanked me away from the table.

"Wait –" I fought to free myself, searching for Bron and Cordelia, but they'd moved closer to the dais.

"*Now, Dove,*" Theo begged, a wild tremor lacing his demand. Faster than I could anticipate, he overpowered my already shaky resolve, rushing me from the throne room without sparing me, or his family, a backwards glance.

I stumbled, collecting my skirts in one hand as Theo pulled me down an empty hallway, the throne room disappearing as we entered a dimly lit passage that smelled strongly of mold and decay.

"Theo, you need to be in there – just...hear your father out." I hurried behind him on wobbly legs. But he only increased his speed and pressure on my wrist, tugging me deeper through the deserted Palace.

"I'm sure your father isn't feeling the best, but I *really* think you should talk to him, sort this out diplomatically."

Theo ignored me, shoving open an iron door.

As I staggered, doing my best not to faint, magic roared to life behind the barricades I'd erected in my soul. With it, heady nausea crashed over me as I fumbled for control of the antagonized power battering against my mental shields.

One blink, and we were outside the Palace walls, running through night-soaked trees.

I squinted through the darkness, the air frigid and sharp, causing my teeth to start chattering immediately.

"Theo, *stop*, let's talk about this – I know tonight was...unexpected, but I'm here for you."

Silence.

"I don't feel good, Theo, I'm going to…" My stomach pitched, in sync with an onslaught of head pain.

"Theo," I locked my knees, attempting to wrench my wrist free. *"Stop running."*

To my horror, purple sparked in my peripheral, sizzling on contact with the cold wind.

Theo didn't notice.

Heart hammering against sore ribs, I stumbled along a stone path that wove between huge yew trees. I couldn't wrangle my magic *and* convince Theo to slow.

He wouldn't even *look at me.*

My anger grew.

Trailing blindly behind Theo, I ran mental fingers along my shields, no gaps or crevices appearing to my mind's eye.

Why did my magic rally?

Theo slowed so abruptly I crashed into his back. He towed me into a clearing, my breath pluming through the freezing air.

It took longer than normal for my lungs to slow, the added factor of being sick not doing me any favors.

"What. Are. We. Doing. Here?" I husked, my inflamed throat burning like I swallowed shards of glass.

A massive lake sat in the middle of brittle grass, the water distorting the reflection of the full moon.

An uneasy sensation slithered through me.

"Theo?" I whispered.

Dim torches fired to life, circling the perimeter of the clearing and illuminating gnarled, barren trees growing away from the dark lake. I jumped backwards with a hoarse gasp.

My hands shook, muscles cramped, and suddenly, I couldn't draw any-thing other than the tiniest breath. The necklace from Theo constricted my sore throat. Pitching forward, I heaved, unable to get air into my lungs.

"*What. Are. You. Doing*?" I croaked, fighting to stay conscious against waves and waves of overwhelming dizziness. Theo approached the bank of the water slowly, as if in a trance, knocking me off-balance.

Without glancing my way, he jerked me closer.

Adrenaline and fear surged through my blood like a battering ram.

And with it, my lineage gift and temper *ignited*.

Fuck this – If Theo refused to tell me anything, I was out of here.

I needed him to let go of my wrist, and I was waning back to the Palace.

"Theo," I yelled, voice cracking painfully. I thrashed, bracing every mus-cle to hinder him from taking another step. Pure anger choked off my sharp shout, though my scream still echoed loudly through the clearing. *"Answer me!"*

Theo froze.

I tore my wrist from his vice grip.

Chaos magic burst from my soul –

And slammed into a shield that was *not* mine.

The mental impact jarred through me like a lightning strike. I sucked in a disbelieving rasp, unable to rally magic to my fingers. My head snapped up. Theo's rigid silhouette was outlined against the torch light. "Did you..."

"Yes," Theo sighed flatly, *still* not facing me, *still* looking towards the lake, over the dark water.

The necklace around my throat emitted an icy pulse of power. Every trace of sickness, ache, and pain vanished instantly.

I doubled over, clutching my chest, finally, *finally*, filling my lungs with air.

The jade sitting snug at the hollow of my throat flared with bright light.

Bright *purple* light.

And that's when I knew something was very, *very* wrong.

My anger fizzled out, replaced with dread. That dread brought me to a devastating realization.

I took a step back.

"*Look* at me," I breathed, refusing to believe it – refusing to believe the *betrayal*...

But this time, Theo turned slowly, lifted his gaze to mine.

And instead of brilliant blue irises ringed with silver starbursts, Theo's eyes were fully blacked out.

Part Three

FORMIDABLE

Chapter Fifty-Two
MERRICK

Was it him? Or shit luck?

Why was this the *second* time in the same year that he stood on the precipice of a bloody battle, fighting for the truth on where a godsdamned crown should fall?

Carra's tits.

Winnie stood slightly in front of him, shadows writhing like fat moccasins around her wrists and forearms while the haughty Queen spat insults from ridiculously painted lips, insinuating the Voronin children corrupted King Velik, forced him to change his mind.

Merrick's nose crinkled in distaste.

Not that he was one to talk since he'd worn the same two colors for the majority of his life, and currently owned only three pairs of pants, but that ugly plum dress with gaudy gemstones strewn about the fabric didn't do the Queen's voluptuous figure any favors.

Maybe the gown would've looked better on Dahlia if she wasn't such a raging cunt.

"You've always been a spiteful, jealous, man," Dahlia screeched, wagging an accusatory finger at Finneas. "I *knew* you were trouble from the moment Vanessa had you."

Finneas didn't bat an eye. Merrick had to hand it to the witch's patience. One nasty word uttered about *his* mother, and Merrick would've beaten the offender to death and beyond.

Dahlia wailed, "My poor, Theodoric! I *told* him not to trust you; *I told him* you had nefarious reasons for coming back here."

"Then you should ask Theodoric why he *ordered* me here." Finneas scowled. "Returning to the Palace wasn't my decision."

"Liar," Dahlia bit back. "You're a liar. Theodoric would *never* sully his pristine reputation with Voronin filth."

The tension grew heavier, a thunderous rain cloud about to burst.

The Coven edged closer.

Winnie's shadows surged, rearing eyeless heads around the rim of the dais.

King Velik was...*humming*?

The old King appeared completely unruffled while his Coven hovered on the brink of civil war in front of him.

Maybe the King *wasn't* as sane as Finn believed.

Or maybe Velik was so used to Dahlia's tantrums he opted to wait her out.

Queen Dahlia threw her hands up in frustration, whirled towards the Royal Guards stationed near the wall. "Arrest the Voronin siblings, and the gargoyle, for treason."

Velik snorted.

Four Royal Guards snapped to attention, light magic flickering to life, sending a crackle of power through the air. But the other three hung back, glancing between each other with unease.

Merrick pulled the thread of his Sentry closer. If Winnie's freedom was threatened, he'd fight with fangs and claws.

"*Enough.*"

A deep, guttural snarl punctuated the hoarse command.

Every witch whipped their focus to King Velik, now standing from his throne, thin stature supported by the massive grimm at his side. The Royal Guards dumb enough to listen to the Queen froze as the beastie revealed dagger-sharp teeth. With her pointed ears pinned to her skull, not a single guard dared move closer.

Painfully, achingly slow, the King took a shaky step forward, and Finn lurched towards his father's unsupported side, only to be growled at by the giant volkhound telling him to *back up*.

"Listen, and know that my decision comes from a clear head and intact mind. I, King Velik, *will* pass the crown to *my* eldest son upon my death. Finneas, I hope you can forgive me for allowing the succession to change in the first place all those years ago."

Finneas exhaled a harsh breath from between gritted teeth, but the sheer angst bracketing his features told Merrick the shadow witch had forgiven his father long before now.

"I have been kept from sight for decades, my absence blamed on an otherworldly sickness that shattered my heritage gift, my health, and as Dahlia prattles on about, my mind."

Dahlia bristled, dodged Master Vole and bolted forward –

The grimm *roared*, spittle flying into the Queen's stricken face.

With a stuttering curse, Dahlia scrambled back so swiftly she tripped on the hem of her dress and crashed to the floor. Vole pursed his lips with contempt.

Winnie stifled a wry laugh.

Merrick angled his horns towards two Royal Guards who'd crept closer once the demon's attention shifted, as if they truly believed they could blindside a grimm, a gargoyle, *and* the two strongest shadow witches in the Kingdom.

He let his Sentry flash through his sight, pupils slitting, his beast lengthening his fangs. The idiots blanched. Bolted back to their positions along the wall.

With a cocky smirk, Merrick's features returned to normal, his Sentry slinking back into his soul.

"It wasn't until the grimm appeared at my bedside that I began thinking about the repercussions my death would have on this beautiful Kingdom. But with every visit from the grimm, more of my strength...*returned*." Velik gave the beastie an appreciative smile, stroking her fur with a gnarled hand.

The grimm released a pleased *chuff*.

Finneas and Winnie traded confused looks. Neither appeared to have known *that* snippet of information.

Clearing his throat, the King continued – his voice stronger, sharper, with each word. "Originally, I believed the grimm was escorting me to the comforting embrace of death."

Velik chuckled darkly, and for a moment, Merrick saw the powerful ruler peering accusingly through the gaunt man's eyes to the Queen who struggled to hoist herself from the floor, her tight dress restricting her limbs. The King stood straighter. Raised his hand to chest-height.

Winnie gasped. Finneas's face cracked, stunned surprise widening his eyes.

Pure silver light magic bloomed against the King's outstretched palm.

Velik settled emotionless eyes on his wife. "And then, a most astounding miracle happened. My light magic came back. *You* of all people, Dahlia, should understand how...freeing... it was to siphon for the first time in nearly twenty years."

Dahlia paled.

The Royal Coven, those who clustered around the Queen to lift her off the floor, sensed the shift and backed away, until an empty ring of accusation circled Dahlia. She fought to stand with difficulty, the hem of her plum dress tangling around the sharp heels of her shoes.

The King laughed mercilessly. "Oh, yes. You see, Dahlia, the grimm wasn't *just* visiting me in the confines of my empty chambers with the containment rune lock on the door, she was shadow walking me *outside* – to the forest, where I could siphon the gift this Kingdom provides in every towering oak, every blade of swaying grass."

Winnie's hazel eyes brimmed with molten rage.

The Coven descended into mutters.

Velik addressed his wife, the Queen, directly. "How long did you think you could get away with it? How long did you believe you'd need to poison me with Laceroot, Dahlia? Did it *frustrate* you when I began refusing the food you *personally* brought me every night?"

He coughed another chuckle as the few witches who remained conflicted fell back, disgust aimed at the disgraced Queen who finally managed to stagger to her feet without assistance.

"But you *couldn't* kill me, right? Because the stipulation of my death meant you'd lose the title of Coven Mother, and the position you wielded with such pretentiousness would pass to Winona." Velik smiled. But it wasn't the kind smile of a benevolent King – it was wicked, *vengeful.*

Finneas's hate-filled expression turned lethal as realization dawned. "*You*," he hissed. Shadows shot from the darkness roiling at his feet, capturing the Queen's throat, wrists, and ankles in inky shackles. His hands balled into fists.

Queen Dahlia's lips pinched with smug arrogance, even as shadow magic forced her to her knees. "*Me*," she answered scathingly. "It's *your* fault, Velik. I gave you an Heir. You bred two bastard children with your *mistress.*"

She clicked her tongue, as if this was all beneath her, though she squirmed against the shadows. "Vanessa made you *weak*. Made our *Kingdom* weak. I did what had to be done to secure Theodoric's reign. Especially once you got that whore pregnant *again*."

Winnie let out a shuddering exhale, her beautiful face dropping into heartbreaking agony. Merrick stepped closer to her, squeezing the bone dagger in his hand until his knuckles ached to stop from wrapping the Princess in his arms.

With a cruel sneer, the Queen flicked malicious eyes to Winnie. "The Laceroot hidden in Vanessa's meals while she was pregnant with you was *supposed* to kill you both – erase the burden of a *second* illegitimate child tainting Velik's rule. Unfortunately, Vanessa was too calculating, too paranoid."

Finneas grasped Winnie's clenched, shaking hand in his and exchanged a sidelong, somber glare with Merrick from over the top of Winnie's head. They didn't have to like each other – but in that moment, Merrick realized Finneas truly loved his sister, that her gut-wrenching, empty stare and quivering lips clawed into his heart, too.

Dahlia cackled. "Obviously I didn't know until it was too late. But I *was* pleased to learn Vanessa ingested enough Laceroot to hemorrhage on the birthing bed."

The first tear slipped down Winnie's chin.

And then Velik placed a reassuring hand on his daughter's shoulder, a pained frown on his face. The grimm slunk to his side.

Unbeknownst to the horrid Queen, this was a trial.

Her trial.

It took another moment for Dahlia to come to the same conclusion.

The Queen's eyes narrowed swiftly as she took in the sight of the Voronin siblings hand in hand, their father standing protectively at their back.

Silver light magic coiled between tendrils of shadow.

The King. The Princess. The Heir.

United at last.

"Your confession has been noted," King Velik rasped.

Every ounce of Dahlia's contempt vanished.

Thrashing harder against the shadow restraints, Dahlia shrieked, "Your asinine decree that we held and lost our titles together was the only reason I kept you alive as long as –"

Velik raised a glowing palm.

And the resounding *snap* of Dahlia's neck ushered in a new line of succession to the Jade Kingdom's throne.

Chapter Fifty-Three

DOVE

"*Heretic*." I hissed between clenched teeth and a stuttering heart.

Theo prowled closer. "We both know there's no such thing as *heretic* magic, Dove. Call it what it truly is." Irritation flashed across his drawn features, those blacked eyes gleaming under the torchlight.

"Fine." I straightened. "Chaos magic."

"Isn't that better?" Theo purred sarcastically.

That foreboding sense of dread died out at his snarky words. If anything, Theo's admittance pissed me off. Not to mention – "What did you do to my magic?"

Theo ran a hand through his hair, smoothing wayward strands away from the crown still sitting on his brow. I had the sudden urge to rip it off and chuck it into the lake. "What do you know about blood runes?"

"Loads," I clipped dryly, glancing surreptitiously around the clearing for an escape route.

My heart hung on a delicate string, tender and raw.

Which was extremely frustrating. Theo obviously didn't care.

The book I'd found in the library didn't go into detail, but Theo wasn't asking for a lesson. And according to his widening grin, he was calling my bluff.

"Do you know how to check if witch blood was used to cast a rune-stone?"

Squinting at Theo, I couldn't marry *my* version of him to this...stranger in front of me. The whiplash of emotions had me edgy, braced, and seething.

The Dove with light magic that believed the world was ultimately good would've crumbled.

With a growl, I shoved the thought away. *That* Dove died on the altar. Her memory wasn't going to help.

The necklace warmed against my skin. I grabbed the chain, attempted to unclasp it and rip it from my neck.

A zinging shock snapped at my fingers. With a pained whimper, I snatched my hand back, squeezed my singed fingertip.

"You can't remove it," Theo said conversationally.

I took mental stock of my body. The symptoms of sickness I'd fought in the throne room were gone, as was the overwhelming urge to apologize to Theo and grovel for his forgiveness. It had all magically disappeared – the key word being *magically*.

Blood runes.

"If I'd checked this necklace, I would've found bloodstones, right?"

Runestones could only hold one sigil each – regardless of size. If rune-stones were etched with witch blood, they were bloodstones.

Four diamonds. One jade.

Theo used *his* blood to etch the runes, *his* magic to imbue them.

There could very well be five blood runes hanging like a noose around my neck, controlled by the Prince.

I shoved bleating panic away and focused on the cold clarity stoked by anger. Being afraid wasn't going to change anything – only hinder me from thinking clearly.

Surveying Theo, I mulled over everything that happened between me placing this collar around my neck and now.

My emotions had been manipulated, and I'd gotten weirdly ill right after.

Weakening rune.

One.

Definitely an illegal blood rune.

I needed time to figure out what bloodstones I was currently under the influence of and hopefully stall until someone stumbled upon us.

"Did you receive your chaos magic through a ritual?"

The journal translations implied the witch who wrote it *hadn't* murdered someone for lineage magic. My heart perked up, asking if we could *please* forgive Theo if he confirmed he wasn't involved in ritualistic sacrifices.

My brain told my heart to have slightly higher standards. He'd already kidnapped me and dragged me through the woods against my will.

Theo's black eyes guttered, revealing blue irises for a beat before darkness swallowed them once more. I caught him off guard.

His momentary surprise at my blasé question was replaced with that blank, emotionless mask within the span between seconds.

"Dove, you *know* the answer to that," Theo replied smoothly, collecting himself too quickly. He closed the distance between us in three long strides. "You were there."

No.

The veil of deception lifted.

No amount of numbness or anger could've prevented the crushing blow to my heart.

Theo *had* arrived to Bramberry Forest before the full moon – just like Bron said.

Theo had *ample* time to slither into the meadow and find a single witch sleeping amongst wildflowers.

He'd lied to me.

The first moment he saw me *wasn't* from the porch of Bramberry Manor, when we locked eyes and I believed, foolishly, that divinity linked us together.

The first time he'd seen me...was when I ran through the forest for my life, when *he* hunted me down.

Theo was the assailant who'd escaped Carra's temple before Neera could kill them.

No, no, no, no.

But the truth forced me to accept the realization. He'd manifested light magic, yet I'd never seen Theo siphon.

He never used his heritage gift.

He never wore runestones.

All those signs – signs I should've immediately picked up on – now mocked me relentlessly.

"You were the one...you carved the King's sigil on the body."

Theo squinted at me. "What are you talking about?"

I grimaced. *No.* The timeline didn't add up – Theo was too close in age to me to have murdered my birth mother, and he'd only admitted to one ritual. Mine.

"I spent years preparing for a lineage gift from Massis." Theo murmured, as if he hadn't just torn my heart to shreds.

There are more witches enacting sacrifices. I remembered Finn saying that, but in the warped vision of Theo leering down at me, I refused to reveal that tidbit of information.

He took a deep breath. "As Heir, power is *everything*. When my heritage gift manifested and I only received a trickle of light magic..." Theo scoffed, a grimace flickering across his face. "Well, you understand the allure. Receive a powerful lineage gift that could kill a *god* in exchange for one measly life?"

I reared back, "I *never* wanted –"

"*And yet, look at you now,*" he snarled. "Not only do you have chaos magic, but you stole power that beings would *debase* themselves to own. Magic *other* chaos witches would fight to the death over."

Theo crowded me, backing us against the trunk of a dead tree, closer to the ring of torches. My breathing turned erratic. "You got chaos magic like you wanted, so why string me along?" I bared my teeth. "Just wanted to toy with the witch who received the same magic as you?"

"We *don't* have the same magic, Dove," Theo gritted out, as if the admission pained him.

What?

He leaned lower, our faces mere inches apart. "Do you know *what* you took?"

I glared at him, mustering as much hate into my eyes as possible. His nearness made bile rise in my throat. Theo repulsed me now.

"You're pathetic, and a liar." I shoved him, but he didn't budge an inch. *I needed magic.* I couldn't even scream down my connection to Neera – everything was blocked.

Nullifying rune.

Two.

If I killed Theo...the bloodstones would lose power over me since his blood was used in their creation.

But in the eyes of the Kingdom, I was a heretic. Who would believe me if I said I killed Theo in self-defense?

Finn would.

Theo opened his mouth, a sneer curling across his lips. With the purple light from the imbued necklace throwing stark shadows across his features, he looked demented.

I needed to get out of here.

Right now.

Before I could talk myself out of it, I slapped him across the face with as much ferocity as I could summon and bolted.

Ten feet from the tree line, I slammed into an invisible barrier, falling hard onto my back as the breath was knocked out of me.

I'd miscalculated Theo entirely.

Containment rune.

Three.

Theo stalked forward, translucent purple tendrils threading through his fingers as the runed barricade shimmered into view, bathing the clearing and the lake in eerie, lavender light. My entire body shook as I rolled onto my hands and knees, gasping for breath.

With a curse, Theo yanked me up by the shoulders and shoved me towards the lake.

"You're going to listen," he yelled, jabbing a finger in my direction. "You're going to *listen*, then you'll get a *choice*."

My hands balled into fists as I steadied myself on my feet.

Two blood runes were still unknown, but I was out of time. The coolly calculating Theo that first dragged me into the clearing was gone, and in its place stood a deranged and dangerous chaos witch.

He'd tried to kill me once, and damn well succeeded that time. I wasn't going to allow him the opportunity again, and I doubted Phades would help me twice.

Shifting my feet, the movement hidden by the skirts of my gown, I bent my knees and prepared to attack. All those self-defense lessons Maude taught over the decades poured through my muscles. I had to be fast and hit hard if I wanted to knock him unconscious. Then I could find the containment rune he imbued that *had* to be somewhere within the clearing, break it, and run for help.

The moment Theo was close enough, I lunged, swinging my fist at his temple with every ounce of strength I could muster.

I slammed *hard* into another barricade.

The breath *whooshed* from my lungs, the impact so brutal I collapsed to my knees, dazed.

Theo laughed wickedly.

Hidden blood runes, cast in the dead, dry ground flared to life, encircling me in a ring of containment runes so powerful my chest tightened under the humming magic.

I was completely and utterly trapped.

And within the span of a single, stuttering breath, my fragile heart iced over and shattered completely.

Chapter Fifty-Four

DOVE

"That's better." Theo paced the rim of containment runes holding me hostage. "*Now* we can begin."

I pushed myself to my knees, heaving cold air into my numb lungs. Under the deadened stare of his blacked eyes, I'd thrashed and screamed until my throat was once again raw and blistered.

The blatant hunger on his face showed unrestrained now.

He never desired *me*... He desired what I *had*.

There was a reason Theo brought me here, and whatever he planned for me...he'd need me out of the nullifying runes to do it. I only needed to get one solid hit on him.

I cursed myself for leaving my dagger back in my bedroom, for once again being caught unawares. If I made it through this ordeal, I'd never go anywhere without a weapon again. And, of course, Theo planned this all out too perfectly – the sheath that normally hung from his belt was conveniently empty.

My teeth sank into my lip.

"What do you know about Avamere?"

I stayed quiet. Theo paced in front of me.

The strained silence seemed to have no effect on him. He kept talking, though there was nothing I cared to hear him prattle on about.

"Massis discovered an old, stagnant god realm while trying to come earthside. But it was devoid of magic, unlike the realm Phades found – and unlike Aurramere."

I huffed a wry laugh. "Why should I listen to you?"

Theo crinkled his nose, squatting down to be eye level with me. "Because the ritualistic spell work briefly connects the sacrifice's soul to Avamere. And Massis imbued Avamere with god magic, bringing it from an empty, useless realm to one containing its own fissure of power."

I blinked slowly.

If Avamere was imbued with god magic... and I siphoned *that magic* to free myself...

Oh, gods.

Vessel.

The echo of Carra's silky voice infiltrated my mind.

Theo's fists trembled with rage. "You stole god magic," he accused viciously, "a *lot* of god magic. The power Massis imbued into Avamere was later used as the core to create chaos magic. But when he gifts his loyal followers chaos magic, he separates *out* his direct god magic."

He rose to his feet. "*You* siphoned chaos magic that still had god magic in it. And *you* became a Vessel. The Vessel of Chaos."

The truth clanged hollowly through me.

During the ritual, I'd siphoned *red* magic.

I'd never seen the red tint again but...I'd never wholeheartedly utilized my lineage gift.

Was that red hue the god magic?

Was it still in my soul?

Behind him, the water lapped furiously against the bank, as if an invisible force below the surface was stirred into a frenzy.

Sheer instinct told me in no uncertain terms that I didn't want to know what was in that water. Cordelia's warning about not going near a lake wafted through my memory. *I should've asked her to elaborate.*

"I had to beg him, you know. After your ritual," Theo whispered, blacked eyes glassy. "He was too enthralled by the *weak witch* that siphoned Avamere and unwittingly became a Vessel."

Theo assessed the ring of sigils holding me hostage. "Massis finally granted me chaos magic after I debased myself and *prayed* to him. But he didn't give me enough. Sure, I'm stronger than any witch with heritage magic, but I got a *morsel* compared to the amount you stole."

Did Theo believe I was thrilled with my illegal, overwhelming lineage gift? Half the time I had to wrestle it for control, and the other half I spent paranoid that it would get me burned at the stake.

This man was delusional.

"I don't like challengers, Dove. Not for my throne, *not* for Massis's favor."

And *gods*, did he enjoy hearing himself talk.

"Did you take me out here to kill me, again?" I asked bluntly.

"Not necessarily," Theo replied. "Though that depends solely on you."

"You failed at killing me the first time," I grumbled, rising to my feet and dusting dirt and dead grass from my gown.

Was goading him brave or stupid? Either way, anger felt better than fear, and I was sick of Theo's smarmy voice.

"Do you know what this lake is?" Theo pointedly ignored me, gesturing to the water behind him. The ripples grew more aggravated.

"During the Witch War, spell work and blood rituals were a common occurrence, and dukhmora were a huge threat. Witches weren't skilled at killing demons, and the dukhmora were a challenge they'd never encountered before. Their solution was to imbue boosted containment runes around this lake and trap the dukhmora below the surface."

"There are dukhmora in that lake?" I wasn't feeling very brave anymore. Still thoroughly pissed, though.

"Oh yes." Theo grinned maniacally. "The Lake of Souls holds *hundreds* of dukhmora, all waiting for someone to drain the containment runes keeping them below the surface and release them."

I grimaced. I hadn't seen a dukhmora before, but the books I'd read gave a horrifying enough picture.

"Who would be stupid enough..." I trailed off.

The Prince who just lost his crown, exhibited unhinged behavior, used illegal spells and blood runes, *and* killed me before, was *definitely* idiotic enough to release a horde of dukhmora on Palace grounds.

"No."

Theo's scowl told me that was the wrong thing to say.

"Too bad," he growled. "I need to see if Massis's god magic truly grants his ultimate power." As an afterthought, he added, "Don't worry, the dukhmora can't hurt you."

"Because nullifying runes work against them?" If so, I was secretly relieved to be stuck in these stupid sigils.

Theo scoffed, "No, those are no more of a barrier to them than a stiff breeze. I meant because your *necklace* is runed against them."

My breath hitched.

"The necklace is runed against demons?"

Neera.

My grimm had been wary of the box since it appeared on my doorstep. I acutely remembered how agitated she'd been when I opened the door.

And once I put it on...

"Yes, it's a very specific type of concealment rune that makes you invisible to demons. They can't sense your presence."

Concealment rune.

Four.

That left one more blood cast sigil to figure out.

"It's a concealment rune cast in *your* blood?"

"Stop stalling," Theo barked, raking his fingers through his hair again.

Concealment rune. Containment rune. Nullifying rune. Weakening rune.

I chanted the four in my head, over and over. If I survived this, I was never going to accept jewelry from a man ever again.

"The fifth rune – "

The question died in my throat as the nullifying runes etched into the ground around me surged with power, and a barrier of magic slammed against my back.

My heart shot into my throat as a new path of sigils flared to life, dotting the dry grass of the clearing, carving a narrow trail from me...to the water.

"*Theo!*" I screeched as magic shoved harder against me towards the lake's now-churning surface.

"When you breach the surface, use your god magic on the dukhmora, command they must listen to *me*," Theo shouted over my screams.

I pushed against the wall of magic with every fiber of my being as it herded me closer and closer to the water's edge. Now, I could see *something* thrashing below the surface, wisps of light grey in the murky water, writhing with excitement.

"No, no, *no* – there *has* to be another way. There's a book!" I shrieked, digging my heels into the brittle earth. "A journal – from a witch who gained chaos magic without the spell work or ritual. It can tell you how to gain more power."

It was a desperate gamble, and a bold lie, since the journal didn't explain how to get *any* sort of magic, and was currently missing, but I'd say anything to avoid plunging into the demon lake.

"That journal is nothing more than the ramblings of a disgraced Coven Mother from the Slate Kingdom." Theo rolled his eyes.

Well, now I can die knowing who stole my journal.

And if I get out of this alive, I have a starting point on where the journal came from.

As the barricade pushed me closer to the water, I called Theo every nasty name I could think of in every language I knew.

He stole the journal– and he knew how to imbue blood runes. Without a doubt, he tucked the journal into a blood rune that protected against seekers.

"This is the *only* way," Theo hissed, the lavender light of the nullifying runes illuminating the planes of his face. "You'll get your magic back. *Underwater.* Tell the dukhmora to line up along the perimeter of the bank. If they do, I'll pull you from the lake."

"And if the dukhmora don't listen to me?" I slammed my shoulder into the side of the barrier so hard my teeth snapped together. It didn't slow, just pressed me towards the lake and the demons inhabiting it.

Theo merely smiled. The smile didn't meet his bloodthirsty eyes.

The nullifying runes on either side of the path thrummed as my foot touched the reed-lined edge. Nails digging into the dry dirt, I tried to gain purchase against the immovable magic, against the inevitable. The edge of my gown grew sodden and heavy, trying to drag me into the depths itself.

My foot slipped from the bank, into the water. I screamed, trying to wrench my foot out, but a magical force held it under the surface.

"Take a deep breath," Theo taunted, "Once you go under, the *fifth* sigil I etched in your necklace will link to the runes that kept the dukhmora underwater for centuries."

Off. I needed this infernal thing *off.*

Panic blurred reason. I yanked at the necklace. This time, it didn't burn my fingers in warning, it *scorched* my flesh so excruciatingly that blisters rose and burst across my throat.

"The necklace will stay on until you fulfill your end of our bargain, Dove." Theo chastised. His voice was a tinny, faint thing over the sheer pounding of my heart.

"The dukhmora must listen to me. *Not* you. *Me.* And don't get any bright ideas. If you refuse to follow my *implicit* instructions..." He touched two forefingers to his brow, a mockery of the sign of respect for the dead. "I'll receive the honor of lighting your memorial pyre myself."

My lips parted on a soundless gasp as everything below my waist sank into frigid water. The shocking temperature smacked the hysteria from my overwhelmed-with-terror mind.

"The *choice* is yours, Dove." Theo smirked.

Sucking in as much breath as I could, mental clarity returned, and my senses honed in on survival.

Linking rune.

Five.

Theo's barricade dumped me into the murky, demon-filled lake.

CHAPTER FIFTY-FIVE

DOVE

TIME STOPPED.

Hair billowing around me in the brackish water, I fought the weight of my dress as the fabric pulled me down, down, *down*. Forcing my eyes open did no good – the faint moonbeams didn't reach this deep. Dark water stretched in every direction. Bubbles burst from my lips in a silent, petrified scream.

As I sank closer to the lake's bottom, pressurized energy sent a warning tingle through my bones.

Time sped up once more.

Against my blistered throat, the necklace shuddered, releasing a nauseating whine that scrambled my already overwhelmed senses. I focused on the bloodstone Theo imbued to restrain my magic. The barrier separating me from my power wobbled as every kernel of outrage, betrayal, and fear became a weapon with the sole purpose of tearing the sigil to shreds while my magic battered against the nullifying rune's control.

The necklace loosened a final, hoarse bellow.

A sharp burn seared across my collarbone as the nullifying bloodstone fissured in half.

Chaos magic surged victoriously from my soul.

Relief barreled through me as I slammed into my thread of magic. My eyes flickered, enhanced sight clicking into place, allowing me to peer through the unending blackness surrounding me.

Brilliant violet light widened my field of vision. The containment runes along the lake's surface meant I couldn't wane, but once Theo siphoned them, their hold over me would vanish. As I swam through the eerie depths, I pieced together a plan, a back-up plan, and a when-everything-ultimately-goes-to-shit plan.

Tall, snakelike grass swayed across the lake bed, their hypnotizing movement giving me something to focus on aside from my pinching lungs as magic explored the bloodstones continuing to blaze with Theo's power.

The jade kept me invisible to demons, and it *was* a true blood rune – extremely illegal to imbue and only castable with witch blood. I wasn't attempting to break the concealment rune until I was safely out of this godsdamned lake.

The last two diamonds still humming with power were bloodstones as well, but they were regular sigils that Theo's blood simply boosted. The nullifying rune was broken, though Theo stated I'd receive magic back underwater. Maybe the sigil weakened under the surface, and that's what allowed it to break it apart.

If that was the case, I wouldn't be able to crack the others easily –

A flash of grey caught my attention through a patch of aquatic plants. I swallowed a terrified scream, fighting to keep air in my lungs, as a dukhmora snaked up from the reeds, giving me a full, unobstructed view of it.

Dukhmora.

Taller by a foot with willowy, elongated limbs, the demon didn't spare me a glance as it slithered past, moving through the water effortlessly – a plume of smoke and spirit rather than a fleshy beast forced to paddle or swim. Grey veins stretched under translucently pale skin, and its shiny, blacked out eyes were depthless and haunting. I clapped a palm over my mouth as it lowered bone-colored horns and sped towards the surface.

In horror, I watched the dukhmora slam into the containment rune stretching over the lake. Its lipless mouth wrenched open in a shriek of frustration as it twisted its limber body and scratched frantically at the invisible magic with split, jagged nails.

I let a whimper, and an aching sliver of air out. Another dukhmora appeared, then another, then three – no, *five* more wove from the grass below my kicking feet and shot upwards, bashing against the surface.

Ducking my head, more dukhmora blew by in a blur of silvery skin and bone horns, until a writhing mass of dukhmora clustered above me, fighting to breach the surface – as if sensing their long-awaited freedom was imminent.

With furious kicks, my numb, bare feet propelled me closer to the cluster of horrific beasts. I dug into my well of power, sinking past purple chaos magic to hunt that red-tinged god magic that apparently made me the Vessel of Chaos.

If chaos magic couldn't break bloodstones...I bet god magic could.

I just needed to find it.

The caveat – I absolutely was *not* breaking the concealment rune anytime soon.

Nope.

My lungs fluttered painfully, reminding me I was on a *very* limited timeframe. Abandoning my search for god magic, I turned towards the dukhmora.

Theo believed I could control them.

Only one way to find out.

Treading water fifty feet below the surface, the aftermath of the weakening rune Theo hid in a diamond caused every muscle in my core and legs to scream as I threw my consciousness wide, following the instinct of my gift, burrowing deeper into my well than I'd ever traveled before.

Like a lock sliding into place, my magic sunk into the spirit-like bodies of the demons closest to me. Eight dukhmora drifted towards me, pitless eyes dazed and maws slack. *"You will do as I bid."* I snarled down my connection to them.

Fuck Theo. If I had to be cold, and wet, *and* drowning, then the dukhmora were under *my* command.

If I survived this, I'd happily double-cross *him* with the same heartless cunning he showed me.

Theodoric Balabanov would learn a bitch of a lesson.

Never underestimate a vengeful woman.

I threw magic wider.

Two demons I snared ripped free of my net and launched towards the surface with an animalistic shriek.

I grappled with the dukhmora I'd caught, now ten in total, pouring magic into them with blind recklessness. Finally, their limbs relaxed. A wave of dizziness sundered through me.

You will do as I bid. And...feel free to eat a witch named Theodoric.

I pressed my order into them, offering my general location in return. Slowly, they sank a few feet below where I struggled to stay afloat.

My head ached as I speared magic out again.

There was no way I could stay underwater, turning ten at a time, *and* get out alive. The bleak, unbidden thought stuck, and I couldn't dismiss it or tuck it into the box of trauma where I shoved everything else.

As the second group of ten acquiesced to my control and sank to the bottom of the lake, a blurry glance to the *hundreds* clustered at the surface had my heart stuttering...or maybe that was the lack of air...

I stared at the twenty dukhmora under my control with hazing vision. Subconsciously, I knew they couldn't see me due to the jade bloodstone, but their blacked eyes and reverent faces followed each lackluster tread of numb legs through water.

My feet faltered.

I was so...*tired*.

Chaos magic exploded through my head, clearing away brain fog. I hadn't realized my eyes were closed. A chill that had nothing to do with the temperature of the frigid water sent a stream of bubbles tearing from my lips, propelling towards the surface with fear-fueled energy.

Theo believed I could turn all the dukhmora *at once*.

But I couldn't.

He was about to release a horde of dukhmora that weren't under my control.

Which meant I'd imbued myself with *some* god magic – enough to make me a Vessel and put me in an incredibly powerful league of my own, but I hadn't siphoned the amount required to place *hundreds* of demons at my command.

Spikes of adrenaline warred with the thinning breath remaining in my lungs. My limbs were heavy, unwieldy, as I desperately swam for the surface.

Linking rune.

Half-conscious and fighting to survive, I directed thick tendrils of chaos magic into the necklace as a last resort. Sparks of purple popped against the collar of painful burns encompassing my throat. It took all my concentration to make my physical body swim while my mind trailed down the threads of magic imbued into the nefarious jewelry.

The moon's beams illuminated the water. I was getting closer. My magic shivered through the silver chain, confirming my desperate, last resort plan was now in full effect.

Theo used the linking rune hidden in a diamond to join the containment rune and the concealment rune *together*.

He didn't connect the nullifying rune – since he needed my magic to command the demons, and the weakening rune, a true blood rune, must've been too heavy of a drain on his magic to keep imbued.

Teeth gritted, a barrage of realization threaded between waves of light-headedness. The weakening rune cut off when Theo imbued the containment runes around the clearing. My health returned *because he wasn't powerful enough* to hold so many blood cast sigils at once.

Theo must've known the first thing I'd do once my magic rallied was break the bloodstones, so he threaded the concealment rune *with* the containment rune. The linking rune acted as the lock banding them together.

Which meant he believed I *could* break the bloodstones with magic, but hoped I'd think twice since doing so would reveal my presence to the horde of bloodthirsty dukhmora trapped in the lake with me. And my magic was granting me a small amount of extra time holding my breath, though the more I used my gift, the less air I had.

But drowning was awful.

Fuck it.

I slammed chaos magic directly into the jade. Theo's magic held.

I was out of air.

Eyes shut, I kicked with everything I had, focused on one goal – survival.

Suddenly, a terrible emptiness swept over me.

I peeled open an eyelid as demons crawled from the surface of the lake.

Theo siphoned the containment runes.

And like a bursting dam, the magic trapping the horde below the surface disappeared completely, and hundreds of dukhmora emerged from their watery prison, elongated limbs clambering from the water.

Twisting my body, I tried to wane, but only managed to shoot a few feet upwards, my lungs cramping as I inhaled water, the shock sinking me back down.

But...If the dukhmora could get out, so could I – right?

I was so close to the surface, I could see Theo. His mouth moved as he shouted something to the horde of dukhmora I couldn't hear, oblivious to the fact these demons weren't under my control. Or his – for that matter.

Through the distortion of the water's ripples, I saw dukhmora swarm the clearing, their movements jerky and uncoordinated. Theo's blacked eyes widened in fear, and he fell to the ground, scrambled backwards, and pressed his bloody palm into a sigil by his feet. With a flash of purple, he disappeared.

Ten feet from the surface, I found out why waning had been unsuccessful as I smacked into another barrier and the silver necklace glowed brighter, mocking me.

Containment rune.

Theo was *never* going to allow me to resurface.

He'd siphoned the containment runes from the lake for the *demons* – but the one collaring me was separate – *not* linked to the lake's runes like he told me. He was forcing me and the secrets he'd admitted into a watery grave.

Time for the when-everything-ultimately-goes-to-shit plan.

I didn't panic, though I was *seconds* from death. Cold, creeping finality weighed down my limbs, whispering to stop swimming, close my eyes, *rest* in drifting, peaceful sleep.

Instead, I poured every dreg of magic from my soul into the jade blood-stone as darkness filled my vision.

The satisfying burn against my already ravaged throat was the most beautiful agony I'd ever experienced, followed by two more as the conceal-ment rune, the containment rune, and finally, the linking rune shattered completely.

With the bloodstones broken, I waned. The looming finality of death pounced, but a flare of purple tore me from the lake, narrowly evading death's cold grasp.

Crashing onto dry grass, I hacked up a belly of water, took one short, rattling breath, and fainted.

Chapter Fifty-Six
MERRICK

MERRICK STALKED ACROSS THE dais, giving the grimm a wide berth. The demon watched his every move while laying protectively in front of the King, head resting atop her crossed front paws. King Velik was seated, his gaunt face the only indicator that he still suffered the effects of poison. But after Dahlia's body slumped over, an energetic, vengeful sparkle lit in his eyes.

Winnie knelt next to her father, speaking softly with their hands clasped together, the concern furrowing her brows a complete contrast to the furious energy palpating from Finneas. The *new* Heir stood rigidly at the base of the dais as the disgraced Queen's body was dragged to the pyre.

There'd be no ceremony, no witches chanting or mourning as the Queen burned to ash.

To the Royal Coven, Dahlia's existence would be ruthlessly wiped away, reduced to nothing more than a passing name jotted down in a scroll and buried amongst the archives. Merrick wondered how many cruel rulers were stuck from the Jade Kingdom's history – if their stories would be more useful as cautionary tales instead of torn almost entirely from record.

He didn't voice the concern aloud.

The witches of the Royal Coven still filled the throne room, though they'd migrated to the tables, speaking amongst themselves in hushed voices. The group of musicians disbanded, as the dance floor was currently filled with high-tier, titled witches and Royal Guards holding truth rocks as Master Vole paced in front of them and barked questions regarding Dahlia's sinister plans.

Even though a handful of ladies-in-waiting, healers, guards, and witches had been unceremoniously arrested and brought to the dungeon, the air of tension was gone, and a new, electrifying sense of ease settled over the room.

To Merrick's surprise, the wizened Master Vole was actually King Velik's twin brother, who advocated for the King for years, studying cures and brewing potions to try and heal Velik – though Vole admitted he was rarely allowed to visit his brother. Turns out, Dahlia bribed multiple healers to tell the Coven the King's "illness" was contagious, that it was too dangerous for most witches to go near him.

From the way Velik and Vole swapped glances packed with relief, love, and somber sadness, Merrick concluded the brothers had a lot of catching up to do.

So far, the consensus was Dahlia acted alone on the poisoning aspect. Multiple witches were charged with accepting bribes from Dahlia, though the truth rocks revealed no one in the throne room was an accomplice to the actual Laceroot procural or use on the King.

Merrick scrubbed at his beard, his Sentry fidgety in his soul – though it was less agitation and more instinctual apprehension that *something* was amiss. Adrenaline pounded through his veins, and he couldn't relax his rigid muscles. It could've been because of the book hidden in his jacket pocket, but he doubted Carra had any interest in imbuing a gargoyle with god magic.

He'd stolen a Vessel Book from the *King's brother*. When he found that familial information out, he wanted to bolt from the dusty library study Winnie shadow walked them into after they danced, but Winnie told him to quit being a whiny bitch while her shadows cracked the nullifying runes on the box securing the Book of Carra.

It was *absolutely* treason.

But then the pale grey book was in Winnie's hands, and she'd turned with a victorious grin and announced his pockets were bigger, so he needed to carry it. It was probably paranoia, but Merrick felt as if it were a test. If it was – he was going to fail. The moment they left the Palace, Merrick planned on escaping to Ruby and trading the Vessel Book for the Oracle – if Lenna was still King Eamon's captive.

If she wasn't...Merrick swallowed. It burned like acid.

If Lenna had already been saved from the evil fae King, Merrick would bring the Book of Carra to Hale to translate...and try to forget the beautiful, vicious witch he betrayed who was burrowing deeper into his heart.

Stretching and folding his wings, Merrick shut his eyes and pleaded with his beast to calm down. When he opened them again, a female witch with a braided crown of mahogany hair stood before him, twisting the sleeve of her dark blue dress between her fingers. Anxiety wafted off her in plumes.

"Sir, um..." the witch stuttered. Fear flitted across her face as he tightened his wings to his back.

"Merrick," he grunted, wincing internally as the witch visibly trembled in front of him.

The witch nodded rapidly, taking a deep breath before saying quickly, like she needed to get the words out before she lost her nerve, "Sir Merrick, I *know* you don't eat witches, and I don't want to bother you or the Voronins – it's probably nothing – but my friend is missing, and I'm worried..."

"What's your friend's name?" Merrick interrupted, crossing his arms and glancing over to Finneas, who marched around the throne room as if he, too, was looking for something.

Or some*one.*

"Dove Koroleva." The witch delicately cleared her throat. "She was here when King Velik was talking, but now she's gone, and –"

"Cordelia, where's Dove?"

Finneas appeared at his side. Aggravation thundered around his edgy presence.

The witch in front of him, Cordelia, shook her head. "I don't know...she *was* here, and then everything happened with Velik and Dahlia. Bron's checking the library and her room, but..." She shrugged helplessly.

Finneas stiffened. "Fuck. Theodoric's not here." With a curt whistle, the grimm materialized in front of them. Cordelia shrank back as the demon huffed her skirts, tail wagging and sending plumes of smoke into the air.

"Is that a gr-"

"I'll explain later," Finneas muttered, shadows curling around his fists as he strode towards the closed doors of the throne room. The grimm gave Cordelia one more gleeful chuff before bounding over to Finneas, ears perked and alert as she sniffed the air.

"What is –"

"Dunno," Merrick husked, following Finneas and the grimm. His Sentry hissed inside his thread of magic, as if it was trying to warn him –

A split second later, the grimm froze, the scruff of her neck bristling. Cautiously, she lowered her head and let out a guttural growl.

Merrick's heartrate lurched as a trickle of unnatural power flowed over him.

Finneas glanced at the beast quizzically, but it was Merrick who bellowed, "*Get away from the doors!*"

Within the span between seconds, Merrick charged forward and tore the gates of his soul open. Power burst through his bloodstream as he shifted into his Sentry. With a snarl, Merrick lowered into a defensive position next to the crouching grimm, scraping his claws against the stone floor, each one now etched with demon-banishing sigils – courtesy of Winnie.

Merrick lashed his tail, each spike sporting the same sigils – the only runes, he'd learned, that a shadow witch could imbue. He raised his maw and roared in warning – just as a flash of purple light, and a horde of dukhmora, flooded the throne room.

CHAPTER FIFTY-SEVEN
MERRICK

THE ROYAL COVEN SCRAMBLED to rally magic as Merrick slashed a runed claw through the first dukhmora that burst across the threshold. To his smug satisfaction, the sigils Winnie etched glowed like embers and smoldered as the dukhmora was sent back to Avamere.

Bone-chilling shrieks, horrified screams, and shouted commands wove into a melodic havoc Merrick knew all too well as hundreds of demons poured through the doors in a wave of fury, teeth, and inky purple magic.

Arrows of light magic speared through the air in a coordinated attack, aiming right at him. Merrick ducked, tucked his wings in, and braced for impact. But each arrow found their mark in the dukhmora's translucent flesh, banishing a group of at least twenty dukhmora in a succession of rapid *pops*.

Maybe he *was* growing on the witches after all.

With a furious bellow, he launched deeper into the frenzy, talons and spiked tail tearing through grey-ish hide, the sigils burning darker with each successful attack.

At his side, the grimm was a blur of smoke and teeth, ripping into dukhmora so quickly a cleared ring of destruction began growing around the pair.

The grimm paused, glanced at Merrick, and vanished, reappearing closer to the dais. At her departure, Merrick shot into the air, landing in front of a group of witches surrounded and overwhelmed.

His claws made quick work of the dukhmora that circled the group. The witches nodded to him with fierce respect before fanning out and synchronizing white orbs that detonated like sparkly cannonballs, blowing demons apart.

Merrick caught a glimpse of Cordelia, barefoot and sprinting across table tops, whips of silver banishing dukhmora with lethal accuracy. It was a far cry from the trembling witch he'd met a few minutes prior.

Leaping back into the air, Merrick searched the throne room for Winnie.

She fought from the stairs with Finneas, the two shadow witches commanding the darkness with deadly precision. Finneas wielded his black-bladed sword in one hand, shadows lunging around him, and Winnie dodged dukhmora chaos magic with dance-like fluidity, her multi-headed shadow snakes striking opponents faster than Merrick could track. At their feet, an ankle-deep black fog seeped outwards – harmless to witches, seeking out dukhmora and tearing their spirit forms apart.

But for every demon sent back to Avamere, more poured into the room.

Already, a few bodies were scattered across the floor, stirring the demons into bloodlust as they screeched and swiped at each other with chaos magic, fighting to drain dead witches of their heritage gift. It was as horrifying as it had been in Shadymoss.

The Royal Coven was being beaten back, deeper into the throne room, edging closer together and closer to the dais, surrounding their King. Even Velik fought – tendrils of silver dancing through his children's shadows, lunging at dukhmora with the force of a battering ram.

Merrick dove into the fray, desperate to reach Winnie's side, to help her, to get to her, heart thudding in his heaving chest.

He landed with a jarring *thud* in front of the Royal Coven, tail banishing a handful of demons in one swift strike.

Glass shattered. A witch screamed as dukhmora crawled through the stained-glass window above the throne, their lipless jaws open and greedy, elongated limbs scurrying across the stone floor, making quick work of surrounding the Royal Coven on all sides.

The grimm yelped from behind the throne as twenty dukhmora converged on her, their jagged teeth and bone horns piercing her fur. Merrick leapt into the air with one powerful beat of his wings, talons tearing through demons as he fought to free the grimm. Finally, the grimm staggered to her feet, ruby eyes dulled with pain as she panted. Merrick took up a defensive position over her.

Runes began humming to life against the still-intact windows, light magic crawling up the colorful glass like vines. The dukhmora horde shrieked with agony and stumbled away, some fleeing outright, others backing out of the throne room on four limbs, their black eyes slitting as if the light caused them pain.

Merrick stood in front of the grimm, breath sawing through his nostrils, lips peeled back menacingly as the demons fled into the Palace, crawling up walls and lurching away on jerky legs.

A shaky finger stroked down his flank. Winnie stood at his foreleg, short hair matted with blood, free hand holding her hip. Gashes trailed down her arms and a dark bruise had already begun blooming across her cheekbone. Before Merrick could say a single word, her lids fluttered, and she slumped against him. There was blood – *too much* blood – dribbling down her side where her hand pressed. In a blink, Merrick shifted his Sentry back into his soul and caught Winnie before she crumpled to the floor, collecting her against him.

"Win," he croaked, shaking her lightly as she buried her head into his shoulder. "Win, you need to stay awake."

"*HEALER!*" Merrick roared, his eyes never leaving Winnie's too-pale face. "I need a healer, *NOW!*"

Winnie groaned against his shoulder, "I'm not dying, bonehead. I'm just tired."

"Insult me when you're feeling better," he sniped, wrapping her tighter in her arms and standing, his wings flaring out to counterbalance the weight of the witch he carried.

Finneas stormed up to Merrick's side and glared at his sister cradled in Merrick's arms. His scowl dropped the second Winnie's blood splattered across the dais. "Winona needs a healer." Her eldest brother's panicked eyes flew up. With a barked order, he gestured frantically to someone as Merrick lightly smacked Winnie's non-bruised cheek to keep her conscious.

"No shit," Merrick gritted out. She needed to stay awake, *godsdammit.* If she passed out, she could go into shock.

Cordelia hurried over, her fingertips glowing silver as she shoved her hand against Winnie's side. With a weak half-threat, Winnie tensed, lips screwed in a grimace.

"I can help," Cordelia snapped the moment Merrick opened his mouth. "Just hold her still until I staunch the bleeding."

Merrick did as the light witch commanded.

The grimm stood with a grunt, limping towards Finneas. His gaze softened as he knelt down to the beastie, speaking too quietly for Merrick to hear. He stroked her fur, checking her for wounds, though by the relief on Finneas's shuddered face the grimm's injuries must've already started knitting themselves back together. Merrick wasn't sure how demon-magic worked, but he was thankful the beastie could heal herself fast.

"Cordelia, tell Master Vole we need witches to power the banishment runes until every dukhmora has been shoved back into Avamere. No one is allowed to leave the throne room." Finneas stretched out an open palm. Darkness pooled and gathered around his forearm as he siphoned. "The grimm's name is Neera, she'll protect the King while I find Dove. I'll be back to gather a group and begin hunting down our uninvited guests."

With a curt nod to Merrick, Finneas added brusquely, "After Winona's on her feet, have her siphon – it'll help her heal."

Finneas barely fared better than Winnie, but the set of his jaw and the ire burning in his eyes meant the shadow witch wouldn't count himself out of the fight for a long time coming.

Especially since hundreds of dukhmora were currently loose right on the other side of the doors. Banishment runes meant the demons couldn't enter the throne room, except for the grimm, apparently, but unfortunately, that meant dukhmora could be *anywhere* amongst the sprawling courtyards, winding corridors, rooms, and tunnels that made up the Jade Palace.

Cordelia focused blankly on the pink scar weaving together on Winnie's side. More to herself than them, she murmured, "It'll leave a mark, but an advanced healer can remove the scar tissue once the Palace is secured. Bron could do it, but he's busy with two witches who sustained even *worse* wounds. For now, Winnie's the strongest witch here – we need her on her feet."

"I'm right here," Winnie wheezed, color returning to her cheeks. Merrick's heart squeezed with sheer relief as she pinned him with clear, hazel eyes, and an attitude. "Put me *down*, you savage."

Merrick lowered the witch to her feet. Still grumbling, Winnie stretched her palms out and siphoned, calling shadows from darkened corners of the room, from under tables and thrown across the floor, even from the cloud-filled night visible through the destroyed mosaic rising behind the throne.

Cordelia surveyed Winnie once more, as if she was assessing how stable the Princess was. Quietly, she said, "Finn is going to find Dove. You're in charge. He ordered the Coven to stay in the throne room, that he'll pull a hunting group together on his return. I need to talk to Master Vole."

Winnie tipped her chin to the witch in thanks, and Cordelia flitted away, the bottom layers of tulle weighed down with gore and sweat. Her hair crown was askew, allowing tendrils to escape and swing around her face. From the way she fought and healed Winnie, Merrick gave the witch a massive amount of respect, warrior to warrior.

"You ok?" Merrick asked.

Winnie let out a foul stream of curses that would've made Esmeray proud.

"Of course. I'm the strongest witch in the Royal Coven, aside from Finneas. I *personally* took out fifty dukhmora, and all I had to show for it was a little scratch."

Merrick slashed her a placating smile, bracing his hands on his bent knees so they were the same height. "That's *very* great, Princess. But I lost count of my kills around number sixty-five? Seventy? And I kept the majority of my blood *in* my body." To add to the taunt, he booped the end of her pert nose with his finger. She tried to bite him.

With a derisive snort, Winnie leaned closer and crooned, "Sure – you've had like, a *century* more battle experience than me. I'm actually disappointed you didn't double my kill count."

Merrick rolled his eyes as Winnie continued sarcastically in that sugar-sweet tone, "But thanks *are* necessary for the *wonderful* runes I etched into your talons. Otherwise, you would've been as useful as an overplucked baby bird."

With a dark chuckle, Merrick wrapped his hand around her waist, dragging her mouth to his. "Then let me thank you," he growled against her lips. With a moan, Winnie threw her arms around his neck, kissing him back desperately, body melting into his.

In that moment, he could've sworn they were the only two beings in the entire throne room. The noise around them muted as he deepened the kiss, realizing how gone he was for the witch in his arms.

And he realized what Esmeray meant when he'd been a hollow shell of a male, and he'd asked her what it felt like when her soul tie to Keerian bloomed.

Merrick was truly awake for the first time in his life.

It dawned on him that this wasn't mere attraction, or lust, or something temporary and fleeting.

He was falling in *love* with Winnie.

Gods, he was so, so, *so* fucked now.

Chapter Fifty-Eight
WINONA

I WAS UTTERLY FUCKED. Especially as Merrick growled against my lips and my breathing hitched on its own accord, as if my soul was so aligned with his that I couldn't unravel where I began, and he ended.

Arching my back, his callused palms skated down my hips, and I knew it was because of the tender new skin stretching across my side that he was holding back.

The Royal Coven wove around us, voices of witches I'd grown up alongside – some who still treated me like family – many who were as disconnected from me as I was from them.

I broke the kiss, hoping he couldn't see that I had to physically bite my tongue to stop myself from spitting out those three little words that would damn me more than any warped *veles* or dukhmora attack.

Love was for people who *liked* themselves, people who were soft and kind, untarnished from loss. I'd lost too much too early. Built walls around my hardened heart that protected me through the years spent on the run from my own family, fighting dukhmora with a Coven that shrunk in members and grew in memorials every few months. Blood had tarnished my soul until all that was left were ugly, jagged pieces that were too raw and battle-hardened to let anyone in.

It was why I'd kept away for so long. Why I was terrified Merrick had already gotten too close.

If I let myself love, just to experience loss again, I wasn't sure I'd survive it.

And after everything Merrick told me about his ghost soul tie...I couldn't do that to him either.

With an ache in my throat, I pulled from Merrick's grasp, needing space to think, to slide into that brutal, calculating role my Coven needed. My father slumped against his throne, surrounded by healers. His face was gaunt, much thinner than I'd like, but he was coherent, and that was better than he'd been in decades.

It made me wish Dahlia was still alive so I could kill her again.

Slower.

Bloodier.

I sidled up to Velik, placing my hand on his shoulder. He smiled warmly at me, dismissing all but one healer – an older woman with pure white hair and bright eyes who *tsk*-ed at his dismissal, her thin fingers glowed as they pressed the pulse point on his wrist threading healing magic into his atrophying muscles.

"Winona, where's Finneas?"

"He'll be back soon," I replied, my gaze jumping between banishment runes to confirm they were evenly powered. The sigils were our only line of defense against the horde running rampant around the Palace, and I knew the Royal Coven was already exhausted.

The mosaic of Massis shattered during the fight, cracking the sigils lining its surface. We only had one back up. The realization was bleak. If one more window broke, if one more rune died out, we'd be overrun.

Witches stood in front of each intact stained-glass window, waiting to imbue magic into the banishment sigils. Many toyed with their gemstone rings and jeweled pendants, siphoning the power stored in their runestones into their souls. Being a shadow witch had its perks – one being the fact I didn't need to carry *rocks* wherever I went.

Another group stood with Cordelia as she spoke with my uncle, Master Vole. For a second, a wave of guilt sundered through me over stealing the Book of Carra, but I had a hunch, and I wanted to see it play out. Plus – Princess perk, who would ever tell *me* 'no'?

Aside from the frustratingly stubborn gargoyle that I was annoyingly falling in love with.

He told me 'no' plenty. *Ass.*

Healers wove through a makeshift infirmary, using tabletops as cots to mend witches who sustained serious injuries during the attack.

It was all so...efficient.

I squinted against the wave of emotion to glance down at my father once more. There were a million things I wanted to say to him, so many apologies I needed to make.

He was trapped in Dahlia's clutches, *poisoned*, since I ran away. The guilt threatened to swallow me whole.

Blowing out a heavy breath, my eyes wandered to Merrick. He crouched next to the grimm, stroking her fur reassuringly as a witch with a bright orange beard checked her over for wounds that hadn't finished healing. Next to the giant volkhound and the mountain of gargoyle, the witch appeared comically small – which was ironic because I knew Bron was taller than me by at least six inches.

"What is your friend's name?" Velik asked lightly, following my line of sight.

"Merrick," I grumbled. "Found him half-dead on our border and saved his boneheaded life."

My father made a humming noise. "He cares for you."

I bristled, the word piercing right through my reinforced walls and right to my tender heart. "He's my prisoner."

The lie felt foreign on my lips, and from the soft laugh Velik let out, I had a feeling I wasn't convincing.

Before I could brace myself and sell another lie, a pressurized energy slammed through the throne room. Screams went up as the banishment runes shuddered, their bright white hue vanishing.

Merrick and the grimm were at my side in an instant, the volkhound pivoting until she stood defensively between my father and the dais steps.

A suffocating silence crashed through the room as my half-brother stomped over the threshold.

His eyes were fully blacked out.

Theodoric's a chaos witch.

"Witches of the Royal Coven," Theo shouted, raising his fist. "I hoped it wouldn't come to this, but alas, your *King* left me no choice."

He threw out his palms. A rush of chaos magic burst from his hands, sliding up the windows and imbuing every sigil with eerie lavender light. The dukhmora sensed the shift in the air and crept along the threshold of the open doors, chittering and screeching with hunger right where the banishment runes cut off at the entrance to the Great Hall.

"The crown will be mine," Theodoric said, matter of fact, those soulless eyes roving the crowd. "If anyone tries to be...noble, I'll rip down the runes that are fully under *my* control and let the dukhmora exterminate every witch in this room."

Loosening a slow breath, I snuck behind Merrick and dropped to my knees next to the throne. The majority of my magic depleted while fighting, but I needed to get the King out of here right now.

I'd burn out.

There was no other choice.

"Father," I whispered urgently, calling the shadows from the dark corners of the room as Theo strode closer. "You need to come with me."

Behind those crumbling walls, my heart thudded painfully against my bruised ribs. I had *seconds* before we were exposed. Merrick shuffled to the side, his wings hiding me and the shadows weaving together into a blot of darkness. I could take them to the cabin...it was the only place I deemed safe.

I'd happily take the agony of burnout over Theodoric sticking my head on a spike.

Theodoric has chaos magic.

Get out. Find Finneas. That's what I needed to do. My shadows wavered. Gritting my teeth, I drained everything I had into shadow walking us out of here.

The yawning maw of burnout grinned from the edges of my flickering vision.

No, no, no.

Suddenly, icy breath fanned across the back of my neck. I flinched. Goody, I was already hallucinating.

But then, ruby red eyes blinked in front of my teeming mass of shadow.

Grimm.

Neera.

She must've disappeared the moment Theo entered to give us the advantage of surprise.

Neera became semi-transparent, black fur smoky, pooling into the darkness I'd collected to shadow walk. I gasped as she fed her magic into the writing depths, shoving my shadows back into me.

The effects of imminent burnout faded.

With a pointed look, she chuffed. I had no clue where the grimm was shadow walking us, but a sense of ease slipped into my soul.

She'd take us to safety.

"Merrick," I breathed to the back of his head, where slate-colored horns ended in points. "King Velik."

It was so slight I would've missed it if I wasn't so in-tune with him. But the subtle lowering of his head told me he was on board.

"The Jade Palace is now under my command." Theodoric's smugness was one of the most punchable things about him. "Anyone who doesn't bow to me will be politely asked to leave the room."

To punctuate his point, he glanced over his shoulder, to the cluster of dukhmora chittering and snapping at each other in the hall, waiting impatiently to feed on witch blood.

"Now," I hissed.

In one fluid move, Merrick lifted my father from the throne and dove into the writhing shadow. The grimm darted behind them, feathery tail wagging.

I scrambled to my feet. Cordelia, hand covering her mouth, gazed from the portal to me. I froze.

But as if she knew my hesitation was on her account, she shook her head and mouthed, '*go.*'

My heart cracked.

There was one thing I could do – to give them hope, to settle my own mind.

In Cravic, a language we'd spoken since we were children, one that merely a handful of witches in the room knew, I gave two curt commands to Cordelia. Her eyes flared in surprise.

Theo roared as he realized what I'd done, though he didn't understand the weight of the words I'd said – only knew I was escaping and King Velik had already been smuggled to safety.

Purple magic exploded towards me.

I was faster. With a running start, I launched into the swirling darkness and disappeared.

CHAPTER FIFTY-NINE

DOVE

SOMEONE SHOUTED MY NAME, though it was muted and tinny, and that made no sense whatsoever to me.

Rough hands rolled me onto my stomach, whacked me hard, twice, between the shoulder blades. I gasped into consciousness – and immediately heaved up disgusting lake water. Tremors wracked my body as I tried fighting back, only to descend into a hacking fit that spotted my vision.

My back bowed.

I threw up again.

"Fucking *breathe,* Dove."

Finn?

It took another minute of panicked gurgling and coughing before I was able to take a full breath, the cold air like daggers against my battered lungs and raw throat.

Finn pushed himself off the ground to stand behind me. The broody Voronin was *definitely* here and *definitely* pissed. "Theo let the dukhmora out of the damned lake," he grumbled, "They overtook the Palace."

My blurry eyesight snapped to the Lake of Souls.

The water was perfectly still.

Unconsciously, my fingers drifted to my throat, where the necklace of bloodstones lay, though the iciness of the silver chain confirmed I'd broken every sigil Theo cast.

"I always perceived you as a woman who preferred yellow gold," Finn drawled, massive hand reaching around to peel my fingers away from the damned jewelry.

"Me too," I rasped, squinting up at him. Finn's lips tipped up into a dark smirk as he towered over me. The full moon peeked out between thick clouds, illuminating the shadow witch and his agitation.

Suddenly, the last hour crashed over me. I let out a strangled yell, tearing at the clasp with numb fingers.

Off. I needed this infernal thing off *now.*

Finn hauled me off the ground, and before I could process it, I was cradled against him, his arm banded firmly across my upper back. "Stop," he said quietly, catching my chin with his free hand. I whimpered. His palm was so warm against my icy skin. It hurt *so* good.

Smoothly, he scooped my wet hair from the back of my neck. I was too drained to do anything except bury my cheek into his jacket, desperate to absorb every ounce of heat wafting off him. He smelled like spicy cedar and smoke. I let it soothe me.

A beat later, the weight of the necklace disappeared.

Pieces of my shattered heart healed, and a stone fortress around my most vulnerable organ solidified swiftly, leaving me with brutal clarity.

And hatred. And spite.

Those feelings for Theo intensified.

I swallowed. It was agony.

Finn hissed, stroking my neck gently with the tip of his finger. "*He* did that to you."

It wasn't a question.

The burn encircling my throat almost took the little breath I had in my lungs. From the sheer wrath on Finn's rugged face, it was easy to assume there was a perfect circle of raw skin from the bloodstones I broke with chaos magic.

I pulled out of his hold, steadied myself on shaky legs.

There were *hundreds* of demons released. "We need to save the Royal Coven." My voice was a brittle, mangled croak.

Finn shook his head, a dribble of blood slid down his temple.

"You're hurt."

"And I found you half-dead on the lip of the lake, barely breathing."

I winced, waved away his gruff reply. "I'm fine."

Finn crossed his stupid, thick biceps. "You inhaled so much water I'm surprised there's still a lake here."

Rude.

My magic hummed weakly below the surface of my skin. But a new…sensation… in my blood made me realize how much power I truly held.

Which made me stumble sideways. Finn *needed* to know everything.

"Theo has –"

"Chaos magic." Finn finished, hands grabbing my shoulders in an effort to steady me. "I'm aware."

I blanched, struggling to wrench free of Finn's grasp. My heartrate lurched as purple sparks shot to my fingertips. Annoyingly, it didn't faze Finn in the slightest. He sighed and let go, though his darkening eyes stayed on my face, worry pulling his mouth into a frown.

"How do you know Theo has chaos magic," I wheezed. If Finn had been a part of the ritual that killed me, I'd murder him.

Without a single beat of hesitation this time.

"I wasn't there," Finn said quietly, reading my tormented thoughts.

His expression simmered with self-loathing and guilt. The rivulet of blood dripped down his brow. Finn slowly raised a hand, wiping the blood away with the side of his thumb, never breaking eye contact with me.

"I suspected Theodoric was hiding something when we were in the Quiet – after Bramberry. Given his history, I figured it couldn't be anything good. That's why I told you to stay away from him." Finn rubbed his bloody hand against his black pants. "I'll swear it on a truth rock, Dove. I *didn't know*."

My shoulders would've relaxed if I wasn't shaking so badly. I could imbue a truth runestone easily now.

"I confirmed he had chaos magic the night of your...*dinner*." A muscle feathered in his jaw as he stared at me with intensity. "Don't give me an 'out' because I wasn't there, darling. I should've kept a closer eye on him."

"You aren't responsible for Theo." My voice was hoarse, but I hoped Finn didn't shoulder the blame for his brother's actions.

"I would've killed him," Finn growled. "If I'd found out Theodoric enacted a ritual the night before, I would have killed him immediately. In Bramberry."

"How did you know it was me?" I forced through chattering teeth. The emotional weight of Theo's betrayal, cold gusts of wind, and my frigid, soaked-through gown created a perfect trifecta of bone-shuddering tremors that settled into my weakened body.

I wasn't sure I'd ever get warm again. Or if sensation would return to my bare toes.

With a curse in Cravic, most likely due to my pitiful shivering, Finn yanked off his jacket and held it out to me. He kept a respectful distance, and part of me was grateful. It helped me not feel trapped. The other part, the part with numb fingers, feet, and, well – numb *everything*, wanted to leech his body heat like a flesh-burrowing parasite.

"Lucky fucking guesswork." He glared at the trees behind me.

Reaching across the few feet between us for the offered clothing took an exorbitant amount of effort with cramping muscles and blue-tinged fingers. I was past the point of exhaustion, and attempting to shove limp arms into the sleeves proved too difficult. Instead, I draped the jacket around my shoulders and held it closed. Instantly, Finn's spicy cedar scent enveloped me.

The heavy fabric warded off the blustery air, but what I really needed was dry clothes. I snuck a glance at Finn, who scowled at the dark trees, clenching and unclenching his fists at his sides.

Since a dukhmora horde infested the Palace, I highly doubted I could sneak into my room. *Gods*, I was so tired waning was impossible. I'd probably miss my bedroom entirely and end up on the roof.

My legs wobbled. Finn lurched forward, catching me before I crumpled. *If I could wane to the roof, I'd fall right off.*

I took a stuttering breath, tipping my head back. Finn tucked me into his chest again, using his other hand to tug his jacket tighter around my shoulders.

Our eyes locked.

Vulnerability and raw emotion flickered through his hooded gaze. Then, his regular, shitty attitude popped back to life with a vengeance.

"Why do you continue getting into precarious situations, darling?" Finn's rumbling baritone was warmth in itself. I'd never admit it, though.

I mustered up the meanest glare I could. "Funnily enough, I lived a pretty quiet life until two Princes showed up."

He scoffed, though his focus had returned to the forest behind me.

A shrill screech tore through the silent clearing. Finn's entire demeanor changed – the vulnerability and arrogance replaced by the cold features he normally hid behind.

He slashed out a hand, gripping me harder against him. Shadows leaped up from the ground. "Dukhmora." He jerked towards the portal. "We need to leave."

I balked. "Where are we going?"

"We're going to Bramberry, darling."

"But –"

Cordelia, Bron – they were in the Palace. Were they alive? Where was Neera?

"I'm a Vessel," I said stupidly, digging my heels into the dirt as if I could be useful at all while shivering like a half-drowned rat with no shoes on. Even though it was a lineage gift, I was so drained from breaking the bloodstones and waning out of the lake, harmless purple sparks were the extent of my oh-so-feared prowess.

Finn replied dryly, "I know."

Before I could ask *how* he knew that, too, he tossed me over his shoulder. I let out an *oomph* and rallied my second-most powerful gift – cursing him out. Though my indignation over being carried like a sack of potatoes died in my throat as he spun around and bolted into the portal of shadow.

That was when I saw the twenty dukhmora mere feet away, their smoke-like bodies nearly silent as they rushed through the dark tree line, spindly fingers extended. Their blacked eyes shone with rabid hunger, mouths agape, revealing way more jagged fangs than I was interested in becoming familiar with.

As Finn shadow walked us away from certain death in a whirlwind of darkness, I wondered how he acted so calm in the face of what I could only assume was me getting into *another* precarious situation.

CHAPTER SIXTY
DOVE

FINN SHADOW WALKED TO the rim of the Bramberry Meadow.

Stumbling from the swirling smoke, I froze the moment I realized where we were.

A bitter rage ignited under my icy skin.

Purple sparks snapped painlessly across my knuckles.

The grassy field and swaying wildflowers used to bring me so much joy.

"Dove –"

Ignoring Finn, I yanked out of his slackened hold and shoved away, driven by a fury that drowned out everything else. My vision blurred as I staggered towards the meadow, tightening Finn's jacket around me. But even the musky cedar and smoke couldn't calm the shrieking in my head.

The last time I'd stood amongst the wildflowers I loved so much had been the night Theo hunted me down, drugged me, and killed me for his own selfish gain. He tore decades of happy memories from me in his quest for power.

Theo didn't care that I'd lay in the meadow and watch stars flicker into existence after one of the high-tier witches placated me with lukewarm interest when I spoke to them.

He didn't care that I used to love the afternoons I brought witchlings here when their teachers needed a break.

He didn't care that he stripped me of my sense of safety, ripped through my illusions of peace.

Theo used me. He never cared for me. Every kiss, every touch, every moment we spent together had been a pretty lie with nefarious intentions. And stupidly, I fell for it.

Since the beginning, Theo only ever cared about himself.

So, I was going to tear him to shreds and reclaim this place, its peace, and its memories for myself.

Tears burned in the corners of my eyes. I stubbornly refused to let a single one fall.

I felt the strength of the banishment runes surrounding Bramberry Forest a split second before I smacked into them.

My breath hitched.

I sank to the ground, tucked my bare feet under the hem of Polina's ruined dress, and pressed my palm delicately against the magic that kept me from my home.

Without a word, Finn crouched down next to me, staying a few feet away, as I fought to reclaim control over my life while everything seemed dangerously fragile. I stared at the wildflowers inches from my fingers. The barricade kept them just out of reach.

The banishment runes surrounding Bramberry Forest keep heretic witches out.

My sanity fractured further.

The purple sparks zipping from my fingertips turned into a glow of dark purple light as my anger struck hotter.

I was not a heretic.

Hope became edged with barbed coldness.

Walls fortified around my heart with every beat.

The chaos magic in my veins sang louder than the screams ricocheting through my head.

The pain I'd experienced at Theo's hand morphed into impenetrable armor.

The embarrassment of being laughed at and pitied by other witches in my Coven, of being made to feel *less than,* and *inferior,* were weapons I confidently sheathed at my side.

My innocent view of the world became calculating, ruthless.

Innocence was a wicked thing.

The memories sharpened as I breathed through grief and fury.

A mere month ago, a weak light witch lay among flowers and slept under the stars.

And then she died.

She *looked* like me.

But now all I saw was a stranger.

And all I felt was rage.

Slowly, I rose to my feet and surveyed the barricade.

I trailed a single finger down it, feeling every roil of power that thundered over the Coven I called home, humming angrily at the forsaken magic churning in my soul.

I was not a heretic.

I was the Vessel of Chaos.

With a soft breath, I closed my eyes, rallied chaos magic, and shattered through every sigil that stood between me and the Bramberry Forest.

And then I walked into the field of wildflowers.

CHAPTER SIXTY-ONE
MERRICK

MERRICK PERCHED AWKWARDLY ON the edge of the lumpy couch, trying to figure out the best way to sit where he could guard the door and see Winnie. Frustratingly, the infernal piece of furniture was in the perfect location – but was too narrow and tall for his wings to drape over.

The couch was even *more* uncomfortable than the terrible floor poufs Sparrow had strewn about her living room.

With a hiss, he shot to his feet in agitation. The edge of a wing knocked into a glass-blown clock poised precariously on the mantle. It fell. He lunged, catching the timepiece before it shattered, his boot tripping over a raised floorboard in the process.

Biting back curses, Merrick released a long-suffering growl. He was too big and cumbersome for the tiny living room. And it was pissing him off.

The grimm gave him a look of smug amusement before jumping gracefully onto the couch he'd abandoned, spun twice, and curled into a ball of fur and shadow, tail draped primly over her snout and piercing gaze settled on the front door.

"You can keep watch then, beastie," Merrick grumbled.

The grimm huffed dramatically.

Cabinets creaked and slammed behind him. Winnie muttered under her breath as she rummaged through the kitchen, finding only empty glasses and thick cobwebs. "Whoever lives here either hasn't been back in a while, or they were robbed, because there's not a *morsel* of food in this place."

King Velik sat at the dining room table, his slight frame hunched against the hardbacked chair. "Winona, the grimm brought us here for a reason. Be *patient.* If morning comes, and the owner of the home hasn't returned, we'll figure out where we are."

Merrick pursed his lips. "What if the being that lives here isn't friendly?"

King Velik shrugged a bony shoulder, gesturing Merrick to the empty chair beside him. "Then it's a wonderful thing you're here to protect a frail old man, Sir Merrick."

Merrick didn't like this one bit. After everything that happened in the Jade Palace, adrenaline was still thrumming hot through his blood. It made him irritated and restless. And it absolutely didn't bring him a beat of relief that the *King* of the Jade Kingdom, with his soft smiles and twinkling eyes, was counting on him – unaware that Merrick was fucking his daughter and had stolen a Vessel Book from him.

One of those actions was definitely treason. Either would probably be enough for Merrick to find himself on the wrong end of an executioner's sword.

Did they do beheadings here? Or were they only into burning beings at the stake?

Merrick rubbed his sternum as anxiety mixed with his edginess.

Winnie stomped away from the cupboards and over to Merrick, looping her arms around his waist. He stiffened, not wanting King Velik to get the wrong idea, but the King didn't pay them any mind, humming along to whatever music he heard in his head.

Beheading would probably be less painful. Quicker – at the very least.

Winnie dragged her palms down his chest, a mischievous gleam in her eyes.

He glared pointedly, flicking his eyes to her father. *Was she really trying to turn him on...right now?*

Even the fact she was outwardly showing him open affection was weird. Maybe she had a concussion after all.

But then Winnie straightened triumphantly, the Book of Carra in her hand.

Merrick winced. He couldn't bring himself to glance at Velik.

Sashaying over to the rickety bookshelf next to the mantle, Winnie stuffed the Vessel Book next to a pile of old tomes.

King Velik merely chuckled, "I see you've been in Vole's study, my dear."

Okay, maybe Merrick wouldn't be charged with treason *just* yet.

She preened, dusting her hands off. "Well, it's a good thing we did since Theodoric is currently bat shit insane."

Merrick shut his eyes and took a steadying breath. Finding out Prince Theodoric was not only a complete asshole, but *also* a massive threat, he couldn't get self-righteous with Winnie for stealing it. Which meant she'd be gloating about her stealthy handiwork for days. He could already feel her ego growing, as if she was siphoning *that* from the corners of the dark townhouse along with shadows.

And he would *not* admit that he was glad they stole it.

Now that it was out of the Palace, Merrick had a better chance of smuggling it away for his plan to free Lenna.

But he resolved to help Winnie and Velik first, praying it would absolve at least a sliver of guilt over inevitably betraying her once Velik was back on his throne, and the dukhmora were banished to Avamere.

Just *thinking* about hurting her caused self-loathing to replace the restless anxiousness.

Carra's tits.

No matter what he did, Merrick was letting someone down that he cared about.

Lenna? Or Winnie?

"*Pick one.*" King Eamon's cruel voice threaded through his memories, from when Lenna was forced to choose between saving Merrick's life or Hale's. Merrick knew who she'd pick, he could read it in the way her breath caught, in the pain etched across her face that had nothing to do with the migraine dragging her into unconsciousness.

But he knew the choice would've haunted her for the rest of her long life. So, Merrick had made the decision for her.

Taking the eye of the King's Guard bastard in the process had been a bonus.

In a twist of fate, Merrick was now facing the same choice. Betray the witch who owned his heart, steal the Vessel Book, and save the Oracle of Terramere? Or stay in the Jade Kingdom with Winnie, and forsake the female he vowed to protect with his life?

Before Merrick could sink into guilt, the lock on the front door clicked, and a flare of blinding light burst through the room.

Chapter Sixty-Two
Winona

THICK TENDRILS OF SHADOWS shot from my palms a split second before the front door slammed open. I darted towards the offender, determined to defend my father, meet this newest threat head-on, as Merrick snarled, the *shick* of metal telling me he'd drawn a weapon.

A high-pitched screech accompanied the light magic. My temper boiled.

Who would dare attack the King of the Jade Kingdom?

Well, Winona, probably someone who came home and realized their house had been broken into by a grimm, a gargoyle, and two strange witches.

I thinned my lips, calling more shadows to me. They slammed through the light magic, suffocating it until it faded.

Though my sight was subpar at best, my hearing was impeccable, and the sharp gasp from the front door had me whirling towards the source.

"Gods above and below, *Polina, stop!*" An older woman roared, and through my half-slitted vision, a figure yanked another from the threshold. "It's the *King!*"

Another harsh inhale, this one more fearful than surprised, and the light magic winked out, revealing two women in the doorway.

"Your Majesty." The older woman fell to her knees, the younger woman next to her numbly mirroring her move, hands raised, palm up, in surrender. "I am *so* sorry –"

My father let out a wheezing laugh, dabbing his watery eyes with the sleeve of his too-large robe. "Oh, my dear Maude, is that your sweet voice I hear?"

"I guess I shouldn't be *too* surprised, you old hag. You *were* always one for coming unannounced." The older woman purred, eyes gleaming with mirth as she straightened and stepped into the living room. Her sharp gaze flicked from me, to Merrick, to the grimm on the couch who hadn't moved a muscle this entire time.

Actually – I could hear the beastie snoring.

What an *excellent* guard dog.

When her gaze landed on my father, Maude's eyes crinkled at the corners, a full smile taking over her angular face.

She moved with grace through the townhouse, grey hair wrapped in a tight bun at the nape of her neck. Expertly tailored pants and a cream-colored jacket with a high neck alluded to her imposing presence, and it took my brain a moment to catch up.

Maude was Coven Mother for the Bramberry Coven.

But why was she here – in this house – in the middle of the night?

The witch who'd arrived with her was pale and stricken with guilt as she shakily moved from the threshold, tears threatening to fall as she covered her mouth with her hand. "Your Majesty, I am *so* sorry – this is my friend's home, and the barricade –"

Velik waved her to a stop, as Maude scooted the chair next to him out from under the table, settling onto it with her ankles crossed. "It's quite alright, my dear. No harm done."

The younger witch screamed, noticing the grimm and the gargoyle near the couch. The grimm – now awake – sat at Merrick's side, her unnerving eyes trained on the younger witch Maude had called Polina. Neera's tail thudded happily against the floor.

Merrick was scowling – but that was nothing new.

"Is that a *grimm?*" Polina looked as if she was seconds away from fainting. I rushed to her side, helping her to the floor as gently and not-awkwardly as possible since I was still covered in blood and had definitely counter-attacked.

Polina stared at my face and instantly burst into tears. "Your *Highness,*" she sobbed, "I – *oh my gods* – I attacked the *King* and the *Princess of the Jade Kingdom!*"

I crinkled my nose as she descended into hysterics, shooting a wide-eyed glance at Merrick who fought off the grin curling the corners of his lips. He cleared his throat and stared at the grimm, struggling to maintain composure. I sneered at him as I patted Polina's back.

"If it makes you feel better, you aren't the first witch to attack me tonight. And you are *definitely* the only one who apologized."

Polina wailed louder, burying her face in her hands.

Maude and Velik were completely ignoring us, speaking in low, hushed tones at the kitchen table while I tried my best to get Polina to quit crying. From my father's slight frown, and Maude's quiet tone, I knew whatever they were discussing wasn't good.

Finally, Maude stood from the chair, pivoting to face Merrick and me. She bowed to me before assessing the grimm and the gargoyle with wariness. "How did you break the runes around Bramberry Forest?" Maude snapped, glaring from Merrick to myself.

I narrowed my eyes as I rose slowly from the floor. To my surprise, Merrick answered first, his darkly wicked growl immediately making my blood heat. "Are you insinuating your *Princess* has done something wrong, Coven Mother?"

Oh gods. My toes curled in my boots.

"Insinuation or not," Maude sniffed, "there are two different barricades around Bramberry. One to banish heretics and the other protects against demons. When they were up, we had no volkhounds in our Coven." She inclined her chin towards Neera. "Now, both the ring of banishment runes *and* the protection runes are down." The grimm chuffed, tail wagging hard enough for smoky plumes to curl through the air. But she wasn't paying attention to us, her focus was to the still-open front door.

"And you believe *Princess Winona* took your runes down to break into some dusty ass house?"

Merrick's rough tone had me biting back my own retort, but Maude stiffened, leveling the gargoyle with a hard stare. "I have no problem with your kind, Sir. But this is witch business. I need to know *how* you broke runes that are *centuries* older than yourself, and I want to know *why*."

Before anyone could answer the furious Coven Mother, the grimm yipped happily, bolting towards the front door where a soft voice rasped, "They didn't break the runes, Maude. *I* did."

CHAPTER SIXTY-THREE
DOVE

WHY IS MY HOUSE filled with...with... I glanced around, half-dried, stringy hair sticking to my throat, irritating the blistered skin.

"The King is in my house," I noted hoarsely. Neera loped over, her bright eyes and happy chuffs meant she was the only one that wasn't staring at me in surprise. I sank to my knees, burying my face in her fur as she enthusiastically licked my face.

I pretended I didn't feel the weight of so many eyes on me at once.

There is a Princess, a gargoyle, my mother, and my sister in my living room. The King of the Jade Kingdom is sitting at my dining room table.

I was too tired and on edge to talk to anyone. I'd been betrayed, heart-broken, half-drowned, and told I was the Vessel of Chaos all within the last two hours.

My breaking point had been somewhere along the bottom of the lake.

"Not now," Finn muttered as he stomped past me and into my house. I peeked up from Neera's silky fur. His stance was squared off, his arms folded across his broad chest, and he was glaring at Maude as if he *dared* her to say something.

Maude swallowed thickly, nodded once, and sat down next to King Velik.

"Let's get you inside." Finn bent down, rubbing Neera between her pointed ears. "You need to get out of those soaked clothes and rest."

I was too tired to do anything except nod.

Numbly, I ignored the lot of people in my house and rose, heading towards my bedroom.

But the moment I passed my couch I froze. My eyes shot to the bookshelf where a feeling of *otherness* wove through the air.

"What is the Book of Carra doing on my bookshelf?" I croaked.

Princess Winona spoke, and I didn't miss the way her gaze slid to the gargoyle standing imposingly at her side. "We stole – no. Merrick and I *saved* it from the Royal Library."

"And you decided –"

The gargoyle, Merrick, interrupted me. "Can you feel a sort of...heavy pressure, a *sentience*, from the Vessel Book?" Up close, he was much bigger than I imagined, but there was a kind aura around him – like he understood I needed space and wanted me not to feel cornered.

Finn, however, growled a warning, and the gargoyle bared his teeth to the Prince in response.

There was a certain type of apprehension carved on his tanned face, and the dregs of my magic grumbled in response, as if it *approved* of the gargoyle's concern.

Too exhausted to speak, I simply nodded again.

Merrick looked around the room. "Can anyone else feel a sort of...of tension, or presence from the book?"

A chorus of "*no's*" went up. Not that I was surprised.

"What does that mean?" Winona asked, leaning backwards to survey the Book of Carra sitting *on my bookshelf*. I shivered, hating the way the god magic in the book seemed irritated at my closeness.

Merrick grunted, cutting his focus from me to the Princess. "There's only three beings I know that have *felt* energy from a Vessel Book." With somber eyes, he said softly, "One's the Oracle of Terramere. The other two are now Vessels of the Gods."

Someone gasped. Probably Polina.

I snorted and stalked towards my bathroom door. "Well, now you know four, since I'm a Vessel, too."

Maude inhaled sharply. "You're –"

Rolling my sore shoulders back, I stopped abruptly. I wanted a shower and to sleep for a full day. Maybe two. Gods, a week would be even better. "The banishment runes didn't work correctly, Mother, because they were made with specific language to barricade the Bramberry Forest from *heretic witches*."

Turning slightly, limp hair falling into my face, I added flatly, "Your protection runes keep out *some* demons, but they won't work on the grimm. She's too powerful. And there's no such thing as heretic magic."

With that statement, a motley of voices shouted over each other at once.

I slammed the bathroom door shut.

Every question aimed my way bounced harmlessly off the worn wood panel.

Chapter Sixty-Four
FINNEAS

"She's a *Vessel*? Did Carra choose her to become the Vessel of Salvation?"

"My Dove doesn't *have* strong magic – there must've been something wrong with the sigils. Polina, we need to imbue new ones before the sun comes up."

"What did she mean *heretic magic* doesn't exist? Of course it does – you've said so yourself, Mother."

"What the *fuck* were you thinking?"

"I stole it to be an asshole – but you're *welcome* for getting it out of our dukhmora infested Palace, *brother*."

"Win, I'm not being a dick – I'm saying if it's affecting Dove, then it doesn't need to be on her godsdamned bookshelf."

Shadows slipped across the floor as Winona stared me down. I gritted my teeth, balling my hands into fists.

"*ENOUGH!*" I barked. Immediately, every conversation ceased.

My father had stayed silent since I arrived, and the light that returned to his eyes was all the encouragement I needed to quickly and sufficiently take control of the room.

With a deep breath, I gestured for Maude and Polina to sit. I knew Dove needed time to herself, and the fact that Neera was missing meant the grimm was in the bathroom with the witch. My heart lurched as I imagined a different scenario where *no one* had been in Dove's house when we arrived, and I'd been able to care for the witch who was slowly making me question my own sanity.

Instead, I gripped the back of the last empty chair and filled Dove's Coven Mother in on my side of the events that led the King, the Princess, her gargoyle...*prisoner*, a grimm, and a Vessel to Bramberry Forest.

Winona filled in the blanks with what I'd missed in the throne room once Theo made his claim, and then we brought Maude and Polina up to speed on everything the crown knew about chaos magic.

I *hated* to admit it, but even Merrick was helpful – explaining the way the Vessel Books worked, telling Maude about the fae with chaos magic that attacked cities in Irridessen.

In conclusion – we were all fucked unless we got Theo's ass off the throne.

And we wouldn't be able to do *that* unless we had support from the Vessel of Chaos currently locked in the bathroom taking the longest shower known to witchkind, and the backing of Bramberry's Coven.

"Bramberry has always supported the Royal Coven," Polina said firmly, her gaze, like mine, continuing to flit to the bathroom where the sounds of running water and a slight sheen of steam floated out from under the door. "If there's a threat to the throne, Bramberry will fight to stifle it."

Maude's long fingernails tapped against the table. "Of course, but this is a three-headed beast to defeat. One," a single finger popped up. Maude tilted her head to my father, "removing the Prince from the throne to place King Velik back upon it. Two – exterminating the demons that are tearing through the Palace halls...and third, battling the misconceptions surrounding chaos magic, heretic witches, *gargoyles, and the grimm* that seem to be...staying here."

"I don't eat witches," Merrick grumbled.

Neera sneezed. I think she was agreeing with the gargoyle – hopefully.

Winona slid her eyes to the gargoyle and chuckled pointedly. But it wasn't annoyance.

In fact, she seemed...smug?

I didn't like *that* one fucking bit.

The contemplative silence was broken by the quiet *shick* of the bathroom door unlocking, and I stiffened as Dove breezed out, the grimm materializing at her side and following her with worry shining in her ruby eyes.

A thin robe was cinched around her waist, leaving her long legs and feet bare. Her dark hair was wrapped into a thick bun at the top of her head, and I could tell from her bloodshot eyes that she'd been crying.

My heart pinched at the sheer exhaustion on her beautiful face.

The ring of burns around her throat made me want to remove every inch of Theodoric's skin and feed it to Neera. I believed the demon would make an exception to eating witches for that. It was a good cause, after all.

"Dove," Polina started, stepping closer to her. I frowned, knowing the pity reflected in Polina's face had good intentions, but it wasn't what Dove needed right now.

I jerked forward, not sure what to do or say, just that I wanted Dove to see that I was on her side.

To see that I wanted to protect her.

That I wanted to support her.

That I knew she was strong, unbreakable – *formidable.*

But Dove held up her palm, sidestepping Polina with a guarded expression. "I will say this once," she said evenly. "I do not want pity. I don't want to be treated as if I'm made of glass."

Dove rose her chin, a gleam of vengeance sparking through her deadened stare. "As of now, I am the most powerful witch in the Bramberry Coven. Before anyone thinks of pushing me to the side, I want you to remember that. I have been through a lot of shit – but I survived. And that path made me strong. I am here. I'm standing. And I'm angry."

"What do you want to do, Dove?" I asked, my voice rough.

She cut hard eyes to me. "I'll help you take the throne back. But Theo's death is *mine.*"

I gave her a slight nod, our eyes meeting briefly. A smirk dragged against her lips.

Maude huffed, her brows narrowing. "Dove...this talk of killing – it's unlike you."

Dove flicked her unique eyes to her Coven Mother. "I *tried*, I truly did, to be the good witch you wanted. But the witch you knew died on the altar, Mother. The witch that came back – the *Vessel* that was born from a pool of her own blood, the *Vessel* that crawled out of the Lake of Souls, is out for retribution. And I'll be taking what I am owed."

"Feel free to stay here," she added with a scowl, as everyone wavered between uncomfortable awkwardness and nervous acceptance. "But get that godsdamned Vessel Book *out* of my fucking house."

And with that, Dove disappeared into the bedroom, the door shutting behind her with a loud bang.

Her words rang through the now silent space. Neera gave us a pretentious scoff as she stuck her snout into the air and disappeared through the closed door after Dove.

"Are all Vessels so..." Winona frowned.

Merrick glanced down to my sister and grimaced. "You think *that's* bad? Wait 'til you meet Esmeray."

Chapter Sixty-Five

DOVE

Waking up in my bed in Bramberry was *almost* enough to trick myself into believing the last month had been a fever dream.

Neera was draped across my hips, her weight comforting and familiar. The sight of the grimm filled me with reassurance that the bloodstones hadn't damaged our bond. My beastie was still very much attached to my soul, and from the way her giant snout was propped against my shoulder, I could tell she was also relieved to no longer be separated.

After the Lake of Souls and Theo's betrayal, I hadn't given much thought to my future. Now that Maude knew I had chaos magic and was a Vessel, the fact I hadn't been arrested told me the Coven Mother had already adjusted her truth, and I hoped that was enough for me to earn her acceptance.

If it wasn't – her loss. If Theo's betrayal taught me anything, it was to *never* settle for less than you deserved.

For example, I deserved a Coven that saw and cared about every part of me, Neera deserved an endless amount of love and head scratches, and Theo deserved to die a horrible death.

I chuckled to myself.

Witches pledged to serve their Coven *until death*. Since I'd technically *died*, my Coven vows were no longer valid. Even though Maude had taken care of me, and I considered her family, I could no longer accept the life I lived before. I'd love her forever, but that didn't mean I'd allow her to decide what was best for me.

Sheltered, innocent, placated.

I wasn't going to shrink myself down to fit the expectations of others *ever* again.

Unfortunately, my mental affirmations and newly discovered confidence didn't stop the tears from building behind my lids, but no one said powerful witches weren't allowed to cry.

I *could* give in to fear. Panic. To heartbreak over dreams of love I stupidly let myself believe in.

Or I could square my shoulders and figure everything out one step at a time.

Neera yawned, rolling onto her back, a giant paw extended into the air as she began snoring once more. I stroked the underside of her chin as I explored my magic. Drowning wasn't the best time to seek out hidden god magic, but I knew it was *somewhere* in my soul since I'd successfully bound twenty of the dukhmora in the lake to my command.

At least I think I did it right.

A loud crash in the kitchen snapped me out of my well. I was out of bed in a blink, chaos magic sparking at my fingertips. My vision flickered into chaos witch sight, though I pushed back, controlling my rallied magic *without* changing the color of my irises.

Flinging open the door, I made it two steps before –

"*Dove!*"

Elijah flung himself at my legs. He'd gotten taller over the past month. A lump formed in my throat and the chaos magic at my fingertips disappeared as I knelt down and tugged the shadow witchling tighter to me. Pieces of my tender heart healed.

"Good morning – hope you're hungry."

My eyes widened as I rose slowly and took in the scene before me.

Finn stood at the stove, stirring a pot that smelled delightfully like spice and peppers, surveying me from the corner of his eye. He must've washed up after I went to bed because he was no longer covered in blood.

Thankfully, someone'd given him clean clothes to borrow – my guess was Arthur since the dark green sweater stretched tightly across Finn's broad chest and the sleeves were bunched up his corded forearms.

Not that I was admiring his muscular frame. *Nope.*

Polina bounced Henir on her hip as she cracked eggs into a bowl. The moment Henir saw me, he clapped his pudgy hands together and screeched. Even after the overwhelming night I'd had, the sight of his golden ringlets and chunky cheeks made me smile.

Arthur sat on the couch with a few children's books laying in a pile next to him – as if he'd been reading to Elijah prior to me walking in.

"What are you –"

Polina breezed over, spinning Elijah off my legs and depositing a wriggling Henir into my arms. "What wouldn't we do for family?" she asked with a shrug. "Plus, I stole all your food before you left. Figured the least I could do was bring over breakfast. And, of course, the little heathens heard you were back and demanded to come."

She glanced sidelong to Finn, before adding quietly, "The Prince refused to leave. Said he'd sleep on your couch so I could go home last night." My sister raised a brow suggestively. "He seems to *really* care about you."

I let out a rough sigh at Polina's very obvious question. "Nothing's going on between me and Finn."

She cackled, "*Right.*"

Fighting to not blush was harder than controlling god magic. Polina cut me a mischievous grin which confirmed I failed spectacularly. "*Sure. I totally believe you.*"

"You are very nosy," I muttered as she embraced me.

"And you are a terrible liar, Dove Koroleva," she cooed to Henir. I buried my flaming face in my nephew's curls with a groan.

Finneas Voronin was wickedly handsome, but after Theo's deception, I was swearing off men for a long, *long* while.

Neera took that moment to enter the living room, claws clacking across the wood floor.

"The grimm isn't going to eat my children – *right*?" Polina asked quietly, tracking the giant volkhound as it trotted over and sniffed her apron.

I shook my head. "We have a bond. She'd never hurt a witchling or anyone I cared about."

My sweet beastie crouched down, nuzzling against Polina's elbow. Tentatively, my sister reached out and stroked the grimm's fur, visibly relaxing when Neera's plumed tail began wagging faster.

"She's a good beastie," I said affectionately as Henir squeaked with glee at Neera.

Before Polina could reply, Neera huffed the air and whirled towards the couch. To my surprise, she darted over to Elijah with a happy yip.

Elijah's eyes grew wide at the sight of the grimm, and I almost called her back when his face broke into a toothy smile and he whispered, "Hi, pup."

Neera wasted no time plopping down to the floor at his feet, resting her head on his lap, and allowing the shadow witchling to lean his picture book against her.

Arthur, gods bless him, looked as if he might faint from terror, but he took it in stride, swallowing thickly as he helped his son sound out a particularly difficult word.

"There's a lot of change happening," Finn said, pulling a stack of plates from the cabinet. "But not all of it is bad, darling. Neera not only protected *you*, but she's given my father his life back, and she shadow walked so Winona wouldn't burn out, saving my family. It tells us there's more to the demons, to this realm, than we believed."

"And she's good with kids," Polina added breathlessly as Henir approached the grimm without a beat of hesitation, crawling into her side to listen to Elijah read. Neera immediately curled her thick tail around him, ruby eyes half-lidded.

I startled, realizing with Finn's words that the other half of this weird-ass welcoming party was missing.

Finn read the question on my face. "Maude brought Winona, Velik, and Merrick to the Manor." He jerked his chin towards my bookshelf – which thankfully no longer held a prissy Vessel Book. "Maude has the Book of Carra, too. She's going to lock it in her study so no one can track its magic."

The moment our eyes met, everything in the room between us appeared brighter, more vibrant, and I mentally double checked that I didn't accidentally switch to chaos witch sight.

I hadn't.

"Breakfast will be ready in a few minutes." Polina held her arms out for Henir. I ripped my gaze from Finn, tamping down the wriggly warmth that bloomed in my core under the weight of his hazel eyes. "Go get dressed, Dove. We're meeting at the Manor after we eat."

"For what?"

My stomach growled.

When was the last time I'd eaten?

And who knew Finneas Voronin could cook?

Finn answered while filling plates with fluffy omelets with peppers and onions. "Bramberry Coven is rallying around King Velik. We're preparing to take the throne back. But we need your help, darling. We need the Vessel of Chaos."

A heady rush of protectiveness made me shiver at Finn's words. This ask...this was so much larger than *just* me, *just* my need for vengeance. My gaze flicked between the grimm, Polina, Arthur, Elijah, Henir, before returning to Finn.

For a moment, it felt as if the realm itself paused for my answer, and every noise, every fear, eddied from my head. And I realized *exactly* what Crown Prince Finneas was asking of me.

Would I use my newfound god magic to save *his* throne?

Could I truly take that killing shot against Theo?

How far would I go to make our Kingdom safe once more – for *every* witch, Coven, human, and child?

I watched Elijah and Henir. For them, for their safety alone, I'd do anything. And they were only part of the group of people I loved.

A sense of resolute steadiness draped over me.

My list of questions was dwindling. It was a startling revelation that some answers were locked inside me all along, and the rest... Well, the rest would come with time.

"You need me? Then, Prince Finneas, *I* need a favor."

Finn slashed me a heated smirk, as if that was exactly what he wanted to hear. "Name your price, Vessel."

CHAPTER SIXTY-SIX
MERRICK

STANDING ATOP THE PORCH that wrapped around the Bramberry Manor, in brand new clothes a seamstress made specifically for him, Merrick pressed the side of his wing against Winnie's back, his intentions to assure her everything would be alright – especially since there was a flipped hourglass counting down with spilling sand that only ended with a rift of betrayal between them.

He pushed his guilt aside.

The choice that dogged him mercilessly had worked itself out. Winona was a *Princess*. Even after the throne was saved, she was needed in the Jade Kingdom.

And Merrick had pledged himself to Lenna's protection.

It was the beginning of the end of his time with Winnie. No matter what, he'd cherish it forever and hope she didn't hate him for eternity.

Finneas and Dove were standing to the left of Velik and Maude, wearing similar expressions of calculating focus. Neera was situated between the Vessel and the King. The Coven Mother was finishing up a speech to gather fighters for this mission, and it seemed every witch *and* human in Bramberry had come to hear the plan and help where they could.

Merrick surveyed the Vessel of Chaos. The hair on the back of his neck prickled in wariness, his Sentry stirring at the tang of her god magic.

Unlike the reckless and volatile aura he felt around Esmeray, or the steady pulses of power that now emitted from Sparrow, Dove's god magic was like the confident, controlled rush one got when fighting – when their instincts snapped into place and adrenaline released.

Then again, Esmeray and Sparrow had been gifted direct god magic from a Vessel Book.

Dove had *stolen* god power.

From a god that wasn't one of the original four goddesses of the Vessel Treaty.

Merrick watched Dove carefully, and when she caught his eye contact, he saw the determined gleam of revenge in her unique gaze. She radiated a ruthless, hardened glint – a warrior readying for battle, a warrior with...

Grief.

He only knew *that* because he'd seen it reflected in his own mirror every fucking day from the moment he'd fled Sparrow's home in Florra like a coward, until recently – when he'd spent those days in the cottage with Winnie.

"I want you to carefully consider joining," Maude cautioned, her sharp tone softening as she addressed the humans and witches standing silently on the front yard of the Manor. "If you are the sole provider of your home, if you are human, or if you do not feel like your gift is strong enough, *please* understand there is no shame in staying here."

A murmur of assent rose from the crowd, and Merrick's heart panged painfully in his chest. Once Maude told the Coven that he and the grimm were not predators, not enemies, every single being in the Coven accepted that as fact. Without so much as a cautious glance aimed his way.

"Bramberry *must* stay protected while we fight to place King Velik back on his throne. Those who choose to stay and protect our Forest, protect the witchlings, the humans, the children, and those who cannot fight, are as integral to this Coven as those who come with us."

He hadn't even needed the truth rock, though he offered, showing the Coven Mother the flat runestone Winnie used during their first meeting. He'd carried the truth rock with him all this time, and now it was safely stored in his new grey leather bag that was incredibly nicer than the second-hand pack he'd bought from the barracks decades ago.

And when Maude found out he was wearing donated clothing, she'd surprised him immensely by calling a seamstress to take his measurements and create multiple garments for him that accommodated his large stature and wings.

Merrick knew his time in the Jade Kingdom had broadened his mind and his heart. He'd advocate for the witches for the rest of his life, and hopefully it would help bring the Covens out of exile. He was confident recanting his time here to Esmeray and Sparrow would sway Irridessen into building a strong alliance with the witches.

Even as a "prisoner," he saw the Jade Kingdom was filled with kind-hearted and strong beings, that rumor and lore from a war that happened a *thousand years* ago spread, warped, and poisoned the minds of the other six Kingdoms.

Kind of like how *some* beings still believed gargoyles ate people and that all fae were vain and pompous.

Merrick tilted his horns.

Actually, he could agree with the witches that the fae were pompous.

That was a well-known fact *regardless* of the Kingdom.

Merrick resisted the urge to rub his beard with his fingers, knowing Winnie would pick up on the fact that he was warring with the thoughts running rampant in his mind.

Maude finished speaking, and everyone's attention switched to Velik seated in a plush armchair Merrick had carried from the Manor to keep the King comfortable. Even though his voice was weak, Velik held everyone's full focus as he explained his intentions to take the throne back from Theodoric, and that Finneas would receive the throne as Heir.

"Now, witches fighting, please stay to review battle strategy. All others, begin emergency preparations to fortify our borders. We depart tomorrow, but Bramberry must stay on high alert until our return." Maude nodded to a female witch with blonde hair. She broke from the crowd and gestured for the beings to follow her down the wooded trail towards town.

It was the most organized, polite, and well-received revolution he'd ever seen, and it increased the guilt surrounding his already-in-motion plan to escape the Jade Kingdom once King Velik was back on the throne and the Palace was rid of dukhmora.

Merrick had the Vessel Book, and the witches were none the wiser. He'd swapped the Book of Carra with another tome after Maude agreed with his suggestion to hide it in her desk for safekeeping. She'd simply put it in a drawer – an unlocked drawer.

With some stealthy sleight of hand, Merrick slipped into the private study after everyone was asleep, nabbed the Vessel Book, and hid it in his new bag under the stack of shirts he'd been given.

The thread of magic would be traceable while he had it, but Merrick hoped either no one was currently searching for it, or if Lenna was, that she'd see the events that landed the Vessel Book in Merrick's hands through the Prism, and know he was coming back for her.

It made him sick to betray the witches of Bramberry Forest, but if they found out it was *his* fault the Oracle of Terramere was in danger, that he wasn't the hero they believed him to be, they'd probably shun him, anyway.

CHAPTER SIXTY-SEVEN
WINONA

I KNEW HE STOLE the Book of Carra.

But his secret was safe with me – because if he betrayed us, his death was *mine*.

Just like my stupid, idiotic heart was *his*.

Chapter Sixty-Eight

Dove

Purple magic illuminated the angles of Finn's square jaw as we sat on the floor of my living room. He flat out refused to let me walk back from the Bramberry Manor alone, even after I reminded him I was a Vessel with a giant grimm at my side.

But his stubborn ass merely shrugged and said since I was so powerful, then *I* could protect *him* on our walk back through the quiet forest that only began humming with heated tension when the two of us were alone together.

Maude, Winnie, the King, and Merrick had stayed at the Manor, speaking with the witches who'd help take the Jade Palace back, making sure they were siphoning enough power and carving sigils into rocks to imbue with additional raw energy so the witches fighting would be able to sustain their heritage gifts for as long as possible.

I'd debated staying at the Manor but so many curious eyes on me made my pulse accelerate.

Agitated trepidation worked its way through me, and I needed to quiet the unrest in my mind to prepare to take on the horde.

Polina was coming. She was a high-tier light witch that wouldn't take unnecessary risks – but seeing Arthur's lips set in a somber line after capturing her mouth in a desperate kiss...

It stuck in my mind.

He supported her decision – even though he was terrified for her safety.

I glanced at Finn from under my lashes as I pushed another tendril of power into the seeker rune glowing against my wood floor. There was unease etched in the set of his square jaw, echoed through the thin creases at the corners of his eyes.

"And you're looking for..." Finn sat a few feet away, his back against the base of my couch, running a hand through his dark hair. He was handsome with that moody, stoic frown, eyes trailing over me, a muscle flexing in his clenched jaw that was covered with a layer of slight stubble. Too bad he spent a month pissing me off because he'd been fairly...nice over the past day. I stretched my back, arching my spine and rolling my shoulders as his gaze seared against my skin. The way he always watched me both thrilled and terrified me.

"A journal," I admitted. The seeker rune flared its search wider. "When I first used a seeker to find information on chaos magic, the rune bought me a handwritten book. The first half was a detailed account of a witch who gained chaos magic, and the last half was a secret diary that I was in the middle of translating."

Finn raised a brow. Closing my eyes, I searched in my well for some sort of distinction between chaos magic and god magic. "I think the witch received chaos magic from something outside of the sacrificial ritual. But before I could finish my translations, the book and translations I'd worked on were stolen from my bag."

"Stolen...while you were in the Palace?"

I nodded as the seeker dimmed. "I tried using a seeker rune after it went missing, but I imbued the seeker with chaos magic – not god magic. And now that I know Theo is a deceitful ass, well-versed in spell work and blood runes, I have a feeling he's stowed the journal in a blood rune that contests a seeker. If I can imbue a seeker rune with god magic, I should *theoretically* be able to summon the journal back to me. God magic broke bloodstones, so it should break whatever blood rune he's protecting the journal with."

"Ah yes," Finn said dryly, "A gripping battle of wit and runes."

"So far it's my favorite type of fight," I grumbled. "I'm not bleeding."

I'm not bleeding.

I startled.

With a sweep of my hand, I snapped apart the seeker rune, the purple glow fading instantly.

"What?" Finn scrunched his brows, leaning forward as I scrambled off the floor and ran into my bedroom.

God magic could break bloodstones.

The bloodstones were sitting on top of my blistered, bloody throat.

My god magic can only be rallied with blood.

It was a wild gamble, but I had to try.

Grabbing my dagger from my shelf, I darted back into the living room.

Finn's gaze flitted along the steel blade. "No."

"Oh, hush." I sliced the dagger across my palm before he could snatch it away. Blood immediately pumped into my cupped hand as I sat back down. Dipping a finger in my blood, I carefully drew a new seeker rune on the wood floor.

And this time, when I imbued the completed sigil with magic, the rune glowed *red.*

Finn shielded his eyes with a curse as ruby light flooded my living room.

My jaw dropped.

God magic.

I hadn't seen it since that night in Carra's Temple.

"There it is," I breathed. "God magic."

Focusing on the journal, I commanded the blood boosted seeker rune to bring the journal back to me.

The air around us vibrated, rattling the plates in the cupboard, the books on my shelf, building in sync with my pounding heartbeat, until the seeker let out a high-pitched whine. My god magic stalled, slamming against some invisible force I couldn't make out.

But I just *knew* they were Theo's boosted containment runes surrounding the journal.

Gritting my teeth, I shoved harder against the barricade, and the moment it buckled, I yanked every morsel of power back into me.

A blinding flash of red surged through the room, followed by an echoing *boom* that seemed to come from the space between the air itself, causing us both to jump.

Smoke billowed along the lines of the seeker. Finn's eyes narrowed onto it, shadows curling around his wrists and fluttering over my skin, shielding us.

Then, with a guttural hiss, the rune fizzled out.

And as the smoke cleared, I scrambled towards it with a gasp.

Because there, in the middle of the rune I'd poured blood and god magic into, sat *A Testimony to Massis and His Hidden Lineage Gift*, my meticulously translated notes tucked neatly inside the cover.

I shot off the floor in excitement, snatching the journal from the middle of the broken blood rune that was *definitely* charred into the hard wood. But I didn't care.

It worked. Which meant I could use chaos magic until I was bloody from battle, then my god magic would come out to play.

Finn rose to his feet with a lopsided grin as I spun in place. "I did it," I said breathlessly, smiling so wide he chuckled, raking a hand through his dark hair.

"I never doubted you for a second," he replied in that wicked rumbling voice.

I laughed, opening my mouth to remind him that he said '*no*' the second I pulled out the dagger, but my boot snagged on a raised floorboard, and I stumbled.

Finn's arm banded around my waist.

My breath hitched.

We both froze.

Chest to chest, I tilted my head back, meeting his wild hazel eyes.

Finn seemed as stunned as I was, and for a moment, we stayed like that – the two of us pressed against each other, neither making a move to step away.

"Dove." His features softened.

At the sound of my name on his lips, a rush of heat tore through me. His eyes flicked down to my mouth and back to my eyes.

Did Finn want to kiss me?

I *wanted* him to kiss me.

That brought a rush of cool, icy panic. I stiffened.

Taking three swift steps backwards, I ripped my eyes from his, from the agonized understanding that crashed over his face, unsure why my stone heart was now thumping erratically against my ribs.

"I can't," I said softly, shaking my head, refusing to allow the ache blooming in my belly to take root.

I couldn't do this again.

Theo's betrayal was too fresh.

I wasn't ready to trust *anyone* with my heart again.

Finn let out a strangled exhale, smoothly putting more distance between us, scrubbing the stubble on his chin roughly. He turned away, as if he didn't want me to see his face as much as I didn't want him to read the anxiousness on mine.

My living room suddenly felt too cramped.

"I...need to go to...someplace," Finn grunted, averting his eyes.

He left without another word, and the moment the front door shut, my damned traitorous heart beat in earnest once more.

My fingers pressed against my lips, as if they could replicate how it would feel if Finn's mouth met mine.

Fuck.

Chapter Sixty-Nine
FINNEAS

Fuck.

I stalked through Bramberry Forest, head spinning. All of my thoughts gravitated around Dove, and I cursed as my mind conjured up the feel of her small body pressed against me, how her wide doe eyes pierced right to my soul and dug its talons in.

I wanted to kiss her.

And the moment her lips had parted, the moment she'd taken that shaky breath and leaned into me harder, I'd almost given in.

But that hint of fear shuttered through her eyes and she pulled away.

I refused to add myself to the list of people who'd let her down. The Bramberry witches coddled her, even after her declaration that she was the strongest witch in the Coven. They treaded carefully around her, always looking to Maude for confirmation before politely asking Dove if she could *handle* the upcoming battle.

Godsdamned they were more accepting of the gargoyle and the grimm than Dove now outranking every single one of them *including* the Coven Mother.

Gods, Dove outranked *me* on the power scale, and I was *thrilled* for her.

It made my skin itch. Dove flourished in the Jade Palace – even though her gentle smiles and bright, keening eyes had been directed at Theo, not me. But she'd impressed everyone from Vole to Cordelia – one of the highest ranking and hardest to please light witches in the Royal Coven.

Dove was a potent mix of cunningly analytical and insanely gorgeous.

When I first saw her standing at the Bramberry Manor in the crowd, I'd been intrigued by her. And then she crashed into me, holding a baby, and I stupidly assumed she was spoken for. I should have talked to her, but my tongue twisted itself around in my mouth and I think I merely grunted at her?

Real smooth.

But when I saw her again as we departed the Manor, she was already swapping curiously affectionate glances with Theo – not to mention she had a grimm following her and was hiding chaos magic.

I lost myself in the memories of every stolen moment we'd shared, every time I'd found myself intoxicated by her, gravitating to her.

When I found out Theo etched a truth rune into her wine glass at that farce of a dinner *date*, I hadn't known he was aware Dove held chaos magic. I just assumed he was being an ass. But when my shadows shattered her glass, breaking the sigil and pissing Theo off royally, I realized how deep she'd sunk into my bloodstream.

And after Theodoric revealed his own chaos magic, I'd spent two weeks trying to figure out where he'd gotten it. I'd left Cordelia with strict instruction to make sure Dove stayed away from Theo, and I thanked my lucky stars the witch didn't let Dove out of her sight the entire time I was gone.

My steps faltered as I stared at the ruins of Carra's temple. I hadn't aimed to end up here, but seeing the dilapidated stones had my blood icing over, thinking of how terrified Dove must've been. I swore upon the hallowed ground that my brother would be dead soon enough.

If Dove couldn't do it, I'd kill Theo for her.

"You look like you're *also* brooding."

Merrick glided down from the temple roof, wings folding and tucking high to his back as he landed next to me.

I grumbled a confirmation. Thinking about Dove had me crossing my arms and widening my stance as I stared at the ruins.

Merrick shoved his hands in the pocket of his pants, glancing curiously at the temple that I glared at with utter loathing. I wished I could burn it down, make every stone suffer for witnessing Dove's pain.

I rolled my neck, shadows pooling at my feet.

Merrick said nothing, just stood like a quiet force of support against the loneliness that plagued me.

Which was annoying.

I didn't particularly like the gargoyle, and I had a feeling he was sleeping with my sister.

"Are you going to fuck over Winona? Are you a spy? Do you plan to betray her? *Us*?" I asked harshly, ripping my eyes from Carra's temple to him.

Merrick bristled. For a tense moment, we appraised each other with pure disdain before he snorted sarcastically. "Your sister terrifies me. I'm her prisoner."

A beat of awkward silence passed before Merrick cocked his horns towards me. "Let's pretend we like each other more than we do at the moment. You're the Heir to the Jade Kingdom. Would you ever be willing to ally with Irridessen if it meant purging Ingotheria of the cruelty that ruled it?"

The question caught me off guard. Merrick's wings rustled as I lapsed into silence, the two of us sizing up the other. We were almost the same height, sans horns, and though he was slightly bulkier than I was, I did have my shadows on my side. I wondered, in a fight, which of us would be victorious.

The unfortunate truth of the matter was – "Irridessen has no desire to align themselves with witches."

"But what if they did?" Merrick hedged, an edge to his words that had me surveying him with piqued curiosity.

I chose my response carefully. "Remember, the Jade Kingdom didn't willingly place themselves into exile. It would take an extraordinary enemy and a very dependable friend to make the witches forget the injustices they've suffered at the hands of the other six Kingdoms over the past thousand years."

Merrick scoffed. "What a politically polite non-answer, your Highness."

I narrowed my eyes. The gargoyle slashed me a lazy sneer, wings snapping open so fast I had to jerk my shoulder away to avoid the talon at the apex glinting under the moonlight. "Well, when you realize Irridessen is the *only* reason your Kingdom hasn't been decimated by Topaz and Ruby, we can reconsider entering negotiations."

With that parting shot, Merrick launched into the sky.

"Fucking bonehead," I growled as his silhouette flew into the star speckled sky.

It was only when I'd begun stomping back towards Dove's home, ready to catch a couple hours of fitful sleep on the most uncomfortable couch in history, that I remembered Merrick never gave me a straightforward answer on if he'd betray my sister.

Chapter Seventy

DOVE

I wasn't sure where Finn went, but relief swept over me when the front door creaked open. He murmured gently to the grimm on the couch, and seconds later, Neera materialized through my bedroom door, curling up at the foot of my bed.

The beastie started snoring immediately.

Unlike the grimm, sleep evaded me.

We were leaving for the Jade Palace at daybreak. The little sleep I'd gotten was filled with dreams of Finn's smile and nightmares of Theo's taunting face.

Both jolted me awake.

The dreams of Finn left me confused and annoyingly aroused.

I refused to analyze why.

But it was the nightmares that made my throat ache as if the necklace was still clasped around it. My lineage magic had smoothed over the burns, and the injury no longer hurt, though a thick band of silver skin remained.

God magic could probably remove the scar where the necklace collared me, but in my quest for vengeance, I decided to leave it. It was a powerful reminder that I'd never allow anyone to control me again.

Tossing off the sheets, I cursed as my hands shook. Chaos magic sparked across my knuckles with the same frenetic energy that buzzed through my mind.

Something about the Lake of Souls nagged me the way an unfinished translation did. Like I knew there was more to do, and the feeling of leaving it incomplete was...wrong.

Giving up on sleep, I paced the perimeter of my bedroom. Switching my viewpoint to one that was purely analytical, I told myself the Lake of Souls was simply another dead language to unravel, and I was merely another scholar hunting for the origins of the dialect.

I mulled over everything. Theo's history lesson, the complex containment runes circling the lake, the way the dukhmora moved like spirits through the dark water, yet how they sank like stones after snaring them with my magic...

My eyes shot to Neera.

Why did the dukhmora sink?

Emotionally, I was a ball of nerves.

Academically, I was thrillingly stumped and overwhelmingly intrigued.

I had to find out.

Tugging a pair of dark breeches and a snug, black sweater from my wardrobe, I pondered an explanation to the dukhmora's odd reaction. Belting leather harnesses across my waist and around my thigh, I shoved the runed bone dagger Winnie gave me into the thigh sheath, opting to store my regular dagger in the new pair of boots Arthur made for me that contained a hidden weapons sleeve.

If I needed to use god magic, I'd prefer to slice my palm open with a weapon that *wouldn't* be bathed in demon blood.

More sanitary.

Neera grumbled dramatically and stretched out across the mattress, confirming she'd shadow walk to me once she woke up. I peppered kisses over her snout and ears, whispering to her how good of a beastie she was. The wagging tip of her tail told me she thoroughly enjoyed the compliments.

Now, I needed a certain grumpy Prince who could easily shadow walk the distance without burning out.

"Finn?" I hovered over him, unsure if he was awake or not. In the dark living room, he was just a big lump of blankets and pillows on my couch. "*Finneas.*"

"I'm sleeping."

Right. Not rolling my eyes was a lesson in patience. "I have an idea."

He groaned something that didn't sound coherent, so I wrapped my hands around his bicep in an attempt to shake him. Trying to move the man was like attempting to pull a boulder uphill.

Resorting to more serious means of getting my way, I flicked my finger at the lamp standing in the corner. A flash of purple flared before turning into a cheery light that brightened the entire townhouse. And a *very* disgruntled Prince.

"Is this a stupid idea?" Finn growled, squinting against the brightness.

"Why?"

"Because it's after midnight, darling. The majority of ideas after midnight are typically stupid ideas."

"There's still dukhmora in the Lake of Souls," I said proudly.

Finn yanked the blanket over his face to block the lamplight. "The terrifying lake demons can wait until morning."

I shrugged, even though he couldn't see me. "Okay, fine."

Finn mumbled in sleepy agreement.

"Good night," I drawled loudly, making a show of shutting off the lights and throwing the front door open.

Finn was off the couch in a half-second. "Where are you going?"

His demanding tone told me he was now fully awake. I couldn't help but smile.

Gods, I was good.

CHAPTER SEVENTY-ONE
DOVE

TRAILING ALONG THE BANK of the Lake of Souls, I surveyed the ground for any disturbances in the dry dirt. Finn was surprisingly receptive with shadow walking us clear across the Kingdom on an academic whim – once I allowed him a few minutes to fully wake up and come to terms with this late-night trip.

"You're looking for something specific." It wasn't a question.

"The dukhmora Theo freed didn't disturb the dirt around the lake." I responded absentmindedly, squatting down to peer closer at the perfectly undisturbed ground.

"They're spirits," Finn muttered. "Dukhmora are both in Terramere and in the veil, able to interact and physically attack beings while being annoyingly ghostly when we fight back."

I hummed, half paying attention to the Prince, half mentally rifling through everything I knew about the demons Massis created to mimic his light witches.

"But some weapons on this realm *can* hurt them. As can magic."

Finn shrugged a shoulder, following a few steps behind as I walked towards where I'd been dragged into the lake. There was disturbed dirt, drops of my blood, and scattered rocks here.

Based on my stellar observation skills, that just meant *I* wasn't in the veil.

"When I pulled the dukhmora to me, they sank down into the lake. But the ones Theo released moved through the water and crawled up the bank without leaving marks in the dirt like spirits." I glanced up at Finn. "Why did mine sink?"

Finn opened and closed his mouth, and the frown that followed told me he was as stumped as I was.

Purple magic shimmered from my palms, sweeping over the surface of the lake. I wasn't sure if god magic was needed to call the dukhmora to me, but for the sake of academic integrity, I used chaos magic first. Less bloody.

Dukhmora crawled from the brackish water, greyish hides speckled with water droplets and horns slick with algae. My jaw dropped as their long nails dug into the brittle ground, leaving gouges in the earth as they hoisted themselves from the Lake of Souls.

Heartbeat pounding, I rallied chaos magic to my palms in case they attacked. In two strides, Finn stood next to me, shadows curling around his hands defensively. We traded baffled looks as we came to the same mind-blowing conclusion.

The dukhmora I poured god magic into were *corporeal*.

All twenty dukhmora slunk from the water, chittering and loosening a series of clicks as their orb-like black eyes settled on me.

I darted my eyes between the demons. And as they huddled together, I was hit with a heartbreaking realization.

My god magic wasn't turning the dukhmora into mindless fighters that I controlled.

I wasn't controlling them *at all*.

With my god magic...I *freed* them.

Inhaling a shaky breath, my magic winked out. These demons weren't going to hurt us. Slowly, I placed my palm on Finn's arm. "They have...they have souls, Finn. I'm not controlling them. My god magic is *releasing* them from Massis's control."

Finn raised a brow, his focus still on the dukhmora standing in front of us. He lowered his hands, shadows weaving around his wrists.

"If they're free," he started slowly, "then why are they *here*? They could've left the water at any time."

I nodded, staring at the cluster of demons quietly chirping and keening, a few wrapping their elongated limbs around the others. *The dukhmora were comforting each other.* A lump formed in my throat. This was bigger than purely commanding demons to fight.

This was...

Liberation.

"Hello," I said softly, stepping closer to the dukhmora. Finn let out a strangled grunt, though he didn't move from his position. Searching my soul, I easily found Neera's connection, but now, more threads were rapidly braiding itself together next to it, creating a cord of connections that I mentally tracked to the twenty dukhmora, their expressions ranging from apprehension to fear.

The one closest to me shrank into itself with a grimace as I extended my hand slowly, removing a string of algae and muck from around its horn.

"My name is Dove. I'm not going to hurt you. Can you...can you understand that? If you do, can you nod?" I showed them the motion, bobbing my chin up and down. Finn watched with thinly veiled wariness from the corner of his eye. I kept my attention on the newly bound cord twining through my soul, the dukhmoras' emotions switching from nervousness to cautious intrigue.

I couldn't control them, but their intentions were open – similar to how my connection worked with Neera. But unlike Neera's single thread of power, the dukhmora acted like a pack, their feelings aligned and attuned to each other.

There were small differences – some were scared, and others vaguely worried, though the demons who were more fearful seemed to draw reassurance from the rest of their horde until the entire cord emitted a sense of curiosity and acceptance to my soul.

Slowly, they began mirroring my nod, some stiff while others exuberantly tossed their horned heads up and down with gleeful chirps and clicks.

"Massis was controlling you, but you're free now. I think I broke the connection that chained you to him."

Finn hissed out a warning, drawing the bone dagger from his sheath, as the dukhmora clustered closer, rising to their full heights, elongated limbs and hunched backs putting them over a foot taller than myself.

"Don't do anything," I breathed to Finn. "If this goes badly, I'll –"

Before I could finish, the demons fell to their bony knees, orb-like blacked eyes pinned on me. As one, they began chattering three short notes, in synchrony, rapt awe on their terrifying faces.

"Carra's *tits*." Finn dragged a hand through his dark hair, pushing the strands out of his face. The shadows at his feet disappeared. I glared at him.

"Don't underestimate me," I said quietly, yet firmly, my eyes changing as chaos magic bubbled up in my soul. "I'm sick and tired of witches not believing in me."

"I'd never," Finn said gruffly, raising his palms. "Dove, you are the *most* powerful witch in Terramere, the Vessel of Chaos, and now, to these demons, you are a god. I'd never underestimate you. Gods, I wouldn't even call you my *equal*. Darling, you're better than I will ever be."

My lips parted slightly at his blunt statement. Finn cocked his head, his intense hazel eyes studying my face in a way that felt more intimate than my stone heart would allow. In my head, a series of images flashed, each one more scandalous than the next. Heat rose to my cheeks and I ripped my gaze from his.

Without a word, I spun on my heel, mentally whispering to the dukhmora at my back my intentions, my desires, what I asked of them.

God magic must be needed to break Massis's hold over them, but once their connections were woven into my soul, neither of my gifts were needed.

The makings of another wild plan flitted through my mind, and I hid my smile under the curtain of my unruly hair, piecing together another perfect idea that, coincidentally, could be a lot easier with a shadow witch at my side.

The dukhmora lumbered silently behind us. I turned back to Finn. "I never wanted this much power," I admitted as I led the horde through the forest, their devotion and loyalty a warm hum through my well of magic. "But now that I have it, I have another plan."

I grinned as Finn shot me a glare. "Twenty dukhmora fighting on our side *will* help, but there's hundreds loose in the Palace. Even *with* the witches Maude cleared to fight with us, we're still wildly outnumbered. I can't turn many at once. Which is why you're going to help me bolster those numbers more."

Finn squinted like he was trying to read my mind. The way his frown deepened told me he was unsuccessful. "Where are we going to find more fighters? We can't confirm other Covens won't side with Theodoric, and it's the middle of the night."

I enjoyed Finn's grumbled curses. He seemed fully supportive of my insane musings even though he acted like he wasn't. With a toss of my hair and a smirk, I recalled a passage from *Terramere's Beasts* by Neera Mellow.

"Did you know, Princeling, that volkhounds hunt in packs?"

Chapter Seventy-Two
WINONA

WITH THE BONE DAGGER gripped in my fist, I sent another wave of shadows slithering through the tree lined path to hunt dukhmora. So far, in position outside the Palace walls, we were safe – though chittering screeches told us we wouldn't be for long if we didn't keep moving.

Finneas shadow walked to us in the Quiet around midday, looking vicious and deadly as he laid out adjusted battle plans and immediately disappeared into another gust of darkness. The lethal determination in his glare was so sharp even Merrick merely ruffled his wings and frowned at the last-minute change of plans – but didn't dare argue.

I wondered how long it would take my eldest brother to openly admit he had feelings for the Vessel of Chaos, or if he would simply growl at anyone who *wasn't* Dove until she put him out of his misery.

She seemed like a brilliant woman. I hoped she made him suffer a *little* before they gave in to the very obvious tension that sizzled between them. Yearning was good for Finneas. It built character.

Maude and Polina followed on silent feet as we prowled closer to the wrought iron gate that encompassed the mosaic-laid road to the Palace. In the distance to our left, dukhmora passed through my shadows, alerting me to danger. "Hold," I whispered, raising my right fist to signal the

Bramberry witches positioned behind a grouping of birch trunks. In my left hand, I brought my dagger to chest height in case a spirit demon shot out of the bushes and attacked.

"Hold position. Advance with signal," Maude called softly, her lithe movements and black bladed sword snagging my attention. *Gods*, I hoped I was as badass as the Bramberry Coven Mother in a few centuries. The fact that she wielded a sword made of spinel, one of two materials in Terramere that could banish dukhmora back to Avamere, made me wickedly jealous.

Especially since the only other black spinel sword I knew of belonged to Finneas, and he'd only ever let me *hold* it. One time. When I was twelve.

I strained my ears for the sound of wing beats. When Finneas asked Merrick to fly the perimeter of the Palace and give us the signal to advance, it was on the tip of my tongue to nix the idea, worried Marrick would flee with the Vessel Book the moment we were distracted.

Instead, I'd stayed silent. No one else knew what he'd done, and I hoped Merrick wouldn't take *this* opportunity to screw us over. Yet every second I waited, my heart hardened further. If that boneheaded ass left –

The soft thump of wings interrupted my venomous thoughts. I hissed in relief as Merrick circled the Palace towers in his Sentry.

He landed on the pitched roof closest to us, spiked tail lashing and runed claws gouging the shingles. Merrick stalked slowly towards the edge, muscles rippling under his slate grey hide, as he used the advantageous perch to check our path to the entrance was clear of dukhmora.

Suddenly, Merrick froze – so still as if he were truly made of stone.

On silent wings, he launched off the roof.

I held my breath as he disappeared and didn't release it until the high-pitched scream of a banished dukhmora pierced the night.

"He got one." Polina commented from my left.

I smiled grimly.

A bark rang out to our left, as a pack of sleek volkhounds loped from the overgrowth to join our ranks. Unlike the grimm, the volkhounds were the same size as a wolf, though the smoky shadows wafting from their paws spoke to otherworldly prowess. Ten pairs of ruby eyes peered at us curiously before shooting off, swift as an arrow, for the Palace.

Polina gawked.

"Dove made more friends," I chuckled quietly. Polina scrunched her pert nose in response.

"Bramberry is going to be *filled* with beasties once Dove comes home," the light witch muttered. "Unfortunately, my kids are going to *love* it."

We exchanged knowing grins.

Maude's second-in-command had apologized profusely to Velik again before we left Bramberry for accidentally attacking him in Dove's home, but the King waved away her groveling and commended her on the strength of her magic. Velik even offered her a position in the Royal Coven – which Maude snapped at him over. And then Polina snapped at Maude for meddling, swearing she would never leave Bramberry, which made Maude grumble.

It all seemed very cutthroat yet loving, and I enjoyed the intricate dynamics of the Bramberry Coven. It was wildly entertaining.

I shivered, adrenaline pumping through my veins and warming me against the chill bringing in winter's arrival. The fighting was coming. I could feel it in the air.

Just as the thought crossed my mind, the Sentry burst through the canopy. With three powerful pumps of his wings, Merrick crouched atop the roof of the abandoned foyer, swiveling around. Pinprickles of awareness coated my skin as he scanned the shadows where our troupe was positioned. We were completely swathed in darkness, but I swore his gaze pinned to mine.

He found me – even when I did my best to hide.

We stared at each other for a long moment, making a lump form uncomfortably in my throat, before Merrick turned his maw to the sky and loosened a bone-chilling roar.

Volkhounds answered the signal with a chorus of eerie howls as our troupe ran from the shadows towards the abandoned entrance.

And as the haunting battle cry faded to an echo, we brought a reckoning into the hallowed halls of the Jade Palace.

CHAPTER SEVENTY-THREE
FINNEAS

I COULD DO NOTHING but trek behind Dove as she wove gracefully through the dark trees, a silent army of dukhmora at her back. Their black eyes glowed with unwavering allegiance to the Vessel of Chaos that not only liberated them from their shackles but gave them free will.

They had *souls*.

Harsh truths were the hardest to face, and I fought internally as I kept my steps quiet. Neera – sure. The grimm had proven over and over that she followed more than a base desire to protect Dove. I'd spent time with the grimm, and I could sense there was more to her than animalistic, surface level needs.

But the dukhmora? With their lipless mouths, their hideous, twisted faces, their taught hides that rippled over thinly veiled muscle, their long, spindly limbs...

That would take more than a single rushed conversation to wrap my head around.

As we reached the abandoned entrance, I saw Winona and the Bramberry witches cross into the foyer. She noticed us too, her lips pressed into a thin line of apprehension as Dove and her dukhmora came into view. A few light witches tensed, but I'd told them earlier in the Quiet that this may happen.

They knew the corporeal demons and the volkhounds with red eyes were allies – not foes.

Wordlessly, the dukhmora filed in between witches, their night-mare-inducing forms adding bulk to our ranks. Some were hunched over on all fours, slitted nostrils flaring as they tasted the dusty air, others stood tall, chittering and conversing in their own language.

Dove palmed the bone dagger in her fist. I unsheathed the black spinel sword from between my shoulder blades, moving towards the courtyard that led into the dukhmora-occupied part of the Palace. From the pressurized power radiating off Dove, I knew she rallied her chaos magic. Dove wanted to free more of the dukhmora from Massis, but there were too many currently rampaging through the Palace, and it was dangerous for her to experiment during the heat of battle. Especially since she could only turn a handful at a time, and freeing the demons from the God of Chaos was a huge drain on her magic. But I could tell it was bothering her that she couldn't save them all.

Glancing over, I almost sank to my knees.

With half her face shrouded in shadow, her silver iris gleamed through the dimly lit foyer. Dressed in all black with her wild hair braided down the small of her back, tight breeches, leather harnesses, and purple sparks dancing across her knuckles, she looked like a dark goddess.

After almost forty years of being forsaken by the gods and never uttering a single prayer, I knew one thing with absolute certainty.

To her, I'd pray.

As if she felt my gaze on her, Dove flicked her chaos sight to me. Around the room, her dukhmora released a synchronized chirp.

I sank into the mindset of battle. My father was safely in Bramberry, protected by witches who had chosen to stay behind and defend the Bramberry Forest in case any enemies saw through our plan. Velik would be brought back home once we succeeded in removing Theo from the throne and the Palace was safe.

Winona clicked her tongue, giving me a barely visible nod. She'd start purging the Palace of demons with the witches and Dove's dukhmora.

I jerked my head to Dove.

It was time.

My shadows rose from the ground, twisting through each other and up the length of the spinel bladed sword as they created a portal that would take only Dove and myself straight to my brother. Straight to my throne.

I slipped my hand through Dove's. She squeezed my fingers.

Silent confirmation. Loaded reassurance.

I dropped her hand and shadow walked into the throne room of the Jade Palace with the Vessel of Chaos at my side.

"Hello, brother," I crooned darkly, as Theodoric shot from the throne with a stunned look on his shitty face as Dove and I stepped into the middle of the aisle that led to the dais. "You're in my seat."

The Royal Coven huddled against the walls, leering at Theodoric.

Witches were a lot of things. But *forgiving* wasn't high on our list of attributes.

Dove regarded Theodoric with calculating impassivity, her chaos sight adding to her savagely demented allure. *Gods, she was gorgeous.*

My half-brother's initial shock curled into a cruel grin. "So, you're still alive, Dove."

Dove didn't respond. Theodoric's glare narrowed, bouncing between us with suspicion. I spun the spinel sword in my palm. A muscle feathered in my brother's jaw, highlighting the sharp gauntness from powering the banishment runes himself.

With an act of disinterest, Theodoric slumped onto the throne, propping his elbows up and steepling his fingers. His eyes blacked out, lips curling mockingly. "Are you here to kill me, *brother*?"

"*Me*? No." I chuckled derisively. Dove took a single step towards the dais. "I promised Dove the honor. She *really* wants to kill you. And I'd love to watch her rip you to shreds."

As if my words were a cue, chaos magic bathed her beautiful features in violet. With pouty lips twisting into a sneer, she appraised Theodoric with disdain.

"You betrayed me," she rasped.

Against the walls, the Royal Coven listened intently as Cordelia murmured orders to power the banishment runes once they fell out of Theodoric's control. Cordelia – Winona's old friend, and very insightful witch.

Theo rose slowly. He'd been using too much chaos magic – not understanding that even lineage gifts burned out.

Dove laughed, tossing her braid over her shoulder as she advanced down the aisle towards the throne. "And to think, this entire time, I *knew* it would never truly work between us. I'm *much* too good for you."

Theodoric bared his teeth at her.

Chaos magic hummed against her palms as she pointed to Theodoric. "Your arrogance is going to cost you everything."

"And your refusal to bow will result in your death." Theo growled back, purple light rallying to his hands.

Dove merely smirked, and I saw the exact moment realization dawned on Theo that he wouldn't win this fight as easily as he anticipated. She was rested, at full power, not at the mercy of any blood runes, and had taken him by surprise.

Not to mention she was the Vessel of Chaos.

Theo, however, spent a full day draining his gift into the banishment runes and believed she was dead.

This was the precipice – if Theo concluded she truly was stronger he could wane, allowing the horde of bloodthirsty dukhmora to enter the throne room and attack before the Royal Coven could re-activate the banishment runes.

I spoke up, "What if we came to an agreement? Peacefully? For you to hold the throne?"

Theodoric's brows furrowed in confusion before relaxing.

He *wanted* to believe he could defeat Dove, and my question aimed to trick him into thinking that I was willing to give up the throne to him.

I strode towards the dais. Dove ducked to pull something from her boot. A flash of silver made me wince, but she only tightened her palm against the blade, using my bulk to hide her plan.

"I never wanted to rule." The lie dripped effortlessly from my tongue just like every other time I spoke those words from the moment my shadows first manifested, and my succession was denied. "What if I tell Velik I don't want to be Heir?"

"Why would you do that?" Theo asked dubiously.

But he was fully focused on me now – and not Dove who squatted behind Bron, whispering to Cordelia and a few other Royal Coven witches. Then, when she was hidden perfectly under the bright purple light spilling from one of the banishment runes, she waned.

I shrugged, dangling the metaphorical crown in front of Theodoric's hungry gaze. All he wanted was power. It made him blind to everything else. My shadows rippled across the floor, hovering a few inches off the ground until the dais rose above a sea of thick, inky black fog. I wanted Theo to think I was threatening him with my heritage gift – though the real reason was simply poetic justice that reminded me to never get on Dove's bad side.

"You've been Heir for decades – I was disappointed Velik changed the succession. I've gotten used to my freedom outside the Palace and don't want that to change."

Theo regarded me with amusement, as if he knew something I didn't. "You'd rather romp around the Kingdom in dirty clothes and get in fights with dukhmora over living in luxury?"

"I've never considered myself materialistic," I replied smoothly. "But if you feel safer sitting in an uncomfortable chair enacting no real change, then Velik should definitely give you the crown." I ran a hand through my hair. "My ego doesn't need to be constantly stroked like yours. I've never struggled with insecurity, and I don't want the burden of ruling."

With a manic laugh, Theo threw his hands wide. His blacked eyes widened at my feigned contempt. "*Burden?* How is it a *burden* to be the most powerful witch in Terramere?"

"Well..." I drew out the word with a long sigh, hoping I'd given Dove enough time. "Wearing a crown doesn't suddenly make you *powerful*. And you aren't the strongest witch in Terramere. Dove is."

Theo reared back, seeking out Dove – just like I knew he would.

"She's a Vessel – and you *only* have chaos magic. Dove has *god* power." I hated the way his eyes flared with hunger the moment they landed on her. She stood behind me, which I hoped meant everyone else was readying themselves accordingly.

And I hated myself even more when I breathed, "I've seen her god magic, brother. Dove can do things you can only *dream* of. She's formidable - *unstoppable*. The sole reason you beat her at the Lake of Souls is because you trapped her in blood stones. But now?" I let out a rough laugh. "What's stopping her from killing you and taking the crown, herself? *Who's* going to stop her? Who would be able to?"

Red tinted magic wove through the purple, brushing affectionately against my shadows.

I raised my hands in mock surrender, backing up and out of the way as I planted more and more seeds of doubt in Theo's mind, seeing each poisonous word land like a blow against his ego.

"I wouldn't stop her." My gaze settled on Dove. I spoke my truth, my vows, to her. "Godsdamned, I'd marry her. Treat her like the goddess she is."

Dove stiffened. When we were going over the plan on how to get Theo to snap, I left out this part.

Theo scoffed, though that flicker of worry in his expression told me we were winning the mind fuck game. "She may be *slightly* stronger than I am, but she couldn't control the dukhmora in the lake. Even though she took god magic, it's apparent she didn't siphon a lot."

"Would you bet your life on that?" Dove piped back, her bell-like voice making the threat sound unhinged. Her eyes were still on mine.

Theo blanched, attempting to recover her attention, to get her to settle her gorgeous eyes back onto him.

"I'd bet the lives of each and every witch in the Royal Coven on it," Theo yelled.

Dove turned away, and iciness broke over me the moment her focus shifted. Theodoric preened, believing his threats got him what he wanted once again.

"Do you know what you taught me?" Dove asked softly, her chaos magic dimming as a fury of red surged at her fingertips. "Aside from the fact you're a worthless, power-hungry leech?"

She raised her hand where a deep, bloody cut slowly knit itself together across her palm. Theo froze. Baring her teeth, Dove purred wickedly, "You taught me a lot about blood runes."

Squeezing her hand into a fist, a few drops of blood splattered onto the throne room floor.

Theodoric lunged forward, but he was too slow. God magic erupted from Dove, imbuing the circle of blood runes around the dais, hidden from sight by my shadows until this very moment. As I called the darkness back to myself, vibrant red magic illuminated Dove's vicious smile and the exact same blood boosted containment runes Theo used to trap her underwater in the Lake of Souls.

Chapter Seventy-Four

DOVE

Three things happened simultaneously.

Theo bellowed a curse as he tried and failed to wane – only succeeding in spinning and stumbling on the slick stone dais like a complete fool.

Every banishment rune he'd been powering died out.

And the throne room doors burst open, letting in a wave of dukhmora that had been waiting for the banishment runes to fall so they could feed.

But we were ready.

I'd given Cordelia succinct and hasty orders before waning around the throne room, painting runes with my own blood. As dukhmora lunged, witches poured magic into the stained-glass banishment runes. The rest of the Royal Coven flanked them protectively, unleashing blasts of well-timed attacks, beating the horde back.

I raised my hands, sending arrows of chaos magic towards the dukhmora, wishing I could take the time to break their collars and free them, but knowing banishment back to Avamere was the only way to save Finn's Coven in the heat of the moment. Tendrils of violet threaded through shadow, shoving demons back towards the threshold of the room.

Theo couldn't get out. He wouldn't leave this room until he was good and dead.

Then I'd drop the containment runes so he could burn.

A flash of pure white light, and the banishment runes powered back up with a roar. The Royal Coven cheered as dukhmora stumbled from the room, shrieking in fury as the runes shoved them out the doors.

Finn gifted me a wicked grin. "That went well."

I rolled my eyes, his brevity grounding me firmly back into reality.

"Are you out of breath?" I asked incredulously as he doubled over, bracing his hands on his knees.

Finn squinted up at me, strands of dark hair falling over his eyes. "Does saying '*yes*' win me sympathy points?"

"Not from me." *I was such a liar.*

"Then, no. I'm not out of breath." He straightened, dusting invisible dirt off his jacket. "Creating enough shadows to fill the throne room and hold them a few inches above the ground was incredibly easy, actually."

Warmth squeezed through the cracks in the wall guarding my heart as Finn winked at me.

Winked.

Swoon.

I shook my head, turning away so he wouldn't see the flush creeping up my cheeks. Unfortunately, I pivoted right in front of Cordelia, who had a brow raised and a shit-eating smirk on her face.

"Don't start," I warned her.

She snorted, wrapping me in a hug. "I'm so glad you're alright. We were worried *sick*. And, I'm so sorry, but what happened to your *magic*?"

"I'm alright," I echoed. "The rest is a long, sordid tale for when we have a minute to breathe, but I swear I'll tell you." Cordelia nodded slowly. She wasn't the only one who'd noticed my magic was purple, but she *was* the sole witch who'd approached me.

The idea of the Royal Coven turning on me had bitter irritation flooding my mouth. I switched my sight back to normal, shifting closer to Finn and Bron.

Bron's normally gentle expression was filled with angst as he murmured in a low voice to Finn, gesturing to the pile of bodies in the corner covered with tablecloths.

Not every witch made it out alive. I glared at Theo – the witch this Coven *should* direct their anger at. The False King.

Theo didn't meet my eyes, just sat on the throne with his head in his hands. There was no smugness to him now, and I saw him for what he truly was – a weak witch with an ugly heart.

He wasn't worth pity or a moment of my time. He wasn't even worth the heartbreak.

"We'll have a memorial once the Palace is safe," Finn grunted in that rough, detached tone that told me he was deflecting – that he felt each death and took the losses personally.

Shouts and screeches from the Great Hall had chaos magic sparking across my knuckles once more, my sight flickering and changing as the sounds of fighting grew closer. A rush of muttering started as more of the Royal Coven noticed I was a chaos witch.

Heretic.

They thought I was a heretic.

I cut my attention to a group of four edging closer, their faces stony and magic glowing at their palms. With slow steps, I retreated backwards, never taking my eyes off them. They whispered something to another group, confirming I was in trouble without some intervention from the Heir of the Kingdom. Cordelia slid in front of me, silver magic glowing at her palms as she faced off against her own Coven.

For me.

"Finn." My back bumped into his hip as the witches advanced, pitting both Cordelia and me in their hard stares. "We have a problem."

Finn snapped his head up, the fury he wanted to direct at his brother now aimed to the witches crowding closer to me. Bron growled and grabbed my upper arm, dragging me behind him before rising to his full height and baring his teeth at the cluster of Royal Coven witches stalking closer. My heart pounded. I couldn't protect myself – if I fought back, I'd be the villain.

Shadows reared up from the floor, forming a protective wall around me as Bron and the Shadow Prince stood with Cordelia, facing off against the witches sneering at me with pure hate.

"Back down now," Finn barked, his hazel eyes burning with dark intensity. "We're going to get one thing straight right fucking now. Everything we knew about heretic magic was *wrong*." Cordelia darted to my side, light magic rallied as she raised her chin and stared down the witches with the promise of death in their eyes.

"Dove is the Vessel of Chaos and the uncontested strongest witch here. You harm *her*, you share a pyre with Theodoric and Dahlia. Any questions?"

The sharpness to Finn's threat had the group backing away, though their outward disgust and morbid curiosity caused my skin to prickle in warning. Master Vole hustled forward, standing with Bron while visibly shaking.

It seemed Bron, Cordelia, and Master Vole were the only ones who wholeheartedly believed Finn. The rest of the Coven regarded me with varying degrees of distrust.

Might as well make it worse, right?

"There are dukhmora fighting on our side," I said loudly, drawing the Coven's focus. In my peripherals, Theo jerked up to stare at me. Ignoring him, I continued, "They are physical beings that were enslaved by Massis. I freed them with my god magic, and they are here on their own free will, boosting our ranks with their magic. If you encounter corporeal dukhmora or volkhounds with red eyes, don't be afraid. They are our allies."

"Don't attack them," Finn added, his curt tone brokering no protest. "You kill one of the demons fighting to save your asses, and you'll catch the same charge as if you murdered a fellow member of your Coven."

Grimaces and frowns followed Finn's declaration as the tension faded. If anything, witches were loyal to a fault. Those that supported Finn's succession over Theo's would follow the new Heir's orders without argument.

The Royal Coven nodded, some more hesitantly than others.

I wasn't being hunted. That was good enough for now. I'd work on the niceties later.

My sight flicked to the False King.

But I *was* going to make godsdamned sure Theo didn't live long enough to watch me win over his Coven.

CHAPTER SEVENTY-FIVE
MERRICK

MERRICK ROARED, SWINGING HIS tail, the sigils etched along each spike flaring as three more dukhmora were banished back to Avamere. Blood trickled from a gash on his side, but the cut was shallow, and his accelerated healing abilities were already knitting his hide back together.

They'd cleared a third of the Jade Palace already and were fighting their way through the second courtyard. Winnie, Merrick, and Maude led the troupe, and Polina commanded the Bramberry witches flanking their sides, banishing demons that evaded their first assault.

"Shift!" Winnie yelled as they cleared the last twenty feet of courtyard. Merrick pushed his Sentry deep inside his soul, shifting into his humanoid form and wrenching the bone dagger from the sheath at his waist as shadows ripped open the doors of the next building.

Silver magic preceded Merrick as he ran into the corridor, launching the bone dagger through the chest of the first dukhmora that appeared. It let out a hoarse shriek and vanished. Merrick dove across the floor, snatching his dagger and slamming it up into the throat of a dukhmora who tried to attack him from behind.

Witches flooded the space, exterminating demons with lethal precision. Maude threw her hand out, a rope of silver snaring two dukhmora and dragging them to her. The spinel blade she wielded with expertise be-headed both in one fell swoop.

Winnie and Polina were right on his heels, taking out two more demons that appeared at close range.

The corporeal dukhmora that fought alongside them chirped and chattered with deranged glee, galloping up the stairs on all fours. Their job was to clear the top floors, and they were excelling at it with brutal efficiency. Dove's dukhmora were also wonderful at fetching his dagger if he threw it too far away, and they always delivered it with their gnarled fingers wrapped around the hilt, and a round of thrilled chittering. It never failed to send a shudder of trepidation through Merrick as they stared at him with creepy blacked eyes and lipless grins that showed off jagged fangs.

But the gesture itself was sweet, and Merrick made sure to thank the dukhmora every time they proudly returned his weapon.

"Almost halfway," Winnie gritted as they hustled down the hall.

Merrick grunted. With each step he took deeper into the Palace, Winnie pulled further and further away. She'd barely made eye contact with him – even when he'd bit through two dukhmora right in front of her earlier while in his Sentry.

A blur of black shot by as Neera and a pack of volkhounds snarled and yipped, brutally tearing a cluster of dukhmora apart with claws and fangs.

He pushed past the sorrow festering into guilt as Maude released a barrage of light magic, blowing out a portion of the wall so Polina and a group of Bramberry witches could banish the handful of dukhmora hiding in one of the private gardens.

The moment of wishing Winnie would look at him allowed a pair of dukhmora to catch him by surprise, their jaws snapping close to his wings. He ducked, evading one of the demons, and before he could do more than curse and raise his weapon, one of Dove's dukhmora tore out the attacker's throat with sharp fangs and an enthusiastic whistle.

Merrick breathed out a polite thank you to the friendly dukhmora as it cheerfully bounded up a set of stairs to his left. Pivoting, he pinned the second demon with a glare as it whirled around and crouched, chittering in frustration.

Merrick cocked his arm back, ready to down the foe the second it lurched from the floor, when a burst of purple magic barreled into it, sending it to Avamere once more.

Which meant –

The purple light surged through the hall, followed by a whip of shadow.

Dove, Finneas, and the Royal Coven rounded the corner, fighting the dukhmora at the other end of the Great Hall – they were meeting in the middle.

Three hundred feet separated them.

This was almost over.

And the hourglass filled with the sands of Merrick's betrayal was almost empty, counting down the last minutes Merrick would have with Winnie before she found out he double-crossed her.

He'd be long gone by then – if his calculations were correct.

Before he left, he'd kiss her.

One last time.

Merrick pumped his wings hard, landing near Winnie and banishing the dukhmora she was fighting. The moment their immediate area was cleared, he grabbed her arm, spinning her around to face him. The wild fury in her hazel irises ignited as she sucked in a sharp gasp. "Kiss me, Princess," Merrick croaked.

Winnie stiffened as she slammed her lips against his. Wrapping his fingers around the nape of her neck with a growl, they battled each other with teeth and tongue as viciously as they fought off the dukhmora horde. Far too soon, Winnie yanked herself out of his grasp to whip shadows across the room and banish two dukhmora crawling through a busted window.

With her lips swollen from the fierce kiss, she glanced back to him, confusion and desperation dancing across her heart-shaped face.

Merrick couldn't meet Winnie's eyes, and he was secretly relieved when four dukhmora rounded the corner and charged them. "After this," Merrick sliced the dagger across the first attacker's throat, leaping away as the spirit's black blood sprayed everywhere, "do you want to meet in the abandoned foyer? We can celebrate your demon-free Palace with our clothes off."

The words were painful, the beginnings of his escape plan. Merrick hated how badly he wished sinking between Winnie's thighs was his *actual* plan. But he'd vowed to keep Lenna safe. And Merrick couldn't give up on the Oracle now.

Winnie laughed, but the sound was hollow. "Of course," she hissed, baring her teeth as she chucked her dagger through a dukhmora that scurried towards her on all fours. It shrieked and disappeared. "It's the only thing you're good for, anyway. Since your fighting is positively dreadful."

Merrick scoffed, whirling around to impale a dukhmora with the runed talon at the apex of his wing. "I've definitely killed more than you, *Princess*."

"You're a terrible prisoner," Winnie sneered, as shadows returned the weapon to her hand. "But at least you're a decent lay."

Polina squeaked in surprise behind them, and Merrick grimaced as the light witch scrambled away to engage another enemy, the tips of her ears red.

Winnie rolled her eyes as Merrick banished the last dukhmora. Without a word, the Princess shoved past him, stalking towards Maude without a backwards glance.

An uncomfortable sensation of dread wound through him. Winnie couldn't know he stole the Vessel Book – *right?*

He shook off the thought, calling it paranoia.

There was no way Winnie knew he was preparing to leave.

Neera materialized next to him, the grimm leveling the gargoyle with pretentiousness as if she didn't approve of his inner turmoil. Merrick rewarded the beastie's judgement with a flat look. Her maw dripped with black gore from the dukhmora she'd slayed, and Merrick could've sworn the grimm rolled her ruby eyes at him before disregarding him with a huff. Proudly holding her tail high, thick wisps of smoke trailed behind her as she trotted towards Dove.

Merrick rubbed his beard in frustration.

The sooner he escaped, the sooner his delusions that everyone was out to get him would fade.

"All good?" Finneas shouted as the Royal Coven and corporeal dukhmora flanking the Shadow Prince fanned out, clearing rooms that branched off the Great Hall.

"Just fucking peachy," Winnie retorted, wiping away a rivulet of blood from a small cut on her brow.

Merrick trailed after Winnie and the Bramberry witches, and they converged with the Royal Coven, hugs and low conversations blooming around them as the Covens reunited.

"There could still be a few stragglers we missed," Maude announced as she bowed to the Heir. "But you'll find your Palace is nearly secured, your Highness."

Dove threw her arms around Polina, the females embracing and scanning each other for injuries. Maude stood a few feet away, a tiny smile on her face as she watched her daughters.

Dove's eyes changed from her rallied chaos magic back to her brown and blue irises. The handful of dukhmora surrounding her chirped happily, scampering towards the entrance of the Palace. "My dukhmora and volkhounds will do a full sweep of the grounds and forest. They sense demons easier, and they'll banish any that evaded us."

Maude gave her a curt nod and pulled Dove into her arms. Dove startled before her eyes filled with unshed tears and she embraced her mother tightly. Relief crossed the Coven Mother's features. Seeing her daughter, now the Vessel of Chaos, command an army of ruthless dukhmora, multiple packs of volkhounds, and the grimm currently sitting at her side seemed to shift their dynamic into a more positive light.

Once mother and daughter broke apart, Dove stroked Neera's back, murmuring something to her before the grimm vanished in a plume of black smoke. A beat later, a pack of volkhounds darted down the hall, baying with glee as they raced to catch up to wherever Neera disappeared to.

Swallowing thickly, Merrick tried to catch Winnie's eye, but the Princess dutifully ignored him. Adrenaline churned from fighting, mixing with the overwhelming unease that his time in the Jade Kingdom was ending. He glanced over to Winnie before wiping dukhmora blood off his bone dagger and sheathing it.

Finneas strode over to where Merrick was propped against the wall. For a moment, Merrick thought the Heir was going to speak with him, but he walked over to Dove and Polina. The females paused as Finneas nodded to Dove. "You still want to do it?"

Dove raised her chin. "Yes."

Finneas said nothing – only offered the hilt of his black bladed sword to the Vessel. Dove took it, her chaos sight returning as she stood slowly with the spinel sword gripped in her fist. Purple sparks crackled down the length of the blade as she cut a dark expression towards the throne room.

Polina and Maude sidled up to Merrick's side. They exchanged grim acknowledgement over the imminent execution of the False King.

Finneas jerked his chin towards them. "Polina, Maude, Winona, Merrick. C'mon. The rest of you, stay alert until Neera returns. Once Neera comes back, the Palace is secure."

Dove was already halfway down the length of the Great Hall, storming towards the throne room. Finneas and Winnie a few steps behind. The fact she still refused to pay attention to him had Merrick's heart thudding painfully against his ribs.

But it was for the best.

Merrick shoved his hands in his pockets, in stride with Polina and Maude.

"Ready to witness a Royal execution, gargoyle?" Maude asked quietly, the tension in the air thick with apprehension.

Merrick snorted, "Would you believe me if I said this is a pretty common occurrence in Irridessen?"

"Killing a Royal?" Polina asked with intrigue as they neared the closed doors. "That...happens a lot where you're from?"

"Irridessen isn't very different from the Jade Kingdom. One day, I hope you have the pleasure of meeting Queen Esmeray. She's truly going to *adore* your bloodthirsty land."

To that, Maude cackled, patting Merrick on the bicep. "Then I hope you're successful in your next endeavors, Sir Merrick. Since it would bring about the end of the Jade Kingdom's exile."

Merrick stared at the witch. Maude merely gave him a knowing nod, a cunning smile working its way across her mouth.

He had to get out of here, right now.

His paranoia was getting worse with every passing second.

Eyeing the throne room doors with apprehension, he flexed his wings. *Was he walking into a trap?*

But even as he assured himself no one knew his intentions, unease remained.

Chapter Seventy-Six

WINONA

Part of me wished I could kill Theodoric, however, after hearing about the terrifying sacrifice Dove survived, she needed this. Reclaiming peace through bloodshed was the way of the witch.

Merrick stayed a few steps behind me; his aura flooded with potent regret and guilt. One day, I'd tell him he sucked at being a thief, but right now I couldn't bear to look at him.

He'd make his escape soon, and I needed to know where he was bringing the Book of Carra. If his actions placed my Kingdom in danger, I'd take the kill shot before he crossed into Topaz.

It would destroy my heart, but I'd do it for my Kingdom. Gods, being a Princess was *all* fun and games.

I hoped Polina was truly as good at imbuing tracker runes as she claimed to be.

Stuffing my hand in the pocket of my jacket, I ran my thumb over the small, flat-faced runestone that connected to the one I'd snuck into Merrick's bag. Because I was a bitch, I tucked the tracker runestone directly under the damn Vessel Book he'd taken.

Once he escaped, my runestone would glow when I pointed it in the direction he traveled and dull if I headed the wrong way. The bonehead wouldn't even see me coming.

And with the way he was acting, he planned to run soon.

Tonight.

While I had unlimited darkness to siphon.

Boneheaded idiot.

Dove's gasp pulled me out from my brooding.

"Where the fuck is Theodoric?" Finneas snarled, snatching Bron by the collar and shoving him against the wall.

Bron raised his shaking hands in surrender. "We didn't – I *swear* we didn't let him out."

I blew past Finneas and a furious Dove to see for myself.

"How?" Dove whispered. The spinel sword lowered, her grasp on it loosening as her shoulders slumped in defeat.

Maude and Polina entered with Merrick. *Not* that I was looking at him. Maude spread her arms wide, light magic shimmering in the air and swirling over the bloody containment runes, dimming the red glow.

"There." Maude pointed to the single sigil that wasn't reacting against her magic. "You said Theodoric knows advanced blood runes. There's your proof, my Dove. That boosted containment rune isn't functioning. My guess – he had a berserker bloodstone hidden on him. It's a true blood rune, and a nasty one at that, but if imbued properly, he could throw the berserker at any sigil and break it."

Dove let out a string of curses as she sank to her knees, the spinel sword falling from her hand.

My fury mounted as I stared blankly at the empty throne, blood boiling.

Finneas kneeled next to Dove, wrapping an arm around her slim shoulders. He'd released Bron, and the Rummerock witch had hurried over to Cordelia, the pair speaking quietly as they embraced.

To add to my ire, Merrick's solid presence stood at my back. My fingers curled into a fist.

"You'll be safe, darling. I promise." Finneas soothed as Dove buried her face in his chest. At first, I thought she was crying, but when I peeked, her chaos sight met my eyes, simmering with pure, unadulterated, ruthlessness.

I dipped my chin in respect.

Vindictive bitches recognized vindictive bitches.

I knew I liked her.

Master Vole wheezed, issuing orders for messengers and Moon Crows to spread the missive that Theodoric was exiled and any witch helping him would be punished severely.

That was witch talk for "you'll burn alive on a pyre."

I smiled bitterly, remembering when that same message had gone out about me.

Now, looking back, I was eternally grateful for the years I spent outside the Palace walls. I took in the stone throne, the delicate stained-glass depicting the gods – more visible now that the banishment runes were down.

When I first stepped foot in the Jade Palace for the Royal Ball, I wondered if I'd gain some semblance of peace over returning home. But that feeling evaded me.

If anything, being here stoked my restlessness. Rolling my shoulders back, the assortment of injuries I'd sustained fighting zinged with burning pain. Scrunching my nose, I caught my brother's frustrated eye contact.

Without uttering a word, I knew we were thinking the same thing.

Theodoric wouldn't be stupid enough to stay in the Jade Kingdom. With lineage magic and the ability to wane, he was long gone by now.

"There's nothing left for him here," I said dismissively as I patted Dove's shoulder. I wanted to comfort her, but I also needed distance between Merrick and I. "Theodoric ran because he's a coward. Don't let this break you."

Dove lifted her head, blowing out a harsh breath as she stood, using my brother as support. Her eyes flicked back to normal, though the edged energy pouring off her said she was contemplating how much fun it would be to hunt Theodoric for sport. She squatted down, picking up the spinel sword and handed it back to Finneas. "Theo can't hide forever."

The patter of claws interrupted us. Neera let out a happy howl, lunging at the Vessel and knocking her over, her plumed tail wagging so fast the shadows turned into a haze of grey-ish fog. Dove laughed, the sound bright against a sordid backdrop.

Maude hummed as she came to stand next to me, tapping a single long fingernail against her lips. The Coven Mother didn't have a single strand of hair out of place, nor a speck of blood on her. Again – I hoped to be as cool as her in a few centuries. The lethal witch had dispatched dukhmora to Avamere with fluid slashes of her sword and silver arrows of light magic. In the aftermath of battle, Maude wasn't even *sweaty*. Realizing she *also* managed to avoid the black gore from the banished dukhmora made me even more starstruck.

In comparison, I was splattered with blood, some of it mine, and didn't want to see the condition of my hair until after three long, hot showers. Minimum.

"You know, with Dahlia's death, you're Coven Mother of the Royal Coven now."

Oh, right.

I deflated. Maude chuckled. But...glancing over, I spied Dove who was petting Neera, cooing softly to her, while Finneas stood at her side with a dumb, lovestruck grin plastered on his face as he gave the Vessel of Chaos moon eyes.

Dove peered over to Finneas. In return, he slashed her a *very* improper smirk. She blushed furiously.

Nudging Maude with my elbow, I tilted my chin towards them. "I don't think the Coven Mother position is going to be vacant for long," I surmised. "My father seems to have fallen for his healer, and something tells me our Heir is bringing a bride with him once Velik relinquishes the throne."

Maude tipped her head towards...Merrick. *Fuck.* "Well, sometimes our loved ones surprise us," she started. "And just when we believe we're doing the right thing by keeping them close, we realize they have their own battles to fight – their *own* demons to banish."

I straightened. *We weren't talking about Finneas and Dove, were we?*

Keeping my face carefully blank, I appraised Maude with renewed suspicion. The wicked woman clicked her tongue. "The hardest thing to do is swallow our selfish assumptions and, instead, give *support* to those we love – ask *why* they're so determined to walk a different path than the one we wanted."

"This is about *Dove*?"

Maude gave me a stern look. "We both know it isn't, Winona."

I groaned, "I'm too tired for life lessons, Mother." With a wry chuckle, Maude gave me a curt bow and glided away, beckoning Polina to her side.

Unconsciously, I immediately found Merrick in the crowded room. He leaned below the stained-glass mosaic of Moirai, the God of Sight, his wings folded tightly to his back – a tell that meant he was agitated. With the moonlight streaming through the fractured colors, it looked as if small sparkles floated through the air between us.

Our eyes met.

My breath hitched.

We stood like that for a long moment – two different sides of the room, two different paths.

He ducked his head as Finneas began barking orders for everyone to clean up and to get some rest. The throne room slowly emptied as Master Vole hurried about, ushering the Bramberry Coven towards guest housing, while the Royal Coven staggered towards the door, some with arms slung around the injured, supporting their weight.

The Elite Scholar paused as he passed me. "Winona, is my brother alright?"

I gave my uncle what I hoped was an innocent smile. "Velik will be home in the next day or so," I reassured Vole. "He's perfectly fine." For a minute, I thought Vole was going to ask why I stole the Book of Carra.

In my defense, sure, I stole it *first* – but Merrick stole it *last,* and by my calculations, that was the worse offense.

Vole let out a strangled sob of relief, and I shoved down the overwhelming urge to cry. My father and Vole were identical twins – and my uncle was a stark reminder of how gaunt Velik became under Dahlia's cruelty.

I tried clearing my throat to stop the tears. "He loves you, you know," Vole added roughly. "And you'll always have a home here, Winona."

Not trusting my voice to come out steadily, I nodded. Vole bowed before rushing away to help the healers.

Guards were carefully levitating the dead towards the morgue to prepare them for death ceremonies while scholars used magic to scrub Dove's blood runes off the tile floor and clean the broken glass and gore splattered everywhere.

A couple of the Palace cooks announced they'd be making meals for everyone, and a few healers still scurried about, palms glowing as they moved the critically injured witches towards the Palace infirmary.

Across the room, Finneas approached Dove, and I couldn't help my smug chuckle as my brother got caught in her orbit once more. She beamed up at him, and though they weren't touching, I would bet my Royal Title that it was only a matter of time before the two got together.

"Win," Cordelia darted up to my side, offering me a sliver of torn parchment. "Sir Merrick asked me to give this to you."

I scanned the throne room, Merrick's absence a dagger to the gut. He was *gone*.

"Thanks," I mumbled, unfolding the note with trembling fingers. Cordelia hovered near me, like she was waiting to say something more.

"That is all, thank you, Cordelia," I snapped, internally wincing as it came out harsher than necessary, though my oldest friend raised a brow and snorted, a contrite expression on her face. "Shoo, you heathen. I love you." I amended, waving her away.

"Love you, too – even though you're a saucy, mean Princess," Cordelia cooed sarcastically, curtsying dramatically low before heading back to Bron.

I ripped the note open, scanning it quickly.

Meet me in the abandoned foyer in two hours.

A thrill danced down my spine as I reread Merrick's note again.

Two hours gave him a head start, and he could fly, but I could shadow walk. Sentry or not, he had to land *eventually*. His wings were too weak for long flights.

If anything, the note confirmed he felt guilty for running.

"You're going to need a new Coven Mother," I announced breezily, tossing the words over my shoulder to Finneas and Dove as I stalked out of the throne room. "I'm not interested in the position."

I didn't know what I'd do once I hunted Merrick down, but I was bringing a dagger and my tender, anxious heart that only beat for him.

Once I heard him out, I'd decide which one I wanted to use more.

CHAPTER SEVENTY-SEVEN
DOVE

THREE DAYS HAD PASSED since the dukhmora horde was banished from the Palace and Theo escaped. Two nights ago, we'd held a much more somber gathering around the Palace's ceremonial funeral pyre to pay our respects to the witches who lost their lives fighting to protect their Kingdom.

But today was for celebration.

I smoothed my palm down the shimmery gown Maude surprised me with this morning. The fabric was a gorgeous shade of violet, with sheer, off the shoulder sleeves.

When my mother broke down and cried while gifting me a dress for King Velik's return, I'd been shocked. But I was completely stunned when Maude said she was incredibly proud of me.

We'd both dissolved into tears then – only brushing them away with shaky laughter once Polina popped into the room and told us we had ten minutes to get to the throne room.

Maude shot back that we *actually* had twenty minutes, and the two descended into their typical bickering. With them, it felt like home.

Today was my last day in the Jade Palace. I'd be returning to Bramberry Forest with them tomorrow morning after the festivities. Velik had no desire to understand the Vessel Book, and was incredibly surprised to learn Theo brought translators to the Palace during his brief Regency.

Which was perfectly fine with me. I never wanted to see the infernal Book of Carra again. The Goddess of Salvation could keep her secrets for all I cared. I had enough going on with my chaos magic and the fact I was the Vessel of Chaos. Bitchy goddesses were *far* down the list of my priorities.

Taking a deep breath, I snuck a peek at Finn from under my lashes. He stood next to me on the dais, in a tunic the same hue as my gown. It was such a contrast from the black clothing he normally wore that I figured my mother had been *heavily* involved in the Heir's wardrobe selection. I looked curiously to Maude who stood across the dais in a jade-colored suit, her hair tucked in her signature bun. When she caught my eye, I inclined my head towards Finn.

In response, Maude simply winked.

I rolled my eyes at her *very* obvious meddling before stealing another glance at Finn. His dark hair was slicked back, with a simple golden crown adorning his brow.

Now that he was the *Crown Prince*, he, well, wore a crown.

To top off the list of things I never believed the shadow witch would willingly don, thick gold rings with teardrop diamonds decorated his fingers. However, with all the embellishment Finn now sported, he'd scowled when Maude slapped his hand and huffed that he wasn't allowed to roll the sleeves of his shirt up until *after* the ceremony concluded.

He'd trimmed his beard short for the occasion, which emphasized his strong jawline and full lips. In the brightly colored tunic with dark grey trousers, his already muscular stature appeared broader. I surveyed his thick, drool-worthy biceps, trailing my eyes down to his –

"Are you seriously staring at my ass right now?" Finn purred quietly so only I could hear.

Dammit.

"You wish," I muttered, averting my sightline entirely to Polina and her family sitting in the first row of pews, desperately trying to wrangle their youngest child under control.

The Crown Prince smirked and, *fuck*, I was blushing.

Henir let out a frustrated screech from Arthur's lap, displeased that he couldn't wander around the room. Arthur and Polina traded exasperated grimaces as Henir thrashed his chunky legs and loosened a frustrated wail since his demands for toddler freedom weren't being met.

Elijah scooted closer to his little brother, opening his palm to reveal a blob of shadow magic that inched across his arm like a fat caterpillar. At the sight of the magical bug, Henir squealed with excitement, his chubby hands outstretched to catch it, though Elijah used his witchling magic to make the shadow insect dart away and crawl playfully around Henir's wrist.

Polina and Arthur made exaggerated shows of relief, wiping the backs of their hands dramatically across their foreheads before laying a soft kiss on Polina's cheek.

Yesterday, Finn asked what I wanted to do, going so far as to grant me a permanent room in the Palace if I chose to stay, but I couldn't bring myself to accept. I missed Bramberry Forest, and part of my plan for vengeance against Theo included reclaiming the places he tainted – like the meadow of wildflowers and the winding trails through the sacred oak trees.

I missed my rickety townhouse on the cobblestone street, and living close to Polina and her boys. There were too many invisible wounds that needed time to heal after everything that happened over the last month, and I would be doing myself a disservice if I pushed my mental health to the side.

Elijah's shadow caterpillar vanished with a *poof*, his little face screwing up in concentration as he willed another into existence before Henir could start howling again. The shadow witchling still needed a teacher, and I wanted to teach. At least a little.

With the new magic in my veins, I could.

Maude offered me a position teaching any subject I preferred, declaring she'd work around whatever schedule I desired. I promised my mother I'd let her know once I felt ready.

Before anything else, I wanted to explore more of my new magic and finish translating the journal on *A Testimony to Massis and His Hidden Lineage Gift.*

A lump formed in my throat. Leaving the Jade Palace was bittersweet, but I always knew my time here would be temporary.

Bron was staying in the Jade Palace. His decision didn't surprise me since Cordelia was promoted to an elite position in the King's Guard, and Rummerock had always been amenable to sharing witches with the Royal Coven. They'd visit me in Bramberry soon, and I looked forward to showing them my home.

There was only one person left to say goodbye to.

If you told me a month ago that leaving the arrogant, cocky Prince behind would move me to tears, I would've scoffed. Now, I fought those stupid tears with everything I had.

"I'm going to miss you," I whispered to Finn, keeping my gaze trained on the door where Velik would enter.

Finn raised a brow in confusion. "Why would you miss me?"

"Because I'm going back to Bramberry," I reminded him. "Tonight."

With a thoughtful hum, Finn faced forward to the witches congregating into the throne room and dismissing me completely. Gritting my teeth together, I returned to ignoring him and his pretentiousness.

Apparently, Dahlia and Theo weren't well liked by the Royal Coven as a whole, and many opted to live in towns surrounding the Palace instead. But with King Velik's return, a sea of new faces had begun streaming through the throne room doors – witches who knew their Coven, their Kingdom, was strong once more with the return of their beloved ruler.

There was so much joy permeating the air, I didn't even flinch as the squat herald blew a squawk though his trumpet and announced the arrival of a Lady Merle and some Lord Something-ton that I'd never heard of before. The herald was slowly turning red in the face as he panted, sucking in short breaths before strangling another shrill bellow from the abused instrument to declare the Coven Mother for Shadymoss entered the throne room.

"It's funny, actually," Finn said, turning back to me, his low baritone making my heart flutter, "that you say you'd miss me – seeing as I'll be staying in the Bramberry Manor for a while, starting tomorrow."

I whirled towards him, jaw dropping. "*What?*"

My question was drowned out by the herald and three sputtering shrieks of his trumpet, signaling the King's arrival. Pulse skittering, I stared incredulously at Finn, though he merely tipped his chin towards the throne room doors.

The crowd rose to their feet, cheering loudly as King Velik appeared. He wore a long, jade green robe with minimal embellishments, and color had begun returning to his cheeks that weren't as hollow as when I found him sitting at my dining room table days ago. King Velik strode down the aisle to his rightful throne with a wide smile on his face – his bright hazel eyes twinkling.

Neera materialized in a plume of black smoke, trotting proudly at Velik's side. A few witches screamed, though I noticed the witches who were already aware of the grimm's existence quickly reassured the newcomers. I couldn't help but laugh as the King paused in the middle of his procession to scratch Neera's chin affectionately.

There was nothing I could do to get my grimm to listen to me. If Neera decided to escort King Velik to his throne, then she was going to. I mean, who was going to argue with a demon beastie that stood taller than the majority of beings in the room?

Once Velik stood in front of his throne, Neera leapt up the steps in one graceful move, sitting on her haunches at my side while regarding the assembled court with coy regality.

"My friends, my family – my *Kingdom*," Velik started, his booming voice an incredible contrast from when Finneas had to speak on his behalf. The celebrating died down into respectful silence. The pure joy radiating from the old King made me tear up. "It's been quite a journey to get here, hasn't it?"

Velik chuckled heartily before spreading his arms wide. "I'm already King, so there will be no stuffy ceremony today." He raised a gnarled finger, tapping the slim gold crown to a round of light laughter. "But before we eat, drink, and revel, I want to speak with you about the reality we live in."

There was a wise sharpness to his words, capturing the focus of every being in the room. "With the reveal of chaos magic, the truth surrounding heretical witches, and now that we have our very own Vessel, I can only surmise that the gods will be more apt to peer into our realm."

"I ask that we, as the mighty Jade Kingdom, not be so fast to judge our neighbors, not be hasty to dismiss new friendships over a set of horns, lineage gifts, or pointed ears. We must adapt to the future unfolding before us, because the time is right for the Jade Kingdom to step out of exile and show the rest of Terramere that we refuse to be beat down over the mistakes of our ancestors."

He nodded. "The winds are changing, yet the goodness in our hearts and the pride we have for our Covens is solid and unyielding. Together, *we* are the Jade Kingdom. Each and every witch, human, and being in this land is special in their own way."

"My eldest son, Crown Prince Finneas Voronin, is my Heir," Velik said, matter-of-fact, "but as of now, he will begin an adventure of his own." I shot my surprised gaze to Finn. "My daughter, Princess Winona –" Velik chuckled, "is forging her own path in the world, but I'm confident her endeavors will better our Kingdom, too."

"There are rumors swirling about my *other* son, Theodoric Balabanov," King Velik waved a hand, bringing the crowd to silence. "His actions reflect his own blatant disregard for this Kingdom. I, King Velik, publicly disown him, strip him of title, and remind every being in this room that anyone caught harboring Theodoric will be considered a traitor and sentenced accordingly."

The softness to the King's face disappeared, revealing the incredibly powerful light witch that snapped Dahlia's neck. Though King Velik was a jovial old witch, the self-assured confidence and power thrumming around him told the crowd he was still a stern ruler who would reign with an iron fist.

"With that being said," King Velik paused, nodding as the kindness returned to his bright eyes, "the Royal Coven will answer to myself until a new Coven Mother is appointed. I daresay you will have one soon." The King eyed the row of healers standing across from us at the base of the dais. I didn't miss how the plump witch with white hair blushed furiously under his heated gaze.

"Well, that's all I have to say, so go celebrate and gods, someone bring me a glass of wine." King Velik clapped his hands together and sat on his throne as the crowd descended into the loudest round of cheers yet.

I had a split-second view of the white-haired healer bustling towards him, the two softly talking to each other, before Finn took my hand and led me towards the exit.

"What did you mean you'd be in the Bramberry Manor tomorrow?" I hissed as Finn wove us through the Great Hall.

"Well, I spent some time in the Bramberry Forest, and I promised the Vessel of Chaos that, in exchange for her services to help my father regain his throne, I'd teach a certain shadow witchling about his gifts."

I blinked as we entered a quiet garden off the main corridor. "You're coming to Bramberry to train Elijah?"

"To be perfectly transparent, darling, I'm coming to Bramberry for *you*," Finn corrected. My stomach flipped, heat humming through my core at the intensity written all over his face. Finn tugged me closer. "Helping a young witchling is the least I can do. But whatever you're doing, wherever you go, that's where I'll be. In whatever capacity you'll have me."

Finn angled my chin up with a single finger. I sucked in a sharp breath as our gazes locked. His hazel eyes burned with desire, the green in them so vibrant against a starburst of copper. They were beautiful, reminding me of the thick oak trees in the Bramberry Forest, and the leaves that changed with the seasons.

I threw caution to the wind. Really, I chucked all caution away as my heart hammered and my entire focus pinned to his lips.

"Kiss me."

Finn's lips crashed into mine without a beat of hesitation.

Instantly an inferno of pure fire exploded through my blood as Finn hoisted me up, rough hands palming the backs of my thighs through my filmy dress. I wrapped my legs around his waist, slanting my mouth to kiss him deeper, harder. Finn devoured me with wicked passion, backing me up until the cool stone wall pressed against my spine. He nipped at my bottom lip, eliciting a breathy moan from me as I pulled him closer, never wanting this moment to end.

At the feel of his hard cock pressing into me beneath our clothes, I whimpered, rolling my hips against him. Finn groaned, fingers digging deliciously into my thighs as we descended into a frenzy of exploring hands, our lips never parting.

This. This was the passion I was looking for. Finn drove me to a dizzying high, and I never wanted to come down. But it was his acceptance over what *I* wanted to do, the way he cared enough to ask, and to ultimately leave the decision to me. With Finn...I didn't feel the need to change anything about myself. I didn't need to hide or alter my life to serve him. He knew my deepest, darkest secrets, and didn't run from them.

And he *didn't* tie me to an altar and attempt to sacrifice me to a dark god so, you know, I really upped my standards on men.

Neera appeared at our side on her haunches, cocking her massive head as if she wasn't sure what we were doing, but was curious enough to make her presence known. She pawed at Finn's leg and let out a playful yip.

We laughed, breaking apart, though Finn didn't release me from his hold as I bent over and ruffled Neera's ears. Finn lowered me to my feet, stroking Neera's back and leaning his forehead against mine.

"It's a shame I already swore off men." I drawled breathlessly, half-slumped against the wall, spun over that single, blazing kiss.

"That *is* a shame," Finn purred, voice drenched in raw heat.

Neera chuffed, nudging us apart to steal affection for herself. I welcomed the distraction from the wickedly handsome man who kissed me in a manner I could only describe as sinful.

Averting my focus from Finn in order to collect my bearings, I tried to ignore the way my core clenched at his close proximity, the dark promises lacing his words, the ache between my thighs, and the inferno of desire simmering in those alluring hazel eyes.

Finn slashed me a roguish smirk, shadows stirring from the ground to swirl around him. "See you in Bramberry, darling."

As shadows whisked him away, I was hit with the uncanny sensation that Finneas Voronin was trouble. And, for once, I couldn't wait to see where that trouble led.

CHAPTER SEVENTY-EIGHT
MERRICK

THE RISING SUN DRIPPED vivid orange through the tree canopy, gilding piles of fallen leaves in hues of amber. It was the first day in a week where the lingering smell of rain was absent, and instead, a crisp chill crackled through the air.

Merrick trudged on, determined to put miles between him and the beautiful witch who stole his heart from his chest.

He hoped Winnie was furious at him. It was better for her to be angry. He couldn't bear the idea that she was crushed. It just made him hate himself more, and picturing Winnie's hazel eyes wet with tears was a dagger to the ribs. Merrick shoved the image from his mind, loathing himself more with every step deeper into the trees.

It had to be done.

She wouldn't let him leave, or she would've tried to get involved and been hunted throughout the rest of Ingotheria for her witch blood. The Jade Kingdom was the safest place for her. As badly as Merrick wished he could stay in the land of witches, guilt over leaving Lenna at the mercy of King Eamon would devour him.

And...the land of witches was no place for a gargoyle.

Star-crossed. They were from two different worlds.

Winnie didn't need him. He'd retrieved his pack with the Book of Carra from the roof of the abandoned foyer, and his Sentry took over, flying hard and fast as the last hours of night gave way to dawn.

The note he'd written her was a distraction. His paranoia that she somehow *knew* he was preparing to leave was so prevalent that Merrick had to be sure she'd stay in the Palace while he escaped. She needed rest, to see a healer and finish mending her injuries.

But imagining Winnie alone, waiting for him and ultimately realizing he wasn't coming about dropped him to his knees – so he refused to think about it again. Maybe he was addicted to heartbreak. Or maybe he was cursed. He was too numb to care.

He'd flown in his Sentry form until his wings ached, and then he'd spent the last few hours on foot, trudging through the outskirts of the Shadymoss Marshes, avoiding cart paths and plotting how to slip into the Ruby Palace without getting caught.

So far, he didn't have a solid plan. Winnie's voice drifted through his mind – her lilting laugh as she crooned, '*no plan...is the best plan.*' Merrick walked aimlessly towards the border of the Topaz Kingdom, the savage little shadow witch with soft skin and bright, cunning eyes infiltrating his thoughts once more.

He could almost smell her now...that heady scent of leather and sage.

Merrick froze, scanning the slowly lightening forest with his Sentry's enhanced sight, cautiously raising the bone dagger in his fist. Instinct told him a predator was close.

He didn't see anything, but that palpable tension didn't dissipate. The last thing he needed right now was to stumble upon a horde of dukhmora – or a witch.

Merrick ignored the apprehension.

Once the forest thinned, and his wings weren't sore, he could Sentry again – and hopefully not touch down until he was hidden away in the Topaz Kingdom.

Keeping his weapon out, he picked up the pace, assessing every shadow and noise that stoked his paranoia higher.

A rustle sounded above him. Merrick crouched into a defensive position, scanning the treetop and squinting against bright glimmers of sunlight that sparkled like jewels against damp leaves.

He saw nothing. That uncanny feeling remained.

Up ahead, a copse of birch jutted from the ground, the base of their peeling trunks half shrouded in shadow where daybreak hadn't chased away the night yet.

But...the shadows stretching towards him weren't natural.

Merrick's heart leapt into his throat.

Ink black hues, crawling opposite the rest –

"Hello, *bonehead*."

Merrick hissed.

Winnie strode from the birch grove, hands fisted at her sides and a scowl twisting her plush lips. Merrick swallowed the yearning desire to pull her into his arms and never let go.

"Go back to your Palace, Princess." Merrick growled with as much malice he could muster, though he shoved his dagger back into its sheath. His heart pounded so rapidly he could barely breathe. If she drew a weapon, he wouldn't fight back.

He turned, storming away.

Black smoke plumed in front of him.

"You thought you could sneak away, and I wouldn't find you?" Winnie shadow walked directly in his path, shoving at his stomach.

He was so much larger than her that he didn't budge.

"Fuck you," Winnie sneered, pointing a finger in his face instead, hazel eyes leaping with fire. Merrick winced. The wrath and devastation across her heart-shaped face was worse than any physical blow he'd ever received. "Why did you steal the Vessel Book?"

Merrick reared back, praying she was merely fishing for a confession over truly knowing he had it. "You think I took it?"

"I *watched you take it*," Winnie screamed in frustration, throwing her arms wide. Dressed in dark clothing and an open jacket, the move revealed the handles of at least four daggers. Merrick tensed.

Carra's tits, what if she was here under orders from the Royal Coven?

"I *saw you* sneak into Maude's study and take it. Did you forget I can shadow walk?"

Merrick pushed away the *relief* of her being here. In his presence.

If she left the Jade Kingdom, she'd be hunted.

Merrick would hate himself even more if anything happened to her.

"I need it, Win." Merrick roughly scraped a palm down his beard, fearing that she'd follow him to the Ruby Kingdom. "The witches have no use for a Vessel Book. I do."

Winnie glared at him, shadows writhing around her clenched fists. "Tell me why you *need* the Book of Carra."

"I just do," Merrick gritted out, wings tightening to his back.

"That's *not* good enough."

They'd hit an impasse. She obviously wasn't going to go quietly back to the Jade Palace.

For a long moment, they stared at each other. Merrick searched her beautiful face, memorizing the delicate slope of her neck, the warm amber flecks that broke up the light green in her irises, every dip and curve of her lithe body. If this was the last time he ever lay eyes on her it would be enough – it'd *have* to be enough. Where Merrick was headed would kill her on sight – regardless of her royal blood.

There was only one thing left to tell her.

The truth.

With a sigh, Merrick braced himself. "The Oracle of Terramere was captured by King Eamon at the autumnal equinox. She is being forced to use the Prism to locate the Book of Carra. And it's my fault she's trapped there. It's my fault she left the Slate Kingdom in the first place." Merrick shook his head rapidly. "When I realized you had the Vessel Book, I figured I could use it to barter for Lenna's release, and right the wrong of leaving her there in the first place."

"Why didn't you tell me?" Winnie asked timidly.

"It isn't your burden to bear."

Winnie blinked. A handful of racing heartbeats later, she rasped. "You bonehead, you really don't get it, do you?"

And then she was shouting again, shadows whipping around her. "First, you thought you had to suffer because the gods took away a soul tie that was never meant to be yours. And now, you believe you have to pay *penance* for the evil actions of a vicious King?"

"Why do you care, *Princess*?" Merrick bellowed, his temper hitting a breaking point. All he could picture was Winnie in the Ruby dungeon, hear her cries as she was brutalized and murdered. He wouldn't allow that to happen. She *had to understand.* "You're needed here to keep the throne of the Jade Kingdom safe. *My* duty is to the Oracle – I was willing to *die* to keep Lenna safe!"

Winnie sucked in a sharp breath. "Don't be a martyr, Merrick."

Hearing his name on her lips was almost his undoing. He looked away. "It doesn't matter. Lenna's the Oracle – she's more important than a single gargoyle warrior."

"You're important, too," Winnie said quietly. Merrick jolted as her hand slipped around his wrist. Then, Winnie was in front of him, her enchanting hazel eyes burning into his soul. "Do not *ever* say you're disposable."

"King Eamon threatened to decimate the Slate Kingdom if Lenna refused his summons."

"Did you, *personally*, demand that Lenna go to the Ruby Kingdom?" Winnie asked, venom lacing her question.

Merrick's brows knitted in confusion. "No? Of course not."

"And did you force the Oracle to leave the Slate Kingdom to go to Irridessen?"

"I did shove her through a portal..."

Winnie huffed in irritation. "Did Lenna beg you to take her back to the Slate Kingdom?"

"No, she –"

"Did she ever tell you to *die* to keep her safe?"

"Well, no, but –"

Winnie's eyes narrowed as she interrupted him again. "And did she ask you to trot back into the Ruby Palace after you were so brutally tortured that you almost *died*, were bedridden for *weeks*, and couldn't fly? Or do you *think*, that *maybe*, Lenna knows she isn't *your sole responsibility* and doesn't want you to lose your boneheaded life failing to save her?"

Merrick opened his mouth, closed it, and opened it again. Words failed him. Winnie stalked past.

"What are –"

"Are you coming?" Winnie whirled around. "We have an Oracle to save, and I can guarantee my plan is better than yours."

Merrick stood rooted to the spot, utterly confused by this entire situation. "You can't come with me, Win."

"Why?" she shot back, stomping loudly through the forest,

Merrick had no choice but to follow. "Because the Ruby Kingdom hates witches. They wouldn't hesitate to kill you."

"Then don't introduce me to any King's Guard by saying '*Hello, this is Winnie. She's a witch.*' Honestly, bonehead," she tutted sarcastically. Merrick jogged to catch up with her. "I hope your plan includes not getting caught."

"I wasn't planning on getting caught," Merrick retorted, albeit half-heartedly.

"So, you *do* have a plan?"

"Well, I was trying out your '*no plan is the best plan*' idea," he grunted reluctantly.

Winnie glanced over her shoulder coyly. "That's a terrible plan, bonehead. *Gods* – it's a good thing I'm coming with you."

Her teasing tone and the challenge in her eye broke the last dregs of Merrick's resolve. He lunged.

Winnie fell against him with a soft *oof.* Merrick bracketed her chin in his hand, tugging her gaze up to his. "I don't want anything bad to happen to you, Princess. It'll destroy me," Merrick pleaded roughly, his free hand skating down her back. Her body relaxed into his hold as his fingers tangled in the hair at the nape of her neck.

"Shut up," Winnie tilted her face to his. "I'm not changing my mind, so either let me come with you, or I'll just hide and follow behind you. You'll have no idea when I get captured immediately –"

Merrick snarled, slamming his lips against hers.

She kissed his back fiercely, nails digging into his biceps as they stumbled across the uneven terrain. Winnie gasped as his fangs grazed her throat.

"You're *mine,*" she moaned, nipping at his bottom lip as he lowered her to the forest floor, swiftly unlacing the ties on her pants enough to tug them down and palm her soaking core. Winnie wrapped her thighs around his waist as Merrick fisted his cock, positioning himself at her entrance.

"I'm yours," Merrick vowed as he thrust into her. Her tight cunt clamped around him immediately, his vision whiting out at the pure pleasure. He groaned as she rolled her hips, her sultry eyes peeking up at him from beneath thick lashes.

She matched him, stroke for stroke, as he fucked into her like the beast he was. Winnie let out a breathy cry as she came, strangling Merrick until he was roaring through his own, following her into bliss.

Spent and languid under him, she breathed heavily, cupping his cheeks with her hands. Merrick shifted his weight so he wouldn't crush her, gently pressing his palm against hers.

"And you're mine, too." Merrick whispered, dipping down to press a kiss to Winnie's swollen lips.

"Good," Winnie responded, slashing him a grin as she wriggled dramatically beneath him. "Now, get off me, bonehead. We have an Oracle to save."

Merrick couldn't help but chuckle as he tucked himself away and Winnie yanked her breeches back up.

He shoved off the ground, wings flaring as he helped Winnie to her feet. Suddenly, the idea of taking on King Eamon together didn't sound so terrible. With the shadow witch at his side, and his Sentry coiled in his soul, Merrick had never felt so powerful.

"You know," Merrick mused as they walked hand in hand, heading south where the border of the Topaz Kingdom loomed. "I think Lenna's really going to like you."

Winnie laughed, swinging their joined hands between them. "She better – seeing as I saved your life and let you steal a godsdamned Vessel Book."

Merrick shrugged, his heart already lighter as the witch gifted him a smile filled with mischief. "In my defense, Princess, *you* stole it first."

And as Winnie rolled her eyes, Merrick smirked.

There was a reckoning approaching the Ruby Kingdom, and King Eamon's time on this realm was limited. For so long, Merrick had given in to his own darkness, let it consume him, devour him. But after falling for Winnie, after fighting demons and meeting the witches of the Jade Kingdom, Merrick conquered his darkness. And not only had he survived against all odds, but he also came out on the other side stronger, more confident, and sure of himself.

Because now, *Merrick* was the monster lurking through the shadows.

Formidable beasts didn't break amidst darkness.

They were *reborn*.

EPILOGUE

Lenna

LENNA KNELT ON THE cold tile floor, heartbeat loud in her ears as King Eamon leered down from his throne.

"Again," he hissed, hard eyes pinned to the Prism she held.

With a shaky breath, Lenna closed her eyes, throwing her consciousness into the past once more. She was acutely aware of the King's proximity as she hovered right on the cusp of the present.

Distantly, she felt her nose begin bleeding, but she ignored it. The King of the Ruby Kingdom demanded she search for the Book of Carra, but Lenna had better things to do during her imprisonment. Right now, she simply had to sell a lie.

A lie that only worked if the King believed her to be meek. Afraid. Cooperative.

Thankfully, King Eamon typically gave up after an hour or so. She wove through the past, finding when she arrived to the throne room today.

Fifty minutes ago.

A hand brushed her shoulder.

Lenna jerked out of the Prism, wary of the King's cronies attempting to anchor her and uncovering the lie. They'd tried before – and she'd taken them so far and fast into the past they'd gotten physically sick. Lenna had, too, but keeping the King unaware of her true intentions only worked if she was able to delve into the Prism alone.

But this time, it was Prince Cillian who stood over her.

"You're requested in the council room, my King," Cillian said, disregarding Lenna completely.

King Eamon scoffed. "I'm not done with the Oracle, yet."

Lenna flinched, though Cillian merely shrugged, stuffing his hands into the pockets of his deep red trousers and striding towards the dais. "Fine. I was just passing the message along. Lord Batair reported a red hydra spotted south."

King Eamon straightened, vengeful intrigue gleaming through his dark eyes.

There was only one hydra in Terramere, and wherever the hydra was, Orla was.

"No," Lenna breathed in horror, eyes flicking from Cillian to the King. "I'll – I'll do *anything*, please don't harm Orla."

A cruel smile played across Eamon's face as he rose from the throne, disregarding her pleading entirely. "Make the Oracle search for another hour. Once she's done, take the Prism away. She's only to use it under our supervision."

Cillian gave his father a curt nod, glancing impassively down to Lenna. *They all had a role to play.*

In the wake of Orla's escape, Cillian was under more scrutiny than ever. Eamon had been suspicious, but whatever happened behind closed doors was enough for the Prince to convince the King of his unwavering loyalty.

Lenna bowed her head as Eamon strode from the throne room.

"South?" Her voice was barely a whisper. Cillian squatted down, tugging a handkerchief from his pocket and offering it to her. Hastily using it to wipe the trickle of blood from her nose, Lenna pressed. "Orla's south?"

Cillian shot her a bemused smile as he helped her clamber to her feet. "Did I say south? Gods above, I meant *north*. Or...maybe it was east?"

Lenna chuckled, brushing off her grey skirts, knees aching. "How long do we have?"

"Not long enough," Cillian grunted, escorting Lenna swiftly towards the doors. "But I have enough witnesses making noise in the wrong direction to keep him away for a day."

Before Lenna could respond, a drone echoed through her temples, causing her to grimace. It wasn't the beginnings of a migraine – it was much worse.

As cold numbness crept through her limbs, she stumbled. Cillian caught her, brows pinched in concern.

"Fuck, hold on Len."

He knew.

They *all* knew now.

"Get. Hale," Lenna gasped as Moirai dug into her mind, raking talons down her defiance until she succumbed to whatever prophecy the God of Sight demanded to bestow.

Cillian hissed, banding his arm around her waist and hoisting her into his arms as deadened, dulled vision shuttered Lenna's sight. This time, she fought to stay in control. She hated it. The deafening silence. The sheer nothingness while she was used as a mouthpiece.

With fae speed, Cillian rushed towards the Royal Wing.

But it wasn't fast enough.

Moirai must've enjoyed her fighting back because he acquiesced, granting Lenna a sliver of consciousness this time – just enough to hear the warning spill from her own lips in a voice that was both her own and not.

"A link is forged on unblemished skin. Another step closer to the gods walking this realm. Be wary of the blood seeping from between fractured veils, as only those with the power of the gods will be able to reverse it."

BONUS EPILOGUE
Adara

NECI DUG SHARP FINGERNAILS into my forearm, steering me into a dimly lit study. Unsure what to expect, I shielded myself behind court-refined etiquette – spine stiff, shoulders back, my expression serenely neutral – though once my focus snapped to the male sitting behind the massive desk, I pursed my lips.

Gods, I loathed witches.

Through the flickering lamplight, the male surveyed me with the same obvious distaste.

"Who is this, Neci?" The dry question was directed to the witch who'd drained my magic daily for the past month.

"She's a Queen with no kingdom." Neci replied bitterly. "Exactly what you asked for."

I assessed the male silently. The less I said, the more I'd learn.

In the wake of it all, I clung desperately to the scattered shards of my upbringing.

Be proper and poised, mind your manners, hold your tongue.

Well, Esmeray never did, and she –

I winced, tearing my thoughts from my twin.

That wound was much too raw.

"What else do they call you, *Queen with no kingdom*?" His mirthless tone didn't match the cunning in his beady eyes as he appraised the dirty dress and cloak I'd stolen, my useless wings, and my limp, greasy hair.

Swallowing thickly, I resigned myself to fate. "Adara."

"*Adara*, the Queen with no kingdom," he mused, rising from his chair. Neci tracked him warily from under her lashes, her grip on my arm tightening. Drawing myself up straighter, my nostrils flared as the reek of alcohol wafted over us.

His thin lips stretched into a leering smile. "Welcome to the Doortan Manor, Adara. You are *exactly* what I've been hunting for. My name is Lord Leon, Coven Master of Veilhaven Hill."

ACKNOWLEDGEMENTS

That's a wrap! I had so much fun writing Dove since she's such a wild contrast to Orla and Esmeray. And, if you couldn't tell, I had the time of my life writing Merrick in this book.

But before I relax and start book #4, I have so many people to shout out!

To Randall – my wonderful husband. Thank you for being my peace, my safe place, and the other half of my soul. At the beginning of this year, you were cheering me on for publishing my first book, and here we are, six months later, finishing a 3rd release cycle! I love you forever and couldn't have done any of this without you. This is our success, our life, and I am so blessed to celebrate every milestone with you.

Mom & Dad – Every step of life, I know I can count on you. I love and adore you.

Carly – Thank you for being you, and for all your awesome social media knowledge.

Tori – Thank you for being the best hype woman ever. I am so grateful to have you as my best friend. Author-ing can be isolating at times, but your stead fast friendship is something I cherish.

Amanda – Thank you for cheering me on and freaking out at every sneak peek. I am so grateful for you.

Tina – My incredible cover artist! You did it again! Thank you, thank you! I am obsessed with this gorgeous cover!

To Heather, Jess, and Rattle the Stars PR – Thank you for making this release cycle so effortless. From editing to street teams, your expertise has been a blessing.

To my awesome Street Team – Thank you for hyping up the Vessels of the Gods series and wholeheartedly supporting the indie community!

To my readers – from the bottom of my heart, thank you. Your support means the world to me. Now, buckle up, because we're heading back to Esmeray and Orla for book #4, and this chaos... Is. Just. Getting. Started.

And finally, to Mellow, Indi, and Pig – my real-life Neera(s).

ABOUT THE AUTHOR

Katerina Stevens is a dark fantasy author who loves writing morally grey characters, creating friendly-*ish* beastie companions for said morally grey characters, and drinking coffee with wild abandon. She currently resides in Florida with her incredible husband, three spoiled dogs, two chunky cats, and a grumpy bearded dragon. She graduated from the University of North Florida after taking pretty much every creative writing class offered. Though she started off as a business major, she quickly discovered that math is hard, which led to her getting a bachelor's degree in Sociology. Outside of being an author, Katerina is a devout Capricorn, a tattoo collector, a Canva lover, and a OneNote enthusiast.